The Laundry Room

It's not what you gather, but what you scatter that tells what kind of life you have had.

Golda Meir

The Laundry Room

by

Lynda Lippman-Lockhart

www.Penmorepress.com

The Laundry Room by Lynda Lippman-Lockhart

Copyright © 2015 Lynda Lippman-Lockhart

ISBN-13: 978-1-942756-10-1(Paperback)
ISBN-978-1-942756-11-8 (e-book)

BISAC Subject Headings:
FIC041000FICTION / Biographical
FIC014000FICTION / Historical
FIC032000FICTION / War & Military

Cover Illustration by Christine Horner

Address all correspondence to:
Michael James
Penmore Press LLC
920 N Javelina Pl
Tucson AZ 85748

Dedication:

This book is dedicated to forty-five unsung heroes who helped change the course of history.

Yehudith Ayalon, one of those heroes and my contact throughout the writing;

Robert W. Lockhart, my hero;

Bogie Lockhart, my standard poodle and muse, who sat patiently by my side during the development of this book, and who left the world a sadder place due to his passing.

Laila sensed it long before she felt it, like so many other ominous occurrences in her short life: her mother's death, her family's flight from Poland, and her call to arms. Each of these events left an invisible scar, not to be trifled with, but none as compelling as what happened next.

Chapter 1

Jerusalem, 1942

The day was much like every other—balmy, busy, and boring. Although Laila Posner had fought her father for the right to run her own falafel stand on King David Boulevard, just to the left of the magnificent pink limestone King David Hotel and at the entrance to the *Old City* of Jerusalem; she hated to admit it wasn't all she had hoped for. Oh yes, people came and went, often stopping to taste her wares, but there were no long-lasting relationships formed. A senior in high school, she had little time for friends. She supposed there were some who might find her standoffish, having lost her mother at such an early age and older sisters to marriage, but she longed for female companionship.

While scraping off the grill, Laila perceived a presence and jauntily turned to take care of her next customer.

"Good morning," said the man, nodding. "I would like one of your famous falafels with everything on it."

The Laundry Room

feeling slightly uncomfortable. She couldn't put her finger on it, but she had the strangest feeling she had seen this man before. A man of average height, but that was where the average ended. His face was round, sporting a rather large nose (not altogether too large). His grey eyes sparkled with mischief. He was distinguished, as if he were going to speak at a symposium. His sandy hair receded a bit, but it was neatly trimmed and not one hair was out of place. There was something about him that stirred Laila's curiosity. Perhaps she *had* seen him at a peace rally, thinking him a hothead, or maybe she was wrong. Whatever the case, she would probably never see him again.

Unnerved, Laila went to work, adding a little more of everything to the man's order. She listened intently to him as he spoke. He had a commanding way about him—intelligent —maybe a little arrogant, but likeable. She was good at reading people even after only a brief introduction. Her father, *Abba,* had said she was blessed with insight and her ability to see into people's souls would take her far.

"Beautiful day—isn't it?" he said. "You know, these are the best falafels in town. How is it yours are better than anyone else's? I've been to a lot of places, but when I'm in Jerusalem, I only eat Abella's falafels."

"Thank you for the complement," Laila said, glancing over her shoulder; but the afternoon sun, reflecting off the pink limestone King David Hotel, made it difficult to take another peek. Laila had chosen this particular spot, next to the hotel, to open her first stand, over the objections of her father—the owner. He had warned her about the closeness to the *Old City* and "those foreigners" who came to Jerusalem for "their own ends." She had persevered, as she usually did, and took the spot away from her brother, who had not put up much of a fuss. She loved the hotel and its elegance. Every

2

day, people from all over the world passed through its doors. There was nothing like it in all of Jerusalem.

Laila handed the man his order. "Do we know each other?"

"I don't think so, but I would remember a face like yours. I'm a connoisseur of pretty women."

Was the man flirting with her? He was older by years, but for some reason she didn't care. He had not, however, mentioned a wife. Laila had little knowledge of men except for her boyfriend Yoel, whom she would marry someday; that is, if they could just stop arguing for a moment. She supposed that if opposites attracted, they were well suited.

"Do you live around here?" she ventured.

"No, but not far. Actually, Hertzlea, and come to Jerusalem often on business. I usually frequent the stand uptown, but today I'm meeting someone staying at the hotel. I'll make sure he stops by."

Hoping to continue their conversation, Laila was annoyed when a group of disorderly students approached her stand— pushing and jostling for position, acting like a bunch of thirsty camels at the watering hole. She feared they might knock something over.

"Children," shouted their chaperone. "Mind your manners; you are not on the playground." The woman, dressed demurely in black, parted her charges and stepped to the front of the stand. She placed her order.

Laila filled it quickly so the children could move on. She had little experience with children either since her mother had passed away giving birth to what should have been Laila's little sister. Instead, Laila would be last in a line of four. Her sisters were grown, married, and lived miles away. Only her brother had remained in Jerusalem with his new wife.

The Laundry Room

With the diversion gone, Laila turned to her mystery man, but he was gone. How had she not been aware of his departure? Oh well, she would probably never see him again. She busied herself replacing condiments that had been used up with new from the ice chest below. She had better things to do than moon over a man. She was a working woman.

Her thoughts drifted to her brother Judah and the reason for his visit earlier that day. He said it was to restock the stand; she thought it might be something else. Usually he arrived at the end of the day to pick up the stand and deliver it back to the warehouse, to be cleaned from top to bottom and all food items removed and replaced the following morning with new; but since yesterday had been so busy, he said he thought it wouldn't hurt to see how things were going. She bet he dropped by to pick up her techniques. Laila knew neither Judah nor Abba could believe she had done as well as she had over the last few months.

Let me warn you, Judah had said in his attempt at being stern, *Abba is in one of his bad moods. It seems one of the workers had not shown up this morning, and Abba had to run the stand himself, disappointing Abba once again.*

Abba's standards were as high for himself as they were for everyone else, but his spit was like a camel's and you didn't want to be within range.

You've been working so hard. Why don't you take the rest of the afternoon off? I'll close up, he had said.

If she had thought he was sincere, she might have considered the offer, but Judah was a bit on the lazy side and any excuse to escape his wife he would take. Laila adored her big brother. Their conversations were easy and often teasing. That's what she loved most about him. Compared to Abba, he was a breath of fresh air. She knew her Abba had taken her mother's death hard. As it were, he never really got over

4

it.

Refreshed by his visit, Laila had returned to her duties. But an hour passed without a single sale, and then the stand became overrun with customers. Then, as Laila served a platter of falafels to a nice, elderly couple, a blast of hot air smacked her in the back, lifting her out of her sandals; sending her heavenward, soaring like a bird over the stand and above the treetops; and then, unceremoniously, dropping her onto a mound of humanity, landing like a broken doll.

It was July 22, 1942. On that day, Laila found herself transformed from a "dove" to a "hawk," but for all the wrong reasons.

Sirens cried, voices wailed, and rubble pelted Laila's head and shoulders, jolting her back into consciousness. She opened her eyes but saw nothing. Was she blind? *Oh God, please, don't let me be blind. Take a limb, my hearing, but not my sight.* Then without thinking, she rubbed the back of her hand across her lids, and looked at it. Her hand dripped with dark red blood. Was it hers? Wait, she *could* see. She whispered a small prayer of thanks and lifted her head to see what had happened. Pillars of grey smoke and scarlet flames shot from the upper floors of the hotel that had, just moments ago, stood elegantly against the cerulean sky. The center portion now lay in ruins along King David Boulevard.

Laila's thoughts were confused, her focus scattered. Were they at war? What about her falafel stand? She coughed and gaged; something was cutting off her breath. She reached for her neck, pulling at what was wrapped around it. Her prized, white apron, sewn by her loving mother, was no longer about her waist; it had become a noose, constricting her every breath, and it was covered in blood. As Laila struggled to

The Laundry Room

make sense out of what had just happened, a searing pain shot through her left leg; she had been injured beyond a scalded right arm.

She tried to move but could not; a body lay across her, pinning her down. It was then she noticed the other bodies strewn along the street like toy soldiers on a pretend battle field. It was a horrible sight; her stomach heaved. Her thigh throbbed, her head swam, her hand burned from where the hot grease must have splattered. She strained to see her stand, but there was nothing left but a poof of smoke like her hopes and dreams for peace. She fell back against one of the bodies and lay in a hopeless stupor. It was all too overwhelming, but Laila knew she had to get out of there; but how? She couldn't move. Perhaps it was the time to use what her father, Abba, an affectionate name for a male parent, had called her *eyshen reash*. Her wise head could figure this out; she was her father's daughter.

All she knew was that she had to free herself from this mound of human flesh, and soon. She took a deep breath, but the smoke-filled air that now blanketed everything in sight made her cough, causing her to convulse. When she tried to cover her mouth with her free hand, she remembered it had been burned by grease and smelled like cumin. She sneezed; the pain excruciating.

With every last bit of strength she could muster, Laila made another attempt to free herself. She pumped up her body and pushed as hard as she could—to no avail. Her right arm was lodged so tightly under the woman's body, who lay unmoved on top of her, that Laila realized she wasn't going anywhere without help. Exhausted, she took shallow breaths like her mother, Emma, had taught her as a small child when she found herself in a difficult situation. She could still hear her mother's words: *the power to survive comes from within; use it wisely.*

What could she do? She closed her eyes to create a better picture of her circumstances, which usually helped. If she could only move the woman above, she might have a chance. Using her free hand, she reached up and ran her fingers along the woman's body to determine how badly she was hurt. Laila contorted her own body for a better look, and what she saw made her fall back, sick to her stomach: blood everywhere. She whimpered silently. Abba always said she could charm her way out of most situations, but this was not going to be one of them. *Use few words, well* he would say. She had to come to grips with her circumstance—she wasn't going anywhere because she was trapped. That was all there was to it. Tears slipped down her cheeks as she considered the possibilities. She made herself think of better times: evenings, sitting by the gramophone Abba had smuggled out of Poland and listening to Abba's favorite composers: Mozart and Tchaikovsky; or the aroma of cinnamon from Tanta's strudel and rugelach; or her elder sister plaiting her long, blond hair. Those thoughts only served to take her mind off her situation for a brief moment.

Her head was a tangled web of conflicting thoughts: *What was the worst that could happen?* She could bleed to death, or be captured by the enemy—but who was the enemy? Why had this happened? It was hard to tell whether it had been the British or one of the many Arab factions that had blown up the hotel, but it really didn't matter because the end result was the same. Was there no one to help? Sick at heart, she knew if she didn't come up with a plan, she was going to die right there. She had to do something. "Can anyone hear me?" she cried out. "Is anyone alive?"

No response.

She thought about praying, but didn't think God would

listen. It had been so long. Laila wasn't even sure she remembered how. Would He punish her for asking for help when she had turned her back on Him? Perhaps this was His punishment. She had nothing to lose, so she prayed the best way she knew—honestly. *Please God, I need your help. I know I haven't done my share of praying lately, but I also haven't had much guidance in praying. Since Emma died, Abba has turned away from you. I guess I have too. I need your help. Would you send a sign telling me you hear me and I'm not all alone? No one else seems to hear me. I don't want to die.*

As if on cue, shredded paper began raining down: some pieces on fire, some like snowflakes wafting through the air. A scrap landed on Laila's forehead. She blew it off; it landed on her nose like a persistent fly attracted to something about her. She peeled it off and looked at it. There was but one word written on the scrap: *Hope.* How bizarre. It was what she needed most, but she regretted she had none left. Had her prayer been answered? Was this the sign she had asked for, her missive from heaven?

Hope. She reflected a moment. It was true; she had allowed hopelessness to overwhelm her. That got you nowhere. Instead of negativity and hopelessness, she needed to get angry. Anger gave you strength. She reminded herself of the consequence of doing nothing, and began to feel strains of anger course through her veins. If she could only get the man under her to move, it would start a chain reaction and she could free herself from her prison. With a new approach and God behind her, she began searching the man below for a pulse. He was large, well dressed, and dead. *Hope* again slipped away and so did she.

###

A sudden shift in weight brought Laila around. The

8

woman pinning her down moaned and rolled to the ground, freeing Laila from her bonds. She moved her leg, but the pain was beyond words. She fell back terrified. She didn't want to die—not here—not alone—not yet. *God, where are you?* She had too much to live for, and Abba couldn't take another death. Her Abba had always been there when she needed him, and she needed him now. *Be strong and of good faith* he often reminded her. She didn't feel strong or so grown up at the moment. Living in Jerusalem, Laila had learned to accept air raids and rockets fired from their neighbors, but had never experienced an attack firsthand. The moaning commenced again. Laila looked to see if there was anything she could do for the poor woman. Why wasn't anyone helping them? She couldn't bear to look at the woman's disfigured face.

All around, bodies lay where they had been flung: some screaming, some moaning, and some silent; those screams muffled her own cry for help. The acrid stench of burnt flesh filled her nostrils, making her all too aware of her situation.

Exposed, and in the middle of the street, they were nothing more than a flock of sitting ducks. Laila was afraid the bad men would capture, torture, or kill her, so she screamed with all her might. "Help, please. Someone help us." Still no one responded. People ran pell-mell, many bleeding, clothing in tatters. All she could think of was dying. She had to act. She would not give up. The air was making it increasingly difficult to breathe. She decided it was all a matter of working up the courage to crawl away. When it came down to it, she didn't really care about helping anyone else. She was young and didn't deserve to die there in the street.

Laila knew suffering. She had watched her mother's last days and, whether she wanted to admit it or not, felt a

The Laundry Room

kinship with the woman next to her. She took a deep breath, and inches at a time, rolled onto her side. Laila became lightheaded from the sight of so much blood but refused to give in to the feeling. Coping with nausea, she propped herself onto her elbow and held her hand over her mouth, just in case. While she searched the woman's body for the source of the bleeding, Laila noticed a cloying odor of cloves about her. The woman must have been cooking before she took to the street. What had she been making, and for whom? She might have been preparing soup or a white sauce. It struck Laila as strange that she would be drawn to the pungent odor of spices at a time like this. Perhaps it was her connection with food.

Forcing her attention back to the poor woman, Laila wondered if a person could survive losing so much blood. *Oh God, she's pregnant.* Laila cried out in empathy, knowing how her Emma had taken her last miscarriage. Without thinking, Laila ripped off her apron and tied it above the wound on the woman's thigh. It was then she noticed blood spurting from the woman's stomach. What should she do? She panicked and then she instinctively placed her hand over the spot, all the while talking herself out of passing out again. All she could think about was the commandment: *Love thy neighbor as thyself.*

The wind had picked up, fanning the roaring flames above, and this time a fiery piece of debris landed on Laila's head, scorching her scalp and setting her hair on fire. She jerked her hand from the woman's wound, but quickly replaced it. Pained, she raised her wounded arm, which had taken the brunt of the fall and batted out the flame. She found her voice and screamed again. "Help. Please help. This woman is badly hurt. She'll die if someone does not help us." Now more concerned for this woman's wellbeing than her own, and knowing the woman had most likely lost her baby, Laila's determination to help swelled. She cursed the people who had committed this crime. Killing and maiming innocent people? This is what came of the senseless use of guns and bombs.

Within her jumbled mind, it occurred to Laila that the man under her had probably saved her life; if she had fallen directly to the street, she would have broken every bone in her body. Who was this man? He might have been a father, a husband, a businessman running errands; and now his life had been snuffed out, leaving him incomplete, unfinished, to be grieved. Wanting to show respect, Laila recited the *Kaddish,* the age-old prayer she had recited for her Emma and others who had left this world:

"Yis'gadal v'yis'kadash sh'mei raba..."

As she finished the prayer, Laila spied a British officer and a group of men in white, carrying stretchers and running toward them. She waved, calling them to hurry. Two of the men stopped beside her; the others dropped to the ground and began working on the woman. The medics lowered the stretcher, ready to move Laila. *Thank you God. You answered my prayer. I will never doubt you again.*

"Where are you injured?" one of the aids asked.

"My leg. My arm." She fell back, hoping they would be kind.

One of the aides left for a moment and returned with a board and bandages. He carefully wrapped her leg and lifted her onto the stretcher. She screamed. Laila had been lucky, all her life, never having been badly injured. Her prayer now was that she would not lose her leg, although she had offered it in place of her sight just moments ago.

As they carried her to the ambulance, the attending officer began questioning her. He must have been high-ranking, because his chest was covered with red, green, yellow, and blue ribbons. His furrowed brow told her he had a lot on his mind. She wasn't sure whether to be afraid or grateful.

"What is your name?" He wrote quickly on a clipboard.

"Laila."

"How old are you?" His eyes never left the clipboard.

"Seventeen. What happened?" She asked, hoping to divert the questioning away from her. Again, her father's words found shelter in her mind: *Use few words.*

"King David ... bombed."

"Why?"

"What were you doing there?" His eyes darted from the clipboard to hers, avoiding her question.

"I run Abella's Falafel Stand."

"Alone?"

She nodded.

"You're just a child."

"I am not a child."

"You're pretty saucy for someone who just lived through a bombing. Did you notice anyone or anything suspicious today?"

Her brain was too foggy to think. Why was he asking so many questions? Couldn't he see she was in pain? "What about the other woman?" she asked. "Will she be all right?" Laila had barely taken her eye off the woman for fear she would lose her. For some reason, the woman had become important to her. Laila hadn't had time for any real friends, and for the first time in her self-indulgent life she was actually worried about someone other than herself. Now, they were in it together.

"She's in a bad way, but most likely will live. Relative ...

friend?" he asked.

"Friend." She lied, hoping he would let them stay together. The woman would need a friend when she discovered she had lost her child. Of course, Laila had no idea what the British were going to do with them. Maybe the officer thought she and the woman had something to do with the bombing, and were really taking them to be interrogated and not to a hospital. Laila was not in the habit of lying, but sometimes, she guessed, you do what you have to do.

Two soldiers approached. One of them neither took notice of her nor the woman beside her. He spat as he spoke. "What have those stupid bleeders done?" His disgust was obvious. The other, young with piercing green eyes, the color of the ferns growing in pots outside her front door, never left hers as he stood awaiting orders—his face, kind and handsome. Laila turned her head, not wanting to make a connection. He was her enemy.

"I have no idea," said the officer in charge. "Get the bobbies rounded up and hurry. That might not be the only bomb."

"Yes, sir," Both soldiers saluted and dashed off in the opposite direction. The younger soldier stopped and looked her way. This time she held his gaze.

The officer turned his attention back to Laila. "I say, you're both going in the same conveyance. We're running out of space. They'll take care of you. Now, did you see anything suspicious?" He turned to the aides. "Could you hurry it up? There are others; we're all in jeopardy."

There *was* something, but she was afraid to mention it.

"Well?" His full attention now focused on her.

"Well what?" her voice quivered. "Can't you see I'm in pain? Why don't you ask somebody who can answer your questions?" She knew exactly what he was referring to.

The Laundry Room

The officer held up his palm and looked her square in the eye. The aides stopped short, causing her to gasp in pain. "I can tell from your eyes you know something. Out with it. There is no time to waste. We're not going a step further until you tell me what you know."

Her Abba always said she was not a good liar, and it appeared this man was not going to let her go without an explanation. "Well, you see, there was a man." She stopped to gather her thoughts. Her leg throbbed so badly she wanted to scream. She closed her eyes and grimaced. "He stopped by this morning. Looked important ... complemented me on our falafels. Kept looking at his watch ... said he had a business meeting in the hotel."

"Describe this man?"

"Nice looking: round face, large nose, distinguished, receding hairline. Oh yes, his hair was sandy brown, cut short, and he smiled a lot." Why all the questions? The man had been pleasant enough. Laila probably shouldn't have mentioned him, but if he had anything to do with the bombing, he should pay. What she chose to withhold was that she thought she had seen him at a Zionist rally a few weeks earlier. She remembered thinking he was a hothead; but today, he had been a customer, and she wasn't really sure he was the same person. Laila decided not to mention the meeting. She didn't trust the British, because they had gone back on their word so many times. The *Balfour Declaration* had given Jews the right to a homeland; then, wanting the oil found in the countries given to the Arabs during the reparation, they changed their wording to say the Jews would have a place inside Palestine. Now that Palestine was mandated to the British, there had been no rest for the Jews, who had taken the British at their word. Abba spouted long and hard on this topic every chance he got; though, what

14

could he do about it?

She would say no more—given her circumstances and mistrust of just about everyone. The officer ordered her transporters to move on. Out of the corner of her eye, she watched as the young officer with the piercing green eyes returned and exchanged words with the senior officer. He was close enough for Laila to pick up a hint of marjoram—a sweet oregano. He must have had lamb for lunch. She craned her neck for a last peek as he walked away. She was embarrassed when he turned around again and she was staring at him. He disappeared into the crowd.

Laila needed a diversion from her pain, so she replayed her conversation with the mystery man.

These are the best falafels in town, he had said. *How is it yours are better than anyone else's? I've been a lot of places, but when I'm in Jerusalem, I only eat Abella's falafels.*

Laila remembered feeling honored and telling him so. He had seemed to be searching her face for something, making her a bit uneasy. It was as if he were memorizing it for future reference. *"Do we know each other?"* she had asked.

"I don't think so. I live in Hertzlea, but come to Jerusalem often on business. I usually eat at the stand uptown. Today I'm here to meet someone staying at the hotel. I'll make sure he stops by."

Had he been flirting with her? He was older by years, but for some reason she didn't care. Now she wondered if he had offered too much information about the mystery man.

Laila remembered telling him she thought they had met. The man had frowned, and quickly retorted: *Perhaps, but I'd remember a face like yours. I'm a connoisseur of pretty women.*

She had blushed, something she rarely did. She liked the man in an obtuse way. There was something commanding,

The Laundry Room

yet gentle, about him, and she had told him she hoped he would stop by the next time he was in town. Had she been too forward? And now, all of a sudden, she was considering him a criminal. No, she would not give out any more information, but she couldn't stop thinking about the mystery man, trying to remember something he might have said or done that would have given her a clue as to whether he was involved in the bombing or not.

Somewhere in their conversation, Laila had been drawn away from the man as a group of young people approached. They were busy chattering amongst themselves, pushing their way to the front of her cart, jostling for position, and acting like a bunch of stubborn camels. She remembered thinking if they weren't careful, they would topple her stand over. She had reluctantly left the mystery man and returned to her new customers and the falafels cooking in the deep fryer, a minute away from burning. When she'd chanced a glance in the mystery man's direction, he was gone. No sight of him anywhere. They hadn't even exchanged names. Were men really that elusive?

Earlier in the day, her brother Judah had arrived to restock the cart. Normally he would return at the end of the day to pick it up and deliver it back to the warehouse, to be cleaned from head to toe and all food items removed and replaced the following morning with new; but the last week had been particularly busy. What was left over, each night, went to the poor. Abba was a supporter of those in need. He had been poor as a child and had made a pact with himself, that if he should ever be blessed enough to have his own business, he would take care of the less fortunate. He had honored his pact the third year in business. Today, he would find only ruins.

Judah had warned Laila of Abba's foul mood. It seemed

one of the men who worked for him had not shown up that morning, and Abba had had to run the stand himself, disappointing Abba once again. His standards were as high for himself as they were for everyone else, but his spit was like a camel and you didn't want to be within range.

Laila remembered how simple Judah's and her conversation had been, about all her responsibilities and how she should take the night off. Sure, he had a wife who cooked for him. Who would cook for Abba if not she? She was glad he had not stayed to help. Knowing him, he would have charged into the hotel looking to rescue anyone trapped inside, putting himself in danger without a thought. He was like that: act and then think. His kind heart was his undoing.

In a pleasant mood, Laila had waved Judah off with a smile. He was a good brother as brothers went. Abba was a good man too, albeit tough on his children. Perhaps he knew something she had yet to learn.

Every so often, the aides would lose their grip on the stretcher and it would bump against their thighs, causing Laila to cry out in pain. There would be an exchange in that Limey accent, which she was beginning to understand from the many times the Brits had stopped by her stand. They were everywhere these days. Stiff people, who rarely smiled or laughed. Why did they hate Jews so? Today, at least, they were being kind.

"Move it up, I say," the officer commanded. "What is taking so long? Get them into the lorry, and be quick about it. There are officers on the top floor who need our attention and a horde of others that we have to get off the street."

The aides fired off a nasty sneer, as if to say they knew how to do their job and didn't need him to tell them anything.

While sliding her stretcher onto the truck, they bumped

the other stretcher and the young woman cried out. A nurse began working on Laila's leg.

I'm in an ambulance. I can't believe I'm going to ride in an ambulance to a hospital. Emma died in our house. Maybe if we had taken her to a hospital, she would have lived. I shouldn't think these thoughts. I must concentrate on what is happening now, so I don't make any mistakes.

"How is she?" Laila asked, directing her energies toward her new friend.

"She's lost a lot of blood. We'll do our best."

"You need to worry about yourself, girly," said one of the male aides, almost out the door. "You have a nasty gash on your leg, and it looks like a broken bone."

Somehow Laila had taken on the responsibility for this stranger. She found herself worrying for both of them: where they were going and what would happen to them. Was this to be her lot in life, always running away from something and never toward it? Look at her relationship with Yoel, her boyfriend. It had been her own fears of losing him like she had lost her mother that had kept her from making that final commitment. All Laila had ever wanted was to live in peace and be able to follow her dreams. As she felt a needle prick her upper arm, Laila reached for her new friend's hand and squeezed it lightly, as the medicine commenced taking Laila to a calmer place. She relinquished all control.

Chapter 2

Laila

Jerusalem, two weeks later, 1942

Judah dropped Laila off around the corner of the hospital. It was as close as he could get her with all the traffic on the street. He had a delivery to make and was running late, so he helped Laila out of the truck and sent her on her way—wobbly as it was. Today, as she limped along the crowded street to visit Zahar, she couldn't help but feel nervous with so many British soldiers milling about, brandishing rifles. They were mindful of every Jew and rude much of the time, making offensive remarks that hurt more than they knew. Their presence and their remarks, however, did not stop her from her mission.

Before Judah arrived that morning, Laila had had a moment to think about her future—now that she assumed she had one. This week she wanted to be a scientist—a great scientist—one who invented things. Actually, there were so many things she wanted to be, she wasn't sure where to begin. Perhaps after her first year at the university, she would have a better grasp of her future. Laila stopped to

1

The Laundry Room

adjust her crutch, which was pinching under her arm, and continued, at turtle speed.

Cars, trucks, and ambulances blocked the road leading to the hospital. Laila came to an abrupt halt when she saw a soldier grab an elderly Orthodox Jew, who was bent and carrying a large book that he consequently dropped to the debris littered street. What terrible thing could he have done to be stopped and searched? The Jews' *Promised Land* was beginning to be their prison, causing doubts as to whether they were better off there in Palestine or back in Russia.

Outraged and not thinking, Laila called in their direction. "You should be ashamed of yourself, picking on an old man. Don't you have anything better to do?" Then, realizing how stupid she had been, she turned and quickened her step before the officer had time to change the direction of his inquiry. It was then that Laila stumbled, losing her balance, only to have a stranger catch her before she fell.

"Thank you," she said, straightening up her clothing that had gone awry.

"Some advice," he said, "you don't have to fight everyone's battles," and then he was gone.

Now that was an odd comment, coming from a stranger.

Berating herself for not watching where she was going instead of minding everyone else's business, Laila thought of Abba and what he would say. *One of your weaknesses, Laila, is thinking you can make everything right. Your other weakness is lack of patience. That is why I love you so much.* They would laugh and then everything would be alright.

Laila hated that she had lost her falafel stand—currently under repair. And worst of all, someone else would be running it for the next month or so, until Laila could stand on her own. There, she was seeing the dark side of things instead of being grateful that she and Zahar were alive. What a brat she was being, her thoughts so negative and unproductive. Laila was feeling sorry for herself because it was possible she might not graduate on time. She shook her head to clear it. She would have to rearrange her mood before she reached Zahar's room.

Zahar was the name of the pregnant woman who was wounded in the explosion alongside Laila. She and Laila had become great friends over the last few weeks. They had so much in common: writing, painting, and listening to classical music for hours. Hoping to lift Zahar's spirits the first time Laila visited her, Laila had brought her a favorite book of poems. Zahar had loved it and lost herself in it. Laila could tell Zahar was doing better physically, but she still worried about her friend's mental state after losing her baby the way she had. It was so easy, drawing a parallel between Zahar and her own Emma. How would Laila have handled such a loss? She hoped never to find out.

Laila's mind wandered as she clumsily continued along the fractured sidewalk, trying to establish a cadence to her step. She had never used crutches before and found them clumsy and painful. Someone had told her it would be easier if she kept to a beat, so she began singing a childhood song until sirens heading her way drowned out the melody. Nearing the entrance to the hospital, Laila reached a resolve about her life and her future. The bombing and the fact she was alive had made her realize she owed it to herself and her family to make something of her life. She would finish high school and graduate at the end of the term and then begin college.

Laila's two favorite subjects, the ones which had kindled a passion in her, were chemistry and physics. Never having taken those courses before, one survey class in high school had changed everything. With her new direction, Abba and she had locked horns since he expected her to major in finance and take over running the business. Laila had other ideas. According to Abba, there would be no more discussion. Although Judah wanted the coveted job, Abba didn't trust him like he did Laila—that *eyshen reash* again. Judah's head was up in the clouds—moonstruck by his wife. Laila had decided to worry about it later, but "later" was fast approaching. What was the matter with her? She had a broken friend to visit, not think about trivialities.

She hobbled on but could not help thinking about her future. The fall months loomed ahead. How many more bombs would fall? How many more deaths would Laila witness? Why was she even bothering to consider a future? Her future was supposed to have included attending the Hebrew University of Jerusalem, but now she didn't know. She was afraid to plan ahead after what had happened the other day. On the other hand, Abba always said: *Our enemies win if we change our direction.* He said the university would give Laila the tools to move ahead, become a thinker; education would mean freedom.

It was time for Laila to make some decisions. When Emma was alive she had made all the decisions: what they ate, what they wore, and how they would behave. She would drop a note in each lunch bag to remind Laila and her siblings to be respectful of their teachers and fellow students. Even Abba got those notes, which Laila was sure he took in stride. Emma was the keeper of their history, a constant reminder of where they had come from and where they must go.

Always interested in history, Laila had done a little research on the university. She found it had been a vision of the Jews of Palestine, and the cornerstone was finally placed on Mt. Scopus in 1918. It had taken seven years to realize that dream, and Dr. Chayim Weizmann, the founding father, made it possible. She also looked up Dr. Weizmann, who had been credited with many other contributions. Like him, Laila hoped her name would, someday, stand for something.

With no mother to continue her personal education, Laila now tended to mimic Abba's masculine traits, like being bossy and overbearing. Yoel must not have seen that in her because he told her he loved her just the way she was. He was just about the perfect boyfriend. They had met at a Pioneer Israel Scout meeting, one she had joined hoping to make friends. Yoel and she had gravitated toward each other, their conversation easy and light. He constantly encouraged her in every way: to be the person she wanted to be, to follow her dreams, yet keep her feet firmly planted on the ground. He was a senior at the university and graduating soon. After a stint in the army, they would get married. It was all mapped out—all except having Emma with her on her wedding day.

As Laila entered the hospital, she remembered why she was there, the floodwaters washed over her. She fought the sensation of drowning and had to sit down to collect her thoughts.

"Are you all right?" asked an elderly woman sitting on the bench.

"I will be fine. I'm getting used to these crutches."

"What happened, if you don't mind my asking?"

"The bombing of the Kind David Hotel."

"You poor darling. Can I get you some water?"

"No, thank you. I will be fine in a moment. I have to catch my breath."

A nurse helped the older lady up and into a wheelchair. It

was then Laila noticed she was missing a leg. Why was Laila feeling sorry for herself? At least she had been able to keep hers.

Lately, nightmares had plagued her dreams: bombs dropping, and people screaming until they woke her up. Abba sat with her most nights until she fell back asleep. The newspapers had given several differing accounts of the bombing, but it was clear who had been responsible. Shocked, Laila could not forgive the *Irgun*, a right-wing, splinter group of the *Haganah*, which was the fledgling secret service of the Jewish resistance, for what they had done. Ninety-one people lost their lives, countless more were injured, all to wipe out the British Military Command. Abba said it had something to do with papers being taken from the Jewish Agency by the British. Not wanting the papers in the wrong hands, the group had acted. He also said that Menachem Begin, their leader, had claimed he made three phone calls: one to the hotel, alerting them to evacuate the other guests; one to the French consulate; and the last to the *Palestine Post*, warning of the impending attack. The British were said to have replied: "We don't take orders from the Jews."

Obviously Laila did not understand politics, nor did she condone killing people, and it did seem to her there was a great deal of killing going on everywhere. She especially didn't like the soldiers standing around with Enfield rifles and Bren machine guns on their shoulders. Laila had learned about weapons at her Scout meetings. Abba said that men carrying weapons had been standard procedure in Russia, and partly the reason their family had they left when they did.

Making her way to Zahar's room, Laila couldn't help but notice that the activity of the past week had not quieted down. The hospital had been a madhouse, with beds in the hallways and doctors stretched to capacity. One atrocity or another was taking place continually around Palestine. Would it ever end?

"Knock, knock," she said as she balanced a bouquet of colorful flowers and her crutch.

"Enter."

Laila prepared her face; it was always so hard in the beginning and so important not to show how much she ached for her friend. Physically, Zahar would never be as beautiful as she must have been before the bombing. The last time Laila saw her, bandages had covered half her face, her neck, her torso and right leg. Laila hadn't visited in a few days, what with getting used to the crutches and all. She was hoping for signs of improvement today. Not wanting to wake Zahar if she were sleeping, Laila opened the door slowly. A handsome, dark-haired young man rose, and motioned for her to take his seat.

"No, no. I'll pull over a chair." Laila pointed to the opposite side of the bed.

"And how will you manage that?" He smiled. It was easy to see why Zarah had fallen in love with him. There was a boyish look about him, one that made you want to mother him. He strode to the far side of the room and picked up a chair like it weighed nothing, placing it next to Zahar. His height and build belied that innocence; and for a moment, Laila experienced a moment of envy.

"Avraham, this is Laila, the kind young woman who helped me. I would probably be dead if she hadn't been so persistent. Laila, this is my husband, Avraham Lemberg."

"Don't be silly. I did what anyone else would have done," said Laila, a bit embarrassed. She extended her hand, but Avraham drew her to him in a brotherly hug. Laila detected the distinct aroma of savory about him. She knew savory well, as Emma used it in her German dishes. She once told Laila the spice had been around for over two thousand years.

"So nice to meet you." Laila sat awkwardly—every bit embarrassed by the hug. She dropped one crutch to the floor, making a clatter that must have awakened the whole hospital.

"You saved my life." Zahar's eyes welled up; she blew her nose. It was easy to read sincerity in her face. She grabbed Laila's hand and gave it a gentle squeeze.

"I am also grateful for what you did," said Avraham. "Zahar told me you stopped the bleeding. That was very brave of you. How old are you, if you don't mind me asking?"

"Seventeen." She had been asked that twice in two weeks. Did she look that young?

"Very brave."

Now she was even more embarrassed. No one had ever called her *brave*. Laila was not sure whether what she had done was bravery or instinct. Whatever it was, something drove her to do it. "Thank you just the same. I didn't feel very brave that day. I was scared to death." She squeezed Zahar's hand and leaned forward to kiss it.

"We were talking about school and Zahar's plans before you came in," said Avraham, brushing back a wayward black curl from his creased forehead. "She will miss the end of the semester and is in no condition to think about it. I suggested she take the year off and start over in the fall. What do you think?"

He had put Laila on the spot. It wasn't up to her to make that decision. "You two will have to decide." She knew she had taken the coward's way out, but what else could she have done?

Zahar openly pooh-poohed Avraham's suggestion. Laila guessed standing up to one's husband came with age.

"What would I do with myself? I haven't taken that much time off in years. If I do, I'll lose the momentum. No, I have to keep my mind busy." Zahar turned her head so they wouldn't see the tears trickled down her pale cheeks. What could Laila do to stop the pain her friend was feeling?

"You can do some writing or painting," said Avraham, sitting forward in his chair, looking a little uncomfortable with talk of the future.

"Oh, I forgot," said Laila, seeing the hopelessness in Zahar's eyes. "These are for you." Laila held them out, slightly crushed. She looked at them in horror. "Sorry."

"Don't be silly. They are beautiful. Where did you get them?" Her eyes lit up for that moment. The first sign she was mending.

"...from a lady who has a stand on the next block from me. She was horrified by your story." Oh no; Laila hadn't meant to refer to Zahar's loss. It just slipped out. She would have to weigh her words more carefully.

"Zahar told me you lost your falafel stand. What will you do?" asked Avraham.

"Fortunately, the business will go on. The stand is being rebuilt, as we speak. Abba is not letting me near it for a while; although, I told him lightning never strikes twice. He said he didn't care. I'm too precious."

"He's right," said Zahar, inhaling the aroma of the flowers.

Laila was glad she had brought them. They seemed to bring Zahar comfort.

"Here, let me find something to put them in," Avraham took the flowers from his wife. "I'll be right back." He left the

The Laundry Room

room.

Laila was trying to picture Yoel in Avraham's place. Zahar and Avraham's relationship possessed a purity that Laila wanted for herself. In the short time she had known the two young people, she had seen a strong commitment and a passionate love. Would Yoel be as protective? He didn't have the same temperament as Avraham. Yoel was a bit standoffish and introspective. Suddenly Laila had doubts.

"What a nice young man, and so handsome." Laila could hear those words echoing from the past. Was she becoming her own Emma? Her skin prickled. Her mother managed to find her way into Laila's thoughts daily—one way or another. If Laila became half the woman her mother was, she would be lucky.

"He is the most wonderful husband a girl could have," Zahar's eyes reflected her admiration. "I hope, someday, you find someone like him."

Laila started to mention Yoel, but something stopped her. Perhaps she didn't think of him as husband material any more. After all, she was only seventeen.

Zahar adjusted her bed into a sitting position. "So, tell me something about yourself, after all, we are going to be friends for life. I believe when you save a person's life, you are responsible for them forever. I could not think of a better person to hold that responsibility, but please do not take it as your mantra."

They laughed.

Zahar seemed eager to know who Laila was. Laila rarely talked about herself; she didn't find herself that exciting. "You're much too kind. I acted on impulse—not meaning I didn't care; it was that I couldn't have done anything different. My parents raised me that way." Actually what she had done for Zahar was a big concession. Normally she

10

would have put herself first, but something happened that day that she still didn't quite understand. Perhaps the understanding would come later, after things settled down. Before that day, Laila realized, she hadn't particularly been a nice person.

"Your parents did a good job. I'm sure they're proud of you."

"So you want to know my story." Laila reached for Zahar's hand. "Well, let's see. My grandparents came to Palestine from Russia in 1920, during the third migration or *Aliyah*. They lived side-by-side with Arab families and everyone got along, for the most part. My mother passed away some time ago, and my sisters got married and left shortly afterwards, leaving me to take care of Abba. I miss her every day." Suddenly Laila felt tears well up in her eyes. She did her best to ignore them and went on. "My Abba is a hard worker but a little set in his ways. I still live with him."

"Show me a man worth knowing, and I'll show you a man set in his ways."

"My Abba will like you. Do you mind if I ask how you two met ... you and Avraham?"

"Not at all. We met at Scout camp. We were both introverts and considered a bit eccentric, so we gravitated toward each other."

The story had a familiar ring to it. "I find that hard to believe ... your being eccentric and introverted." Were Yoel and she going to end up like them? The doubts kept mounting. Their dreams were becoming further apart.

"Were you born here?" Laila was sure that Zahar found Laila nosy, and maybe tiresome, but Zahar seemed to be interested in her too.

"No, I was born in Poland shortly after my parents had emigrated from Russia. My father was a diamond dealer and owned his own business. Someone broke the glass one night and stole everything on display. Fortunately the important pieces were in the safe, but they wrote terrible things on the wall and worse."

Laila could see how painful this was for her, so she held up her hand. "I didn't know. Sorry." Their friendship was new and delicate. They were family now.

"Of course you didn't know. I want to tell you the story anyway; it's interesting. My father asked my mother to sew loose diamonds into a false hem in the collar of our shirts. We were searched at every checkpoint and expected to be caught and killed. It was a miracle we made it intact. Once we reached our destination, my father was able to sell the stones and, with that money, he was able to buy a small business here."

"That sounds like the makings of a good book. You should write it down while you can."

Zahar laughed. "I doubt I have the skills to do justice to the story. Perhaps someone else will write it for me someday. The ending of my parents' lives is an unhappy one."

They talked for some time until Avraham returned. He brought sweets and tea and the flowers in a glass vase. Laila tried to make Zahar laugh when she could to take her mind off her sorrow. Although the child was never mentioned, the subject hung heavily about the room like a shroud. Laila glanced at the clock on the stand and realized she had stayed longer than she had expected. She would have to find a phone to call Judah to pick her up. As much as she hated to think about it, Laila had homework and tests to study for. She had a lot to make up for the weeks she had been out of school, so she began gathering her belongings.

"You know," said Avraham, "we are the generation that will have to deal with what is going on right now, so why don't we begin before we have no choice? Look what is happening to the Jews in Germany."

Avraham surprised Laila. She had taken him for an academic, not an activist.

"What is on your mind?" asked Zarah, suddenly more alive than Laila had seen her since the unmentionable day.

"The Scouts have begun organizing group meetings to discuss this topic. I have hesitated getting involved because of school, but I no longer have an excuse. Not after what happened to you two. What do you think, Laila?"

"I belong to a Scout group, but haven't been in some time, what with school and work. I've been on hikes, learned how to plant vegetables, and sat through lectures on irrigation. Right now I don't have time for friends—that is, other friends —but if you two are going, I might join you. Yes, count me in." Laila rose awkwardly from the chair. "I hate to leave, but I must run."

They all laughed at the thought of Laila running anywhere. She would not be doing any running for a long time. She had fractured her femur in two places and her knee had been badly bruised. Her right arm had been badly burned and the left had minor contusions. "I'll be back tomorrow if I can. Do you need anything?"

"Only you. Hurry back." Zahar's face had regained its color in the last few moments. Laila hoped it would last after she left.

Laila leaned over and kissed Zahar's cheek, which had been restored to its beautiful desert tan—the part that was not bandaged. Zahar kissed Laila back, and they hugged as best they could. Laila held out her hand to Avraham, but once again he gathered her into a bear hug. "We are family." Those were her sentiments exactly.

"Thank you. That means a lot to me. *Shalom.*" Laila stood

at the door, almost wishing she didn't have to leave. She felt so comfortable with Zahar and Avraham, almost like they were her brother and sister.

"Do you have a ride home?" asked Avraham.

"Yes. My brother will pick me up." Laila left Zahar and Avraham, feeling uplifted until she stepped into the street. Another British soldier was pushing an elderly Jew out of his way. The soldier cursed him, hitting him with the butt of his rifle. The old man cowered. An angry woman intervened and the soldier knocked her to the ground. People began screaming at the soldier, surrounding him, and spitting on him—some kicked him in the ribs. They managed to overtake him, when a car pulled up, separated the crowd, fired into the air, and helped the officer to his feet and into the vehicle. The soldier driving the car glanced Laila's way. She froze. It was the same soldier who had been so kind to her during the bombing. Those green eyes stared back at her and then he disappeared like a mirage.

Laila's mood turned black. At that moment she felt she had to do something to stop the intentional attack by British soldiers on older Jews who could not defend themselves against those actions. She wasn't sure what that would be, but she thought about what Avraham had said. Maybe it was time to get involved.

Chapter 3

Ezra

Jerusalem, 1942

Ezra Ben Hayim had struggled with his studies for the past two years. His parents had such high hopes, but he was restless, and had little interest in history, mathematics, or political science. What he wanted most was to write poetry. Small slips of paper containing beginnings, middles, and ends of poems were spirited away in a copper-covered tin box, stowed under his bed in his modest dorm room. Ezra had hidden his secret for years, as he and his parents moved from one place to another ... his father the "war hero," his mother, the worshiper of a war hero. Ezra had no desire to fight anyone. He was a pacifist, but knew, as long as he remained in Palestine, he would sooner or later have to physically fight for the freedom of his new country. And so he did the best he could, despite his restlessness, to get top grades and remain at the university.

A dreadful paper was due in political science: something to do with the rise and fall of great countries. He had chosen times, and there was plenty of information in the library. Although he had completed the research part of his paper, Ezra could not get started knitting it together. His heart just wasn't in it. What he did like was writing for the university press. He had his own column on current affairs in the art world. His father said it was a waste of written space.

Of course Ezra's father would think his writing was insignificant. His father's life was a series of hostile encounters, one of which being the reason for immigrating to Palestine. Basically, his father got along with no one; that is, except Ezra's mother. Born in Manhattan, Ezra remembered little about the States. What he remembered most was never being afraid a bomb would land on his head. Was his father's pull to defend someone else's land that strong, or was it the need to fight? Ezra vaguely remembered his father in one battle or another, the last with his boss. The boss had landed in the hospital with a smashed jaw and Ezra's father had landed in jail. The boss didn't press charges because of what he had said to provoke his employee, but he had made it clear: Ezra's father would not work in the state of New York again.

And so, they packed up their belongings and arrived in Palestine in time for Ezra's father to be trained for the Jewish army. His rise through the ranks had become legendary and his son's resentment had grown even wider.

A knock pulled Ezra from his despair. He was not expecting anyone, although the interruption—any interruption—was timely. Maybe, he thought, he could return with more vigor after a brief respite. Ezra rose, stowed a few stray pieces of clothing behind throw pillows, and headed for the door. His father had insisted a peephole be drilled into his dorm door, so Ezra could be warned of an enemy and escape if necessary. Ezra's father was always looking over Ezra's shoulder.

David Stern's face appeared, somewhat distorted through the peephole. Ezra threw opened the door to welcome his best friend. Ezra and David had met a year ago, and shared the love of poetry. Ezra thought David would be famous someday. David's poetry was much more involved than Ezra's, as Ezra struggled with each piece.

"Anna's downstairs and she would like to talk to you," said David. "She doesn't look happy either. You better throw some clothes on and come quick."

"I didn't expect her; she knows I'm studying. I wonder what is so important. I'll be right down." Ezra pulled a shirt from off the threadbare couch, and his pants from the dirty clothes pile in the corner. He really needed someone to take care of him. Ezra put one leg in the pants and hopped across the room to the door, where he stopped long enough to struggle into the other leg without falling over. He took the stairs two at a time, continuing to wonder what his fiancée wanted. She almost never came to his dorm.

Anna's sweet face appeared as he rounded the corner. Well, Ezra thought she was sweet, but Anna worked hard keeping that a secret. Why she felt she had to put on such a show of anger and strength was a mystery to him. Today, her fiery red hair was exceptionally neat and from what he could see, she was wearing something other than her usual baggy pants and her brother's even larger paint-streaked shirt from her oils class. Why was she here?

Ezra approached, wanting a hug but knew how she felt about displaying affection in public. She had been acting strange of late; but midterms were upon them, and she had to make all "A's" for her parents. They demanded nothing less.

Instead of the waltz, her gait was more like a farcical

funeral march marked by elongated strides until she stood next to him, taking his hand and walking him to a private corner.

"What a pleasant surprise." He was hoping it was going to be pleasant, but her face told him otherwise. He was not in the mood for a confrontation, not today when he had this wretched paper to finish. They had done nothing but fight lately. She wanted to conquer the world; he wanted to savor it.

"I have something to say to you." Anna stood, playing with her curls, eyes blazing with passion.

"That sounds serious. Please sit down."

"I prefer to stand; and it *is* serious. I'm breaking our engagement."

"You are? Why?" Ezra ran his slender fingers through his disheveled raven waves, stepping backward, almost knocking over a wooden chair behind him.

"We have different goals," she said, almost in a whisper.

"We've always had different goals. That hasn't changed." Ezra took her hand and walked her to the couch. They sat. He tried to put his arm around her, but she resisted and his arm eventually draped the couch.

"We'll be seniors next year. I want to do something with my life, and I want someone who wants the same things. It's becoming clear you'd be happy remaining home writing while I go to work. I want a man with drive, a man who wants to conquer the world. A man ... with some guts."

"Wow," said Ezra, doubling over as if he'd been punched in the gut. After the shock of her words sunk in, he raised his head to search her eyes for the truth. "When ... did this ... all occur to you?"

"I guess it's always been there, but I loved you so much I

hid it." She lowered her eyes for a moment and then blurted out, "I need to be honest with you, so I'm going to tell you the truth. Someone has come into my life; someone I believe shares my passion. I think he and I are far more compatible after knowing each other just a month, than you and I after five years."

"Do I know him?"

"No."

"Where did you meet?"

"...at a Scout meeting of the *Be'eri*. I've joined."

"But we were involved in the *Tzofim Aleph, Scout Alpha,* soon to be graduates."

Her lip pouting. "I can belong to more than one Scout group."

Ezra sat dumbstruck. How could this happen? He'd been so happy with Anna. Apparently she hadn't felt the same way. He could feel his heart crumble. How could he live without her? What would he do?

Ezra had heard of the *Be'eri* group and only knew them to be interested in forming *kibbutzim*. These groups had become increasingly popular with youth who wanted to farm the land or fish the sea. Ezra had joined the Scouts because of his father, who wanted to make a man out of him, and he had seen the obligation through. He wasn't much on long nature walks unless he could write a poem about them, and he didn't care whether he could start a fire from scratch or not. When it became obvious that the camping part of the Scouts was just a cover for a covert spying agency, Ezra had become momentarily interested. It seemed the teens were gathering a database of geographical, topographical and planning information concerning Arab villages, to be used in future raids if necessary. Fortunately for Ezra, he had done very little of that. The glow had soon worn off and he'd

The Laundry Room

returned to his poetry.

What he had been interested in knowing was that when the British restricted land purchases to Jews entering the country, many parentless youth looked to join forces with others for guidance and security; and in 1927 the United Kibbutz Movement, *HaKibbutz Hameuhad*, was established. Some of the kibbutzim became political entities, while the others were merely for commerce. Some formed kibbutzim to escape the orthodox ideology of their parents. All members worked for a common cause, all equal in every way. As a poet, the whole idea appealed to Ezra, but he hadn't taken into consideration that Anna would not share his passion.

Anna was right about everything. Ezra had dreamed of their time together as man and wife—sitting side by side, holding hands, or reading; him writing poetry in the morning, having dinner ready when she returned from her job. It was all there, but apparently she had other thoughts. He wasn't the conquering type.

"I think you better leave." He rose and pulled Anna to her feet. She began to speak, but he put his index finger to his lips and shook his head. Ezra walked her to the front door and closed it behind her. Returning to his room, he threw himself down on his bed and gave way to a flood of tears. He cried for what seemed like an eternity; although he knew it was self-serving. He didn't care. When he thought he had gotten it out of his system, he searched for something else to think about. He'd show her he could do just fine without her.

Ezra's eyes drifted to the table next to the couch and a pamphlet he had been reading, which focused on what would happen to Palestine when the British pulled out. The British Mandate was coming to an end, sooner than anyone wanted to accept. The Zionist movement talked about statehood:

running their own country, protecting their right to practice their religion as they saw fit, and providing freedom from tyranny. Ezra had written poem after poem about freedom.

He had revisited the United States for a month one summer, when he was fourteen. His grandfather, a bigwig in the freedom movement, had brought Ezra with him to America to meet those who had clout and money. A visit to Washington, DC, the capital, opened Ezra's eyes to what freedom was supposed to look like. Ezra couldn't believe Americans' lifestyle. It had changed so much since he was last there. His family was fairly well off, but they lived in crowded apartments in an even more crowded section of Tel Aviv. Ezra was aware his grandfather and father were part of the *Haganah,* an underground military training movement, which was preparing for what everyone knew was coming: a struggle between Arabs and Jews for the land. Perhaps Ezra should consider doing something other than dreaming; but he was scared of facing death head on, and that was his undoing.

Chapter 4

Ari

Jerusalem, 1942

Ari Bitterman had a dream: improve his ancestral home so his descendants could live freely on the land God had promised them in the *Torah*. That dream included a soul mate, but unfortunately for him, he had managed to conclude his junior year in engineering school at the university without catching the eye of any young woman, and finding his true love didn't look promising. Ari's hopes were dwindling away. Even his participation in the Pioneer Israeli Scouts hadn't garnered many friends. Most people thought Ari antisocial. He couldn't help that he preferred building skyscrapers to hiking through the woods; and besides, he was shy. And another thing, he would often experience piercing headaches while studying that left him spent and not up to socializing, and so he supposed he would be single for the rest of his life.

To assuage his angst, he had thrown himself deeper into his studies as he designed bridges, temples, apartments, and banks. The blueprints scattered about the floor of his dorm room were proof that he was serious about putting his energies in something other than finding a mate. It was just that everyone was pairing up and seemed to be so happy.

Ari removed the small, wire-rim glasses from his profoundly hooked nose and rubbed his sore eyes and bushy brows, tired after a number of nights without sleep, studying for exams. He glanced about his depressingly beige dorm room and witnessed a disaster in the making. He was not much of a housekeeper. Noting his attention wandering from his studies, he decided to take a break. His right hand had cramped from holding a pencil too tightly for too long, so he sat clenching and unclenching his fist to rid himself of the tension. It occurred to him that he might change his study location—perhaps the library—but with the unusual amount of rain lately, Ari preferred staying close to home. The problem was that he lacked human companionship.

Ari shivered. One of those wretched headaches was forming in his temples. His hands left his forehead and traveled to his thick, black curls where he began massaging the pain away. How long had it been since his last haircut? Weeks. Not a religious zealot, Ari generally tried to keep his hair trimmed and neat, but had put it off way too long. He had no one to remind him to do such things.

He could hear his grandmother, in the distance, calling him one of her many endearments: *Leben ahf dein keppele,* something to do with being smart and doing things well, or a *bisseleh kop,* little head. As Ari grew older, she would say it mattered not, the size of his head, only that it was crammed with knowledge. There was no denying he was smart—first in his class his first two years. But girls just weren't interested in smart; they wanted good looks and muscles. Later, when they grew up, they would come looking for a good provider.

The Laundry Room

Who was he kidding?

As Ari left his room to grab a bite, he ducked, as had become a ritual after learning a sore lesson the first day he entered the doorway. Being tall had its advantages and disadvantages. Tonight he was on his way to a local boardinghouse that allowed college students to dine with the guests. Ari supposed it helped out with the expenses of running the place. After losing several pounds the first few months he was on his own, Ari had discovered the boardinghouse and found it far more appetizing than cooking on a single burner he would have to pull from under the sink. Skinny by most standards, he was at least visible, now that he ate regularly.

One thing had led to another and Ari had begun waiting tables, hoping the owner would augment his meager allowance. Since his father had passed away, money was tight; not like his friend Itzhak, who never had to worry. As roommates, they had been poles apart. While Itzhak threw his money around, Ari sent money to America to help his mother, sister, and brothers. The family had been taken in upon arrival from Poland by a distant cousin, but there had already been too many people in the small apartment. Ari had struck out on his own, leaving America and his family behind. Bound for Palestine, the *Land of Milk and Honey*, via *Youth Aliya,* a movement that placed orphaned Jewish children in kibbutz-like settings in order to build up the country and give the children a home.

Ari's mother had found it difficult finding a job because she spoke only Polish, Russian, and a little *Yiddish*. Even the few English words she had picked up on board the ship to the States were difficult to understand, so she took in laundry and ran errands for the homebound. Fortunately, a local widower had been very generous. Ari thought he might have designs on his mother. It wouldn't upset him one bit if she remarried. He knew she had loved his father, and it would make life easier for him knowing she and his siblings were secure.

"Ari." Mrs. Malkin called from across the room. "Don't forget to bring out the strudel for dessert. You know how Mr. Nadler loves my strudel." She sniffed as she passed. "Have you been into the basil again?"

Ari couldn't help that basil was his favorite herb. He loved the citrusy fragrance when it was being chopped; so what if he had a little of it in his pocket? Call him nuts.

Mrs. Malkin was a widow, who out of sheer necessity had turned her own home into a thriving business; she also wanted to help young people any way she could. She had lost her son to one of the many skirmishes as they fought to form their homeland. Mrs. Malkin often reminded Ari of his mother: both ample and still handsome to look at.

"I remember." Ari picked up a tray full of dirty dishes and headed for the kitchen, almost colliding with a young woman, hair covered with a drab scarf, eyes downcast, and wearing what his mother would call a *schmatte*. Her eyes flew open, revealing the darkest orbs Ari had ever seen. She immediately lowered her lids, her lashes the color of desert sands as she hurried past. Where had she come from? He hadn't seen her before.

When the meal was over and the dishes put away, Ari approached Mrs. Malkin. "Who is the new girl?"

"That's my niece, Leora. Isn't she a beauty? Both parents gone. What a pity." She imaginarily spit between her forefinger and middle finger to frighten off bad spirits. His mother would have done the same thing. It was an old wives' tale that seemed to put things in their proper prospective.

"I hadn't noticed; I was too busy making sure I didn't

drop anything." Now he felt embarrassed. He could have found out other ways. Surely it would get back to the girl.

Leora...a lovely name. Ari thought all the way back to his room. That night he had a disturbing dream. He and Leora had found themselves in a small room and couldn't get out. He made advances and she rebuffed him. It became uncomfortable until some banging noise woke him.

"Ari, wake up. It's Izzy. You'll miss your exam if you don't wake up."

Izzy Switzer was a past roommate. Izzy's family was one of the movers and shakers amidst the Jewish community, and Izzy knew where all the meetings were being held for Zionist youth organizations. He had tried to get Ari to attend, but Ari had lost interest after the last group meeting. All Ari wanted to do was build, not tear down. In the end, Ari had given up and joined anyway, discovering this group was far more than he had expected. Not only did they go on nature hikes, explore different terrains, and talk at length about their country; they took part in some clandestine operations that stimulated Ari's imagination. There were a lot of firebrands in the group, touting independence and freedom. Eventually, Ari had allowed himself to be drawn back into the passion of the most recent speakers.

As he shook sleep from his head, it suddenly occurred to Ari that his roommates had never lasted long. Maybe he *was* boring, but they all remained his friends.

"I'm up. Thank you." Ari pulled the covers back, slipped his feet into his worn slippers, and strode to the door that was never locked. Even so, it was an unwritten law to knock first. You never knew what was going on behind closed doors.

"Oy vey, you saved my life," yelled Ari, pulling on his threadbare robe. I don't know what I would have done—

probably failed the class." He scurried about the room like a mouse in a maze, tripping over books and blueprints. "How about coming to dinner with me tonight?" said Ari as he gathered whatever he could find for clothes.

Izzy laughed his good-natured laugh. "I'll save your life every day if I can get a free meal." His over-stuffed belly shook with delight. Izzy didn't believe in exercising. It was against his religion. Besides, he was going to be an accountant, and why waste the effort exercising when the only thing he would have to lift would be a pencil?

Ari couldn't argue with that; after all, it was his choice. Ari, on the other hand, was lucky not to have to watch his weight. His tall, delicate frame often brought on other endearing names like *faygala,* which was Yiddish for bird.

Izzy patted Ari on the shoulder and headed out the door. "I'll be back for dinner. I'm holding you to your word."

Ari laughed, tossed one of the small sofa pillows at Izzy on his way out, and as the door closed, quickly donned his recycled clothes. He opened the door and called after Izzy, "Don't worry. I always honor my commitment, even if it is to you." He glanced at the tarnished mirror and realized he looked like he had slept in his clothes. Who would notice? He wasn't exactly a Beau Brummell.

Izzy's head reappeared inside the room "Did you hear the news?"

"What news?" asked Ari, closing the door and heading down the hallway.

"The Zionist Organization put out the *Biltmore Program,* a platform to establish a Jewish Commonwealth."

Ari stopped and shifted his rucksack. "And exactly who is going to listen to that?"

"It's a start and a step beyond the *Balfour Declaration.*

The Laundry Room

Remember, Rome wasn't built in a day."

"So I've been told."

"Oh, and the Peel Commission is coming to an end. They lifted the embargo. My mother's family will be able to come live with us next year. Isn't that wonderful? My uncle is a fine baker." Izzy rubbed his stomach.

Ari laughed. "That's wonderful. Now if you don't stop with the newscast, I will miss my exam." Ari could hear Izzy chuckle all the way down the hall.

As Ari strode to his exam, he thought about Izzy's news and what the zealots from the last scout meeting had said about what was happening in Russia, Germany, and Poland; and that the annihilation of Jews might spread throughout the world if Hitler had his way. It was something to worry about for sure. Somehow his exam didn't seem so important anymore. What good would a degree do him if he were dead?

The rain that had begun as a fine mist was now coming down in torrents. Already soaked to the skin, Ari stopped trying to dodge the drops, and instead, embraced them, drinking in God's gift. As he entered the classroom, he noted to his dismay that the only vacant seat was by an open window. The cool, sodden air chilled Ari to the bone as he fought to concentrate through the exam, which was harder than expected. His mind kept wandering back and forth between Izzy's words and those of the zealot's. Ari's body began to shake as he felt one of those headaches start at the base of his neck, working its way to his forehead. Midway through the exam he started filling in blank areas with made up drivel. At this point, he was sure he had failed. Maybe it was a sign he was on the wrong path. Maybe he would forget about school and throw his energy into helping his new country survive. It had been his dream to build anyway. He already knew enough to do what was needed to be done. All of a sudden the stress lifted off his shoulders and he was able to finish the exam, feeling more confident of his future than he had in his life.

Chapter 5

Itzhak

Jerusalem, 1942

Itzhak Schwartzman sat in class, bored by the current lecturer. They were studying medieval French politics and the professor was putting him to sleep. Why couldn't professors find a way to make the topic more interesting? He could make it interesting, given the chance. Instead of dates and incidents, Itzhak would have his students delve into the lives of the men and women who had made history and carved out the political world. He loved when he had to do a project or present a political situation with an impasse. His life was spent in the library doing research. Someday it would pay off—he was sure.

Two years in America, studying at Harvard University had shown Itzhak what education was supposed to be. He had been sent to America to study the democratic process, known to have worked well for the United States. The new Jewish homeland was hoping and preparing for its own independence and was in the process of deciding how to build the basic foundation for its own democracy. Itzhak had immersed himself in the culture of America, his adopted country, and promptly embraced some of his fellow students' bad habits, which included drinking and carousing.

Unfortunately for Itzhak, his father had called him home to help out with the business when he had his first heart attack. Fortunately for all, Itzhak's father had recovered quickly and gone back to work, freeing Itzhak to complete his education locally. It didn't take long for Itzhak to see his present education equal to that of Harvard's, except for this class, which dragged on for hours. In his head, he was planning the new Jewish state. He had studied enough successful and unsuccessful governments to know what would work and what would not. "The rise and fall of world governments" would be the title of his dissertation in graduate school. Itzhak already knew he would be going. His family had plenty of money, and the prestige of having a son with a masters and possibly doctorate, would be his father's crowning glory. Itzhak, like his father, was tall, with thick, sandy-blond hair, a throwback from Polish ancestors; but he was blessed with his mother's stormy blue eyes. His family had come to Palestine via Russia a number of years earlier, hoping to make a difference. They were one of the few families with money. His father, a member of the committee planning the independence of a Jewish homeland, had quickly risen through the ranks of the *Haganah*.

Itzhak knew his father meant business in everything he committed himself to. Hadn't he bounced back from that heart attack? His doctors called him a miracle. No one told his father *no*.

Itzhak had not wanted to be a moon that drew its splendor from the sun. He wanted to shed his own light. Realizing he had been travelling down a negative path,

The Laundry Room

Itzhak switched gears to something more to his taste—Sonya. They had been introduced shortly after his return from the States by family friends, and had been dating ever since. Even though things were beginning to get out-of-hand sexually, Sonya managed to keep him in line. She came from a wealthy family, one that had given her many benefits— much like himself. Following in her mother's footsteps, Sonya had been taught—early on—how to direct others' lives; and it was she who directed their relationship. Itzhak believed he was in love, but was keeping his options open. They were both young, and neither seemed ready to make that final commitment.

Someone cleared his throat. Itzhak looked up, suddenly aware he was the last one left in the room.

"Either you were mesmerized by my presentation or off fighting the war."

"I wasn't doing either." Itzhak realized how curt that sounded. He was embarrassed, not because it was true, but because he hadn't had a better comeback. One thing Itzhak's father had drilled into his head was to be respectful of his elders. He had forgotten his manners. When he was three, his father had taken him to Haifa on a business trip. One of the men his father did business with tousled Itzhak's hair and Itzhak brushed his hand away, embarrassing the man and his father. He'd never heard the end of it.

"Well, perhaps you'd like to take over my class next week. We'll be looking at the Byzantine Empire." The professor's smug expression made Itzhak believe he was pleased with himself, as if he had come up with a brilliant plan. "Yes, I like that idea. It's in your hands. You can try and entertain this uninspired mass."

What had he gotten himself into? How could he get out of this one? Maybe he didn't want to. Maybe he'd show this man how boring his classes were.

"I'd be delighted. How far into the chapter should I go?"

"A wise guy, huh? We'll see what kind of teacher you are when you stand before your peers." The professor turned and stormed off in the opposite direction.

Had he bitten off more than he could chew? No, by God, he could do it, and do it well. Wasn't Itzhak his father's son? And hadn't his father implanted confidence within him from infancy? Besides, he had already studied much of this at Harvard; presenting it shouldn't actually be too difficult. Itzhak gathered his possessions and headed for the door; he paused and walked to the podium where he struck a pedagogical pose, observing the room from a different prospective. He clutched the podium as a moment of fear gave way to utter exhilaration. Yes, he would show the professor how to teach. Itzhak left the room, lighter than he had been in years.

Itzhak's friend Ari accosted him as he exited the building. "What kept you? I almost left."

"My professor caught me daydreaming and challenged me to teach the class next week."

"What!"

Itzhak and Ari had been roommates for a short period of time early on, and although Itzhak and Ari had little in common, they remained close friends. Itzhak was handsome, with an aristocratic facial bone structure and compact body, while Ari was tall, lanky, and his face was not memorable by most standards. Ari's family was poor while, Itzhak's was well off, and even though the list continued, the two men were still drawn to each other. Both loved their country and were willing to do whatever it took to defend it. They had met the first day Itzhak entered the university. Ari had been Itzhak's orientation leader. His job was to take a group of new students around the school, pointing out interesting spots and giving unsolicited advice about social activities, of which there didn't seem to be many. It hadn't taken long for Itzhak to find outlets for his outgoing personality such as student government, the debate club, and a few other worthwhile organizations. Lately, Ari had gotten Itzhak involved in the Israeli Scouts, a group that took young people who had entered the country with no parents and gave them the skills necessary to survive. Actually having parents sometimes got in Itzhak's way. Did he just think that? He shuddered.

"I'm going to show him how boring he is and how the subject should be taught," said Itzhak, wanting to purge the previous thoughts from his mind. He did love his parents; they were just difficult and demanding.

"You realize it might give him a reason to grade you harder. If these professors don't like you, they can make your life a hell on earth."

"If that happens, I'll challenge him. If my grades drop, he'll be sorry. My father will have a word with the president of the university. Let him try."

"My, you're cocky today." Ari often joked with Itzhak, but this might not be a joke.

"No more than usual."

The two men walked for a while without talking. Itzhak was already planning his presentation. He loved a good challenge and couldn't wait to get started. Itzhak had promised Ari he would study with him, this afternoon, for an upcoming test; and Itzhak wasn't one to go back on his word. He was anxious, though, to begin putting his presentation together. Then he remembered why he had asked Ari to meet. "Have you heard about the secret rallying tonight at the boarding house across the street from your dorm? The

34

word came down from Reuven. My father told me to stay away, but you know I never listen."

"Sounds interesting," said Ari. "Do you always go against your father's wishes?"

"Most of the time."

"Mmmm. Okay then; let's go. And about Professor Friedman, you might want to reconsider. They have our future in their hands."

"No, Ari. It's we who have our futures in our own hands. Isn't that why we're going tonight? Things are happening around the world and particularly in this country. We need to be aware of them and not taken by surprise. Say, did you hear about Avraham Stern's death?"

"Who?"

Itzhak looked at Ari with utter astonishment. "He was the head of *Lohamei Herut, Lehi*, 'Fighters for the Freedom of Israel'. Some people refer to them as *The Stern Gang*. Stern was fighting for unlimited immigration of Jews to Palestine. They split from *Irgun* because of differing ideologies. Stern's group was siding with the Bolsheviks, while *Lehi* was favoring Germany. The British called him a terrorist, arrested him, and shot him under suspicious circumstances. You know what that means."

"I suppose I do. Listen, I have to get to Mrs. Malkin's to help with dinner. How about studying for an hour before the meeting?" asked Ari.

"Okay. And since when did you become a busboy?" Itzhak stopped again and stared at his friend. "Ah, a girl. I've never seen you blush."

"Well, maybe." Ari continued to walk in the direction of the boarding house. "She doesn't know I'm alive."

"After the meeting tonight, you're going to get your first

lesson in wooing."

"I don't want a harem, just one girl."

Itzhak landed a soft punch to Ari's arm, and Ari reciprocated with one to the stomach. Itzhak doubled over feigning pain, and both men laughed as they parted company.

As Itzhak walked in the opposite direction, it occurred to him, he might have erred by volunteering to take over the class. He'd better do well with the lecture, or he'd be the laughing stock.

As Itzhak continued on, he found himself bouncing from one thought to another as he realized Reuven hadn't said what tonight's meeting was about. Reuven had only said to make sure Itzhak was there and to pass on the information to Ari. Itzhak could feel his pulse race as he anticipated tonight's topic. There had been talk about establishing a kibbutz, but Itzhak didn't think they were old enough or experienced enough to strike out on their own. Besides, he had other responsibilities at the moment, like showing Professor Friedman up.

Chapter 6

Zahar

Jerusalem, August, 1942

The last dish dried from their meager evening meal, Zahar stretched and scanned the kitchen for any telltale sign of disarray. Neither she nor Avraham made enough at their part-time jobs to call what they did a living, and with her out of work to recuperate from the bombing of the King David Hotel, times were tough. Zahar and Avraham were in their first year of graduate school, majoring in science: she in biology, he in agronomy. They had met first in the Scouts and then in an undergraduate physics class, where they had realized they were meant for each other. Subsequently they spent all their time studying and making love.

Zahar had been promised to a young man of a wealthy family, but shrapnel from a detonated bomb had put an end to the engagement. She hadn't even met him, so she felt only pity for his parents. There had been nothing vested one way or another. As fate would have it, their third chance meeting was at the library and what might have been construed as rebound, turned into a full-blown love affair. She and Avraham were entirely compatible: they had a healthy sex life, similar taste in books, music, and art; of course, neither had time for any of those extravagances.

Both were mutually happy in their loving relationship. The one thing Zahar longed for was a child. The fact that she had lost the first one in the bombing hadn't deterred her from trying again. Her doctor said that her injuries had been close to ending her hopes; but, he reassured her, with time, she would be a mother.

Zahar glanced into the smoky mirror she had found at the bazaar and turned away quickly. It was difficult to look in a mirror straight on. She had been left with a scar on the right side of her face that traveled from her upper lip to her left eye and had drastically changed her appearance. She had feared Avraham wouldn't want to look at her or would shy away in bed, but that had not happened. It was as if he saw none of her disfigurement. Zahar hoped it were so.

"Zahar, please come here. I have something to discuss with you."

Zahar detected urgency in Avraham's voice. He was a serious young man, but possessed a slightly skewed sense of humor. She wondered what was on his mind. Leaving the kitchen, she wheeled herself down the hall in a borrowed wheelchair. She stopped to rearrange her thick, black hair so it would partially cover the left side of her face before entering their small, cozy living room. Before she died, his mother had given them some old furniture that had been stored in her attic, and after Avraham refinished it and painted the walls a warm cream, the room actually took on a new personality. A few of Avraham's original paintings strategically placed about the room created a homey effect. He hadn't painted in years, not having the time, but said he hoped to pick it back up once he graduated and felt secure in his profession.

As Zahar approached, she noticed the set of Avraham's body. She was right; he had something on his mind. She rolled to his side and flipped on the corner lamp, draped with an old grey shawl that added a bit of drama to the room. Avraham often said that everything Zahar touched turned golden. She wished it were true.

Zahar paused to study her husband. He was the epitome of Michelangelo's *David* in all its splendor: strong hands, a mass of black ringlets, and a body to be worshipped by her alone. She felt blessed to have been the one to catch his eye. They had a wonderful marriage—not like her parents, who had argued from dawn to dusk while they were alive. Avraham's only flaws were that he lived in a constant state of clutter—Zahar always having to pick up after him; and, on occasion, displayed a bad temper. But if those were his only flaws, she could live with them.

A pen stuck out of Avraham's black curls and an ink smudge stained his chin. With his pensive eyes, full of concern, he shifted his attention to her.

Speaking low, as if there were someone else in the next room, Avraham said, "I was approached yesterday by someone I've known for some time, but not socially. I don't think you ever met him. He's not someone you would take to —a bit gruff.

"Yes?" said Zahar, a bit impatiently. Earlier Zahar had noticed that Avraham was more distracted than usual. She hoped he was about to clear the air.

This man, Reuven, told me something was brewing, and asked if I wanted to be a part of history—he said he had just the thing. I was a little reticent to even bring this up, but I know you want to know everything that's in my head at all times, so I'm sharing this with you."

"Is that all?" she laughed, relieved that it wasn't personal. "What exactly is the meeting about?"

"Reuven said he was not at liberty to say more. They would explain everything when we got there. He asked me not to share this with anyone else. I don't think he knows I'm married. He said the information had to stay inside the Scouts."

Zahar sat quietly for a moment, taking in what Avraham had said. She knew he wouldn't have brought it up if he hadn't been the least bit interested. "Are you thinking of going?"

"I don't know. I'm not usually one to jump into things, but my curiosity is piqued, and you know what that means."

She chuckled again, something she did rarely anymore. "Yes. All too well. I guess it wouldn't hurt to see what the meeting is all about."

Avraham smiled his charismatic smile, and she melted. When he smiled like that, Zahar would probably agree to anything he asked of her.

"Should I go?"

"Of course, I would never consider anything that you didn't agree to; of course, unless you weren't interested and didn't care if I went alone." He paused as if rethinking his position. "Let's see for ourselves. How about it? Then we can talk it over and decide if it is for us ... or not." He shrugged.

Zahar chuckled again. He was always so formal. She thought he was better suited for the diplomatic corps than analyzing soil.

"Alright, let's go."

Avraham tidied up his papers while Zahar returned to the kitchen. As she passed the calendar on the wall, she couldn't help but note the 22nd of July circled in red—the day of the hotel bombing. Zahar stroked one hand lovingly across her belly, as if she were still with child and then cried silently. Not able to help herself, she often replayed that day over and over again, and it always ended the same.

###

The day showed its colors; a crystal blue sky with wafts of pink running through it, and not a cloud to be seen. It was July 22nd, two days before her twenty-third birthday. Zahar felt she had everything she had ever wanted, that is except a child; and, she reminded herself with a smile, that would change in only a few more months. Today she had an errand to run in the Old City of Jerusalem. Her class didn't start until 1:00, and Avraham had already left for the day. Zahar had promised to pick up a tablecloth for her mother-in-law for the upcoming holiday, and hoped she would make the right choice. Her mother-in-law, a retired pediatric nurse, volunteered a few days a week at the hospital and had little time to run errands. Zahar, wanting to please her, tried to give her whatever time she could to helping out. She felt blessed having Ruth as her mother-in-law and got along with her better than she had her own mother while she was alive.

Early into her education, Zahar had decided to major in biological science, while Avraham had chosen agricultural science. They both wanted to give back to their country and felt that, in order to progress, science was to their best advantage. Both had promising careers, and were being sought after by a number of independent companies. They would graduate with honors.

A sudden chill passed through Zahar's body. Six months along and experiencing some spotting, she worried about anything abnormal. Her mother-in-law had assured Zahar

The Laundry Room

that she was doing just fine. She did have experience in that field. Since Zahar had no car, she was always using public transportation, which might be a bus or taxi depending upon whether she felt flush or not. Today it would be a bus. She took a seat next to an older woman, covered from head to toe in black muslin. The woman's eyes never met Zahar's, as Zahar took the only vacant seat. Zahar was used to this behavior; Jews and Arabs seldom gave each other the time of day anymore, with Palestine a volcano waiting to erupt. Every day, some sort of skirmish took place around the country. If anyone should be bitter, it should be Zahar, having lost her parents to this hatred, but she had made peace with the world and hoped to find a better way to solve their indigenous problems.

The bus headed down King David Boulevard, fast approaching the King David Hotel. When the bus came to an abrupt halt, Zahar rose, grabbed her purse, and followed those exiting the bus. The thought of not having to be in class that morning made her giddy, giddy enough to decide to skip the rest of the day. The aroma of freshly-cut grass wafted past her as she strolled toward the hotel. She loved all the greenery recently planted, but most of all, she loved seeing children playing on the grass. To her, the grass represented a miracle, because it grew in the middle of a desert. Zahar patted her stomach. Someday soon, she would watch her own child play in the grass.

Zahar passed a food stand and inhaled the distinctive aroma of falafels. They were her favorite. As she deliberated whether she had time to purchase one, something exploded, sending her airborne like a leaf caught up in a sudden wind storm. She rose higher and higher and then dropped, landing on something soft that blanketed the ground. The force of the impact had parted her from her belongings.

Lynda Lippman-Lockhart

###

"Are you coming? We'll be late," Avraham called.

Zahar, reliving that horrible day, hadn't heard Avraham enter the kitchen. "I didn't realize it was tonight."

"Yes, sorry. I thought I mentioned that." He reached for the jacket he had left on the back of the dining room chair and absentmindedly knocked over a glass of water. He reached for a towel to mop up the mess, but Zahar shooed him away with her free hand.

"It's all right. I'll be ready in a minute." She really wasn't in the mood for a lot of people tonight. She had hoped for a peaceful evening at home. Although he said otherwise, Avraham sometimes jumped before knowing the consequences, which kept her on her toes. She hoped he would consider her before throwing himself into something that would affect her. Getting over the loss of the baby would take time, and Zahar needed time to heal. She realized men reacted differently, and that Avraham was keeping the loss bottled up inside. She supposed he needed a diversion. She would try and be open-minded.

As Avraham wheeled Zahar out of their building, a massive roar from above sent them reeling against the building. Zahar grabbed Avraham's arm, pulling him down to her level. They looked up to see a plane, the unmistakable sound of a bomber, passing out of their line of sight. Zahar trembled.

Avraham wrapped his arms around her. "It's all right; they're gone. Just a show of power. You're all right. We're all right." Avraham held onto her until she stopped trembling. "Let's get to the meeting quickly. I'm afraid it's time to leave Jerusalem."

Zahar nodded. "I'm okay. Just a little shaken." She pulled her shawl about her. "It's just the memory of the last time ...

you know? Yes, let's leave while we can." All she really wanted to do was return to her room and her bed.

As Avraham pushed Zahar along, they passed hoards of others still huddled together from sheer fright. The going was rough; the sidewalks were cracked in most places from previous attacks. Zahar was now more resolute than ever to leave Jerusalem behind.

Chapter 7

Laila

Jerusalem, same evening

Upon entering the boarding house where Laila had been told the meeting would take place, she was shocked by the number of young men carrying machine guns. Zahar, Avraham and she were spirited through a side door and down a winding stairway; through a dark, cold hall; through a hidden door that slid to the side; and into a dimly lit room filled with other young people. Bandaged and supported on crutches, Laila hobbled into the room, wondering just what was going to happen that required armed guards. Since Avraham had to carry Zahar down the stairs, Laila found herself having to make her own way; and at the bottom she was propelled to the front of the room, where she located three empty seats together. Laila recognized a number of the Scout members from previous meetings, but knew few. She was not what some called a social butterfly. Funny, she loved English idioms and devoured American newspapers even when they were months old, but at this moment, she didn't

The Laundry Room

America had taken its time entering the war, hence, allowing Germany to continue its annihilation of the Jews; and Great Britain was doing nothing to abate a future conflict between Arabs and Jews once the British Mandate came to an end. Was there no one to come to their aid?

Laila was partially recovered from what had been a defensive move at the King David Hotel by a militant Zionist group called the *Irgun*, although she had heard other stories with different takes on who was to blame. She was told that the British had set up headquarters in the hotel and that much of their secret paperwork had been stored there, and that they had held clandestine meetings with those opposed to a Jewish state. The *Haganah* apparently had tried to warn the British, but ninety-one people died that day, including the man on whom Laila had landed; while forty-six, including Zahar and her, had been injured. The only good that had come out of the bombing was Laila's friendship with Zahar. And so when Zahar called to tell her about the meeting, she agreed to go. The two of them looked like they had been in a war of their own.

An especially thin young man strode to the front of the room and held up his hands for quiet. "Please, we don't have much time, so let's get started. You are here because someone else thought you could be trusted and that same someone believed you had something to offer. We are at a crossroads in the formation of a Jewish state; and if we do not step forward to do our part, we will not have the right to criticize those who tried and were unsuccessful."

Laila looked about her and noticed all eyes focused on the young man. She felt the room charged with electricity, yet wasn't completely convinced this was for her. Yes, she wanted to do her part, but what did these young men know about fighting a war? She thought there might be other ways more covert and less dangerous.

"Many of you have come to Palestine, orphaned by a cruel dictator who wants to 'wipe the Jews off the face of the earth.' This is your chance to do something about that, a chance to live in a land where everyone is Jewish and no one is your enemy. How many of you saw your parents die? How many saw them turn their backs on you as they marched to their grave? Are you going to go silently or are you going to fight for your right to be free and die of natural causes when you're old? Look about you. There is potential here. There are great minds that have not been tapped. You can do anything you set your minds to. You can make this the greatest country ever imagined."

"Yes," responded a voice from the back of the room.

"Where do we sign?" yelled another.

All of a sudden the room became riotous, ready to follow the leader without thought of personal welfare. Laila found herself caught up in the moment, ready to sign herself. She turned to Zahar and Avraham who were among those cheering. There was no doubt the young man had found his audience. Laila's eyes caught Zahar's; they were ablaze with enthusiasm. The tall, thin young man to Laila's left with the pronounced, hooked nose and small, close-set eyes looked scared to death; but seemed to be as moved as Laila by what was happening in the room.

The first speaker sat down and the next moved forward, pacing back and forth in front of his audience. "We have heard firsthand what will happen in months. As David said, when the British leave, we'll be on our own. We are offering options today. One is to form kibbutzim about the country that act not only as specialized agricultural, manufacturing, and creative centers, but as independent armies that patrol and protect their own sector. As David also said, the Jewish army is small and cannot be everywhere at the same time; they need help. They need *our* help. *You* can help. Whether you are interested in fighting or growing, your help is needed. What can you do for your country? That is what we want to know today. Who is in? Let me see a show of hands."

Hands shot up around the room. Laila found herself joining the others. She was sold on the idea of doing her part. So what if she didn't go to college right away, it would always be there; and what an opportunity to do something monumental. Yes, she was in. Where did she sign?

"I mentioned 'options.' That will depend upon you and will come later. I am not at liberty to divulge anything beyond the kibbutz today. First, we have to know how involved you want to be." The speaker turned at the waist, motioning the next speaker on, and then he stood with his comrades.

The last radical to speak was short, stocky, in his late teens, and appeared worldlier than the others.

"We have already spoken about the coming upheaval once the British leave. We can either act as our parents and grandparents did when they believed their countries: Poland, Germany, and Russia would protect them once the battle had begun; or we can stand our ground and prepare for the battle that will come. That is why most of you are here today. We will never lie down again to be tread upon. We will fight back any way we can. Most of you belong to Scout groups. We want to expand on the foundation that has already been laid and extend that experience, making you all self-sustaining, and prepared to guard our borders. The Jewish army is small and spread thin. We need to help the cause. We are young and able. Let us band together to show the world what we are made of."

A cheer and thunderous applause followed his speech.

Everyone stood, fired up, ready to fight for what was rightfully theirs—"The Promised Land." Laila felt the stirrings of something big about to happen. She glanced at the young man next to her; he smiled and nodded feverishly.

It was then a few people rose and walked to the door, mumbling under their breath. One was heard saying: "This is not for me." They obviously did not want to be a part of the movement. Apparently they were not ready to quit college or strike out on their own. Starting their own kibbutz was not in their plans, but there were plenty who remained.

The first speaker, David, apparently the leader, stood and shouted: "*Sheket*! Quiet! Please. We need order. Please, those of you who are leaving, we ask that you keep our secret or you will be placing us in grave danger." The few who stood ready to leave nodded and then filed out. "Those of you who are interested and would like to be notified of the next meeting, please come forward to record your names and how we can reach you. We will meet here again in a week or so unless you are notified otherwise. You will be contacted in time to make your plans. Any questions? See one of us after the meeting. Thank you for coming and thank you for loving your country." He turned to speak with his comrades and then turned back to his audience, his finger to his lips, his other hand motioning to stay put.

A fracas outside the door brought conversation to a halt. The lights went out. It was forbidden for Jews to congregate without permission, according to some British mandate. Laila's eyes widened as she and everyone else huddled together, trying not to make a noise or fall on top of each other. The door to the basement was concealed and difficult to find, but not impossible. She held her breath as a loud conversation outside the room became even more heated. It was difficult to see, but fright had an odor. It occurred to

The Laundry Room

Laila what might happen if they were discovered. Abba would kill her, if someone else didn't first.

Muffled voices continued. Had they been discovered? She was sure her heart would give them away; it was beating outside her chest. Laila pictured the sober British soldiers, stiff backs and necks prowling the building, looking for an excuse to arrest or shoot a wayward Jew. The thought sent dreadful chills down her spine.

Time dragged on as she and Zahar clung to each other, praying not to be discovered. Laila glanced from one person to another in the dimly lit room, strangers looking to one another for strength or protection if the unthinkable happened. Laila found herself constantly asking herself why she had been spared during the bombing, only to die months later. Would the British soldiers shoot them on sight, or haul them off to prison? She wouldn't be able to stand being shut up like a caged animal. How foolish she had been to come without considering the consequences! Yet the adrenaline pumping through her body was magnificent.

The shuffling outside finally faded. Everyone remained silent until the door opened and closed. What did that mean? Was it all over? Laila couldn't stand it any longer. Her underarms hurt from leaning on her crutches for so long. Strands of hair not caught up in her braid were soaked from perspiration and plastered about her face. Thank goodness she had braided her hair tonight.

"All clear. They're gone," whispered someone as he made his way through the crowd. "It was a close call. You can turn the lights back on."

Laila let escape the breath she had been holding. The person delivering the 'all clear' became visible. He must have been on watch; otherwise, Laila was sure she would have noticed him earlier. He was very handsome, with extraordinary navy blue eyes that resembled a stormy Mediterranean Sea. His thick, curly blond hair stood out in all directions, making him look like a kid that had just tumbled out of bed.

Laila began to wonder if being involved with the movement would be fraught with surprise after surprise. Of course, if this curly-haired young man would be part of those surprises, she thought she might be able to handle it.

"Can I help you to a seat?" asked the tall man with the hooked nose and glasses, and who had been standing next to her. "Do you have a way home? Wasn't that something?"

"I'm fine, thank you." She wasn't really fine. She was a mess. "And I have a ride. My friends will take me. I hope we don't have to hide much longer."

"Oh, me neither." There was a long pause. "My name is Ari Bitterman." He offered his hand. His fingers were long and thin like a pianist or surgeon.

Laila had to crane her neck to see his face. "My name is Laila." She didn't bother with the rest. "Thank you just the same." How did he think she had gotten there? Laila winced; she could tell he was ill at ease from her tone. Hadn't she made a pact to be a nicer, kinder person? After all, weren't they going to be seeing a lot of each other when they joined the resistance?

"Do you mind me asking what happened? Your ... crutches?"

"I was at the King David Hotel when the bomb went off. I had a falafel stand outside the hotel."

"Oh."

Laila decided the man had no personality and turned away, looking for Zahar, who was behind her.

"Oh, there you are," said Zahar. "What a fright. It seems

this whole evening has been a fright." She must have directed her comment at Avraham because he looked uncomfortable.

Laila couldn't help it; she was relieved not to have to continue the conversation with Ari any longer. She was too on-edge to be polite to anyone. And didn't she have an excuse for her behavior? She was sure the pain killers she was still taking made her jumpy.

"Laila, who is this nice fellow you're talking to?" A chair blocking Zahar's way made it difficult to maneuver the wheelchair through the crowd. Laila watched as Avraham moved the chair out of her way. He was always there for her. It made Laila jealous not to have someone like that in her life right now. Yoel and she had been drifting apart ever since the bombing and she didn't understand why. Laila guessed her relationship with Zahar and Avraham had made him feel like an outsider. She didn't always understand men.

Laila shrugged. She didn't really want to get involved with this Ari person. Knowing she would be seeing a lot of him, Laila didn't want to give him the wrong impression. He wasn't her type. But then, what was her type?

The tall young man extended his hand to Avraham. "Ari Bitterman. Nice to meet you."

Avraham offered his. "This is Zahar, my wife, and I'm Avraham Lemberg. Interesting meeting."

"Yes," said Ari. A muscle in his right cheek twitched, accentuating his nervousness. He did a good job hiding his shock after Zahar turned her face to him. He kept adjusting his thin glasses.

"Did you have any idea what the meeting was about before you came?" asked Avraham.

"A little."

Avraham stole a look at his wife and then Laila and

probably figured the three of them had experienced enough. "Well, I guess we should head home. Don't forget the curfew. Be careful on the streets," he said to Ari.

"Thank you. You, too." Ari nodded and walked away.

"Strange fellow," said Avraham, "but he seems nice enough."

"I think he could use a friend." Zahar said, looking at Laila.

Laila rolled her eyes.

The meeting had concluded early, but the impassioned tone of the speakers seemed to put new life into Laila's friend. Laila had no idea what Zahar was like before the bombing, but Laila saw a young woman desperately trying to recover from a terrible tragedy; and so Laila had done her best to cheer Zahar up.

Zahar had mentioned something about saving a person and owning her soul for the rest of her life. Laila didn't want to own anyone's soul; she just wanted to be a friend. Her eyes drifted around the room until they came to rest on that good-looking young man who had issued the 'all clear'. He was deep in conversation with a very attractive young woman. Laila couldn't help but notice how commanding he was, how charged with electricity. She was determined to meet him, one way or another. The challenge was on.

Chapter 8

Ezra

Weeks later, Jerusalem, 1942

The next Scout meeting took place in the basement of an old boarding house not far from the university. The walls, heavily whitewashed and peeling in spots, only added to the overall aura of a clandestine meeting. Rows of folding chairs faced a shabby wooden table. No doubt the resistance group expected a crowd. Ezra had been talked into returning for a second go-around by an acquaintance, who had told him it was time to stop moping around like a sick puppy and get out and meet other women. Since his breakup with Anna, his days had consisted of class, Scouts, and poetry. Naturally, all his work focused on heartache. At some point in his dreams, Ezra had visualized himself up there with the most famous of writers: Keats, Shelly, Byron, Poe, Alterman, Amichai, and Hameiri. He was sure he had suffered as much as they, and possessed the words to prove it. Unfortunately, this preoccupation with poetry found his studies suffering.

Ezra scrutinized the room, finding familiar faces from

past Scout meetings. Of course there were others, unfamiliar to him, and who he cared less to meet. His eyes came to rest on Anna, whose arm was wrapped around a handsome, young man with a storehouse of muscles. A dull ache began in Ezra's stomach and radiated out to his extremities. He turned, having seen enough, and walked to the back of the room, hoping to become invisible. Compared to her current flame, Ezra must look like a *schmatta*—washed carelessly and hung out to dry. It had never occurred to him she would be there. And so he took a seat next to a young woman whose girth claimed her chair and part of his. As she smiled, a pair of matching dimples appeared.

"Isn't this exciting?" Her dark eyes twinkled and her body jiggled.

"I don't know." Ezra wasn't in the mood for small talk.

"You go to the university? What are you studying? I'm going to teach. My name is Rivka." Ezra figured her to be about seventeen and a long way from teaching.

"How noble." He hadn't meant to be rude. It was obvious his social skills were lacking. She was only trying to be friendly. "I'm sorry. I'm not in the best of moods." He purposely left out his name.

"Girlfriend broke up with you?"

"How did you ... ?" His head jerked around to face her. He hadn't meant to say that either.

Rivka kept up a running commentary until someone banged something hard on the table and everyone dove for a seat. Another person of equal girth to Rivka ended up sitting on Ezra's right; he felt like a *gefillte* fish crammed into a bottle. The young man had a pleasant face and hungrily eyed the *zaftig* young woman, next to Ezra. He could see a *shiddach* between the two. It would be the perfect marriage. A voice rang out to take a seat.

The Laundry Room

As soon as the room grew quiet, three rumpled young men took the center stage. The trio wore tattered coats: one sported a small; squashed, visored cap; and another, wire-rim glasses, which made him look slightly more intelligent. If this were to be the uniform of choice, count Ezra out. He was not a maven of fashion, but he knew poor when he saw it. They were either trying to evoke sympathy or fade into the background. It was apparent they were recent members of the *Haganah,* looking for recruits to start new settlements or fight a war.

Something had happened to Ezra since the last meeting. He couldn't put his finger on it, but he thought it had something to do with individuality. Ezra was a poet, not an activist; and he could see where this group was headed, and it was not exactly where he had intended. All fired up by the speaker's rhetoric at the last meeting, as were most of the rest of the attendees; Ezra had not been able to maintain that fervor. Perhaps today he would be able to make up his mind, and so he glanced around him and what he saw were a bunch of kids being led by the *Pied Piper*.

"My fellow compatriots," began one of the young men, whom Ezra had seen at the last few Scout camping trips. "We are here to bring solidarity to our cause. We are here for the right to be free, the right to worship as we please, and the right not to be persecuted or owned by anyone other than ourselves. This will be one of many organizational meetings before we can rightfully take our place in our own kibbutz." He went on to extoll the praise of working on a kibbutz.

The second of the three men took his place beside the first speaker. "That's right. You have an opportunity to give back to your country—be productive—on your own. Many of you have no families and no direction. We can form our own families, plant crops, decide what we need, and produce it. "

Lynda Lippman-Lockhart

Ezra was beginning to loosen up and really listen to what the speaker had to say. Okay, so he wasn't exactly a polished speaker, but his passion made up for it. What he said made sense, sounded reasonable, maybe even appealing. Ezra was beginning to tire of school, perhaps ready to give life a whirl. The students had all heard enough rhetoric from the British over the past years of servitude, and were eager to take up their own cause. According to Scout leaders, negotiations weren't going well amongst those countries making the decisions as to what would happen with Palestine; and it was foolish to believe Arab and Jew could ever walk hand-in-hand into the sunset. The sooner those assembled realized it, the better.

As the men continued their speeches, Ezra felt the first stirrings of patriotism. He had never experienced the need to stand up for anything, but he began to believe he was in the presence of greatness. Words were forming in his mind, and he wanted to run back to his room to write them down, but his feet were riveted to the floor. People were standing at this point. Ezra was forced to rise or look conspicuous. So Ezra rose, his thoughts disquieting. He was ambivalent.

Ezra was a reluctant revolutionary and feared discovery. If they were discovered, the British might consider those in the room upstarts—extremists. What then? He was not into pain. Just how fervently did he want to be involved in this movement? Ezra searched the room for those he knew. The erect bodies, the blazing eyes, and the intermittent outbursts told Ezra his comrades had crossed the line into insanity.

The third man stepped forward. "This is your chance to be heard. You are the generation that is going to take back Palestine, one respected by all, one independent from the fetters of other tyrants. We, the youth, have a right to be heard, seen, and felt. It is up to us to grab the baton as it

The Laundry Room

passes from our fathers, and carry the flame of freedom to our people."

The crowd yelled, stomped, and waved their arms. It was like a revival of sorts—at least, what Ezra had heard a revival was like. He couldn't help but be swept up by the furor, against his better judgment.

The three scruffy speakers knew how to keep a crowd on its feet. The foot stomping and hand clapping lasted a full minute, and then the first speaker raised his hand for them to sit. They followed his command—the first step toward total obedience.

Ezra stood a moment longer, trying hard to resist being a follower and losing his individuality, but it was hard to contain the excitement he was feeling. An icy, blue electric shock ran the length of Ezra's body as it occurred to him that this was big, bigger than anything he had ever been privy to. He was going to have a hand in creating the future. He knew his father wouldn't believe his change of heart. For that matter, he didn't understand it himself.

Ezra felt a tap on the shoulder and looked to his right, into Anna's eyes. Then the lights went out—again.

Chapter 9

Itzhak

Jerusalem, a week later

The podium looked different today, Itzhak thought. That was because he was standing behind it instead of looking at it. The research had been easy; the method by which he would administer the information was easier; what was not easy was standing in front of one hundred-plus fellow students and one professor who was probably hoping Itzhak would make a monumental fool of himself. Itzhak's overweening pride hadn't taken into consideration the fact that, when he criticized the professor in front of the others, he might experience the fear of possible failure he was facing now.

Itzhak ran trembling fingers through his perfectly combed hair. What was the matter with him? He had gotten what he wanted, challenging Professor Friedman like that. Itzhak was prepared and knew his subject, and could do a better job teaching the Byzantine Period than boring Professor Friedman—he was sure. Itzhak had something to

The Laundry Room

Instead of looking at his fellow students, Itzhak focused on the clock on the back wall. That would get him through the presentation.

He took a deep breath and began. "Today we're going to get to know Constantine I, or Saint Constantine, who ruled the Byzantine Empire from 306 AD to 337 AD. Who amongst you knows what he became famous for?" Itzhak scanned the auditorium looking for a raised hand. There was one in the back row. "Please stand and share your answer."

"He brought Christianity to his people."

"Very good. Those who knew and didn't raise your hand, shame on you. He gets all the credit." There was a mixture of scoffs and laughs. "Please feel free to take a stab at the answers. I won't bite your head off." He saw enough nods by the students to know what he was getting at.

"Yes, Constantine was considered one of the greatest rulers of his time—so much so, that the next ten rulers were named after him. He singlehandedly eliminated Christian persecution in his realm." Itzhak paused to catch the eye of his professor, who was busily taking notes. All he saw was the top of Friedman's bald head.

"Does anyone know what supposedly happened the night before the Battle of Milvian Bridge?" Again, Itzhak surveyed his audience. This time there were a dozen or so hands up. "The young man in the middle section, about ten rows back in the black shirt; what is your answer?"

The young man stood and looked around. "He was told by his advisors not to go into battle?"

"Close. Thank you for being brave enough to start us off." The young man smiled from ear to ear and sat down.

The next nine took their stabs, and each came even closer.

"Those were all good answers, but not complete. This tells me you must have been out drinking instead of reading the chapter." Laughter filled the audience, and Itzhak knew he had the students in the palm of his hand. Whatever fear he had harbored at the start had taken flight.

Itzhak went on to explain the vision Constantine had had the night before the battle, and how he had told his men to paint crosses on all the shields of his men. In later years Escubius, a Roman historian who wrote Biblical canon and was much respected for his insight into religious rules, came out with a slightly different theory. "He claimed that upon marching into battle, Constantine and his men saw, in the sky, a cross of light and the saying: 'By this sign you will be victor.' Escubius took it a step further, when he said Christ appeared to Constantine and instructed him to place the heavenly battle standard on his army. This standard was then known as *labaru,* displaying the 'Chi-Rho,' Greek letters that stood for Christ."

Itzhak continued for the next hour, until the professor stood, thanked Itzhak, and dismissed the class. Itzhak waited patiently for a response. Professor Friedman gathered his belongings, stood, and walked out of the room without a word, leaving Itzhak dumbfounded. Itzhak had expected the man to at least say something.

"Damn." Itzhak slammed his fist down on the podium, sending his notes flying in all directions. Had he won? If so, it didn't feel as good as he had expected.

Outside the building, Itzhak was besieged by fellow students.

"Great job," said a curly haired girl who usually sat in front of him.

"You showed him," said a short, stocky young man standing next to the girl.

The Laundry Room

"How about taking over the class?" said another, patting him on the back.

A sense of euphoria swelled through Itzhak's body, taking the place of the anger he had experienced at Professor Friedman's brusque dismissal. Hadn't he been looking for the approval of his fellow students, and not Friedman's? He chuckled, grinned, and walked on, inches above the sidewalk. It wasn't until later, when he ran into Ari, that Itzhak was to hear of the far-reaching effect he had had on his class.

"You are a hero!" Ari slapped him on the back. "Everyone is talking. They're saying Friedman better step it up or you might have his job." Ari laughed. "Hey, there's a meeting tonight. Are you in?"

"Of course. I like what I'm hearing, and who wouldn't miss the opportunity to bask in more words of praise?"

"You egotistical bastard. I'll pick you up at eight."

The two faked a few jabs and Ari took off. Itzhak was thinking he hadn't seen this much excitement in his friend in a long time.

###

At precisely seven-thirty, Ari showed up at Itzhak's door to take him to the meeting. Ari talked nonstop as he maneuvered the truck over the bumpy road, as he serpentine down back streets to their secret rendezvous. Itzhak, his mind elsewhere, tuned Ari out for the moment until they hit a deep rut.

"Say, where did you get this piece of crap?" asked Itzhak.

"Mrs. Malkin. She said I could use it as long as I filled it back up and made sure it wouldn't be stolen."

"Fat chance of that."

"Look, it hauls food and staples for her establishment. It

does the job and it's getting your sorry ass to the meeting faster than if you walked, so quit *kvetching*."

Itzhak raised his hands in surrender.

As they navigated the back streets of Jerusalem, Itzhak couldn't help but smell the remnants of something spoiled. Who knew what had fallen, over time, between the wooden slats of the flatbed of the truck or between the tattered seats? He preferred not to think about it, but he couldn't get the thought, much less the smell, out of his head.

"Reuven said this was going to be a very important meeting. Someone special was speaking." Ari kept his eyes focused on the road as he spoke.

"Who?"

"He didn't say. He just said, 'Be there'."

"Since when has Reuven become our leader?"

"He hasn't. The word just came down to him. Each time someone else gets the contact. That way nobody has too much authority."

"Probably wise."

The two men rode in silence until they arrived at the building, which looked like it had been struck by a rocket sometime in the past. It wouldn't win any prizes for architecture. Itzhak hoped there wouldn't be another blackout because if there were, it would mean the British were on to them. Ari pulled behind the building and parked next to a dozen or so assorted vehicles. It was dark; a sliver of moon could be seen peeking through the clouds, adding to the mystery of the evening. For a split second, Itzhak felt the forces of nature guiding him into something over which he had no control. It both frightened him and stimulated him.

"Hurry, or we'll miss the beginning of whatever is going on." Ari knocked on the door—some sort of secret code—a bit

The Laundry Room

much, maybe too much drama for Itzhak; but after the last two close calls, they weren't taking any chances.

The door opened a crack; Ari said something to the man standing there and they were admitted.

One would think it was a big reunion from the hugs, pats on the back, and kisses shared by the group. They were becoming a family with a united front. Itzhak watched Ari's face light up as he made eye contact with a girl across the room. Itzhak opened his mouth to chide Ari, but closed it before something cruel escaped. Itzhak got the feeling this was serious.

"Please take a seat so we can begin," said Reuven as if directing traffic. Folding chairs were set up in rows, forming a tight semi-circle. One of the original three men stood before them, helping people to their chairs. The room settled quickly; it seemed those assembled knew this meeting was supposed to be important, but Itzhak had no idea how important.

As he scanned the room, Itzhak's eyes came to rest on an attractive young woman with silvery blond hair plaited neatly in a long braid down her back. When she turned to speak to someone, he noted that her icy blue eyes were almost the color of his. They could almost be sister and brother, but he sure as hell hoped not. He intended to meet her. Had she been at the last meeting?

Reuven spoke. "We have been temporarily given a piece of land by *HaSochnut HaYehudit L'Eretz Yisra'el* or JAFI, the Jewish Agency. We will be learning how to run a kibbutz until a permanent location is found. The piece of land is seventy miles north of Tel Aviv and thirty miles south of Haifa. The closest city to the property is called Pardess Hanna. The Agency will teach us to plant citrus trees; raise cattle, chickens, and lambs; and how to fish from the sea. We need to write a charter, and we will need a name for the kibbutz."

Voices rose as suggestions poured out, several at a time. Itzhak watched, with interest, the people who contributed. One was that physically fit young woman with blue eyes and blonde braid. He hadn't noticed she was using crutches until she stood. His eyebrows arched as he studied her.

Ari jumped out of his seat and nearly knocked over the person in front of him. "Since we are part of the Hebrew Scout movement, we should use the word *Hazofim* for Boy Scouts; and since we are the first group in the Boy Scouts to form a kibbutz, the letter "A," for *Aleph* should be part of it. Maybe *Hazofim A.*"

"What do you think?" asked Reuven. Again voices rose to be heard. "Please. Let's keep this orderly."

A hand went up in the back of the room. "What about ... never mind."

The room broke out in good-humored laughter. "*Never mind.* I like that," someone mocked.

"Now settle down. This is serious," Reuven scolded.

A few more hands went up, a little more hesitantly now, and then others dove in as the discussion escalated to a high pitch. Names were being thrown out in all directions.

"Please, let's have some order," said Reuven, banging his hand on the podium.

One of the older members of the group, a stout young woman of twenty-two, stood to air her views. "I think *Hazofim A* is a perfect name. It identifies us, yet leaves a little mystery."

Everyone nodded. She beamed as did her husband. It was clear; she would become one of the most vocal of women.

Itzhak kept waiting for that *important* person to show up.

The Laundry Room

He finally figured Reuven must have thought himself important enough. Hadn't Itzhak placed himself in a similar position earlier that day? He had been lucky enough to come out on top.

"You should know the *Lehi* are on the move to force the British out of Palestine. They have instituted skirmishes throughout the land, kicking up dirt everywhere they go. There are those who would prefer to sit out the wait, let the British Mandate come to a peaceful end; there are also those who see it as a tactic to build up the Arab force, giving them the advantage. I'm assuming those of you here tonight want peace, and are willing to build this country without bloodshed. You have a lot to think about."

The meeting continued, ironing out many of the rough spots such as leadership, assignment of jobs, if and where religion fit in, and other pressing matters Itzhak hadn't thought about. He found himself torn between two worlds: academic stability and a new adventure. He was so close to graduating; maybe he could wait and join later, but if he did, he wouldn't be in on the ground floor. This would require some serious thought. Unconsciously, Itzhak began drumming out a beat with his fingers, as he often did when finding himself at a crossroads. He'd have to become involved without his parents' blessing, because he knew they would say, *No.* But this was his future, and he was going to be the one to plan it.

As the meeting broke up, he searched for the girl with the braid, but couldn't find her. He wondered why the crutches.

Chapter 10

Ezra

Jerusalem, 1942

The meeting over, Ezra rose and scanned the room for Anna. He knew in his mind she'd moved on, but he hadn't mistaken the look in her eyes as he caught her staring at him earlier. Perhaps it was wishful thinking. Maybe while working together on the kibbutz, he might persuade her he was every bit a man, maybe even a better man than she thought possible.

As he strolled out the door, Ezra caught sight of the student who had taken over his political science class. "Hello," he said. "You did one hell of a job in class."

"Thank you. You are ... ?"

"Ezra Ben Hayim. If my classes were all like that, I might be a more enthusiastic attendee."

"It wasn't that hard. I just attacked it the way I would want to be taught."

"A novel approach." Ezra hadn't meant it to sound so sarcastic. "I mean, shouldn't that be the way to teach?"

The Laundry Room

"Well, according to Professor Friedman, you teach by the book. I can imagine looking out at a sea of disinterested faces every day. It could become disheartening. I had one professor at Harvard who inspired me to do my very best. He made teaching an adventure."

"How lucky for you." Again Ezra caught himself sounding haughty. Was it because he had heard of Itzhak's reputation? Everyone knew he thought himself superior. Funny, he wasn't picking up that attitude.

Another student joined them. "Sorry, but I couldn't help but overhear your conversation. You're *the* famous Mr. Schwartzman."

"Probably more infamous by now. We've met ... haven't we?"

"At several Scout meetings. That's probably it. I'm married and don't get out with the single fellows much." Avraham held out his hand.

"I guess that's a blessing and a curse at the same time," said Itzhak, adjusting the books he had brought with him and shook Itzhak's hand.

They laughed and continued walking.

"The name's Avraham ... Avraham Lemberg."

Ezra caught Itzhak giving Avraham the onceover. Avraham was a handsome son of a gun, but didn't seem to know it. He was also a very serious student. Ezra had been in several classes with him in the past.

"What do you think of the kibbutz idea?" Itzhak stopped, took off his cap and stowed it under his arm, leaving his unruly blond curls to blow in the wind.

"I'm not sure, but I'm interested. I've never been much on planting and harvesting. I'm a poet, not a farmer," said Ezra, still looking for Anna.

Ari joined the group. "Got a clandestine meeting going on here?"

"Hardly," said Itzhak, who continued with what he was about to say. "Well, the prospect of our own kibbutz sounds interesting enough for me to leave college behind and get my hands dirty."

"Say, men, I have to find my wife. Nice meeting you, Itzhak." And Avraham was gone.

"Comrades, do you men need a lift? It's not a limo and it stinks, but it works." Ari walked toward the dilapidated truck he had parked across the street, in the shadow of a large sign that had fallen from the roof above, and eased into the driver's seat.

Itzhak followed. "That would be great; beggars can't be choosers, so they say." He chuckled. They laughed ... even Ari, who seemed to be brooding.

The men piled into the truck and talked all the way back to the university. While on King David Boulevard, they stopped for a glimpse of what was left of the hotel.

"What do you think is really going to happen once the British pull out?" Itzhak asked as he tried to get comfortable, squeezed between the two men.

The conversation had drifted off to lighter topics, but the sight of the hotel was sobering. "I think we will have problems, the likes of which we have never seen," added Itzhak.

"What do you mean?" asked Ezra.

"I mean, we have the British pulling out, and internal conflict within our own *sochnut*, shadow government. If we don't put aside our differences, we will fall into the hands of the Arabs again. It seems we're always pawns in the sea of discord," said Itzhak.

The Laundry Room

Ari pulled the truck over to the curb and stopped. "Have you ever considered politics?"

"No," answered Itzhak, emphatically. "I'm too unbending for that, and I'm not a good liar."

"Those are not bad traits," said Ezra. "We could use someone with those credentials."

Itzhak sighed. "Too bad my father isn't here to hear your word. He's wanted me to take an interest in something other than being a playboy."

"I think he might be right," said Ezra. "Parents usually know what's best."

"Boy, someone did a good brainwashing job on you," Itzhak chuckled.

"Not really. Every time I did something against my parents' wishes, I rued the day." Ezra wished he had paid more attention to his parents, even though he didn't want to admit it. How many arguments had he had with his father over everything? "I'd be more prepared for what is about to happen. You know, there isn't much call for poets these days, leastways not in Palestine."

Several days passed before Ezra heard anything in the way of news about the kibbutz. It was Ari who stopped by to alert him that they would be meeting two days hence, and that if Ezra wished, Ari and Itzhak would pick him up.

The next morning while Ezra was catching up on his studies, a knock at the door brought with it an undeniable foreboding. When it continued, Ezra decided he must answer it even though he didn't want to. He took measured steps to the door. He couldn't put it off another moment, as it would disturb others either sleeping or studying. He took a deep breath and opened the door.

"*Nu*, well, you certainly took your time."

"Father! What are you doing here?" Ezra noted how dapper his father looked in a double-breasted tan suit. His father's short height, that Ezra had inherited, belied his father's larger-than-life ego. What kind of trouble was he here about today?

"Is that a way to greet your father who drove here to see you?"

"Sorry, Father, please come in. To what do I owe the honor, and how is Mother?"

Ezra's father walked in, eyes scanning the room. He stood in the middle of the mess and shook his head. "Your mother would have a fit if she saw how you have chosen to live."

"You didn't say why you are here."

Ezra's father cleared debris off the only piece of furniture suitable to sit upon and patted the spot next to him. "Sit."

Ezra sat; he knew this wasn't going to be pleasant; it rarely was with his father, who he seldom pleased.

"I understand you have been attending secret meetings held ostensibly by the Scouts. What does this mean?"

"How did you know? Are you having me followed?"

"No, I don't have to. Anything that has to do with the *Haganah*, I know."

Ezra found his couch especially uncomfortable. He wanted to be anywhere else than in his room with his father at the moment.

"I'm not at liberty to say. I was sworn to secrecy."

"Well, well. And what about your poetry?"

"I'm still writing, but it has evolved."

"Yes? Into what?"

"More patriotic."

The Laundry Room

Ezra's father stood and walked toward the door. "Please don't do anything that will besmirch my name. I have a reputation to uphold." He put out his hand to shake. Ezra rose and shook it. There was no warmth between the two men. That had died years before when Ezra's father had besmirched his own reputation.

"You take care of yourself. You don't want to upset your mother," and he was gone.

Ezra sat back down on the couch, dropping his head in his hands and cried—something he had been doing a lot lately. This pain, though, was unbearable.

#

The next two days found Ezra agitated. It became more and more difficult to concentrate. The agitation played out in nonstop writing, while poem after poem flowed from his troubled mind, down his arm, and onto the vacant page. He even questioned his direction, especially since his father's visit. Was he crazy to get involved with the kibbutz movement? What did he know about farming, and did he even care? Had he made a terrible mistake? After all, he wasn't that far from graduating. Basically, was being with Anna worth this much angst? After all, she barely noticed him anymore, and was it really Anna he was trying to please?

A racket outside his building made Ezra push back from his desk, overturn his chair, and run to the window. Shots were being fired into the air by British soldiers, who seemed to think it was funny. Didn't they realize what went up must come down? He had a mind to tell them, but his courage waned as he grabbed for his pen.

What I need is a backbone, he thought miserably.

Chapter 11

Laila

Jerusalem, 1943

Commitment made, Laila couldn't put off telling Abba her plans any longer. She prepared herself for the onslaught of tirades, incrimination, and total disregard for her feelings as she approached her house. Would he yell? Would he disown her for being selfish? He *had* raised her that way—always getting her way. She had rehearsed all her answers, so there would be no hesitation. Now if she could only remain calm.

Butterflies circled Laila's stomach as she anticipated the confrontation. If Yoel had taken her news about joining a kibbutz as poorly as he had, what would Abba do? Yoel and she had verbally fought to the bitter end. She could still feel his darts and arrows.

"What are you thinking?" he had yelled. "You're only eighteen. What about our plans?" Yoel had stood, body rigid, eyes blazing.

"We can still plan. I'll just be at a different place for a

year. It's not like I'm going away forever. After all, you're going away to fight. What if something happens to you? I supported and respected your decision and didn't carry on about it; and maybe I should have. Did it ever occur to you I might not be happy with your decision?"

"I can see where this is going, and it's not going where I planned." He raked his fingers through his thinning hair, as he often did when confronted.

"That's it... they are all your plans," Laila snapped. "I just went along with them. I want to be your equal, not a floor mat. We are living in a modern world where women have a voice, although small. I'm not ready to sit in a closed up classroom just yet. Maybe after a year tilling the land, I'll be ready for a change, but that has to be my decision."

"Who are you?" asked Yoel; the flame had gone out of his eyes. "Not the girl I fell in love with. I think we need to stop this right now, and take a few days to calm down. I'm sure you'll see things differently by then." And he had left without another word.

Laila hadn't known whether to be sad or glad.

As she turned the corner to her house, she noticed British soldiers on either side of the street, rifles in hand, two of them jostling a teenager and his girlfriend. They were picking at his clothing and making jokes about his nose. Laila couldn't believe how cruel they were. She hunched her shoulders and walked as softly as she could, hoping to make herself invisible. It was her crutches that gave her away.

A soldier approached. "Where are you going in such a hurry ... sweetheart?"

The memory of the bomb blast at the hotel made Laila wary, and besides, she hadn't been in a hurry either.

"I'm not your *sweetheart,*" she hissed. "What do you want? And what are you doing here?" Laila's English had improved over the last few years, enough to carry on a conversation. She had been good at languages and had considered studying international relations, but changed her mind as she often did in quest of a future. The soldier stepped closer. Laila took a step back, extra vigilant of British soldiers. They liked to pick on those who were not able to defend themselves.

"What's the matter, Jew girl on crutches ... afraid of me?"

"No, and let me pass." Laila stared the soldier straight in the eye.

"And what if I don't?" he moved even closer, touching her arm in a proprietary manner, and then began moving his fingers upward. No man had ever touched her so.

"I'll scream and get you in trouble." Laila yanked her arm away.

"I like girls with pluck. Why would I get in trouble? You're a pretty girl. I'm just admiring you. There's no law against that. I'd like to loosen that braid of yours and let that yellow hair fall about your shoulders."

She shook with disgust. The idea of his touching her ... "Well, if you're done admiring, kindly let me pass."

He started to grab her arm again when another soldier called him off. Laila couldn't believe it was the same green-eyed soldier, coming to her aid once more. Even at a distance she could see his aristocratic face and warm smile. He was different from the others. There was something human about him. He motioned her on. Laila nodded and hobbled as fast as the crutches would allow, all the way to her house at the end of the block. Did the soldier know where she lived? If he hadn't—he did now.

Panting, she yanked the door open, stepped in, locked the door, and slumped to the floor, crutches and all, almost forgetting her mission. Laila gave herself permission to take

The Laundry Room

a moment to calm down. Her life had become a series of mishaps since the bombing. She was beginning to believe the aftermath of that day would be felt for a long time. She needed to take charge of her future before someone else did it for her.

Using a crutch, she managed to get to her feet as her eyes adjusted to the dim lighting. She could see Abba had already turned the place into a shambles. How could he do such a thing? She now understood Emma's indignation when he dropped his clothes, like breadcrumbs, everywhere he went.

Laila took a long, deep breath and called out. "Abba?"

"In the kitchen."

Following the familiar aroma of spicy food, Laila found Abba in his favorite place in the house; wearing that same old stained apron, holding a dishtowel in one hand and a ladle in the other. Laila was amused. Her Emma would have found the scene entertaining if she had been blessed with a longer life. Abba had been a peddler of tools and household items, and shared a stall with an Arab neighbor in the "Old City" until Emma's death. And then, like manna from the sky, the falafel stands fell from Heaven, and he had become fairly successful overnight. Laila wished Emma could have lived to enjoy that success.

"What happened? You look like Tanta Channa's ghost chased you all the way home."

"Soldiers ... outside." Laila gasped, hoping to disarm him. "One confronted me ... scared me."

"You? Scared?" he chortled. "He must have been a monster. What were they doing out there?"

"... taunting some teenagers. They don't need an invitation to drop by. Thank goodness there was another soldier with manners. He called off the monster."

"I'm glad to hear that. I would have had to go out and give him a piece of my mind."

"I'm fine. You don't have to protect me anymore. I'm eighteen."

Abba put the dishtowel down on the table and sat. "Just. Something's on your mind. Am I right? Come tell Abba what's wrong."

Laila's birthday had come and gone with little fanfare. No one wanted to call attention to their lives these days, so it was just another day. Zahar had knitted her a beautiful scarf, in shades of blue to match her eyes.

"Well, yes." She sniffed the air. "Something smells good. What are you cooking?"

"I'm experimenting on a new recipe for the stands."

"What?" She clapped her hands like a young child.

"You'll see when I'm finished, and don't try and change the subject."

The kitchen resembled a mad scientist's lab, not a kitchen. There were pots, thick with sauce crusted over and down the sides, vegetable peels scattered about the floor, and more breadcrumbs.

"All right, my daughter, what do you want to discuss? I haven't got all day." Another of his favorite new expressions. He thought it made him worldlier. Laila had no intentions of taking that away.

"Please hear me out before saying anything." As she stood in place, Laila felt her throat constrict. She tried to speak but nothing came out. She hated to upset him, but she was eighteen and could make her own decisions. Judah cowered from him, as did her sisters. Her Abba and she were made of the same fabric, probably the reason they got along so well.

"You have my full attention. Sit." He patted the chair next

to him.

Laila remained standing, in case she had to make a swift exit. "My Scout group has decided to start a kibbutz. We have met on several occasions, and the government is willing to finance the project. I think it is time for me to try my hand at something other than making falafels before I settle down. The details of the kibbutz are being worked out. We have our own property, and we'll be farming the land. It's the future of our people."

"Is that it? May I speak?"

"Yes."

"What about school? What about our business? What about Yoel?"

"I'm getting to that." Realizing how that sounded, she changed her tone of voice. "I just finished this semester and will pick up when I return ..."

"If you return..." His eyes pierced hers. She could tell he was holding back; something he rarely did.

"I *will* return. They said there was a limited amount of danger, but we live with that every day. As for the stand, I already spoke to Judah—"

Abba took what appeared to be a menacing step forward. "You spoke to Judah before you spoke to me?" His voice boomed, churning Laila's stomach to butter.

"I had to know if he was willing to help me out before I committed myself. He reluctantly agreed. I suggested Elana take it over, and he blew up in my face."

Her father burst out laughing. "Elana? Work? Unheard of." The first semblance of a smile broke out over her father's face. "I suppose if you've worked it out with Judah, it's okay with me."

"That's it?"

"What were you expecting? You're eighteen. Your education is taken care of. It's up to you when you finish it. A little adventure never hurt anyone. I often wish Judah had wanted some before he saddled himself with a family." He sighed deeply, as if unable to stop the momentum. "I guess you're the real male in the family. Everyone else took the easy way out. You didn't mention Yoel in the equation, so I guess that's none of my business."

Laila couldn't decide if Abba's blessings were a compliment or surrender. A measure of relief washed over her as she never dreamed it would be this easy, since Abba had always had the last word in all discussions, and it was usually *no*. Yoel was like that too. It was the one irritating thing about him she couldn't get over. But that was probably a moot point after their fight. Laila wanted a man who respected her thoughts and would grant her the last word once in a while. She had a need to grow, and she was beginning to see that wouldn't happen with him.

"When do you leave?"

"Soon."

"Come give your old father a big hug and then off to bed. Someone has to keep the business going."

Laila hugged him with all her might and caught his meaning. He would just have to do without her for a while. Maybe he would appreciate her more when she returned. Let's see how well Judah does with the new stand, she thought. He better not outsell her.

As Laila left the room, Abba had to have the last word. "Just remember, if you don't return, I'll never speak to you again."

Laila closed the door to her room and exhaled. Half the battle had been won.

Chapter 12

Ari

Jerusalem, 1943

The anticipation of starting a new life both thrilled and scared Ari to death. Tonight's meeting would be one of the last, before sojourning to the kibbutz. Ari hoped he would be given the opportunity to use his artistic skills instead of sketching pretend structures in his dorm room. He could see it now: drawing up plans for a small community, one with a school, place of worship, and small homes. His imagination had been at work since the last meeting, and he could not wait until tonight.

He had asked Mrs. Malkin for the evening off. She was easy to work for; never demanding. Ari's feelings were ambivalent, as it was hard to stay focused when you knew your education would be put on hold. Since he didn't have to report to anyone, he could only blame himself if things didn't work out right. Still, he was sure they would.

Mrs. Malkin's truck sat by the curb, an eyesore to be sure but transportation, nonetheless. Ari had tried cleaning it up, but the stench of dried vegetables trailed behind like the stench of a Dromedary camel. Some day he would have his own vehicle. He and Leora would go for rides on Sunday with the kids in the backseat. They would take a picnic lunch, and something special baked for dessert. The children would tease each other playfully while he drove, and he and Leora would discuss the kinds of important matters that couples discussed.

The dark sky foretold a storm was brewing. It seemed to rain every time their group met. Was that an omen? He wondered what they would discuss tonight—more plans for their new kibbutz? He was talked out and wanted to put those plans into action.

Deep in thought, Ari turned the corner, not prepared for what came next—a car that had come to an abrupt stop in the middle of the street. What was the matter? Ari sat as patiently as he could, despite knowing he would be late picking up Leora. That would make them even later to the meeting.

Traffic was not moving. He opened the truck door and stood on the running board. A rogue raindrop smacked him in the forehead, splattering his face and hair. He wiped it away without giving it much thought, dropped back into his seat, and slammed the door—another roadblock. What was it with the British? Couldn't they leave them alone? Jews couldn't go anywhere without papers these days. It was like being back in Poland. They said it was for the Jews' own good. Since when did they need to be told what was good for them? Look what happened in the concentration camps. The ugly truth had been seeping out between the cracks as Germany was being invaded. At the last meeting, they had been told of more Arab skirmishes throughout Palestine, and after the bombing of the King David Hotel, all Jews were suspect.

The car in front of him, a 1940 Packard from the States, moved through the stop with no trouble. He was next.

"Papers?"

Ari opened his jacket and riffled through the pockets for his identification card. It wasn't where it should have been. He checked another pocket—not there either. His glasses began fogging up. He removed them, wiping them on his vest and pushed them back up his nose.

"Well? We haven't all day," said the British officer with a jagged scar running from his eye to his upper lip, bringing a chill to Ari's already stone-cold body.

"Sorry, I know I have it on me; I just don't remember where." He fumbled through his clothes.

"Pull over," demanded the officer.

Ari did as told, and as he parked, another officer approached. Ari was scared out of his mind; beads of perspiration had drenched his shirt, his shorts, and what was left of his now unruly hair. How could he appear in public like this? If asked, he could say he had been caught in the rain.

"So you have no identification. What's your name?"

"Ari Bitterman."

"Ah, a Jew."

"Yes." Ari wanted to add *what of it?* but he held his tongue.

"Where are you going?"

"To pick up my girlfriend for a date."

The officer looked Ari over carefully. "*You* have a girlfriend?"

"Amazing as it may seem, yes."

"A wise guy, ha?"

"No, I'm just trying to lighten up the situation." By now, Ari had exhausted the inside of his jacket and went to pull out his wallet.

"What is this girl's address?"

Ari froze. He didn't want to implicate Leora but knew if he didn't come up with something, he'd be in worse trouble. So, he dropped the wallet. Leaning over to pick it up, he hesitated a moment too long.

"What are you doing? Sit up slowly, no funny business."

By now Ari was hyperventilating. His hands had become bear paws, unable to get a grip on anything. He realized he wasn't thinking clearly and he needed to think clearly to get through this checkpoint. "Ah ha! Here it is; right where it was supposed to be." He waved it in the officer's face like the whole thing was a joke.

The officer opened the wallet and studied it. He shook his head. "A student? I have a suggestion. You might consider entertainment. It's been painfully amusing talking with you. Now be on your way; and next time, don't forget where you put your card." He waved Ari on, calling after him, "Don't forget curfew."

How could he?

The gears ground as Ari started the truck. His foot was shaking so badly, he could hardly step on the clutch to keep the truck from stalling, which would be a disaster. Clutch in, he let it out slowly, gave it some gas and crept away from the roadblock. From that point on, Ari watched the speedometer and didn't take his eyes off the road. He was a mess. Tired of close calls and living from one disaster to another, which only made him more resolute about changing his present circumstances, he proceeded with a renewed vigor.

To calm his nerves, Ari switched his thoughts to Leora, who always brought a smile to his face. They were moving along smoothly in their relationship, and Ari had never been so comfortable. Leora was his best friend and staunch supporter. He had encouraged her to pursue her dream of opening a bakery someday. She was an incredible baker. The first time Ari tasted a bite of her strudel, he was transported back to the old country. After that, every time he was around her, he got the impression she smelled like the cinnamon she used in her baking.

Ari had talked Mrs. Malkin into letting Leora bake their desserts. She no longer waited tables. He had never seen anyone come out of their shell like she had, but she still had a long way to go.

As Ari approached the boardinghouse, he saw Leora standing on the porch. She waved and smiled when she saw him. He was about to jump out and offer his coat, but she ran and jumped into the passenger seat before he placed his hand on the door handle. She leaned over and kissed him.

"I was so worried. Are you okay? You're drenched."

He debated whether or not to tell her what happened, and decided that if they were going to be a couple there should be no secrets. "I was detained by a blockade. I don't know what they were looking for, but I couldn't find my card and was pulled over. It's perspiration, not rain that did me in."

"You poor dear." She took out a handkerchief and wiped his brow. "We're doing the right thing, aren't we?"

"Yes. We need to be in charge of our destiny. Away from the city, we'll have peace and quiet."

"I hope so," said Leora, settling back in the cracked leather passenger seat.

"How was the dinner crowd tonight?" Ari reached over to pull Leora closer to him.

"The usual. Mr. Nadler was not there. Mrs. Malkin said he had not been in his room for two days. We are all worried about him."

"Maybe he had business elsewhere."

"None of his clothing or toilet articles were missing."

"Mrs. Malkin went into his room?" Ari thought that was an invasion of privacy.

"After not seeing him for two days, it is her policy. People disappear all the time."

"All the more reason to have our own kibbutz."

They drove the rest of the way in silence, Ari wondering what might have happened to Mr. Nadler and hoping for his speedy return. Eventually he shrugged to himself, sure that he would show up sooner or later.

The meeting place had been switched at the last minute. Sol Shiller had allowed the Scouts to use his father's tire shop. Apparently, it had a secret room that few knew about. Sol's father was a military man, who was rarely home anymore; so Sol took over running the shop. He was sympathetic to the cause, but until his father retired, he would be stuck running the place. Sol had said he hoped to join the rest sooner rather than later.

Ari parked the truck in the last available spot. He ran around to open Leora's door and the two walked arm-in-arm to the entrance. Ezra was standing waiting to let them in.

"What kept you?"

"A long story. I'll tell you later." Ari liked Ezra. For that matter, he liked everyone involved. Well, Reuven could be overbearing at times, but he meant well.

Ari and Leora found seats in the back of the room, which smelled like tires, and they sat quietly. The meeting had already begun.

The Laundry Room

"As you well know, more and more clashes are taking place around the country. After the hotel bombing on the 22nd, it didn't get any better. They have issued strict orders about Jews congregating. This might be our last meeting for a while. Information will be filtered down to you."

Someone Ari couldn't see on the opposite side of the room called out, "What exactly did happen? Not all of us are in the know."

"Pincus Solomon has the inside scoop of this. Let him tell you."

A short, stocky young man, with thinning blond hair, goatee, and mole on his chin stood as he heard his name called. He walked confidently, taking his place next to the speaker, who Ari identified as one of the young men from their very first meeting. Pincas' wife Shaina radiated pride in her husband. They hadn't been married long. Since Ari and Leora were late getting there, Ari hadn't caught the first speaker's name.

"Pincus knows everything going on in Palestine." The speaker stepped back to let Pincus have the floor.

"Well, yes. You want to know what happened the day of the bombing. A little history will help you understand how it came about." Pincus's eyes scanned the crowd, as if deciding which version to tell. "First of all," he continued, "the hotel was the central office of the British Forces in Palestine. It was also the office for the Secretariat of the Government of Palestine. It seems the British headed a series of raids on a number of the *Haganah's* operations, one of which took place on a Sunday, now called "Black Sunday." They raided the Jewish Agency, the heartbeat of the *Haganah*, where they confiscated documents about past and future activities detrimental to their forces, and documents related to the ban on immigration of Jews to Palestine. The hotel bombing was

86

in retaliation for that."

A hand went up.

"Yes?"

"Did they take into consideration there might be Jews at the hotel and in the surrounding area?"

"Three calls were made that day, one of which went to the hotel's switchboard. It was ignored because several false alarms had been sounded in the past. Even someone from the *Palestine Post*, who had received the same warning earlier, had called the hotel to pass on the information. The British obviously didn't think the call was worth heeding. The attack on the hotel was a joint effort of the *Palmach, the Irgun*, and the *Haganah*. Due to a mix-up between groups, the time of the bombing, which was supposed to be later in the day when the offices were empty, was moved up and thus, the casualties. Menachem Begin, leader of the *Irgun*, has been quoted as saying warnings were sent out at least twenty-five minutes before the explosion. No one was supposed to get hurt; only the inner workings of the mandated government were to be disturbed. It was, indeed, a tragedy, and I know two of our members were directly involved. We all are sorry for that. If the British had heeded the warnings, no one would have been hurt. We also lost two of our best men: Avraham Abramovitz and Itzhak Tsadok— shot as they fled the hotel."

All eyes turned toward Laila and Zahar. Ari felt badly for the women. He knew Zahar had lost a baby and it was apparent she had been physically scarred for life. He wasn't sure either of the women would ever get over that day; but hoped it would make them stronger and more determined, like he was, to make a change.

The meeting eventually reverted back to the speaker, who began filling them in on information pertaining to the

The Laundry Room

kibbutz. Somehow the earlier excitement Ari was feeling on the way over, dulled. If his own people were responsible for killing Jews, did he really want to get involved in something that sounded so dangerous? All he wanted was to be a part of establishing a new way of life for the living. Leora must have caught his mood and squeezed his hand. Come what may, they were in this together.

When the meeting was over, Ari started the truck to go home, but nothing happened. It was dead. He said a prayer, thanking God for the truck not dying at the roadblock. Then he got out and inquired where he might find a ride for Leora. She would go home with the group headed to the university. Ari and another group member would work on the truck—in the rain. They were all too aware of the curfew.

Chapter 13

Laila

Jerusalem, 1943

Laila was enthralled with what she was hearing. This would be their last meeting before they left. She couldn't get over the fact they were actually going to be given the opportunity to run a kibbutz! It wouldn't be exactly their kibbutz, but it would be a start. After getting to know some of the members of their Scout group better, Laila was sure they would succeed. She listened intently to last minute instructions; some of which was repetitious, but she didn't care because she was so excited.

She was still having a problem understanding Yoel's reaction; they had barely spoken since their last encounter. He finally told her he wasn't interested in continuing their relationship, if she didn't want any more out of life than tending the soil. Laila was glad she had finally seen his true colors, and in any case, she had her eye on someone else. But still, a part of her didn't like being rejected.

The meeting finally came to an end, and Laila would have

The Laundry Room

to find a ride home. Avraham and Zahar had left early because he had a test the next day; however, before Avraham and Zahar left, they made Laila promise to call the minute she walked into her house. Laila had agreed, not knowing how much later she would be. At the time, she had had high hopes that good-looking young man named Itzhak might walk her home. It occurred to her she could take a public transit; but it was too late at night, they were too close to curfew. Obviously she had been crazy to think Itzhak might be interested in seeing her home.

"Anyone need a lift?" One of the leaders of the group stood by the door, hands cupped in front of his mouth.

Laila rose unsteadily and walked toward him. Although she had physically mended from her injuries, she still walked with a slight limp. It was her mental mending that had been the most difficult with the nightmares and the constant vigilance.

Again, she waved, having difficulty catching the eye of the bearded man in the rumpled vest. A group of enthusiastic Scouts, deep in a heated discussion, were in her way. "Please. I'm trying to get to the man at the door. You're blocking my way." As Abba liked to say, *Honey always works better than vinegar,* but she was not particularly in a good mood.

As she was about to reach the bearded man, she saw Itzhak across the room, talking to that same, attractive girl. Laila's heart took a dive. What had she been thinking? As Laila's group left, all of that enthusiasm she'd been feeling about their own kibbutz walked out the door with Itzhak and the girl.

"Excuse me," said Laila, hoping not to miss her ride. One of the men stepped aside and tapped the other on the shoulder. They exchanged questioning looks and the second one moved out of her way. She finally made it to her destination, just as the vested man turned and walked out the door.

"Please wait. I need a ride." As she passed through the door, she saw to her dismay that it was pouring. Fortunately, she'd had the good sense to bring a raincoat. Retrieving the rumpled poncho from her cotton shoulder bag, Laila wrapped it around her body and pulled the hood over her head. She followed the driver, bumping her head as she boarded the van.

"Are you all right?" he asked, helping her in.

"I'm fine, thank you." She wasn't fine. In fact, her head throbbed, and she was embarrassed.

"How many of you are going to the university?" he asked.

The majority raised their hands.

"You?" He pointed to Laila.

"I live nearby. I'll show you."

"Good. Only one stop ... well, maybe two."

Bullet-like raindrops hammered the van. Laila hoped the sound wasn't an omen of things to come. Her enthusiasm was as mercurial as the weather: one minute sunshiny, the next, bleak. Laila couldn't stop asking herself if she had made a monumental mistake. Her future had been so well planned: four years of college, marriage, whatever came next.

Laila took a seat next to a girl she had noticed at the beginning of the meeting. Laila had seen her several times before, but they had never talked. The girl glanced her way and then turned toward the window. She said nothing, so Laila introduced herself. "Shalom. My name's Laila. It looks like we'll be getting to know each other."

"Mine's Leora." The painfully plain girl with the now-stringy, sandy blond hair smiled halfheartedly. Looking her over, Laila thought a strong wind would blow the girl across

The Laundry Room

the Jordan River and decided to make a point of looking after her, like Zahar was doing for her. Other than her Emma, Laila had never had anyone to look after. Well, there was Abba, but he really didn't need looking after. They would all look out for each other. Laila missed her sisters, living so far away: one in Elat, the other in Safed. They met once each year for *Pesach*, but that was it. Judah, her only ally, served as mentor and mediator between Abba and her. The biggest breach in relations had come after Emma's death, when Abba disavowed God and the family became secular Jews. It wasn't until Laila's sisters married orthodox men, who followed the letter of the law, that the real trouble began. As it is written in the *Torah: A woman cleaves to her husband and his family; and so, her sisters were more-or-less lost to her.*

Two voices rang out above the rest. Laila could feel a current of energy surge through the van alongside the talk of adventure and intrigue. Speculation about the future increased in volume, as they found their voices and cemented new relationships.

Leora and Laila were last to exit. "Would you like to join me for lunch tomorrow?" Laila ventured, covering her head in preparation for the torrential downpour. This was going to be an all-night affair, Laila thought; hopefully not forty days and forty nights.

"I'd love to. I have a break from eleven until two. Where would you like to meet?"

Certainly not at her falafel stand, Laila reminded herself. Tomorrow was her day off. She had been allowed to help Judah two days a week while she continued to recover and reconstruction began on the hotel. "How about that new café down the street? You know the one I mean?"

"I do. It's near the boardinghouse where I work."

"Oh? You'll have to fill me in. Bye." They parted, Laila suddenly happier, and like a small child she jumped the puddles forming on the street. She had mended well, but when the weather was like this, she felt what they called a *phantom* pain in her leg. Arriving at her house, she removed her raincoat under the porch cover and shook off the excess moisture like a sodden mutt.

Suddenly Laila felt a presence and then heard a pebble scuff the ground as someone moved closer to her. She feared it might be one of those trouble-making British soldiers looking to do mischief. Laila fumbled for her keys and dropped them. She bent down, but the shadow picked them up and handed them to her. She stiffened. What did he want? Her breathing, already labored from running, came in gasps.

"Are you all right?" asked the shadow who was wearing a full-length coat and hat.

"Yes, thank you." It was that same soldier—the one with the green eyes. He stood erect and seemed eager to talk as he unbuttoned his heavy coat. His uniform—impeccable—his demeanor arresting. Had he followed her?

"Where are you coming from?" he asked.

"A friend's. We were studying for a test tomorrow." Laila couldn't believe how easily the lies rolled off her tongue. She had changed—learned to survive.

"It's not wise to be out so late." He smiled as if he were a friend. "I can't always come to your aid."

Laila stared dumbfounded at the young man whose green eyes sparkled with amusement. Tonight, instead of fern green, they were the color of ripe pistachios, most likely because of the porch light above. What did he mean by that? They couldn't be friends. It wasn't allowed. His proximity made her uneasy, but she couldn't help but feel drawn to those eyes, cool like an oasis watering hole. She could swim in them. Laila caught herself foolishly swooning. Was she that desperate? It could not be. She needed to disengage herself from this young man before both of them were sorry. "Thank you," she said, opening the door and disappearing into the house before she made a complete fool of herself.

The phone rang, and she ran to pick it up before it awakened Abba.

"Hell...o?" she whispered, out of breath.

"It's Zahar. Just checking to see you made it home all right. Are you okay? You sound winded."

"How sweet. I just walked in. I would have called, but we were somewhat delayed; and yes, I'm fine. I was dodging the raindrops, trying to stay dry." Laila saw no point in worrying Zahar. She had her own worries having just dealt with a second miscarriage.

Zahar laughed. "I was worried about you not having a ride."

"Thank you. No one has worried about me in years. It's nice." That was painfully true. Since Emma's death, she had been on her own. No wonder she had become so independent. Laila remembered being picked on by a boy in her class, and Emma telling her that boys who picked on you, liked you. *It's a complement.* Laila hadn't understood it at the time.

"Avraham and I would like to have you over for dinner Friday evening. It will be simple. Avraham says I'm a darn good cook."

"Then I look forward to it. What time?"

"Is five-thirty too early?"

"No. I have a light load on Friday. Can I bring something?" After graduating high school, and unsure about the time frame for moving to their kibbutz, Laila had begun classes at the university and found she really loved them. At the same time, mixed emotions, about starting something and not finishing it began haunting her. Abba didn't need Laila to help Judah anymore since he was doing so well, so why was she having so much trouble dealing with her plans? It seemed she needed a little more incentive.

"No. Just come," Zahar said. "That will be present enough."

Classes ended at noon for the Sabbath, and Laila couldn't wait for Friday to come. She was excited and looked forward to an evening with her friends. Now she had two.

Friday night arrived, and Laila walked to Zahar and Avraham's apartment carrying a package of dried fruit. She didn't know if they drank wine or if they kept kosher, so she brought what she thought might be appropriate. Emma had taught her, as a child, that it was proper to take a little something when you were an invited guest.

It was still light out and a gentle breeze followed Laila down the street, whipping her skirt about her legs, on her way to her next adventure. Laila saw all new experiences as an adventure. Although the bombing had happened a year ago, she was feeling stronger every day both physically and mentally.

Traffic was almost nonexistent with the Sabbath quickly approaching; everyone needed to be where they were going by then.

Laila's steps were buoyant as she thought about her future and how she was going to get there. The idea of starting a new kibbutz and being with others who shared her vision was exhilarating. It would be hard work and long hours, but that didn't matter. It was an adventure nonetheless. There hadn't been time for friends, what with school and the falafel stand, so Laila looked forward to not only making friends, but embracing a new family. Her sisters had been virtually out of the picture for years, and besides, she had nothing in common with them anymore. Leora and Zahar would be her new sisters. Laila had enjoyed lunch with Leora. She was pleasant company and there was more to her than Laila had expected. It just needed to be drawn out, and Laila was the one to do it.

The steady gait of someone behind her, made Laila chance a glance over her shoulder. It was a man, wearing a coat that flared at the bottom as he approached. His gait had stepped up as he inched closer. Laila increased her step, hoping it wasn't the green-eyed soldier, or someone else looking to do harm. She hadn't seen the soldier in days and hoped she had made him understand, at their last encounter, that there was no future for the two of them. Laila had heard a number of women in the neighborhood had been accosted and unnecessarily searched. She wouldn't tolerate that.

Laila was now at a lope as a sharp pain shot down her leg. She stopped, grabbed for a lamppost, and kept her eyes downcast. The footfalls of the stranger grew louder as he advanced. Had she done something wrong? She felt sick, scared, and sorry she had ventured out of her own. Maybe she wasn't as well as she thought she was. The man was just about even with her when the street lamp flickered and cast a beam across his face. He smiled, tipped his hat, and continued on his way. Laila crumbled in relief. *Silly me.* She continued to cling to the lamppost for support, waiting for her heart to slow down. After a moment, she gained control and almost felt disappointment that it hadn't been the green-eyed soldier. There were so many conflicting feelings where he was concerned, Laila didn't know what to think. She shook her head and walked on. The pain in her leg subsided.

Laila paused at Zahar's door to straighten out her only good skirt and matching blouse. She wore mostly pants or shorts during the day and seldom had a reason to dress up. She did not wear makeup; according to Abba, only low women wore makeup. She decided not to mention the incident.

She knocked, and Avraham answered. He was balancing a tray of pita chips and hummus. It was hard to get past his rugged good looks and his engaging smile.

"Come in, please," he said holding the door open. "You look a little pale. Is everything all right?" He hugged her with his free arm.

"I'm fine—just a little excitement on the way over which proved to be nothing. Really ... I'm fine. Thank you."

"Well good. Care to try Zahar's homemade hummus on toasted pita?" He shoved the tray toward her, so she could hardly refuse. Laila plucked a little gem from the plate and popped it in her mouth, where it melted like a chocolate covered cherry she had once tried. "Yum." The combined flavors of tahini and basil rolled around her tongue until she had to swallow. "That was the best thing I've ever tasted. I brought a little something ... Wow, she *is* a darn good cook."

Avraham looked askance at her and laughed. He took the package. "Thank you. You didn't have to."

"Everything smells delish." It had been a long time since she had eaten a meal prepared by someone other than herself. Now that she had tasted Zahar's hummus, her expectations were considerably higher.

"Let me have your jacket." He motioned for Laila to follow.

The Laundry Room

The apartment was small but cozy, much like her home. Though, she couldn't imagine where the furniture had come from: old and worn, but clean and polished. Family photos decorated the walls, adding warmth to the place—lighting in tones of sepia. Laila leaned in to study a wedding photo. *What a handsome couple*, Laila thought. They seemed madly in love. She hoped she'd find that special someone.

Hand-knit scarves draped the back of the furniture, and religious artifacts sat in niches and on shelves, adding to the hominess and permanence of the apartment. Her eye stopped at a beautiful bronze menorah. Laila had not lit the Chanukah candles since Emma died.

Zahar hobbled out of the kitchen. She, too, was now walking on her own. The two women clung to each other for a moment of true camaraderie. They both had made a lot of progress in their healing. "We're so glad you came. It's not often we have guests."

Laila inhaled that unmistakable scent of cloves that she had smelled on Zahar in the past. Was it a new perfume, or was she using it for medicinal purposes? Funny, Laila also noticed that savory aroma about Avraham when she first entered the room. This obsession with herbs and spices had to stop. She supposed since she was around condiments so often, her nose had become like a pig's, sniffing out truffles.

Laila glanced at the table. It was set for four. *Who could the fourth person be?* She didn't have long to wait. The knock came just moments later.

Avraham placed the tray on the counter and excused himself, and Zahar and Laila exchanged pleasantries until the men entered the room. Laila felt a shock immediately. It was that young man, Itzhak, with the icy blue eyes from the Scout meeting. Could it be? Laila forced a breath. It seemed all she ever did lately was gasp for air.

Lynda Lippman-Lockhart

"Laila, I don't know if you and Itzhak have had the opportunity to talk much at the meetings, but Itzhak is in one of my classes, and I thought it would be nice to have him join us this evening." She caught Avraham wink at Zahar.

It was an awkward moment for both. Laila thought he was extremely handsome, and certainly someone in a league above her own; he probably wouldn't be interested in a restaurateur's daughter, especially one who only ran a falafel stand. His parents would probably be horrified if they met her father: rough, loud, and aggressive, but he was her Abba nonetheless.

"We did speak, but for only a minute." Itzhak stepped forward and made the overture of shaking her hand. Awkwardly, she met his.

"Yes, we did." *He remembered!* Laila tried not to make a fool of herself. *I had thought he barely noticed me.*

Itzhak faltered as Zahar and Avraham left the room. They stood like two salt pillars, neither knowing what to say and certainly unable to move.

Then they spoke at the same time and laughed. The ice was broken.

"I understand you will be a freshman at the university next year."

"Actually, I've decided to start a few classes." Why was she having so much trouble getting her words out? She had never been shy around men ... but this one ... well, she didn't know.

"I don't mean to be rude, but you look awfully young."

"I just turned eighteen."

Itzhak moved toward the sofa. "Why don't we sit? I don't think there's room for all of us in the kitchen."

Not wanting to seem too anxious, Laila found an old

The Laundry Room

armchair across the room. Itzhak sat on the loveseat. They couldn't have been further apart if they tried. Laila remembered clearly the first time she had laid eyes on him. He had looked out of place; most of the young people at the meeting were crudely dressed and lacked manners. They were loud and uncultured ... but Laila wasn't being fair. Many had lost their families and were there as orphans, searching for a place to belong. Laila was lucky; she had Abba and her siblings.

Avraham returned with a tray and napkins. They helped themselves to an assortment of appetizers and a sort of discussion began. Zahar joined them between disappearing back to the kitchen. With every trip came a new aroma. Laila was able to identify cumin, cinnamon, turmeric, and a host of other Middle Eastern spices, but Zahar's arrangement of them was spectacular.

"Dinner is ready. Please take a seat," said Zahar, wiping her hands on her pale blue-and-white apron. "Avraham and I are used to sitting there and there." She pointed to the chairs across from each other. Itzhak pulled out one of the side chairs and waited for Laila to sit. She was shocked at his formality. He had impeccable manners. At home, it had always been every man for himself.

Avraham carried out the first course on a large, wooden tray. The aroma of steaming chicken soup brought with it bittersweet memories of Laila's mother and how she had loved to make chicken soup. Hers was the best, with the exception of Laila's grandmother's—*May she rest in peace,* Laila thought fondly.

Avraham ceremoniously placed a bowl before each of them and then took his seat at the head of the table. Zahar covered her head with a circular piece of lace, lit the candles, and recited the first blessing. Next, they lifted their goblets and sang the blessing over the wine. Laila wasn't much on wine, but she took a sip to be sociable. Avraham removed a linen cloth, covering a loaf of braided egg bread that sat in the center of the table and broke off a piece, passing it first to Laila, who broke off a small piece and handed it to Zahar, who, in turn, handed the remainder to Itzhak. They recited the prayer: *Blessed art thou, oh Lord our God, King of the universe, who bringeth forth bread from the earth.* The soup was as good as it smelled. Itzhak and Laila raved, agreeing Zahar was a talented cook. "When we get to where we're going, I vote you in charge of the kitchen," said Laila.

They laughed, putting an end to whatever tension was left. The rest of the meal: roasted chicken with herbed stuffing, cinnamon-scented apple noodle *kugel,* honey-glazed carrots, and stuffed eggplant with meat and pine nuts served as the feast. To top it all off, at the end of the meal, Zahar brought out a chocolate applesauce cake.

"You must have used up your rations for the month," said Itzhak, wiping his chin with a damask napkin.

"Very close," said Avraham, rising to help Zahar with the plates. "But tonight we're celebrating our next adventure."

Zahar rose, and Laila started to get up; but Zahar motioned for Laila to stay seated, leaving Itzhak and Laila alone again. Was this intentional?

"Do you know how to cook?" Itzhak asked, handing his plate to Avraham and directing the question to Laila.

"Yes. I've been the cook of the family since my mother passed away." Laila still withheld the falafel stand, not ready for full disclosure.

"I'm sorry. How long has your mother been gone?"

"A few years. My sisters are much older and married. They've moved away. I have an older brother who lives in town with his wife."

The Laundry Room

Avraham made several trips to and from the kitchen while Itzhak and Laila talked. Laila felt herself relax as they slipped into an easy conversation—her initial shock over.

Avraham and Zahar finally joined them, and they chatted easily, like old friends.

"Itzhak, Avraham tells me you're quite the orator." Zahar passed a bowl of nuts to Laila.

"If you're referring to my moment of fame months ago, I guess it was obvious I like stealing the limelight. My parents want me to be to go into international law, but I think I might prefer being a teacher."

"I had thought about teaching, but I've change my mind so many times it's probably a good idea I'm taking time out to find out what I really want to do," said Laila.

"Ah the idealism of youth," said Avraham. "I'm sure whatever you put your mind to you'll do well. You're quite an amazing young woman."

Laila began to feel a bit uncomfortable because of Avraham's praise. She had noticed him staring at her during dinner and tried to slough it off as friendly interest. Now, she wasn't so sure. She would watch herself a little closer with him. She didn't want to upset her friendship with Zahar.

The conversation continued for another half hour, before Itzhak mentioned he had studying to do and regretted having to leave. He asked if he could walk Laila home; and she said yes, not wanting the evening to end. They left after many hugs and a number of glowing comments about the meal.

Outside, the world was aglow for Laila. She couldn't believe her luck at having Itzhak join them for dinner. It had been fun, like being a couple.

"How long have you known Avraham and Zahar?" Itzhak asked as they walked along the street.

"Awhile. Remember they mentioned the blast at the hotel? Well, that's when our friendship began. I don't like to talk about it much." Though, at the moment, she was ready to spill her guts to him.

Laila realized how easy it was to talk to Itzhak after getting past his looks and the initial butterflies in her stomach. Besides, she had just eaten the best meal of her life and was walking home with a wonderful fellow. She decided right then and there that she would marry him.

"How long have you known them?" Laila asked, edging a bit closer to Itzhak, not really wanting to revisit that dreadful day.

"... since last semester, Avraham and I seemed to have shared a number of classes but this time ended up sitting next to each and decided to grab lunch one day. He's completely devoted to Zahar. They're lucky."

"Yes, I guess luck has something to do with it, but for me there has to be passion and shared interests." Laila averted her eyes away from Itzhak, hoping not to give herself away.

"Interesting."

"What's interesting about it?" Laila might have overreacted. On second thought he was rather know-it-all and a bit abrupt for her taste.

"You're young. You'll find mutual respect is the most important ingredient for a good marriage."

"You sound like you know something about it."

"My parents have that kind of marriage, and it has worked well for them. My mother isn't the passionate type."

Laila decided he knew little about women.

They continued to walk along in silence until they reached her street. Again Laila was sure he wasn't the least bit interested in her, and she couldn't blame him. She had

The Laundry Room

little experience with men other than Yoel, who had even less experience with women.

Laila stopped before her house, which she noted—to her horror—was in need of repair. Since Abba had begun his business, there was little time for anything else; and besides, he wasn't much of a carpenter. Priorities.

"It was nice getting to know you. I'm sure we'll be seeing a lot of each other once we move to the kibbutz." Itzhak took her hand and squeezed it. The full moon shimmered in the mottled, sapphire-and-ink-black sky. Out of the corner of her eye, Laila saw a shadow move across the street. Itzhak noticed it too because he glanced in that direction and then back at her. Laila hoped it wasn't that soldier. She didn't need an English guardian angel hovering about.

"Well ... yes. Good night." She didn't wait for his reply. Just like that, she was in the door and on her way to forgetting him. So much for the wedding.

Chapter 14

Ezra

Road to Pardess Hanna, 1943

The departure was rough. No one had expected such conflicting emotions all the way to Pardess Hanna. The young women whimpered and sniffled; the young men, who had considered themselves silent observers, found themselves having to console others—keeping their own sentiments in check. Throughout the bus, tired bodies swayed from side to side as they rolled over uneven terrain, filled with ruts and loose stones, skirting areas washed out by the last torrential downpour. The dreariness of the day matched their dismal dispositions. Ezra observed Anna and her present boyfriend huddled together, her head on his shoulder, his arm around her. Didn't she realize what she was doing to Ezra? She couldn't keep leading him on only to reject him all over again.

The trip was long, longer than imagined. Highway One had been carved out by the ancient Romans, but not maintained as it should have been. The travelers hadn't been through and the threat the villagers held over travelers. It wasn't until they had boarded the bus that they found an armed guard sitting in the front seat.

The tired lot passed through many small towns, some no more than ghost towns, blown to bits by the Arabs or British. It was becoming more difficult to be a Jew in their own country, even though they had fought for it time and time again. No one wanted them there. For that matter, it seemed no one wanted them anywhere.

Their first stop was outside Tel Aviv, where they were allowed to stretch and use a convenience area. Ezra and Itzhak waited for the others to use the facility before they entered.

"I haven't been here in years," said Itzhak, surprised at the condition of the buildings and streets. Apparently this area had been the sight of numerous bombings, since only portions of buildings stood on most streets. "So far we've been lucky to escape the brunt of this."

"I'm hoping that where we're going, we won't have to experience any of it." Ezra wiped a handkerchief across his brow. It was a scorching day with no breeze. The Scouts were all feeling a little irritable. Most had taken turns napping.

Itzhak motioned Ezra on; he would follow. The bathroom was dank and reeked of urine. It was nothing more than an outhouse with no flush toilets. Both men exited quickly. Ezra searched for Anna, who was talking to Laila near the bus. He casually walked up to them, leaving Itzhak to look for Ari.

"How are you two doing?" Ezra asked, trying to strike up a casual conversation.

"We're fine." The girls smiled. Anna's eyes averted as if looking for her boyfriend.

Ezra wasn't sure how to broach the subject, so he dove in. "Could I sit with you after the next stop?"

Anna's face cringed. She didn't say anything for a moment. "I guess that would be okay."

"I think Itzhak would like to sit with you," he said to Laila, hoping he would be forgiven for his lie.

Laila's eyes grew large as she scanned the area, her face a mixture of emotions.

"Do you have a problem with Itzhak?" asked Ezra.

"No," she said hesitantly, "but he might have a problem with me."

"Don't be silly. He asked me all sorts of questions about you." Ezra was sure he had exaggerated their conversation and might have placed himself inside a beehive, but the incentive to spend time with Anna far outweighed the risk. Surely Laila and Itzhak would forgive him if they found out.

Laila's face lit up. "Oh?"

The driver and guard checked out the bus before the group filed on. The girls proceeded to their previous seats. The men followed.

Ezra and Itzhak picked up a conversation every now and then. Although Itzhak wanted to appear brave and confident, Ezra could tell he was as scared as the rest. Of course, this was an adventure, and of course they would be in charge of their own destiny, but the Scouts would be on their own, except for the men who would help them get started. This was the first stepping stone to owning their own kibbutz. They had to prove their worthiness. Ezra did wonder how Benjamin, Isadora, and their infant, who sat two rows up would be able to brave the hardships that Ezra knew would follow.

Once they were seated. "How did it go with your father?" asked Itzhak.

"I think he had mixed feelings. On the one hand, he was

proud of me for striking out on my own. On the other he couldn't understand why I couldn't wait until I graduated. How about yours?"

Itzhak's face clouded over. "My father tore his shirt ... declared me dead. I'm on my own."

Ezra shook his head. "I'm sorry." And he had thought Itzhak had the world by its tail. "It seems we can never please our parents. That being the case, we must please ourselves." In the time Ezra had gotten to know Itzhak, he had gotten the impression that Itzhak was someone who needed to feel important—respected. He also got the feeling Itzhak's father ruled with an iron fist, and Ezra could well imagine the scene where Itzhak told his father about his plans. Ezra actually felt sorry for Itzhak; he carried a heavy weight on his shoulders.

"The thing is, your parents will be there if things don't work out," said Itzhak, his eyes revealing his pain.

"Yours will too. You'll see," said Ezra reassuringly. "I can't imagine them abandoning you, under the circumstances. Your father was just testing your sincerity."

"You're such an optimist." Itzhak patted Ezra on the shoulder. "Let's hope you're right."

The two men settled back to watch the scenery change from mountains to the shore, as the bus skirted the Mediterranean Sea. One of the women began singing a familiar tune. Others joined in. Ezra wasn't much for singing.

Their last stop would be Netanya, which Ezra knew meant "gift of God." Actually the name had been an attempt to encourage Nathan Straus, the co-owner of Macy's Department Store in New York City, who had gifted two-thirds of his wealth to projects benefiting both Jews and Arabs in Palestine, to subsidize them. When the people who had founded the town approached the endowment, they had discovered there was no more money. They named it after him anyway.

Just past Herzliya, Ezra felt the first rock hit the window, just missing his head. He immediately rose to lift the window, which was stuck fast. He and Itzhak tried to pry it out of its fixed state, but the glass wouldn't budge. Suddenly, hellfire and brimstone rained down on them, and then sticks followed. The scene was surreal as a group of Arab rebels, robes flapping in the breeze, tongues trilling their tribal chant, chased the bus as if determined to do it harm. Ezra found it almost comical, like watching an American Western, although he knew there was nothing comical about it. If they were successful, everyone on the bus would be dead. The Arabs didn't take prisoners. He was sure of that.

The armed guard hollered: "Get down. Keep your heads down." The guard lifted his Sten gun, a small machine gun, and began firing out the window. Just as Ezra was lowering his head, he watched one marauder go down. By that time, the bus was weaving from side to side, bodies bouncing off their seats and onto the floor, while the bus driver tried desperately to avoid the crude missiles meant to distract him. Babies were crying—mothers were trying to quiet their children, while trying to keep calm themselves. Ezra was sure the driver was doing his best not to overturn the bus. At this point, it wasn't just the babies screaming and crying; many of the younger women were shrieking while the others made an attempt to keep some semblance of order.

"Get the bastards," yelled one of the young men from the front of the bus. "... before they get us."

"What can we do?" yelled another.

"Just keep down and out of my way," barked the guard.

Apparently, the band of rebels hadn't counted on an armed guard but still didn't retreat. The next shot shattered the back window, sending shards of glass throughout the bus, cutting some of the very scared passengers, who now realized these attackers meant business.

Ezra couldn't contain himself any longer. He had to peek. A camel and rider were headed in their direction. The rider yelling what Ezra thought might be Arabic curses. They sounded guttural enough to be curses. Ezra watched the awkward cadence of the camel and rider as it drew near. The man's arms and legs were at odds with each other as the camel clip-clopped its way closer to the bus, the rebel's headdress waving like a sheet on a clothesline. Ezra ventured a look at the guard, who was now at the back of the bus, machine gun aimed in the pursuer's direction. Now within shooting distance, the guard took aim and slowly pulled the trigger. The bus must have hit a rut, because it veered to the right and the shot went wide, making it possible for the rider and camel to shorten the distance between them and the bus. Those in the bus, foolish enough to be watching the insurgence, collectively muttered their own private curse. It was almost impossible to maintain equilibrium as the bus careened all over the road.

The camel rider was now holding a rifle, which was aimed at the bus. He let off a shot at about the same time the bus hit another rut, missing the bus altogether. This time there was a collective sigh of relief. Ezra said a silent prayer. This was not a movie. This was a real life situation, and he was scared to death.

Ezra shifted his attention back to the guard, who was steadying himself for another shot, but nothing happened. Ezra watched the horror-stricken look on the guard's face as he checked his ammo. It must have been empty because the guard cursed loud enough for all to hear, sat down hard on the back seat, and then slid to the floor where he crawled back to the front of the bus, to reload another round of ammunition. The screaming never let up. Ezra covered his ears. It didn't help. Meanwhile, bullets continued to ping off the side of the bus, causing continued pandemonium and abject fear. Again, a bullet from the pursuer sailed through the rear window, embedding itself in the frame of the backseat, and causing everyone who had already moved out of the guard's way to hit the floor. Again the children screamed.

Watching the guard crawl to his previous position seemed an eternity. Ezra felt for sure they were doomed. No one on the bus was equipped to fight hand-to-hand combat, let alone use a gun that they didn't have. The young women carried on a persistent wail, while the young men tried their best to silent them. Ezra wanted to go to Anna, but it looked like the boyfriend seemed to be intent on calming her down. Ezra noticed Itzhak straining his neck to check on Laila. Ezra prayed they would make it out of this alive; they had so much to live for. What a tragedy it would be: a bunch of pacifists losing their lives unnecessarily. Ezra now wished he had changed seats with Laila during the last stop.

The guard's next shot landed his mark. The camel and rider must have been hit simultaneously, as the camel crumpled, while the rider fell backward, in what looked like slow motion, onto the ground, dust flying in all directions. Ezra managed to see the whole thing, breathed a sigh of relief, and closed his eyes for another prayer. When he opened them again, the band of marauders was out of sight, and the bus was on its way. Ezra stretched his upper body to search out Anna. She was actually looking at him. He smiled. *What a fool I am.*

The bus full of Scouts thanked their guard and slapped each other on the backs.

When they arrived at Netanya, everyone filed off the bus

The Laundry Room

without talking, many having trouble finding their land legs. Then, as if on cue, they all began squawking like a bunch of seagulls looking for bait in the Sea of Galilee.

Anna, now standing next to Ezra, said, "I was worried about you. I thought it was our end." She smiled and then went in search of her boyfriend.

For the moment, it was enough. Then Ezra thought to himself: *If the guard hadn't been on board, it might have been our end.* He hoped the rest of the trip to Pardess Hanna would go a little smoother. He certainly had something to tell his grandchildren someday—if in fact he ever got married.

Chapter 15

Itzhak

Road to Pardess Hanna, 1943

As Itzhak walked down the aisle of the bus, he saw Laila already seated. *This is going to be awkward,* he thought, not wanting to get involved with anyone at this time. He liked her, but he was just beginning this venture and wanted no ties, and he had a feeling this young woman did. Yes, she was pretty and smart, and there was something about her enthusiasm he found refreshing; but that didn't matter, not just yet. They were both young, and he didn't have the same passion for her that Ezra had for Anna. This was *definitely* going to be awkward. Reluctantly he sat down next to her, eyes fixed on the scenery passing by.

Laila said nothing. Her eyes seemed to be focused on the Mediterranean, which today was particularly blue, almost aqua. The calm belied what they had just gone through. Itzhak ventured a quick glance her way and then he caught himself staring, his discomfort growing. Were they going to remain silent throughout the trip or should he say

The Laundry Room

"Well, that was a close call." He finally found his tongue.

Laila slowly turned her head until her cool blue eyes and long, luscious lashes were even with his. "I thought we were doomed."

"Me, too. We should be grateful someone had the sense to supply us with a guard. He saved our lives."

"Look," said Laila, her eyes shifting from right to left as if searching for the right words, "you don't have to feel duty-bound to talk to me. I only traded seats so Ezra and Anna could be together. It wasn't my idea."

Itzhak hadn't expected that. She was a girl who spoke her mind. He liked that. You always knew where you stood with her.

"I don't feel duty-bound. I enjoyed the evening we met. I thought you were someone special. It's just that I'm not looking to be tied to anyone."

"Me either. How about friends? That takes the strain off both of us. We are going to be spending a lot of time together; and I, for one, don't want to feel I have to avoid you."

"I like that ... friends." He mulled it over for a moment and felt the pressure subside. They could be friends. She was like a younger sister, someone with whom he could tease and joke. Well, that was settled. Itzhak slid down in the seat and closed his eyes. The strain of the last few hours had taken him by surprise with the strength of the fatigue he felt now. He fell asleep.

Hours later the bus full of Scouts arrived at Pardess Hanna, tired but somewhat relieved at finally reaching their destination. Pardess Hanna was an agricultural village, surrounded by citrus orchards and eucalyptus groves. The young hopefuls would be given the outskirts of the village to farm.

"What a mess," said Laila, feeling for her backpack under the seat.

"I guess I hadn't expected something quite this disorderly," said Itzhak.

From what they could see out of the dusty window, their accommodations were a bit of a shock, as all they saw were tents and crude cabins. Apparently the last group had left the place in shambles. Well, it didn't really matter because this kibbutz was only a stopover until they earned the right to establish their own place. Itzhak had never lived in such squalor, but he would keep that information to himself. He doubted any of the others had been born with a silver spoon in their mouths either.

Most of the young people had come over in waves of *Aliya,* the fundamental Zionistic approach to the Jewish plight of returning to the Holy Land—the land of Abraham, Isaac, and Jacob. Itzhak was familiar with the history of the *Aliya* as his grandparents had been a part of one of the earliest movements. The first *Aliya,* he was told, began in 1882 with the exodus of approximately 35,000 Russian Jews immigrating to the southwest corner of Syria and then to the Ottoman Empire. Later, it became the only way surviving Jews could escape the Holocaust and find refuge in the country God had promised them in the *Torah.*

"Do you know anything about this place?" asked Laila, backpack on lap, disbelief written across her face.

"What I heard was that Pardess Hanna had been purchased from the Arabs for 400,000 francs (two million US dollars) in 1913 by the *Hachsharat Hayishuv,* a Jewish Land Company. I also heard that Pardess Hanna changed hands a number of times until the Jewish National Fund took it over for much less money. Apparently, to get around a Turkish law allowing the Ottoman Empire to confiscate undeveloped land, the people living on the property had planted eucalyptus trees. That is why we passed so many groves on our way here. It seems they grow in abundance, and as you can see, separate our kibbutz from our nearest neighbor. Did you know the site was named after Hannah Rothschild, the daughter of Nathan Meyer Rothschild, of the prominent Rothschild family?"

"I did not. You're just a wealth of information. Are you this thorough in everything you do?"

"I guess," said Itzhak and smiled.

Laila shook her head. "You're a very unusual young man. I bet no one else knows any of what you just told me."

"Oh yes, the town boasts of an agricultural high school that was established in 1934, but I didn't see it on our way in. Perhaps it is on the other side of town." Apparently Itzhak didn't know a complement when he heard one.

Itzhak helped Laila with her belongings and both stood, as it was their turn to disembark. Itzhak watched as Laila slung her backpack over her shoulder and followed him off the bus.

Itzhak looked the place over as his shoe hit the dusty ground. With a renewed enthusiasm, he now saw an opportunity to do something worthwhile with his life. He thought, perhaps, he was growing up—until he watched Laila rush into Avraham's arms.

Chapter 16

Laila

Pardess Hanna, 1943

"Welcome to Pardess Hanna," said a rugged, tanned, and balding man, who wore khaki shorts and matching shirt. He looked like he belonged in a kibbutz setting. "My name is Tal Rabin. I understand your journey was not without incident, and I hope the rest of your stay will be less stressful than your trip here. You have a long way to go before becoming self-sufficient, so there's no time like the present to get started. Volunteers from the surrounding area will help you find your way. They have a lot of experience in growing fruit and vegetables in a barren wasteland." The Scouts shared a moment of relief; the strain of the trip subsided. "We're aware of your training through the Scouts organization, but this is real life with all the hazards that go along with it." His eyes scanned the group, as if measuring their capability to do work. It was hard to tell what he thought because his face showed no sign of emotion.

Chattering voices echoed off the dilapidated buildings, as

the group of weary travelers commented on their introduction. It was obvious many felt as Laila did, and were ready to get back on the bus and return to Jerusalem, but they didn't. They had lived through a near disaster, not easily forgotten. Things could only get better, so said Zahar and Avraham as she clung to them for support. Suddenly she was feeling homesick.

"Let me have your attention," Tal continued. "I'll show you around; then you can choose your sleeping quarters. I'd suggest the ladies buddy up, four in a hut; that way, only a few of the men will have to sleep in the tents." A buzz followed.

It occurred to Laila that she hadn't been friendly enough with any of the girls other than Zahar and Leora, and Zahar and Avraham would be sharing their own room. Leora wasn't outspoken enough, so it looked like the choice was up to her.

The weary travelers followed Tal from one hovel to the next, and Laila really meant "hovel." Each hut was worse than the next. The tents weren't any better. *My God, this isn't a camping trip where we can return home after a week.* This *was* home. And the men didn't seem too excited about the tents. Still, Laila had a feeling they wouldn't be spending much time indoors by the looks of things. And really, it wasn't forever. Eventually, they would build their own place—on their own land.

The guided tour continued.

"This is the main hall where you will take your meals and meet for planning. A crude kitchen is just off the left side of the building. You can do your cooking on a primus stove with fuel burners." He wasn't just kidding about the crude part. Abba would have a fit if he saw the conditions under which Laila and her friends would be working and living. Emma would turn over in her grave. The new tenants had a lot of work ahead of them, just to make the place habitable.

Disbelief appeared on everyone's faces. Leora was now standing next to Laila. "I had no idea it would be this bad." She shook her head and sighed. "Did we make a big mistake?" Her body slumped; she looked crestfallen.

Zahar edged toward Laila. "This is not what I expected either."

"Or me," said Laila shaking her head. "But we're here, and we'll have to make the best of it, and we have each other." The girls locked arms and squeezed. In a short time, they had become sisters. Laila watched over Zahar like a hawk; today she was pale, and Laila was worried about her.

Tal took the new kibbutzniks around back to show them where the cattle would be housed, once they were able to afford them. Like everything else, it was crude and in dire need of repair. The stalls were in shambles and the wire fence was torn in several places. He pointed out the pastureland and where the group would plant crops. There were already citrus trees in abundance; the scent of their blossoms filled the air with possibilities. It was obvious the last inhabitants had done well by their groves, far better than their living quarters. Tal also pointed out the town of Pardess Hanna, and the lush grove of eucalyptus trees separating their kibbutz from civilization, making them somewhat isolated.

"I can almost see myself up on a ladder, dropping oranges down to Avraham," laughed Zahar, tickling Laila in the ribs. Laila could see a change in her friend already. Zahar would bounce back quickly. She must have caught Laila's smirk as Zahar's head wobbled from side to side. Laila would share her thoughts later.

The Scouts made their way through the cattle pens— minus cattle—to the groves and pastures, and back to what

The Laundry Room

would be their housing. Tal stopped next to a long building that had more windows than the huts. "This is where the children will stay. I understand there aren't many of them yet, but I'm sure that will change soon enough. Nurses will be in charge, caring for them and teaching them. They will lodge here. After all, kibbutz children belong to everyone, and you will not have to worry about them while you work. It's the new way. They will take their evening meals with you and then retire here with the nurses."

Zahar and Laila read each other's minds. No one would be raising their children, if and when that blessed event took place. Laila knew the mention of children was a difficult subject for Zahar with two miscarriages behind her.

"Those who are interested in seeing the interior, follow me; the rest can look around on your own," said Tal opening the door to the nursery. A few of the women followed Tal inside. Laila noted the cots lined up like army barracks. Two nurses stood by the small office next to the sleeping quarters. Their faces were pinched and stern—their bodies, just as stern—no curves to cuddle up to. There were two adult beds next to the office and cubbies next to each cot. The place needed a coat of paint and some cute pictures on the wall. It looked too much like basic training. Tal was right about there being very few children. After all, this was a young group, the youngest being only fifteen. But Laila knew Tal was also right about there being more by next year after people paired up out of necessity.

Laila had heard about the *Beit Yeladim* method of raising children—separating them from their parents—and so, she was glad she didn't have a child. To be sure, Laila didn't know if she could handle raising her child that way. It seemed cruel and unemotional.

Tal introduced the nurses and then the group of

disillusioned women continued on. Those with children clutched them to their bodies.

Reassembled in what would become the patio, Tal cleared his voice and said, "I'll leave you to decide who will room with whom. Obviously, the married couples have been allocated their own rooms. As I said before, single men and women might have to have four or five in a room. Some of the men will take the tents until we can build more sleeping quarters." He stopped to check his notes. "Would the married couples follow me? The rest of you might want to start thinking about choosing a leader and divvying up the rooms. There are eight left."

Zahar and Avraham, Benjamin and Isadora, Pincus and Shaina, and two other couples that Laila didn't know well left the group. Laila watched them gather their belongings; their well-mannered children followed.

"All right," said Itzhak, stepping forward and picking up on Tal's suggestion to choose those who will lead, "we need to form a core group who will govern the kibbutz. That's what they do at the other kibbutzim. We'll need to talk this over and vote people in, but we have to know who is interested in holding a position." Itzhak stopped and looked about to see who was listening. "I talked to Benjamin, Pincus, Avi, and Lebel. Only Pincus is interested in politics, but doesn't want to be the leader."

A buzz filled the patio as suggestions flew from one direction to another. Laila was astonished at Itzhak's apparent show of authority. He never ceased to amaze her.

"Avraham is the oldest and wisest," said Yehudith from the rear of the group. "I think he should be in charge."

"What about you?" directed one of the men at Itzhak.

"I don't want the job, thank you; but I agree with Yehudith; we'll ask Avraham when he returns—if that is how the majority feels."

They took a straw vote and Avraham won unanimously.

"Good. In the meantime," said Itzhak, "let's choose roommates."

Friends chose friends. Those not having made strong bonds also managed to pair off and go their separate ways, leaving Leora, Mazel, Carmel, and Laila standing alone.

"Well, ladies," said Laila, facing her new roommates, "looks like we're a group. Let's see what's left." The forlorn, young women followed Laila, the youngest, as she took note of her new roommates. Leora, plain by most standards, reminded Laila of an *onager*—a wild donkey, indigenous to Palestine, and so named because of its big, black eyes and sandy mane. Leora's hair, Laila had noticed early on, cascaded down her back almost to her waist, and was always hidden under a faded kerchief, most likely to hide her somewhat protruding ears. There was a graceful hook to her nose, but anyone paying close attention would find a womanly figure enviable by many. Laila supposed some might think her assessment harsh, but honest.

Mazel, short yet cheery, with perpetually rosy cheeks and hazel eyes, shaded by heavy brows, was pretty in a way most men might not appreciate since she carried her weight predominantly on her hips. She did have nice legs, often showing them off when she wore gored skirts. Mazel had been separated from her parents at the beginning of the Holocaust, and smuggled into Palestine by a Jewish organization. Her story was harrowing.

Carmel, well, it was difficult to be honest without sounding cruel. She had not been kissed by an angel, but she would give you the shirt off her back. Her five-foot-ten frame carried her two hundred pounds with effort. She might have been Slavic with her light complexion and blond hair, flecked with silver threads, and which most women would give their eyeteeth for, but she was as Jewish as the rest of the members of the kibbutz. Laila thought that perhaps with a little makeup and some grueling exercise, Carmel's inner beauty might emerge. She never talked about her beginnings. It seemed too painful.

Together, the four young women found the only empty room and dropped their belongings on the floor. The girls stood silently, as if waiting for Laila to choose her bed. She guessed they had made her dorm mother. The room was sparingly furnished with open cubbies by each bed. Laila noticed, to her chagrin, there was no attached bathroom. *Oh my—another inconvenience. But it is an adventure, and I had better remember that.*

After Laila chose her bed, the others picked up their belongings and stowed them in the closest cubby. Carmel fell to her bed and began to cry. "I don't want to seem ungrateful, but I thought it might get better once we were settled. My mother would turn over in her grave, if she saw how we will live," she sobbed. "It is; however, far better than the concentration camp where she died. We are going to be okay, aren't we?" Her imploring eyes looked to her new roommates for reassurance.

"Of course," said Leora, sitting down next to her and wrapping an arm around Carmel's shoulder. "We will help each other get through this."

It was then Laila decided Leora would make a good mother. Laila wasn't so sure about her own prospects. She didn't have the nurturing spirit Leora had. Perhaps that would come with time. Emma had been born to be a mother, with ample hips and large breasts to nurture her children. She also possessed the right temperament. Laila had not been blessed with either. Laila could remember, vaguely,

The Laundry Room

when she had moments of fear, that her mother would lift her on her lap and Laila would smell a hint of cinnamon left behind after making a yeast cake or strudel. Perhaps that was her draw to Leora—the cinnamon. She also remembered how safe she felt enveloped in her mother's arms, but those thoughts must be stored away like the faded photos of her mother.

Mazel joined her new roommates on Carmel's bed. It must have been a sight because one of the women passing their door stuck her head in and laughed. "What's this? A hen party? We're returning to the patio. Come on, ladies." She backed out laughing.

Beds taken, belongings stowed, they gravitated back to join the rest of the group for their next round of instructions.

Laila couldn't help but notice Itzhak had placed himself in the middle of things. He was making it easier and easier not to like him.

"Everyone," he said confidently, "I have spoken to Avraham, and he has agreed to be our leader; but he says this is a democracy, and he will only do what is necessary to maintain order. He expects us all to pull our weight." Laila guessed that made Itzhak second-in-command.

Tal returned. "This is where I leave you for an hour or so. I have business in Pardess Hanna. It is up to you to iron out any wrinkles before I return." Tal waved and headed toward his vehicle.

"Where is he going?" asked Ezra, just joining the group.

Avraham spoke up, "Tal's giving us some time to get organized before parceling out the duties. We have a lot to discuss, like whom among you would like to be in charge of the kitchen?"

Laila watched as a few hands went up: one was Zahar's, and then Leora's; so Laila hesitantly raised hers. Avraham pointed to three of them. "You are in charge of putting together the next couple of meals. Tal brought the makings for the next few weeks. After that, we're on our own. He also left seeds for planting and tools for hoeing. Decide who's in charge of what and let's get started. Someone from the next town will check on us periodically."

A hand shot up in back. Sherry Silverman moved forward. "Am I to understand we are sharing a bathroom with the men?" Laila was pretty sure Sherry would find life here difficult. She was altruistic and most likely wanted to believe she could live the Spartan life, but Laila doubted it. Laila was hoping Sherry would prove her wrong. Sherry had come over from the States with her parents looking for the "Promised Land": her father was a rabbi, and her mother, a teacher. Sherry had struck out on her own, to establish a bit of independence.

"Until you can build another," one of the men mocked. It was difficult for the rest to keep a straight face, but they did.

"I see," she said and backed into the fold of the group. A new buzz began in the back of the ranks.

"What we must do first is prioritize our needs: food, lodging, bathrooms." Avraham picked up a clipboard, looked it over, and began speaking again. First, they discussed rules and regulations for safety. He spoke of a division of labor and how they would need committees for education, industry, general housekeeping, security, and so on.

The discussion went on until they felt somewhat secure in their plans.

Tal returned and picked up the knapsack he had inadvertently left behind. "How did things go?" he asked Avraham.

"I think we're on the right track. What next?"

"I'm sure you all are interested in eating, and soon.

The Laundry Room

Cooks, follow me. The rest of you can clean out your sleeping quarters." The three that Avraham had pointed out tagged along. Laila was thankful to remain with Zahar and Leora. Schmuel, the only man who raised his hand, seemed confident in what he was about to do. It was probably good to have a man in the kitchen. Abba was a pro; far better than Emma had been. Laila wasn't surprised when Ari joined the kitchen patrol, probably to spend more time with Leora, but it didn't matter. He would be a lot of help.

The kitchen was separated from the main dining room, Laila guessed as a precaution in case of fire. It must have been an issue at some point. The building was constructed of concrete block with very little mortar holding the blocks together. A single light bulb hung from the ceiling in the center of the room.

Using huge tongs left in the back of the covered truck, Ari and Schmuel emptied ice blocks into wheelbarrows and carried them back to the kitchen.

As Laila watched, she decided she liked Ari; he was genuine. It irked her, though, that Itzhak wasn't more like him. She would have thought Ari's kindness might have rubbed off.

Once the rest of the groceries were unloaded, the cooks began planning the next two days' meals. Zahar was good at that. Laila was better at organizing where everything would go on the shelves, which needed a good cleaning.

Laila found a box with some old rags left on the top shelf in the back of the room. She lifted the box from the shelf and something black, with pincers, crawled out and fell to the floor, landing on her shoe. She kicked off the culprit, after many attempts, and ran screaming, from the storage room; Leora ran after her screaming: "What's wrong? Are you hurt? What was it?" She caught up with Laila and grabbed her

126

shoulders.

"I don't know." Laila's heart was galloping a mile a minute. "I think ... a scorpion ... big and black." By now she was gasping for air. This was too much. She was ready to return home.

"Don't worry; Ari will kill it," Leora said holding onto Laila. "I've never seen you react like that. You're always so resilient."

"It just took me by surprise. My nerves are a bit frayed."

"Take a minute to gather your wits and then come on back. Maybe you can work outside today." She left Laila feeling silly, reacting so. Laila had managed a bomb, but couldn't manage a scorpion.

When Laila returned, no one mentioned the scorpion or her reaction. Ari and she went on an expedition in search of a well pump. They found it hidden in the overgrowth behind the building. Laila was not particularly excited about venturing through the weeds after her recent encounter, so she backed up and let Ari take over.

Ari seemed to be taking note of the situation and said, "I'm going back to the storehouse to find some clippers. I'll be right back. You might want to see what else is back there."

"You go; I'm fine." He hurried off, as if not trusting her sudden show of courage. Laila just hoped she wouldn't be challenged by another surprise.

Together they cleaned away the debris until there was a path to the pump and the extra growth was manageable. When they returned to the kitchen, the place shone from top to bottom. "My, oh my, you could almost eat off the floor," said Laila, nodding her head in approval.

Ari entered behind Laila. "It probably hasn't been this clean since the day it was built." They all laughed as if they were feeling a little more positive about their situation.

After Laila's mishap with the scorpion, Schmuel and Zahar finished organizing the meals by shelf: rice, flour, matzo meal, and corn on one shelf, canned vegetables on another. The fresh vegetables were stored in wooden boxes with secure tops until they needed them.

Laila picked up a knife and joined the others chopping radishes, carrots, cucumbers, red and green bell peppers, and parsley. The chopped items were transferred to a small metal tub, which had been scrubbed until it glistened. Next, they mixed a little coriander, chopped green onions, olive oil, fresh lemon juice and ground pepper to make a dressing.

Schmuel had turned on the burners while they chopped and prepared the food. He took eggplant, tomatoes, onion, and zucchini and placed them in the heavy pan, along with some olive oil, and sautéed them until they emitted a mouthwatering aroma. It was obvious the kibbutzniks wouldn't have this many fresh vegetables again until their own crops came into season, so they used what they had sparingly. "Why don't we dry out some of the vegetables and spices?" he suggested. So they hung what was left of the herbs and spices from the squat ceiling.

Zahar and Laila cleaned off the long wooden tables and benches in the dining room, and found some old, leftover tablecloths that had been tightly packed. Laila shook and banged the boxes against the wall.

"What are you doing?" asked Zahar.

"Making sure there are no more surprises."

Schmuel chuckled as he carried the salads into the room. "You girls are regular comedians."

Leora had discovered some wildflowers and placed them in a cracked vase. Ari opened the windows for ventilation and suddenly the dining hall sprang to life.

Lunch was ready in no time. The rest of the group filed in, deep in conversation. Laila caught Itzhak walking in with Livia, that same girl she had seen him with at the meeting, and on one of their stops. Strange, their paths had not crossed. The girl was smiling and looking at him with something close to adoration. It was obvious she was smitten. Laila returned to the kitchen to retrieve a platter of food, determined to get him out of her head.

The aroma in the kitchen was disarming, and Laila felt her spirits lift. A round of applause greeted her as she carried in that first platter of food. She blushed.

Someone called from the back of the room, "This is marvelous. I haven't eaten like this in years."

"Yes. Let's give our cooks a hand," said another. Raucous applause rang out across the room.

Someone went into the kitchen and pulled the cooking crew out for a bow. More applause.

It appeared they would have no competition in the kitchen. Schmuel didn't strike Laila as a hard laborer, with his small build and lack of muscle tone, but he sure knew how to grill. Abba would have been delighted to hire him on to one of his stands. Good workers were hard to come by, Abba always said.

Laila was beginning to think each one of the kibbutzniks would find their place before long. Schmuel sat next to Laila; Leora and Ari sat across from them. Zahar and Avraham perched to Laila's right. It seemed they had created their own family. Laila refused to look in Itzhak's direction.

Chapter 17

Ezra

Pardess Hanna, 1943

Weeks later and deeply entrenched in making the kibbutz a home, Ezra began feeling the enthusiasm return. He and Anna were still playing a cat and mouse game, partly because her boyfriend seemed to have shifted his affections to another member of the kibbutz. The place was beginning to shape up: buildings scrubbed, crops planted, grounds tidied, and most encouraging, chickens laying eggs. All this was positive and yet, for him, something was missing.

Ezra had watched a number of romances bloom. Itzhak's interest in Laila grew as they gravitated toward each other in the fields and during meals. In their room, at night, Itzhak did nothing but talk about Laila until some of the roommates left to find refuge elsewhere. Ezra couldn't help but feel a bit jealous. He could tell Laila was holding back, and he couldn't blame her with Itzhak, the lady's man. There was something poetic about a budding romance, though, one Ezra felt inclined to commit to paper, even though it wasn't his romance. He had attempted to capture the passion of the kibbutz in his latest poem, entitled "Hardships and Discovery". For that matter, a number of others had paired off, with so little else to do besides work. Zahar had miscarried after the trip, generating a great deal of sympathy for the young couple. The group had rallied around them, trying to raise their spirits. To Ezra, Avraham was a man of vast extremes: sweltering with emotion one minute and totally devoid the next, and like Mt. Sinai, apt to erupt when least expected. Yes, their kibbutz experienced many of the same dynamics any small village might encounter.

Ezra thought long and hard about his personal situation and wished something would happen that would force him to let go of Anna once and for all. Maybe then he would be able to pass through the grieving process and finally mend. He had made this quest, not because of her, but to find his own purpose in life. *Oh well*, he uttered, *there is no looking back now, certainly not where my father is concerned*. His father didn't take the failure of others well.

After dinner, Ezra left the dining hall before dessert and ambled back to his room to do some writing. He heard his name.

Itzhak called to him, "Wait, I want to ask you a question."

Ezra stopped and waited for his friend. "What is it?"

"Maybe I'm paranoid, but have you seen Laila talking to Jacob a lot lately?"

"No more than I've seen you talk to the Slutsky girl. What's that all about?"

Itzhak stared at Ezra as if he had slapped him in the face. "You know as well as I, she means nothing to me. We're old friends."

"I'm not sure Laila understands that. Maybe it's her way of making you jealous—talking to Jacob. Sometimes you both can be pathetic. Now, I have writing to do. Go work it out." Ezra turned and continued to their bunk. *Honestly, Itzhak can be a pain in my tuches sometimes. That girl is crazy about him and he can't even see it.*

Ari, Itzhak, and Ezra had chosen to be roommates. Their devotion to each other grew daily, creating a bond unbroken by anyone who might try. Physically stronger and tanned by the sun's unrelenting rays, they made quite the trio. They worked side-by-side in the orange groves, planting, harvesting, and picking the golden orbs that Ezra wrote so glowingly about. Just in the last month, their production had doubled, and so had Ezra's verses. He found a new release in his poetry, which flowed like the swift Jordan River, as each day unraveled a new adventure of challenges and rewards. What Ezra loved most of all, were the evenings when the kibbutz had time to do what they wanted or met to sing or dance. Ezra had never been much of a dancer, but he found the simple dances easy to learn, it was the only time he had the opportunity to get closer to some of the young women— Anna being one of them.

At the end of one of these evenings, a storm rolled in from the west with uncommon speed, dumping buckets of water on the kibbutz and flooding the ground. The crops bent at the waist like old men, the sheep stood knee-deep in water, and a minor flood found its way into the sleeping quarters. Disturbed by the torrential downpour, Ezra awoke to find his shoes floating across the room. He donned his poncho and boots, and headed out to do what he could to help. He was surprised that more people hadn't been awakened by the deluge. Grabbing a bucket, he joined the brigade as they went to work, scooping up excess water from the sheep pen and transferring it to a trough. He was so busy that at first he hadn't noticed Anna by his side.

"Why aren't there more people helping?" she yelled over the howling wind.

"I can't hear you." Ezra continued what he was doing, never sure how to act around her. She waved him off and continued bailing out the pen. There was nothing much they could have done about the crops, as the tarps hadn't arrived yet.

The two worked feverishly until others began to join them. By five that morning, the storm had moved on and the bailers had gained the upper hand.

Anna stopped what she was doing and yanked back a stray clump of hair from her face. Ezra didn't care what she looked like; to him she was still the most beautiful girl he had ever known. He took her arm and guided her toward the dining room.

"You're a hard worker," she said, pulling back the hood on her poncho. "Maybe I misjudged you. I see a new passion in your step—a zest for life I never saw before. Are you happier here?"

Ezra wiped away beads of moisture from his forehead and removed his poncho to air it out. "Yes, I am. I was walking through life unengaged, somewhat in a stupor. Now I have a reason to get up every morning. I have a purpose. I'm creating something other than dirty laundry." He started to say that his reason for living had died when she left him, but he felt that would be overdramatizing things. "I've written more poetry since we've arrived than I have in years. It's good, too."

"I'd like to see it. Would you mind?"

"You would? No, I don't mind."

"Yes, I'd like to read some."

"Wait just a minute. I'll be right back." Not thinking how

pathetic he might seem, Ezra grabbed his poncho, threw it over his head, and ran to his bunk. He rummaged through his things and was about to leave when he heard a voice.

"What are you doing? The rooster hasn't crowed yet." Itzhak sat up and looked around. No one else was in the room. "What happened?"

"You slept through a terrible storm. We were all out bailing water."

"Why didn't you wake me?"

Ezra stood poised to leave, not wanting to explain his sudden appearance and even more sudden exit.

"You were sleeping so soundly, we didn't have the heart. I have something I have to do," and he was out the door.

Finding Anna where he left her, he thrust the notebook into her hands. "Any page," he said excitedly.

The notebook opened naturally to a page he had pored over day and night. It captured his emotions of love and loss. Now that he thought about it, having her read it might be embarrassing. Ezra tried to take the notebook from her, but she pulled away and continued reading. When she finished, she looked up at him with tears in her eyes.

"I'm sorry," said Anna, handed the notebook back to him, and ran toward her room.

He watched her go. *What have I done?*

Chapter 18

Laila

Pardess Hanna, 1943

Months had passed and the kibbutz no longer needed monitoring. The kibbutzniks had recovered from the freak storm, mended fences, rounded up the livestock, and prospered. Weekly reports filtered in, along with visitors who either replenished their needs or came to purchase what the kibbutz had successfully grown on their own. It seemed the citrus crop took more of their time than expected. Laila had heard from her family via long, newsy letters. Abba had suffered a mild heart attack and let Judah take over the business. Apparently he had the talent after all, but had been overshadowed by his domineering wife and successful father and sister. Laila was glad he had found his niche.

One particular letter caught her attention:

My dearest daughter, I grow stronger with each passing day and have been allowed to tend your stand. Judah reluctantly turned it over to me. I have

135

The Laundry Room

more than I can handle. You were right placing it there. Now, for why I wrote you. I have noticed a young British soldier hanging around the house and my stand. It was the same young man who found me and took me to the hospital; for that I owe him my life. He says little, but is very intense. Once, he asked about you. Have you neglected to tell me something? I don't need a shadow, and certainly not an English one. He seems to think he is my guardian angel while you're gone.

I have not told him where you are or what you are doing. I'm afraid he would be there to make sure you are all right. Since you just wrote, I do not feel the need to ask you what you are doing, but I would like an explanation of why this soldier is so interested in you.

Take care of yourself and stay safe. Every day I hear disturbing news. When will this be over?

Your loving father,

Abba

The news came as no surprise. It seemed the young soldier had been keeping tabs on her and her father. Before coming to the kibbutz, Laila had seen him coming and going to work, heading out in the evenings, and just in general. Afraid he might follow her to one of her meetings and cause trouble, she had taken to being very cautious when she left the house, and had found many ways to get to where she was going. Having lived in Jerusalem all her life, its streets had become a stored part of her memory, one that had served her well. The problem was she had to recall them more often over the last year. Leaving Jerusalem had been a kind of relief; no more looking over her shoulder.

Lynda Lippman-Lockhart

It was Laila's day off. The kibbutz had decided to rotate the work schedule, so that every task was covered except at sundown on Friday night to prepare for the Sabbath. The kibbutz was mostly secular, but there were a few who tried to keep their ancient traditions alive; like Laila, who was trying hard to fulfill her promise to God to be more devout for him having saved her. As she finished reading Abba's letter for the tenth time, Laila heard a rap at the door. She rose from her bed and stepped out the room with no thought as to who it might be.

Itzhak was leaning against the door frame, looking a bit nervous. He had been more attentive lately; Laila often found him working next to her in the fields or harvesting the orange trees. "Good morning. I heard you had the day off, and I thought we might go for a walk. That is, if you don't have anything better to do." He stood like a British soldier on watch. Laila couldn't help but notice a pulsating vein in his neck, just at the collar line. He was obviously nervous, and she suddenly realized her hair was down and she was in her sleeping clothes.

Although it felt as if her heart would flutter out of her chest, on the outside Laila remained calm and nonchalant. She hesitated, scrunched her forehead as if running through all the things she had to do, and then agreed. "Let me get a jacket; it's cooled down."

Laila disappeared into the room and came to an abrupt halt. Again she berated herself for stepping out of the room in her pajamas. How embarrassing. Had he noticed? She supposed not, since his eyes had never given him away. Laila grabbed a pair of clean khaki pants, her underwear, and a shirt and ran into the corner to dress. They really didn't have much privacy since they left the door open at night for cross-ventilation. *I should have closed the door, but it's already too late.* She fell over once trying to get her leg into the secondhand workpants they had been given. Dressed, she glanced into what was left of a mirror that had not fared well on their trip, and ran her hands through her wildly curly hair. Desperately looking around the room for something to tame it, she noticed one of Leora's scarves at the edge of her bed. Though almost colorless, Laila snatched it up and tied it around her head, pulling her hair away from her face. As she reached the door, a cool breeze reminded her she should take the jacket she'd told Itzhak she was fetching. It would also act as a disguise for her unsightly clothing.

"That was fast."

"I didn't have much to choose from, so it was easy. Is it safe to leave the grounds?"

"I think so. No one said otherwise."

They walked toward Pardess Hanna, as they weren't as familiar with the route in the opposite direction, and after what had happened on the trip there, they certainly didn't need to look for trouble. That same brisk breeze propelled them down the dusty road, which was covered with tire tracks and oil spills. Laila was amazed that anything could grow in such an arid land. And this was the *Promised Land*? On the trip to Pardess Hanna, she had noticed the disparity between Arab-owned properties and that of the kibbutzim. Why was that so? She had heard of oil wells and the sudden wealth found in the land given to the Arabs during the division of territory by the British and French. Apparently there was no oil, to speak of, in their portion of land, just barren soil. She wasn't complaining, just wondering why she hadn't seen more green on their journey there.

Itzhak cleared his throat. "What's on your mind?"

"My thoughts are simple. I was just wondering about the difference in our land compared to that of the Arabs."

"I think your thoughts are far from simple. You're a deep thinker. Most of the other girls are worried about their hands getting rough and their hair drying out. You never complain."

"What good would it do? We chose our lot and should have known it wouldn't be easy. I find simple joys in watching the lambs give birth or a hot pepper appear. I haven't decided what I want to do with my life yet, so I have no regrets."

They walked on in silence, admiring the lush copse of eucalyptus trees until an open jeep passed by and then stopped short a few feet beyond. The jeep waited for them to catch up. A British soldier stood, giving them the once over. "Where are you going?" he barked.

"For a walk," Itzhak said nonchalantly.

Laila held her breath. It had been over a year since the bombing, and she was still gun-shy. What did they want? She felt like a prisoner in what was supposed to be her own country. Leaving Jerusalem had been a healing balm, working the soil, repairing their souls, and now this. Living at the kibbutz, she had allowed herself to become complacent where the British were concerned. Since the scouts had arrived, the British hardly ever bothered them. Today it all came back: her fear, her dislike, her disdain. Itzhak grabbed her hand.

"Are you members of the kibbutz over there?" The officer pointed back to where they had just come.

"Yes," said Itzhak, positioning himself between Laila and the jeep.

"I suggest you turn around and return to your kibbutz. It isn't safe out here. We've had an Arab uprising on a kibbutz not far from here."

"What happened?" asked Itzhak.

The Laundry Room

"They killed a few of the unsuspecting kibbutzniks, but didn't get away unscathed. It seems that particular kibbutz has a fairly good system in place for such an occurrence."

"Shall we haul them in?" asked the driver.

The officer said nothing, as if to add to the drama, Laila thought.

"No, they're harmless. Now hurry before we have to cart you off for disturbing the peace."

Itzhak tightened his grasp on Laila's hand and pulled her back the way they had come. He whispered, "What kind of 'disturbing the peace'? We weren't doing anything. That upsets me. It's getting harder and harder to be a pacifist."

"I suspect it was their way of exercising their power and scaring us into returning without force."

"I suppose you're right. That still concerns me. We don't really have anything in place in case of an attack. I thought we were fairly safe out here." He let go of her hand. "We have some work to do." Itzhak turned, his thoughts easy to read, and Laila followed.

Laila's heartbeat sped up as they picked up speed. Itzhak was right about being vulnerable. They were open to anyone who might wish them harm. Since she had lived through an assault, she decided it was important that she be on the committee to defend themselves. She was sure Itzhak would work with her. She would like that. Laila mused for a moment as she pictured working together. She had to admit, it was not easy to relax around him—he was so wound up, but today had opened the door of communication between them.

###

By the end of the week, the kibbutzniks knew what they had to do and preparations began in earnest to step up

140

security. Itzhak, Avraham, and Laila had worked out a drill that they practiced at different times of the day. When Tal Rabin returned to check on them, he was pleased with their progress, and with him came the latest news from around the world.

"Gather round," he said, his arms waving everyone in. "The world is changing quickly and you need to know what is going on. I understand you have a plan in place for emergencies. I didn't think we would have to worry about that, but we do. I commend you for stepping up to the situation. Lebanon is now an official country. They've fought for their independence for the last few years, and found a way to secure it. As for us, the British have gone back on yet another promise. They have stopped the immigration of Jews into Palestine. Pressure by the Arabs on the British in the form of oil embargos have spoken loudly. Unfortunately, we do not have the luxury of handing the British something they want. Our only consolation is that American Jews are speaking up for us."

"What can we do about any of this?" someone piped up from the back.

"Nothing. I am just apprising you of world events. If you prefer not to know, I won't mention it anymore."

Itzhak stepped forward. "Some of us are interested. Those who want to hear what Tal has to say can meet in the dining room. Those of you who prefer to get back to work ... by all means."

A number of people left the courtyard, while the rest followed Tal into the dining room. Itzhak sat next to Livia Slutzsky, who made a big deal of where Itzhak had chosen to sit. Ever since the first time Laila had seen Livia and Itzhak together at the Scout meeting, she knew the girl was trouble. Laila couldn't help but feel crushed. She had thought Itzhak

The Laundry Room

was over Livia and had transferred his affections to her. Zahar glanced her way as if asking, *What is going on?* Laila shrugged. She had no idea.

Tal stood at one end of the building while those eager for news found seats nearby. Laila made sure she was as far from Itzhak as possible. That was it for her. She had given him his last chance. If he was interested in someone like Livia, Laila was not interested in him.

"Let's see, where was I?" asked Tal.

"You were talking about Lebanon," said Ari.

"Oh yes. It seems that even though Lebanon declared its own independence in 1941, the French continued their mandate over them. At the beginning of this year, Lebanon formed a democracy and amended their Constitution, which ended the French mandate. The French arrested and imprisoned the Lebanese president, prime minister and the rest of the cabinet. Outraged, Lebanese Christians and Muslims united, putting pressure upon the French, who released the prisoners and granted Lebanon its total independence. That is what we are aiming for. What we need to do is put the same kind of pressure on the British."

"And just how are *we* to do that, so far from anyone and anything? The only time we hear what is going on is when you visit," said Sherry Silverman. "What can we do?"

"You have parents and friends. Use your influence," Tal responded.

Laila shifted uncomfortably. The fact was, many of the kibbutzniks had no parents, and the only friends they had were there.

A discussion broke out amongst the young people who had stayed to hear what Tal had to say and continued, for Laila, until she had to excuse herself to start lunch. Zahar had asked to trade weeks, so even though she had the day off, she didn't have lunch off. Laila stole a glance at Itzhak and locked eyes. Then she shifted her glance quickly, as if scouting out someone in the room. Laila nodded to Leora and left.

In the kitchen, pots and pans clanged away, knives chopped, glasses clinked. Laila took out her frustrations on the homegrown vegetables. "Take that ... and that ..." she said as she chopped the bright orange carrots and the crisp celery until they were barely usable.

The kitchen staff had become gourmet cooks—or at least, they thought they were. Lunch was ready in no time.

"What do you say we start a sewing group?" asked Leora. "What clothing I have are worn bare. It could be fun if we were doing it together." Leora dropped the vegetables into a steaming pot of water. "Say, you know, I was thinking; why don't you just come out and ask Itzhak about Livia? I'm sure it's nothing. You're working yourself into a spin."

"Do you mind if we don't talk about Itzhak right now. I'm just not in the mood. Sorry." Laila had no wish to discuss Itzhak with anyone. He was openly humiliating her, and she had had it.

Dishes cleared, Laila left the kitchen and made her way to the barn. Her day off already ruined, she thought she might as well make the rest of it constructive, so she decided to practice the skills she had just learned milking a cow. The kibbutz had recently been given two dairy cows, and everyone had a hand in milking them. Laila had never milked a cow in her life and found it strange, touching something so private; but the cows didn't seem to mind. She leaned into the cow's flank; its warmth gave her a sense of wellbeing, and she began the rhythmic massage of the cow's teats. She was doing well when something caught her off guard.

Itzhak's spicy aftershave, containing a hint of what smelled like paprika, entered the barn at the same time Laila heard her name called.

"Laila, you're a natural. With that kerchief tied around your head ... well ... and your small, strong, little hands ..." Itzhak stood over her, a smirk on his handsome face. His square jaw reminded her of some movie star she had seen in a small theater in Jerusalem, but since it had been so long ago, she couldn't remember his name.

Wanting to wipe the smirk off his face, she folded the cow's teat and squirted Itzhak in the face. His reaction was priceless, as if it had been her hand and not the cow's milk that had struck him. That would teach him to sneak up on her and make foolish comments about how she looked. His face read like a book—one that you would never forget—and he left without a word. It would be interesting to see how he took the joke. Right now she didn't much care.

Laila finished milking and went on to planting. A group stood around a cleared tract of land watching while Zalman, their resident farmer, demonstrated, using their latest purchase, a broken-down mule that had come with a crude halter. Each took turns making a furrow in the dry soil, dropping a seed here and there, with someone else covering the seeds with the freshly plowed earth. Laila had been thinking they would need plenty of vegetables to feed the kibbutz come fall. It remained a miracle, to her, how things grew from such small seeds in such arid soil. She had been amazed at how quickly plants had sprouted up in the vegetable garden.

Leora was next. She wasn't as strong as Laila, so the mule gained control, and Leora found herself on the ground, being raked over the coals—so to speak. No one dared laugh, although Laila couldn't help but think it was incredibly funny.

"I'm alright," she said, red-faced and covered in dirt, as Ari helped her to her feet. He had begun spending all his spare time hanging out around the room she and Laila shared with their other roommates, unlike Itzhak, his best friend.

The rest of the day was labor-intensive, as they knelt on the hard ground to plant corn, cabbage, beans, and a bunch of other vegetables needed to get by. Once that was done, Laila returned to the kitchen to prepare dinner. Schmuel was already there. He had learned his tasks quickly and never complained about being asked to do what was considered "women's work." After all, he had volunteered for the job. Laila was surprised one of the girls hadn't made a play for him already. For her part, Laila felt that she and Schmuel had become too close, thanks to working together almost every day; and besides, her heart was already taken—even if her interest did seem to be in vain.

Meals were always a success, or so Laila was told; but supplies began to run out, and the cooks had had to improvise until the second crop of vegetables matured. The kitchen staff was forced to come up with some strange combinations, like beets and sweet potatoes, or string beans and radishes. If anyone complained, they knew what that meant. They would be relegated to the kitchen, themselves. It almost became a joke amongst the kibbutzniks. It took so little to amuse them.

Today was no different even though it was the end of the week from when Laila and Itzhak had taken their walk and a week since they had said much to each other. With her bones aching, Laila stumbled back to her room, ready to collapse—until she saw a figure leaning against the outside wall of her

The Laundry Room

room. Itzhak looked pretty sure of himself, posed casually like that with his legs crossed at the ankles. Laila devoured every inch, like she would one of those juicy oranges in the grove. He had become tanned by the blistering sun, and his hair had lightened; his eyes, dark pools of cavernous water, were brooding as if he had something on his mind. Laila loved that he towered over everyone except Ari, who could have played basketball.

Itzhak had caught Laila off guard, but then, it seemed like he always caught her off guard. Was that his intent? Laila was tired, dirty, and her nervousness around him was left her feeling vulnerable besides. What was he doing here?

She urged one foot in front of the other, hoping not to look too anxious. Was he still angry at her for the milk squirt? Laila thought she'd had every right to do what she had done. Hadn't he taken her by surprise? Anyway, he deserved it, flirting with Livia for all to see. But then, what did that say about Laila? She hoped her face hadn't given her away, as she wanted to appear cool and unaffected, which was the total opposite of how she actually felt.

"Shalom. Would you like to walk with me?"

Laila remembered the last time they walked and was not in the mood to revisit that day, nor was she in the mood to pretend she was happy with him; but something made her say *yes*. She glanced down at her clothes and shook her head. Her hair must have been a sight, what with flour, grease, and spices clinging to the ends; her shirt and shorts were stained beyond belief, and her sandaled feet ... well, they were still dirty from early morning plowing. Itzhak had managed to find time to clean himself up. She must be crazy.

"It's all right. You look fine. As a matter of fact ... you look very good." His hand waved Laila forward—away from the kibbutz and toward the citrus groves, where evening was

146

settling and the first flicker of stars appeared in the velvety black sky. Laila found it difficult to study his features—night made them all equal. She could, however, make out the furrows in his brow. Something definitely was on his mind.

They walked in silence, and then Itzhak stopped between the first few rows of orange trees and grabbed her hands. "It is hard for me to say this, but you've been on my mind more than I want to admit."

Laila's head spun. What was going on? She wanted so badly to come up with something clever. Instead, she blurted out, "Is that supposed to be a compliment? Because if it is, I don't know how to respond."

"You always have a smart answer for everything. I envy your ability to put your emotions into words. I can put almost anything else into words; in fact, I'm quite glib, but emotions escape me. I like you ... a lot." He turned to face her. "I respect how you've jumped in here at the kibbutz, and have been such a good sport about everything. You just plod on."

Laila had heard similar words from him before, but this time they sounded more sincere. Itzhak never ceased to amaze her, in that he hid his emotions so well, unlike her, who wore her feelings on her sleeve. Thank goodness he couldn't see her body shaking, she thought. She must control herself. She wouldn't let him win so easily. Their relationship so far, if it could be called that, had had its peaks and valleys. She didn't care what anyone said—dating was like a game of chess: a girl moves forward and backward, depending upon her opponent's next move; and one was always a jump away from being checked. He would still have to pay for rebuking her, she thought, and for making her look like a fool. Well, maybe a little—Laila tried to imagine how difficult this was for him, who was always so sure of himself.

The Laundry Room

"I like you too ... sometimes ... especially when you aren't sneaking up on me and scaring me to death. Or ..." Laila paused, knowing what she had almost said would reveal too much of her feelings.

"What were you going to say?" His eyes pierced hers.

"It doesn't matter."

Itzhak reached for her hand and held it tight. Laila prepared herself for their first kiss; it did not come. She felt foolish; on the other hand, maybe he just respected her too much. Then he took off his jacket and placed it over the damp ground and helped her onto it. He continued holding her hand as she took her seat.

"I would like for us to take this time to get to know each other. I know so little about you. Tell me about your family, your likes and dislikes, your favorite book, what you did for fun ..."

Laila was almost too stunned to speak. The words came out in staccato. "Hmmm. Well ... I live with my Abba ... in a house near the university—but you already know that. You know about my Emma ... passing ... and that I have a brother and two sisters." From then on, her words flowed like olive oil. "I like people, animals, the world, and my favorite book is the *Torah*—I love the stories. Let's see, what I did for fun? I didn't have much time for fun." Was this where she told him about the falafel stands? She guessed. "My father owns a number of falafel stands in Jerusalem. I ran one of them."

"Do you mean Abella's Falafels?"

"Yes."

"I love them. Oh, it was your stand that was blown up during the hotel bombing!"

"Yes."

"Now I understand."

He didn't have to tell her what he understood. She already knew.

"So, you're a businesswoman as well as cook, organizer, and good friend."

"I guess you could say." Laila still wasn't sure how he took her Abba's occupation.

"I think your parents have done a fine job raising a self-sufficient woman who isn't afraid to get her hands dirty. I admire that about you. At first I thought you were just cute ... even pretty, but too young. But I have watched you closely and find you're a complex person with many talents. Not to boast, but there have been a lot of girls in my life, but none as challenging as you."

"I'm never sure when you are giving me a compliment or mocking me."

"Believe me, this is a compliment."

They talked for hours, and something magical happened that night that Laila hoped would cement their relationship forever. They walked back to her room holding hands. She guessed this was serious.

Over the next few weeks, their blooming romance was no longer a secret. Laila noticed that Itzhak avoided Livia like the plague, while he and Laila settled into a routine of working side-by-side when they could, and spending free time in the grove—alone. They found it more difficult to keep their kisses from moving to a dangerous conclusion. Itzhak was better at resisting temptation than she.

Ari and Leora became engaged, as did a number of others. The kibbutzniks settled into a peaceful regime of labor, camaraderie, and purpose. The tightly bound group shared a love of nature and freedom, and was more resolute than ever to own their own kibbutz, not simply biding their time or working for someone else. Their potential was great,

The Laundry Room

with the abundance of brainpower, brawn, and youthful idealism, not to mention the ability to more than survive. Laila was happier than she had ever been.

Chapter 19

Laila

Pardess Hanna, 1944

A year had passed, and although Itzhak and Laila spent every possible moment together, nothing had been said about marriage in all that time. The original forty-five kibbutzniks had paired off; some of the couples were no surprise to anyone, but some were unexpected. The biggest surprise was that Livia—the most beautiful and once-companion of Itzhak's—was still single. It appeared that she and Itzhak were keeping their distance from one another, but Laila was not always around to be sure. She wanted to trust Itzhak. Wasn't a relationship supposed to be built on trust? Wasn't a relationship sacred? If Itzhak had been like the other men, Laila wouldn't have been so concerned, but he was very handsome, commanding, and oh-so-sure of himself. Still, Laila wanted what she believed her parents had in the beginning of their marriage, before Emma became sick and noisy children filled the house. Laila's father, although gruff with others, was always gentle with Emma. It was as if

The Laundry Room

Over past year, Laila had noticed a change in herself; she was kinder, she thought, more settled in her routine, and starting to think about having a family of her own. When she had the opportunity, she would visit the nursery and play with other people's children. Somewhere over the last year, Laila realized visiting 'other people's children' wasn't enough. She observed the women who were now wives, and she had seen how they glowed and seemed to be more content. She wanted that for herself. What was Itzhak waiting for? What more could she do? She was taking more pride in herself, washing her hair more often, making her own clothing of brighter materials. What would it take for him to ask her to marry him? She had thought about asking him, but that was highly unconventional, and what if he said *no?*

And what about her own future? Hadn't she wanted to be something ... make a name for herself? She had considered pursuing something, maybe in the sciences. Would she still be able to do that as a wife? She had a lot to think about, so when Itzhak suggested a walk to their favorite place, the orange groves, she put her discontent aside and decided to enjoy the life she had chosen. Married or not, it wasn't so bad.

As they walked away from the kibbutz and all its tumult, Laila felt a wave of tranquility wash over her. Itzhak had taken her hand and walked purposefully but quietly, toward their spot. It was a beautiful evening, with stars sprinkled about like seashells scattered about the shore. Laila had loved it when she was younger, and her family would pick up and journey to Tel Aviv for a brief respite while Abba did a little business. They would pack a lunch and throw an old sheet down on the hard-packed, tan crystals along the Mediterranean coast. Laila had loved finding whole shells along the shore. She would take the shells home and place them in a jar on a small stand near her bed and watch the morning light enhance the sparkle of the pastel colors.

Itzhak had brought a large towel with him, which he dropped to the moist grass. He helped Laila down and then walked to the nearest tree to pluck two oranges for them, bringing them back and ceremoniously handing one to Laila as if a prized gift. On the walk to the groves, Laila had noticed Itzhak seemed distracted, and she was growing concerned. Perhaps she was making things too easy for him, being so available. He had just about everything he wanted from her—well almost. But Laila wanted more. She was determined to have more. Suddenly the evening didn't seem so perfect.

Then, as if he were reading her thoughts, Itzhak went down on one knee, holding out a ring fashioned from a grapevine that he had taken out of his pants pocket.

"I know this isn't a diamond, but my heart beats just as true. Will you marry me?"

Unable to contain herself, Laila rose to her knees and threw her arms around his waist, which had narrowed with toil during the past year. Itzhak had been one of the hardest workers. It was as if he were trying to obliterate his lavish background—to prove he was worthy of being a genuine part of the kibbutz.

The happy pair fell over laughing. "Of course I will," said Laila, tears streaming down her cheeks. Suddenly she felt awful for her previous thoughts. After all, she was trying so hard not to be that spoiled brat, the one who had gone into this adventure with her eyes wide shut.

They lay side-by-side, locked in each other's arms, making plans for the future.

"What kind of wedding would you like?" asked Itzhak,

The Laundry Room

smoothing a strand of wayward hair from her forehead.

"Something simple. I know my father will want to invite the world, but I prefer it be our families and our friends."

A shadow seemed to cross Itzhak's eyes as they began to lose their sparkle. "If things were different, my parents would help, but they won't, and that is that."

"You should invite them anyway. Perhaps they will have a change of heart, knowing that you have settled down and are making a life of your own. There is nothing like a wedding to mend fences."

"That's the problem. They want to control my life—pick my profession and my wife. That is why they disowned me."

"I'm so sorry. This should be the happiest day of our lives. Let's not let negative thoughts outweigh the positive ones. We are embarking on a long journey—one that I promise will help make those unpleasant thoughts easier to accept."

"That is why I love you. You are so resilient, so sure of yourself. We will live happily ever after. I feel it." He gathered her in his arms, cocooning her in a web of love. They lay quietly, Laila listening to Itzhak breathe. Every once in a while, one would awaken to kiss the other and then fall back into a contented slumber.

At dawn, noise from the kibbutz woke the lovers. There would be no trouble over having slept in the orchard. Here it was different, not having to worry about parents and curfews; they were free to mold their lives as they wished. Laila was going to make sure the molding continued to go slowly. She was determined to be a virgin bride, not like some of the women who had had to get married. Not that she was judging anyone, but it was her own decision. She didn't ever want Itzhak to think she had trapped him into anything.

Itzhak grabbed her shoulders and peered into her eyes. "I love you with all my heart. I will always protect you and take care of you. I pledge to respect your strong will and help you find your way. Please feel free to put me in my place whenever necessary."

"Can I have that in writing?" They laughed again. Laughter came easier to them lately, especially when away from their chores.

As she looked at the grapevine ring on her finger, Laila found she was so excited she could barely contain herself. She couldn't wait to write Abba. He would have to come to their wedding. She wasn't sure her sisters would be able to make it, but Judah would be there. Zahar would be so pleased. Hadn't she and Avraham brought them together?

Laila jumped up, pulling Itzhak with her. They kissed and kissed and kissed until neither could breathe. Their urges were getting harder and harder to control; Laila knew what came next, but she didn't want to think about it. Laila's poor mother—may she rest in peace—had never discussed relations between a man and woman with her daughter. A friend had blatantly filled in the delicate details, making Laila want to wait as long as possible for that blessed event. It would be different with Itzhak; she knew it. Her body responded with a shudder.

And then, for some reason, a pair of dark green eyes appeared before her, eyes she should not be thinking about. Especially now. Laila brushed the uncomfortable thoughts away, hoping never to be confronted by them again. She had no business letting someone she didn't really know enter her thoughts. The British soldier was a figment of the past, a mystery that did not need to be solved. Hadn't she insisted Livia be exorcised from Itzhak's life? It was up to her to do the same. She owed it to both of them if they were going to be happy together.

"What's wrong?"

The Laundry Room

"Oh, nothing. I'm just so happy. I can't believe we're going to be married. Wait till Zahar and Avraham hear. You know it was really their fault. They were the ones who saw it before we did. Remember how awkward we were at their apartment that evening, sitting as far from each other as possible, for fear we might find we actually liked each other?"

"All I could think about was your long, thick braid, and how I wanted to untangle it and shake it free."

Laila had once heard those words from a soldier, the rude one who had accosted her near her home; but coming from Itzhak, those words didn't sound quite the same. With Itzhak, the words were intimate and sensual, not degrading or sexual, when he said such things. Again, Laila decided she would have to let go of the past and its uncomfortable memories, or she would ruin her future.

"Really, you thought that?" She blushed at the implication.

They walked back to the kibbutz together, and lingered by Laila's room. A rooster crowed in the distance and a goat bleated. They were truly farmers, she thought. She was getting used to the idea, but there were still things unrelated to farming that she wanted to try, everything from a career in science to traveling the world. She knew Itzhak would encourage her to do so when the time was right.

"Shall we tell Zahar and Avraham?" Laila said excitedly pulling Itzhak in their direction.

He pulled her back and kissed her. "Why don't we keep it our little secret, just for today? We have plenty of time to share our good news."

"You're right, of course. I'm not sure I'll get any work done today, though. All I'll be thinking of is moving into our own place." Suddenly Laila found it difficult to take her eyes off him. He was really hers, although she didn't understand why they had to keep their engagement a secret.

Chapter 20

Ari

Pardess Hanna, 1944

Time had flown by and the kibbutz had fallen into a comfortable routine, Avraham keeping them on their toes without seeming to be a taskmaster. Tal Rabin's visits had tapered down as tensions continued to escalate between the Jews and Arabs. The war was in full thrust, and Germany had been exposed to be what the Jews already knew—murderers. The ban on immigration had been lifted and Jews flocked into Palestine in high numbers, escaping tyranny from the four corners of the earth.

Ari had felt secure in his surroundings, enough to ask Leora to marry him. They would be married before Itzhak and Laila, due to Mrs. Malkin's health. As Leora's only living relative, it was important that Mrs. Malkin attend the ceremony. She had suffered another stroke, this time losing her speech. She insisted she was able to travel with a companion, though, so Ari and Leora were in the middle of planning a wedding.

Lynda Lippman-Lockhart

Ari, Itzhak, and Avraham had done some scouting for a place for their future kibbutz and found a spot along the Mediterranean that would suit them for fishing and farming. They had asked to borrow a truck from Tal for the journey north to Ma'agan Michael as soon as they heard the land might be available to purchase. Ezra had wanted to go, but he had come down with a fever, so just the three of them took the trip. The kibbutz crops had been lucrative, especially the citrus, and the kibbutzniks had been able to save enough money to make a down payment on the abandoned property, if it suited their needs.

The truck, devoid of glass in the windows, made the trip that much more challenging with gnats, flies, and other insects bombarding them every step of the way. The scouting party had layered their clothing, not having proper attire to handle the dip in temperature. Halfway to the site, Ari wrapped the scarf around his nose and mouth as he had gotten tired of removing the pesky gnats from his teeth.

"How much further?" asked Itzhak like an impatient child, and the one most susceptible to illness. He had come down with a fever earlier in the month, making them have to postpone the first trip. Ezra wouldn't hear of postponing it again after he got sick; so instead, he had given them his blessings and gone back to bed. Ezra's illness stemmed from late night scouting parties for the purpose of locating their enemies and keeping track of their activities. It seemed too many of these expeditions had brought with them the cold night air, not to mention inclement weather. Only those who had been designated by Tal were aware of what that particular group was doing. It was dangerous, but it added a bit of intrigue to the humdrum days of planting and hoeing. Ari hated that he couldn't share what he was doing with Leora, but he understood the added pressure placed on the small group's loved ones. The mission was teaching him discipline and survival skills he might need in the future.

"The property is not much farther ... Here ..." Ari removed the scarf around his face and handed it to Itzhak.

"No, I can't take that. You'll catch your death."

"As I remember, it was you who were at death's door only last month. Don't be a fool. I'm fine. Leora knitted me a vest to keep me warm. If she only knew that I was using it during our evening reconnaissance missions, she would be angry." He opened his shirt to reveal the sweater vest. His eyes twinkled as he showed off her work.

Itzhak and Avraham poked Ari from either side, laughing the rest of the way.

Arriving at the site, they turned the truck onto a sandy road that led down to the sea. Long, wooden buildings, left over from the last occupants, stood in disrepair. Ari parked the lummox of a truck and eagerly exited the windowless door, noting the difference between their rather morbid, landlocked property and this airy, inviting, seaside village. Yes, there was much to do, but these eager young men had all the time in the world on their hands.

"I can already see the children playing in the water," said Avraham, who had just become a father. Half the trip had been spent extolling the praises of his wife and new baby, which was unusual for him since he kept his thoughts close to himself. Ari had worried about his friend after the bombing. Zahar's scars were so prominent, he hadn't been sure Avraham could get past them. And so when it appeared there was no friction between the couple, Ari was proud of how Avraham had handled himself.

"What do you mean, children?" said Ari, bending down to roll up his pants, forgetting how cold the water would be. "Are you holding out on us? Is there already another one on the way?"

"No. I meant the other children of the kibbutz, you nut." Avraham punched Ari in the shoulder.

Not waiting for an answer, Ari plunged into the salty Mediterranean, carrying on like a child who had been given his freedom for the first time. "It's freezing. I don't suggest you come in, Itzhak." His teeth were chattering.

"Are you kidding? I'm no fool. Get yourself out of there before you turn into a block of ice," Itzhak chided.

The distant roar of a plane stopped them all in their tracks. Ari quit his antics and lay quietly at the water's edge. Before they could take cover, the plane buzzed them, coming so low they could actually see the grin of the pilot's face. Lately more and more planes were being spotted across the skies, making the kibbutzniks leery about the property.

"What was that?" yelled Ari, unsure whether to run or stay put.

"That's a Bristol Beaufort torpedo bomber with two seven-millimeter machine guns mounted on the nose, and two on the dorsal gun position. Notice the wings mounted low, on the fuselage," yelled Itzhak over the lingering drone of the plane." Probably out of Ramat Gan ... stopped to refuel. I heard they ran out of space in North Africa and carved a portion of land out for themselves east of Tel Aviv."

"And where did you get all that information?" Avraham asked. "You're a regular walking encyclopedia of inconsequential information."

"Inconsequential? Hardly, if it decides to drop a bomb on us or use those machine guns ..."

"Well, I'm impressed," said Ari, sidling up to Itzhak. "Seriously, how do you know that?"

"Remember, I'm a student of history. I cut my teeth on

The Laundry Room

wars and everything revolving around them. If we don't study them, we can't conquer them."

"I didn't mean to be dismissive," said Avraham, "I'm just overwhelmed by your knowledge. You're a silent wonder."

"Maybe we're not supposed to be here," yelled Ari over his shoulder, as he ran back to the truck to get changed. "Come on, men. Let's get out of here."

"Look, we came to look the place over. No one said we couldn't." Avraham pointed toward one of the huts. "Ari, you and Itzhak check out the building over there. I'll look at the other one." He was already on his way.

Itzhak shook his head, palms spread to the heavens as Ari caught up with him. "Do what he says. Remember, he's the boss," said Itzhak flippantly.

"Do I detect a bit of sarcasm? Remember, we put him in the position. I don't think anyone else wanted it. You sure didn't."

"I only meant since the baby, he walks around like a bantam rooster. Haven't you seen a change in him?"

"I hadn't noticed. I've been too busy with plans for our new kibbutz and keeping the chickens in their pens. Besides, he's been through a lot. Give him a break."

The wind picked up, and Ari could see that the weather was about to take a turn for the worse. Black clouds were rolling in from the north; the parched fields were about to be drenched, and they were in an open truck.

Ari jumped out of the rattletrap and broke out in song to *Mayim, Mayim*. Itzhak joined him as they locked hands and danced around in a small circle. *Mayim* was the Hebrew dance for rain, usually performed when rain was scarce, but today, it was part of the camaraderie the men were feeling for each other.

"What are you two clowns doing? We are here on business." Avraham ran toward them, broke the circle, and took up the step. There on the beach, three grown men danced and sang with abandon. Before they finished the tenth round of the song, a heavenly faucet opened and the rain came down in buckets. Already wet, they continued their rain dance until they were certain it wasn't going to stop any time soon. Only lightning would have ended the festivities.

Having seen enough and decidedly too wet to do anything else, the three headed back to Pardess Hanna to make their report. As they approached Tel Aviv, two bombers crisscrossed overhead, flapping their wings to make sure they were noticed, and then disappeared.

"Our lives are not our own anymore," said Ari, upset by his own revelation. Things were changing too quickly and they were not prepared. "Our every move is being observed."

"Do you suppose they have found out about our nightly expeditions?" asked Itzhak, as the joy of their time together turned into a harbinger of the future.

Upon returning to the kibbutz, Itzhak, Ari, and Avraham were mobbed by anxious kibbutzniks, hoping to hear good news for a change. News from abroad had only gotten worse, with the discovery of millions of bodies buried in deep graves in concentration camps throughout Germany. Whenever the members of the kibbutz saw Tal coming their way, they didn't know whether to hide or be hopeful. The collective death toll of the parents of just those in the kibbutz was astounding. Were the powers that be getting any closer to a decision about a Jewish state?

Avraham shushed the crowd. "We have good news and not so good news. What do you want first?" By now Zahar,

The Laundry Room

Laila, and Leora had pushed their way to the front of the circle.

"Good."

"Good."

"Not so good."

"The *goods* have it. The plot of land is right on the Mediterranean and has great potential. There is room to build anything we want. The *not so good* news is that if we bought the property, we'd have our work cut out for us—not that any of us has shied away from hard work. This time our efforts will be for us, not others."

"Now, what's next?" asked Benjamin Perlstein, who had been chosen for night activities with Itzhak, Ari, and Ezra to reconnoiter the Arab camp. Ari hadn't had much hope for Benjamin at first, being small and slight, but he was as tough as they come when pressed to carry out a job. The group had decided that, since Avraham was running the kibbutz, it was too dangerous for him to do the scouting too.

Avraham cleared his throat. "We count our money; and if there is enough money after having put a new roof on the dining room and mending the animal pens, we sign the papers. Then the work begins."

A number of other questions were fielded and answers given, until almost everyone was satisfied with the report. Benjamin approached Ari, took his arm, and guided him away from the crowd. "We go tonight."

"Okay. What time?"

"Midnight," said Benjamin looking square into Ari's face. "You better get some rest. You're looking a little tired."

"I'm fine. I'll pass the word to Itzhak. I don't think Ezra is up to it yet. Where shall we meet?"

"Behind the dining room, like always." Benjamin reached

up and patted Ari's shoulder. They were becoming fast friends, but it was Itzhak, who had become attached to Benjamin's oldest son Avi, who was six and followed Itzhak everywhere he went. Ari was thinking it might just be the boy who speeds up Itzhak's date for a wedding.

Ari returned to Leora.

"What was that all about?" she asked, locking her arm through his.

Ari hated lying to Leora, but he had sworn an oath with the rest of the men not to tell anyone. It had been Tal who had prepared them for this particular job, and he had told them that he'd handpicked each of the men he thought could be trusted the most. If the secrete escapades got out, there could be some sore feelings as to who had been chosen.

"Benjamin wants to do something special for Isadora's birthday. I'm not sure why he came to me; I'm not the best party planner." Ari watched Leora's eyes for a reaction. He had been hard-pressed to come up with a better excuse, and now he could tell she wasn't buying it. He would have to be extra nice to her tonight.

"Isadora's birthday has come and gone. Are you sure that's what he wanted?"

Now, Ari was feeling like his back was against the wall. They never fought. He wondered what had gotten into her. Leora had started giving him the third degree; perhaps one of the other women had planted doubts in her mind. He would have to sit down with her later and get to the bottom of her distress.

"I can only tell you what he told me. Maybe it's a surprise. Maybe he forgot the last one and is making up for it. I don't know. Come on, let's get ready for dinner. I'm starved." He grabbed her arm, perhaps a little too gruffly, and guided her toward the room. He kissed her soundly and left her standing at the door. "I'll be back in half an hour." He kissed the wind and headed away.

###

The ground was damp from the rain that had fallen that day, and it made crawling more difficult because the mud stuck to their clothing like thick glue. Ari had volunteered to take care of the dirty clothes after each night watch, and to have them ready for the next use. Tonight, Itzhak, Ari, Ben, Pincus, and Schlomo Bar-Lev elbowed their way along the ground, keeping their bodies as close to the earth as possible. They kept within eyesight of each other as they fanned out to do their patrolling.

Tonight it was Itzhak's turn to lead. Itzhak stopped and raised his hand, and then ran the light of a small flashlight along the ground so that each man knew to halt. Ari watched as Itzhak crawled ahead, leaving them to remain where they were until he motioned for the men to follow.

Ari, second in command, edged forward until he was just behind Itzhak. "How much further?" he whispered. "I'm soaked all the way through."

"You'll need to take a hot shower when you get back. We all probably should take showers. It's difficult explaining to someone who might wake and have to use the facilities. We'll have to take turns and keep watch. But anyway, it's not much further. Tell the men to fan out a little more. We're coming upon a campsite. I'm not sure whether it's British or Arab. Also tell the guys to check out weapons and artillery if they see any."

Ari edged back to the rest of the men to relay Itzhak's orders. Ari knew Itzhak would have preferred Ezra by his side. They were like minded, in that Ezra had no problem following whatever Itzhak told him to do; whereas, sometimes Ari or one of the other men had something to say about how they would handle a given situation. What a shock it had been when Ezra was chosen to join the group. Ari had never suspected his potential. Ari wondered if Anna had anything to do with his newfound bravery. Ezra's confidence had grown exponentially since they had gotten engaged again. Apparently Tal was a better judge of character than Ari.

A snapped branch stopped Ari and the rest of them. Someone was patrolling outside the camp. The kibbutz night patrol had been instructed never to take the offensive. If they were caught, they were to plead their innocence, say they were patrolling their kibbutz and got lost, whatever worked.

More snapped branches and more breaths held.

"Did you hear something?" one man said to the other in Arabic. Ari had studied enough of the language to be able to understand and converse minimally.

"You're jumpy tonight. What's the matter?" said one of the Arab soldiers, knocking the other in the head with the butt of his rifle.

"I'm always like this before a raid."

Ari panicked as one of the soldier's feet came down less than a foot from Ari's outstretched hand. If he held his breath, maybe he would stop shaking. Ari never took his eyes off Itzhak as Itzhak turned to see what was going on. It was Itzhak's eyes that held Ari's gaze and calmed Ari, as Itzhak transferred a silent nod to say *stay put*. Ari continued to hold his breath until the man walked in the opposite direction. When he thought they were gone, he let out that held breath a little at a time. So that was it; there was going to be a raid. Ari hoped the two men would have let slip more information, but all he heard was some more mumbling, and the men moved out of earshot and Ari missed what else they had to say. He decided he was not cut out for this and hoped they

The Laundry Room

wouldn't have to do this much longer.

Ari dropped his head to the ground as he fought for composure; another close call. Each time they went out, something different and more challenging happened. They, both the scouts and the kibbutz in general, had been lucky so far, but who knew how long that would last.

Hoping each man had gathered enough information, Ari watched as Itzhak inched back toward him after giving the retreat signal. Like inchworms, the men continued on their bellies until they were safely inside their own grounds.

Night patrol didn't get any easier, no matter how many times they went out. Ari was itching to move onto their new kibbutz and hopefully start a family.

Chapter 21

Laila

Pardess Hanna, 1944

The wedding would be small; just members of the kibbutz, Laila's father, brother and one sister. Her other sister was too pregnant to travel. Zahar had made Laila's dress, cut from Laila's mother's treasured lace tablecloth, Carmel's ivory kimono, and Zahar's own aged prayer shawl. The dress was beautiful, considering what she had to work with. Laila was counting down the days. She had received another newsy letter from Abba, letting her know that the green-eyed soldier had stopped him on the street to ask how Laila was doing. Abba said he asked the soldier to let his feelings for her go and move on. He did say she was spoken for. She couldn't imagine how that went over. Laila had a feeling she hadn't seen the last of him.

The kibbutzniks had been in Pardess Hanna over a year and doing well. Zahar, Schmuel, and Laila, with the help of a few others, had taken over the kitchen. Leora joined them on occasion, making her now-famous desserts. The rest of the

The Laundry Room

Leora and Ari had married before her and Itzhak, and Leora was already pregnant. A number of weddings had taken place, and it looked like an epidemic of swallowed watermelons had taken over the kibbutz. But then, what else could they do with their spare time—the little they had?

Their entertainment was simple: campfires; song fests, old and new; dance. Tonight they were sitting around one of those campfires singing their favorite song: "Don't Sit Under the Apple Tree." This was their third time around.

Don't sit under the apple tree with anyone else but me,
Anyone else but me, anyone else but me, No No No
Don't sit under the apple tree with anyone else but me,
Till I come marching home.

Some of the men liked to tell stories about their experiences before they had arrived in Palestine. Tonight Sonya, one of the originals from Laila's Scout group, finally got up the nerve to tell her story. She sat nervously next to Laila, who had befriended her.

"This is hard for me. I haven't told this story to anyone. I try not to think about it, but I can't seem to let it go. Please bear with me." Sonya's audience waited in anticipation.

"This will be good for you," said Laila, as she took Sonya's hand. Leora supported her on the other side.

"After my mother and father and the rest of the adults in our barracks in the concentration camp hadn't returned from taking what the Nazis called a *delousing*, two boys, a girl I had befriended, and I started plotting our escape. Every day, the four of us would go outside for exercise with the rest of the parentless children. One of us would disappear behind a small building and dig under a fence using a discarded tin

170

cup, while the other three kept watch. When we were ordered to return to the barracks, we would cover the hole with a piece of tin that had ripped off the roof of a nearby building and join the rest.

"We did this for weeks, and one day, while the guards were distracted and we were outside running around, the four of us disappeared behind the building, uncovered the hole, and crawled through—never looking back. I remember thinking as I ran, *a bullet will find me and kill me*; so I ran until I collapsed. By then we were deep in the woods and had no idea which way to go. Our only thought was to be as far from that horrible place as possible. We had talked about the possibility of our parents having been taken someplace to work for a short period of time and returning to find us gone, but then decided that hadn't happened.

"Our next few days were spent taking turns sleeping or standing guard. My friend Anna had been losing weight for months before we left and had refused to eat what we were given. I tried to make her understand that she had to stay strong so we would be the winners, not the Nazis. On the fourth day of our escape, she dropped to the ground and did not move. We coaxed her to get up and fight for her life, but she just lay where she fell. That night, she died, and we buried her in an unmarked grave in the forest. I had lost my only childhood friend.

"I cried through the night, and the next morning made my resolve to survive this ordeal. We stumbled upon a farm and two of the nicest Germans God had ever created. They nursed us back to health, and Max ended up staying with them. He was the weakest and youngest of the three. The Schmidts helped David and me join a group booking passage to Palestine. When we arrived, we were separated; I never saw him again."

The Laundry Room

Only the crackle of the bonfire could be heard. It was some time before anyone spoke. Finally, Laila guessed, Abe Silverman found the courage to relate his crossing of a Russian mountain peak wearing nothing more than the simple clothing they had on their backs. He went on to say how the snow had been up to their knees, making the trek that much more arduous; so much so, his mother died during the crossing, and his father became so infirmed by the lack of food and the bitter cold, Abe and his brother took turns carrying their father on their shoulders until they could make a sling.

The stories went on and on. When all was said and done, Laila decide if she had a choice, she would stick with her own life. Yes, losing a mother was monumental, but her mother hadn't suffered long, and her Abba did his best to fill the void.

Laila awoke earlier than usual the day of her wedding—there were so many things to do. She sliced apples, dates, and nuts, heated the oven, found the cake pan, and began making her own wedding cake. She wanted it to be just right.

"You shouldn't be making your own cake," said Schmuel, wiping the sleep from his eyes. "There's something ungodly about it, but if you insist ... Zahar, Leora, and I will prepare everything else. Zahar gave us our list."

Knowing how capable Schmuel had become, Laila had little concern about the food preparations. He made chicken so many different ways that you didn't know you were eating chicken.

Zahar and Leora peeked around the corner. "What are you doing here?"

"I said I would make my cake." By now the small room was toasty warm, perhaps too warm for more than one. "You three have been so wonderful to me, but I want to feel like I did something." Laila gathered the remaining ingredients from the shelf—no more scorpions—and carried them to the preparation table.

"It will probably be better than either of us could make anyway. Enjoy. We have other things to do. Come on, Leora. Schmuel, you are needed elsewhere."

"Yes. You've made it perfectly clear." He left in a huff.

"Men," the women said together and laughed. Leora and Zahar walked out arm-in-arm singing another favorite tune.

Laila spent the rest of the morning making the wedding cake. She measured the flour, added baking powder, salt, and cinnamon. To the apples, she added a drop of grape wine, more cinnamon, a dash of cloves, sugar, and finally the nuts she had chopped earlier. She grabbed the milk from the icebox and measured a cup. With no mixer, she plucked a large wooden spoon from the earthenware jar and began pouring in the milk, stirring constantly. She broke two eggs into the bowl and continued stirring. She did this all by memory, having watcher or helped her mother make the cake for them or others. Once everything was well mixed, Laila poured the batter into the pan and added a pinch of cinnamon to the top for measure. The oven, set for the proper temperature, was ready to receive her offering. Laila slid the pan inside and stood for a moment taking stock of all the ingredients, hoping she hadn't left anything out.

With an hour to kill, she ambled back to her room, and when she entered took a last look at single life. After tonight, this room would no longer be her home. She would be sleeping with Itzhak: the thought brought a smile to her lips and a blush to her cheeks.

For that moment, though, Laila had the room to herself. Her dress hung on a wooden peg beside her soon-to-be-

The Laundry Room

vacant bed. Lovingly, she ran her hands along the folds of the material as they cascaded to the floor. Zahar had taken pains to make the gown memorable. At the last minute, she had taken her lacy prayer shawl and worked in the remaining fabric into the bodice, rendering it festive and a little more provocative. Laila wasn't used to showing cleavage the way some of the other women did. As one of the youngest adults at the kibbutz, she watched the others carefully, molding herself into the person she most wanted to be. Zahar was the best yardstick by which she judged herself and others.

With no chair to sit upon, Laila plopped down on her bed and plumped a pillow behind her head. She couldn't help where her mind traveled: to the after part of the wedding, something she hadn't let herself dwell upon. She was uneasy, never having experienced a man in that way. Although she had the basic knowledge and had watched the goats, lambs, and cows, she hoped it would be more than that. She and Itzhak had kissed and been fairly intimate but nothing more.

Shying away from the thought of intimacy, Laila made herself skip to the following day. With no other room available, they would begin married life in a tent. The first available room would be theirs. There were two cots in the tent; not very romantic, but she would make it romantic with candles. Zahar had confiscated a few from the larder. Zahar and Laila had spent the last two days sprucing up the tent, trying to make it as homey as possible. Their attempt had not gone unnoticed. A number of other women had stopped by to admire their handiwork. She and Zahar had taken the day off a week earlier and gone shopping in the next village. With meager funds, they had managed to work miracles by bartering with oranges for their purchases. The tent had ended up looking like a sultan's retreat.

By noon and only a half an hour since she had returned to

her room, Laila was bored. In search of something to do, she left the room and headed toward the orange grove to their favorite place, where Itzhak had proposed. She wasn't mindful of where she was going when a figure stepped out from behind a copes of trees.

"Good day, Laila."

She froze, not knowing whether to run or stay. What was he doing there? How did he know where she lived? And he knew her name. She didn't know his.

"Are you surprised to see me?" Those green eyes flashed in the sunlight. They mesmerized her; she couldn't help it even if she weren't supposed to be interested in anyone other than Itzhak. Why then did she feel a thrill, imagining the trouble he had gone through to find her?

"Yes." Laila turned, ready to bolt; but something stopped her. She was curious about this man who would not leave her alone. "What are you doing here?"

"I'm here to stop you from making a big mistake."

"And what mistake might that be?"

At that point, they were standing too close, and she felt uncomfortably aroused. No one was around to protect her from herself. Laila didn't think he would hurt her, for if that were the case, he would have done it already. Hadn't he protected her and Abba?

"Marrying the wrong man."

"And who are you to make such an assumption?"

"I am the man you should marry."

"But I can't marry you. You're the enemy." Tears welled up in her eyes. This was her wedding day. Nothing was supposed to spoil it.

He took her hand. Laila pulled it away.

"I am not your enemy," he pleaded. "I want to be your

friend and more."

"That cannot happen. You are not Jewish. I can't marry a non-Jew."

"And why not?"

"It is written."

"Where?"

"In the *Torah*."

Laila realized she had given him more encouragement than he deserved by answering his questions. She was marrying the man she loved. This man was a stranger—a non-Jew, and worse, an enemy of her people, who had brought nothing but lies with them. How could he imagine she could love him? She might have harbored an attraction, but that was it. No, that wasn't true. She couldn't help the feelings she had for him. Maybe he really did care about her.

"You must go. You're not supposed to be here. Go back to your English girls. Find someone who is of you faith and ideals. I am not that girl. Please go."

His head dropped to his chest as he covered his chin with his hand. Slowly, as if searching for the right words, his head lifted, those eyes piercing hers: "If you ever need me. If he hurts you ..."

"He will never hurt me."

The soldier turned and walked away. Laila stood rooted to the ground, shaking. Was this a sign of things to come? Would he make trouble for her and her people?

Hurrying back to the kibbutz, Laila desperately used every means of distraction to keep those green eyes out of her thoughts. As she approached, she saw signs of frantic preparations. The *chupah* was being moved inside because rain clouds were gathering. The wedding wouldn't be under the stars. She was disappointed. Mazel and Carmel pitched in as they took over the kitchen and Laila's usual chores. Laila realized how lucky she was, having such good friends and marrying the man of her dreams. She was young, but had grown up fast—she'd had to. Over the last two years, and with Itzhak by her side, Laila had come to feel she could conquer the world. Yes, she was indeed lucky. Why would she look for trouble? The girls had told her over and over how happy they were for her, but that they would miss having her for a roommate. With Leora gone to Ari and Laila to Itzhak, it would be just Mazel and Carmel, but she didn't see that lasting long.

###

The evening arrived, and with it Tal Rabin and the *hazzan* from Pardess Hanna. Apparently the rabbi was administering to a death in his congregation. What a sight—a *hazzan* riding in a milk wagon and Tal driving it. The kibbutzniks weren't exactly heavy into tradition because they didn't have the time or wherewithal, so they had opted for something simple but beautiful. Itzhak decided not to use the traditional *kittel*, a white robe usually worn on Yom Kippur. He and Laila also dispensed with the formal veil ceremony, where the groom and his family covered the bride's face with the veil. It symbolized the groom's commitment to clothe and protect his wife from that time forth. The veil was supposed to represent modesty and the fact that the soul was far more important than outer beauty. The tradition dated back in time to when Rebecca covered her face before marrying Isaac. Today Laila wore a simple veil that Zahar had managed to create from scraps.

Laila waited in the drab kitchen with the new metal sink and icebox, while Ezra and two other men from the kibbutz played the wedding march on guitar and flute, those being the only instruments available, and the only musically

The Laundry Room

talented members of the group. The men had worked up quite a repertoire for a thrown-together band. Zahar entered and shut the door quickly so no one would see Laila in her wedding attire.

Zahar reached for Laila's hands and held them tightly. She was shaking, and her words were mixed with sniffles. "I wish you ... the same happiness I share with Avraham. I couldn't wish ... you any better. Remember to always talk to each other as much as possible. Never go to bed angry. If he suggests something that makes you uncomfortable ... wait a day or two before saying what you think. Always respect each other and be there for each other. Jealousy can kill a marriage. If someone shows interest in Itzhak, talk to that person and tell her to find someone else to share her charms."

Naturally Zahar was referring to Livia, who had made no excuse for her show of affection from the beginning. The first thing Laila had noticed about Livia was her breasts. You couldn't help but notice them; they were so out of proportion to the rest of her body. Her legs went on forever, especially when she wore shorts, and her frame was narrow—in fact, everything about her was narrow, from her hips, to her back and her mind. She had only one thing on her mind—men, but Itzhak was no longer available.

Laila did not care that Itzhak and Livia were childhood friends. That did not make Livia immune to his charms. If Livia persisted in pursuing Itzhak after they were married, Laila *would* have that talk with her. If that did not work, she would have a talk with Itzhak.

She caught her train of thought and consciously cleared her mind of anything negative. Today was her wedding day and it was going to be perfect.

Chapter 22

Laila

Pardess Hannah, 1944

"You look lovely," said Zahar, kissing Laila on both cheeks like her mother would have—may she rest in peace—before pulling the veil over Laila's face. Zahar, one of the eldest, of the kibbutzniks, was called upon to help in many ways. She had become the matriarch of the kibbutz, heading the education committee and the food distribution. She was their rock, and only twenty-three. At this point in time, Avraham had become, more or less, the titular head of the secretariat, and both of them were held in high esteem.

Zahar nodded. It was time. The tension Laila had felt in her stomach was beginning to subside. She was doing the right thing by marrying Itzhak, she knew it—or was she trying to convince herself? Was this the last-minute wedding jitters she had heard of? She and Itzhak had cast their fate to the wind, trusting that their love would blossom and grow like the citrus trees they tended. The two of them, like the braided *Havdalah* candle lit at Sabbath sundown, had

The Laundry Room

hand into the future. Now was the time to banish all doubt.

A clash of thunder followed closely after a bolt of lightning, threw Zahar and Laila into each other's arms. Zahar held Laila as she would a small child. "God has ordained it. It is good luck to have rain on your wedding day. It cleanses both of your lives so that you can begin anew, building the future together."

"How lovely. Is that true or did you make it up?" Laila asked, knowing Zahar was trying to calm her down.

"It sounded good, didn't it?" Zarah hugged Laila one more time.

Whatever misgivings Laila might have had were now gone; she was ready to walk down the aisle. She and Itzhak were going to have a wonderful wedding and life together.

Laila's heart fluttered, picturing Abba, dressed in his best suit, waiting patiently outside to escort her down the aisle. When Zahar opened the door and Laila stepped out, Abba's expectant eyes lit up like the brightest stars in the evening sky. His face reflected the pride he must have been feeling, and Laila almost broke into tears. He smiled, locked his arm in hers, and kissed her cheek over the veil. "My *shayna maidel*. My beautiful girl."

Laila remembered the last time she had seen Abba dressed so and wearing that same prideful face, at her brother Judah's wedding three years ago. Perhaps her father's youthfulness today could be attributed to the woman he had brought with him—the woman who must have brought love back into his life after so many lonely years. If this woman made him happy, Laila was happy for him.

Yesterday, her father, the woman Malka, Laila's brother Judah, and his wife arrived amidst the preparations. Her father asked to speak with Laila alone, so she took him to the sacred orange grove and stood in the shade holding his hands. It struck her that she felt as secure with Itzhak as she did with Abba.

"I declared a holiday today," he said with pride, "closed my stands for your wedding, and gave my staff a token of my appreciation. It is not every day a daughter is married. I can only wish your union will be as beautiful as your mother's and mine, and that you are as fruitful."

He handed Laila an envelope. "Please do not open it until we are gone."

The request puzzled her, but she would respect his wishes. "Should I thank you now, if a thank-you is appropriate, or wait and write a note?"

"It is up to you."

Laila wrapped her arms around Abba and hugged him like she would never see him again. The thought was overwhelming. The world being what it was—unsettled—and his health precarious, Laila no longer saw Abba as a threat to her future. He had become a tired, old man, who had been lucky enough to find someone to fill a long time void left by her mother's death. Laila's mother had been gone so long, and Abba was entitled to some happiness.

Abba disengaged himself and held Laila at arm's length. "I feel I must explain Malka. She is a good woman. I was lonely. She cooks and cleans for me, and took care of me after my heart attack. Her nursing skills have helped make my life bearable. I'm not asking you to love her, just be nice to her."

"If she makes you happy, Abba, I like her already."

"That's my girl."

Laila supposed more than enough time had gone by since Emma had passed, and with no one else at home anymore, Laila understood her father's loneliness.

The Laundry Room

They returned to the kibbutz, arm in arm. "There is something else," he said, turning to her before they reached the patio. "That soldier of yours stopped by my stand the other day for a conversation. He really is a nice chap, and under other circumstances, I would not have objected to his being our friend, but he worries me. He talked about you nonstop, and I told him you were getting married. My intent was to get him to move on with his life. He didn't seem to understand you would not be free to marry him. He left despondent."

Laila's head lowered to her chest for a moment. Her eyes raised, a little cloudier than before. "He showed up here today too. Did you tell him where I was?"

"No. I would never do that." Abba's eyes flared. "Why would I do that?'

"I'm sorry I questioned you, but he seems to know everything about me." Laila nibbled on her lower lip like she used to do as a child. "I hope he doesn't make any trouble."

Abba wrapped his arm around Laila, squeezing her shoulder. "I'll keep an eye out, just in case. I think some of your men friends here should be warned."

Laila looked around to see who she might trust. "I'll leave that to you, but please do not mention this to Itzhak. I don't want him upset today. It's enough that we know. I'm hoping this will all blow over and the soldier will respect our tradition. You know, I don't even know his name—the soldier's." Laila suddenly thought about Livia Slutzsky and her relationship with Itzhak and how irritated Laila had been with the two of them. Laila wanted all of this to stop.

"It's probably better that way," said Abba as a shadow fell across his face. Then, as if he removed one mask only to replace it with another, his face changed to reflect the joy of the day. "I would like to have a word with your intended."

What would he say to Itzhak? Would he tell him how spoiled Laila had been as a child? Would he tell Itzhak that she cowered before lightning? Would he tell him she had been playing house since she was little?

Laila looked around for someone who might know where Itzhak was and spotted Ari sweeping the sidewalk. "Ari, where is Itzhak?"

Ari put aside the broom and joined Laila and her father.

"Abba, this is a close friend, Ari Bitterman. Ari ... my father."

"So nice to meet you," said Ari, pumping Abba's hand like he was priming a well. "I feel like I already know you from all of Laila's ravings." Ari dropped Abba's hand, looking embarrassed by his outburst of emotions and took a step back. "Itzhak's poring over one of those history books someone sent him. He said he wasn't supposed to see you, so he's staying out of the way."

"Would you please take Abba to him?"

"My pleasure." Ari dropped the sprig of eucalyptus he had been grasping and waved Abba on. Bodies in close proximity, the two men began talking like coconspirators. No telling what they were plotting.

"I'll be there to walk you down the aisle." Abba called over his shoulder as he and Ari disappeared down the walkway to the rear of the kibbutz.

"You better," Laila called, feeling it was the best day of her life. As she hurried back to her room, she thought she saw her nemesis, Livia—the slutinsky—scurry off in the opposite direction. *Nah*, she said to herself, brushing it off as mistaken identity. Why would she be anywhere near Laila's room? Excitedly Laila turned her thoughts to last minute preparations for her wedding. As she entered the room, Laila noted someone had deposited a large tub in the center of the room. She bent over to test the temperature. *How nice!* she thought. She wondered who had conspired. It was the closest thing to a *mikvah*, a ritual immersion, she was going to get, under the circumstances. Traditionally, a young girl would attend a *mikvah* the day of her wedding to cleanse herself of all impurities for her groom. It had also been used after a girl's menses to purify the body.

Closing the door and placing an old steamer trunk in front of it, Laila stripped down to her bare skin, grabbed a towel from the cubby, and stepped into the piping hot water. What a luxury. It had been years since she had taken a bath. Even their showers at the kibbutz had been crudely thrown together at the last minute. As she lay basking in the warmth of the water, Laila couldn't help thinking about her future with Itzhak: their children, home, friends. She knew Pardess Hanna was but a stopgap to owning a kibbutz, and she didn't mind. It had actually been fun learning to be self-sufficient— proving their right to run their own kibbutz someday. Laila really loved Itzhak, and it didn't matter where she was as long as she was with him. She would not allow the soldier with the green eyes or Livia to ruin their future.

As Laila toweled off and began organizing her wardrobe, she heard a knock at the door. Who could that be? She was supposed to be left alone. Annoyed, she grabbed her robe and padded to the door. Moving the trunk out of the way, she opened the door, expecting to see Zahar. When she saw who it really was, however, she thought her eyes were playing tricks. Laila blinked to adjust to the bright light of the day. Could it be? She must be dreaming. She wouldn't dare.

"May I come in?"

"Are you sure you're at the right door? Itzhak's is on the other side of the compound."

"I guess you think I deserve that, but I don't," said Livia, wringing the stems of the flowers she was holding. "Itzhak is like a brother. He's been there for me since I was a baby. I just want to make sure you understand that, and if I look at him with adoration, it's because I do adore him—but as a sister would her brother. I came to offer my services. I'm pretty good with hair, and yours is so lovely. I would like to be your friend. Please let me fix your hair for this special day."

Laila's tongue was tied in knots. Today had been one shock after another. Here Laila was, trying to be that woman she wanted to be and not some spoiled brat. And now here was Livia, testing Laila's resolve, offering friendship; the least Laila could do was to accept. It probably wouldn't be easy since she had spent so much time trying to believe Itzhak was telling the truth about his relationship with Livia. Laila didn't want to admit it but she might have been wrong.

Laila made a hasty decision. "I would be delighted, and we are friends ... from now on." Laila reached for Livia and pulled her close, feeling the woman's body stiffen.

"I'm so happy," said Livia, pulling away. "Now let me make you even more beautiful than you already are. I can see why Itzhak is so much in love with you."

Laila wanted to believe this wasn't an act and that Livia wasn't going to do something awful. Laila was allowing that old, skeptical side of herself to enter the room, when she was trying so hard to keep her outside. Wanting to trust, Laila took a seat on the edge of the bed and turned her back to Livia. It was so hard not to look suspiciously over her shoulder at the other woman. What was she doing?

Livia held a bunch of orange blossoms in her hand. "I'd like to arrange them in your hair. I understand they mean a lot to you."

So, she knew I would let her do my hair. She came

prepared. They probably have bugs in them, and how did she know orange blossoms are important to me? No, Laila chastised herself; she was not going to succumb to the old hag who whispered naughty things in her ear. This was the new Laila. "I'm so grateful," she said. "I didn't know what I was going to do with it."

"Leave it to me."

Laila couldn't make herself relax, convinced that Livia would sabotage her wedding. Why was she letting Livia do this?

Livia moved Laila's hair this way and that, until she came to what Laila hoped was the best approach. It seemed like she spent hours with hairpins appearing from nowhere, being stuck here and there, with Laila unable to see what was going on. Once or twice Livia poked Laila's scalp. Laila was taking a big chance, and Zahar would be coming to help her any minute.

"There. You look lovely. Where is your mirror?" Livia stepped back, as if marveling at a masterpiece.

Laila was embarrassed to say her mirror was just a shard of glass, but she stood and walked to the wall just the same. What she could see was amazing. Livia had taken a hardworking farm girl and transformed her into a storybook princess. "Oh, my," was all Laila could say.

"Do you like it?" asked Livia, as if she really cared what Laila thought.

"I love it. I look sophisticated. You are a wonder. Thank you." Laila approached Livia and encircled her in a warm embrace. "You are truly talented." This time Livia seemed to welcome Laila's embrace.

"Thank you. Now hurry up and get dressed. You won't want to be late for your wedding. Do you have someone to help?"

"Yes, my maid of honor should be here any moment." Why hadn't she just said Zahar? What was the matter with her? "But thank you for asking, and thank you again for fixing my hair."

Livia hugged Laila again like Zahar might, with no hesitation. Laila stood in disbelief. Had she been wrong all along?

The next knock reminded Laila she had a wedding to attend—hers.

All thought of the luxurious bath and Livia's surprise visit quickly faded with the announcement of the bride. As Laila stood next to her father, waiting for the music to change, she had a moment of discomfort as she allowed thoughts of the green-eyed soldier and his earlier visit to wander into her thoughts. What drew one person to another, she wondered. Would he always be a fleeting question in her mind? Laila was familiar with the term *obsession,* and hoped she wasn't harboring a secret obsession, one that might undermine her relationship with Itzhak. Today she should be happy. No— today she *was* happy, and was not going to let some stranger cloud her wedding day. Laila tightened her grip on Abba's arm and the procession continued down the center of the dining room to where Itzhak waited. She took a deep breath and let her thoughts of the soldier fade into the night.

Boughs of citrus blossoms and eucalyptus branches decorated the long, wooden dining room, creating a mixture of soothing aromas and nature's grandeur. As Laila glided down the aisle, she breathed in the medicinal scent of eucalyptus, the sweet, pungent blend of fruit and wood. She would always remember that scent when she was in need of comforting. This was as prepared as she had ever been for an important moment in her life. Itzhak and she were meant to

The Laundry Room

be.

Familiar faces lined the aisle as smiles and kisses sailed her way. Laila glanced several times at Itzhak as she made her way toward him. He was so handsome in his finery, but to her he had become an old slipper whose sole had been carved out to accept only one foot—hers.

The *chuppah*, swathed in tulle and fresh greenery, served as the focal point of her journey. Itzhak stood under the *chuppah*, her Greek god dressed in a black suit and tie, both handmade by Simca, their only tailor. The suit would serve for all occasions the rest of their married life. They had given up the luxuries of the past and would live a simple life. Itzhak and Laila's father would have already signed the *Ketuba,* the marriage contract which would be more ceremonial than binding. Basically, Itzhak promised to support and take care of all Laila's earthly needs.

Itzhak's parents had refused to attend. They continued their disavowal of him because of the path he had chosen, and sent nothing, not even a telegram. Laila knew how it hurt him, but he never said a word against them. Her only hope was that one day they would relent and want to see him and meet his new family. In the meantime, those around him would have to fill the void.

Further down the aisle, Laila caught Livia Slutsky watching her. What was she thinking? What was her ulterior motive: to really be friends or to make a way to spend more time with Itzhak? Livia smiled. Laila smiled back and nodded a thank-you. If she were pretending, Laila decided, she was doing a good job. Livia appeared to be genuinely happy for Laila.

Further down the aisle, Laila caught Leora and Ari sharing a loving glance. Theirs was a marriage made in heaven. Each brought out the best in the other, and since they were first in each other's lives, it made the match so much stronger.

Her brother Judah stood next to Itzhak, his face glowed with pride. His wife, Elena, sat stiffly next to Laila's sister Zelda, who had aged through four children. Her husband Bernard's hair had receded like the Red Sea, leaving a bare path from his eyebrows to the fringe at the base of his head. Laila hoped the years would be kinder to Itzhak. She would see to it.

Only a few steps separated them now, and neither could suppress a smile. Itzhak's passionate eyes narrowed as if he were focusing on a singular feature of hers. She wondered which. Most likely her décolletage. He had never seen her dressed in such finery. She blushed and took her final three steps that signified she was willfully entering into this marriage.

Chapter 23

Laila

Pardess Hannah, 1944

Laila took her place next to Itzhak. Abba placed her hand in Itzhak's, symbolically handing her over to the man who would take his place as her protector. Laila caught a wink exchanged between Abba and Itzhak. It warmed her heart to know they could be friends.

Zahar stepped forward and lifted the veil over Laila's head, so the Itzhak could make sure he was marrying the right woman. This tradition supposedly began when Laban tricked Jacob into marrying Leah, his eldest, instead of Rebecca, who he loved. Zahar kissed both of Laila's cheeks, replaced the veil, and reverently retrieved the bouquet of orange blossoms from Laila's hands and backed away. The blossoms were also a symbol of their time together in the groves. Itzhak reclaimed Laila's hand and they stood before the *hazzan,* soon to be man and wife. Laila determined, at that very moment, she would be the best wife that ever existed. She would stop being petty, selfish, and self-centered. Itzhak made her want to be that person. She would live up to her resolve.

Itzhak and Laila had written their own vows because the *hazzan*, who would be marrying them, didn't know them well. Itzhak went first. He surprised Laila by saying: "I pledge myself to you forever. You have become my life's blood and brought me direction. I look forward to sharing a life of love and devotion, understanding, open-mindedness, and adventure." As Itzhak continued, Laila drank in every word.

Then it was Laila's turn.

Laila had thought long and hard about what she would say. Somehow it paled in comparison to Itzhak's litany of praises. "To you I pledge my heart, my soul, and my mind. I pledge to follow you to the ends of the earth as Naomi did Ruth. I pledge my loyalty, trust, and most of all my understanding. I will love you forever."

The *hazzan* continued his part of the service. Then Laila and Itzhak shared the ceremonial cup of wine, the *Kiddushin*, sanctifying one to the other, blessing their union with a long life together. The *hazzan* took the wedding ring from Ezra which had been inscribed with the words from the Song of Solomon: *I am my beloved's and my beloved is mine*, and handed it to Itzhak who placed the ring on Laila's forefinger.

Itzhak recited the ancient vow: "Behold, you are consecrated to me by this ring, according to the ritual of Moses and Israel." The *hazzan* then read the *Ketubah*, marriage contract, handed it to Itzhak, who then handed it to Laila. According to law, once the ring was in place, the marriage ceremony was complete.

A second cup of wine was poured and the Sheva Berachot or Seven Blessings was recited by several members of the

The Laundry Room

kibbutz who Itzhak and Laila had chosen. Ezra began the first blessing: *Blessed art Thou Lord our God, King of the universe, Fashioner of the man.*

After Ari completed the seventh blessing the *hazzan* placed the ceremonial covered glass on the floor for Itzhak to break. Laila had been told many stories about why this custom was part of the wedding ceremony. The one she liked best told of how the breaking of the glass reminded a marrying couple that life had its sorrows as well as joys; that by standing under the marriage canopy, the couple was at the apex of their happiness and had created a bond that couldn't be broken, even by a shattered glass.

Itzhak took his job seriously, breaking the glass into a thousand pieces. A resounding "*Mazel Tov!*" rang out. Just as the *hazzan* pronounced them man and wife, thunder shook the building and lightning illuminated the room. Again, Laila was not sure whether they were being blessed or invaded.

"*Mazel Tov!*" yelled everyone again.

Zahar stepped forward, lifted Laila's veil, and gently pulled it over her head. Laila turned to Itzhak, who kissed her soundly amidst applauds and cheers. United, they ran from the *chuppah,* down the aisle, headed for the door, and then remembered it was pouring. Instead, Ezra directed them to a small table where the wedding contract would be signed by both the bride and groom.

Prior to the reading, Laila had had no idea how clearly the contract outlined the responsibilities of the husband toward his wife. It was then she remembered her responsibilities and cringed. Suddenly, the ceremony had become a blur, as she concentrated on what would come next. She was scared and expectant at the same time. What if she couldn't perform? Itzhak had held her hand throughout the ceremony as if knowing her thoughts. He must have understood that if he let go, she might collapse.

The reception went on for hours as they danced, sang, and kibitzed. At one point, Itzhak and Laila were hoisted onto chairs, elevated above their guests' heads as the women danced in circles around the room, turning their chairs until Laila became dizzy with happiness ... Itzhak eating up the attention.

The door flew open, the music stopped—quiet fell upon the room. Four soldiers barged in, carrying rifles and scaring everyone to death. The men lowered Itzhak to the ground and huddled together. The women almost dropped Laila. Avraham cautiously approached the soldiers, and in his best English, asked what they wanted. The wedding party moved to the back wall, waiting for their demise. One of the British soldiers pointed his rifle at Avraham. A collective intake of breath vibrated throughout the room.

"We heard a ruckus and came to investigate. What is the meaning of this gathering?" he snapped.

Another soldier approached, his eyes devouring Laila's body while he leisurely ran his palm down her cheek. Those piercing green eyes fastened on hers, telling her what he'd like to do to her. Laila couldn't believe the change. She never would have expected such behavior from him. She had wanted him to be different, but she had smelled the liquor on his breath, and she was scared. What would he do?

The green-eyed soldier turned back to his comrades and made what must have been some English wisecrack that none of them understood. The soldiers laughed uproariously. This was what the Jews in Palestine had come to expect of British soldiers, but this soldier had a special motive, and Laila knew what it was. She feared him like this, drunk and riled up. He must have thought he had nothing to lose—

nothing but her respect. She hadn't wanted Itzhak to know about him. Now, there would have to be some explaining.

Zalman and Ezra grabbed Itzhak, trying to keep him from doing something stupid. Abba moved from behind, placing himself between Laila and the soldier. A whispered exchange took place. The green-eyed soldier focused his gaze upon Itzhak, and Laila's stomach roiled. Was she to lose her husband of mere hours? What were these madmen after—a little fun?

The green-eyed soldier took a step toward Itzhak, as if in a challenge. They were face to face. Zalman and Ezra let Itzhak go. That small vein in Itzhak's neck had popped out from the strain of holding himself back. Laila knew the sign. For the most part, Itzhak was mild mannered and more used to using his words than his fists; but when pushed to his limit, he could become frightening. Laila had seen the result only once, when another soldier had made an offensive comment about Jews. Laila never wanted to see that side of him again.

The room barely breathed, and when it did, the exhalation sounded like thunder to her ears.

The tension built to an impasse as words passed between the soldier and her husband, who understood every word. Laila missed most of their meaning, but not their intent. She prayed Itzhak would control his temper. He had nothing to worry about; she was his. This intruder was drunk, upset, and would be sorry in the morning. Please, God, she prayed; she had asked so little; spare her love, the man she planned to spend the rest of her life with, the man who would help raise their children, the man who she would laugh with, cry with, love and sometimes disagree with.

Laila could not stand it any longer, not used to letting others fight her battles; even so, no matter how unbearable, she realized this was a time to use restraint. Her temples throbbed, her throat constricted, and she felt faint, much like the day of the bombing.

By then, each soldier had chosen one person to aim his gun at, making the assault even more personal. Contorted faces looked on in anguish, some revisiting scenes they had left behind in Germany, Poland, and Czechoslovakia, all expecting the worst.

But the worst didn't come. The green-eyed soldier brushed past Itzhak, like someone on a busy street, and then stopped abruptly. He was heard to say: "You better be good to her," and then strode out of the room. He stopped once more at the door, turned, eyes glaring at Laila. She looked away, wanting Itzhak to know the man meant nothing to her. The other soldiers laughed, helped themselves to food, and followed their leader out the door. They never said what they had come for. Laila, of course, knew.

Intent on not letting the British ruin yet another celebration, the festivities continued through the night; however, not for Laila. The scene from earlier would be a memory she would never forget. Faces, only moments ago filled with dread, now were masks of relief. They were all pretending to have a good time, but the intrusion had taken something away from Itzhak and her, something that would take a lifetime to mend. A grey pall shrouded the room, wrapping everyone in a veil of gloom. Laila knew a discussion would follow when they were alone. Her heart was broken, and on her wedding day.

Chapter 24

Avraham

Jerusalem, 1945

In the days, weeks, and months that followed, the kibbutz lived in relative harmony. Their production had doubled from the previous year, and the cry of babies could be heard coming from the nursery. Zahar was pregnant again, and this time the pregnancy was going well. Laila had relieved her of all her chores, and Leora fussed over her like a drone for her queen bee. The kibbutzniks were closer to obtaining the property by the sea that Avraham, Itzhak, and Ari had looked into. Avraham couldn't have been any happier.

Then in early August, word came down through Tal that the *Haganah* was interested in speaking to their group. Tal hadn't said why, just that they wanted two select representatives to journey to Jerusalem for a meeting with a Yosef Avidar, head of the *Haganah*. He had passed limited information on to Avraham.

Avraham assembled the group, which in the beginning had been a combination of mostly two Scout groups: *Noar A* or Youth A, made up of children who had immigrated from Germany and Austria to Jerusalem in 1933 without parents; and the other, *Noar B*, who had immigrated from Germany, Austria, and Czechoslovakia in 1943 and joined with Noar A in 1945. A smattering of other youth in the group were lucky to have at least one or more parents still living. Each young person had a story to tell, one more harrowing than the other; but time and circumstances had brought them together to form a cohesive, respected kibbutz with clout.

"I've called you here to discuss something that has come to my attention," said Avraham, somewhat subdued. "It seems representatives from our kibbutz have been called to Jerusalem for a talk. I know nothing more. I can't imagine that we've done anything to displease of benefactors; perhaps they are ready to sell us the Ma'agan Michael property. Either way, someone has to go."

"You should go," said Rivka, as outspoken as ever and now seated on the general assembly.

"All right, I'll go, but they asked for two representatives. I will need someone else. Who do you suggest? It would only be for the day, I suspect."

Zahar made her way to the front. "I think Laila should go. She is an original member of the secretariat and knows the inner working of the kibbutz better than most. My vote is for Laila." A number of other women came forward in support.

"Is there a consensus then?" asked Avraham, looking to Laila for a nod. "What do you say?"

Avraham knew this was a great honor and responsibility. Laila had risen through the ranks and was a top member of the secretariat, but how would Itzhak take the news that Laila had been selected and not him? It was Itzhak who seemed to bask in the rays of honor. Would Laila need his validation? Could she make up her mind by herself without

The Laundry Room

his support? Now was as good a time as any to find out.

"I would be honored to represent the kibbutz," said Laila, her eyes revealing her delight.

Avraham was, however, less than delighted. He would have preferred one of the other men. His feelings for Laila were mixed. Sometimes being in close proximity with her confused him. Avraham loved Zahar, but something in him also longed for a woman like Laila—strong, resilient, and sexy. Zahar had lost that spark he had fallen in love with after repeated miscarriages; and so, he would have to keep his emotions in check.

A discussion went on for some time, as it did whenever anything had to be decided. The men were not in favor of a man and woman traveling together without being married.

Rivka piped up, "Avraham and Laila have known each other a long time, and there is nothing improper about them making the trip to Jerusalem together, especially for something that appears to be important, and I suppose there would be a driver escorting them."

An accord was struck, and Laila was the kibbutznik's choice.

Avraham decided to stay out of the discussion. He was not particularly in favor of their choice for other reasons. Laila could be outspoken at times; her youthful enthusiasm might find her speaking inappropriately. He would have to monitor her. It was settled, however—Laila and Avraham would represent the group and leave for Jerusalem the following week.

As the days passed, Avraham became more agitated. He hoped the trip would be quick and without a power struggle between him and Laila. She had shown her true colors many times during their secretariat meetings, sometimes being bull-headed and opinionated.

A week later, a transport truck picked Avraham and Laila up early, the morning of their departure. The journey was uncomfortable, but less complicated than the kibbutznik's first trek trip to Pardess Hanna. No one would dare attack a vehicle that looked so menacing. Avraham and Laila spent the first leg of the ride speculating on what they had done wrong. As they talked, Avraham decided he might have misjudged Laila. She was quite smart and seemed to grasp their situation well. He was beginning to feel better about her part in the excursion.

"I've tried to come up with a reason for our being called to Jerusalem," said Avraham. "It has to be important. This general could have come to the kibbutz to speak to all of us at the same time."

"I agree. Maybe he wants to get a feel for what our group might think through us. Hopefully, it is about Ma'agan Michael. I can't wait to see the settlement. From what Itzhak said, it's a paradise."

"Maybe the view, but it's in a worse state of repair than our present quarters. Yes, we will be able to fish, and yes, the earth appears more fertile, but it will be more work getting started. There isn't enough housing, either. Let's take this a step at a time. The summons could be about a million things."

It was hot and muggy, and the close proximity of three bodies only added to the stress of the ride. Avraham marveled at how Laila handled herself, under the circumstances. Most women would be complaining by now. She was one of the youngest of the group, yet she seemed to possess the most common sense, with the exception of Zahar, who was as steady as a rock. Avraham's feelings for

The Laundry Room

Laila waivered all over the place, probably because of an internal struggle brought on by some unexplained attraction he had for her—one that he needed to do something about.

With someone else present, it was difficult to talk frankly, so Avraham and Laila spent the rest of the trip speaking only when they stopped for gas or a bathroom break. They had passed through several road blocks and had been asked for identification. Fortunately, they both had been reminded to bring theirs. Just outside of Jerusalem, the truck pulled behind a line of vehicles about to pass through the last roadblock.

"Have your papers ready," said the driver. "More than likely it will be as the rest—nothing to worry about."

As they approached the checkpoint, Avraham couldn't help but worry. The drive so far had been without incident. He was beginning to expect the worst even under the simplest of circumstances. It was hard to forget their journey to Pardess Hanna, with bandits chasing them down on camels. The members of the kibbutz had already been through so much. What next?

The driver handed his papers along with theirs to the guard. The guard looked them over, turned to another guard, who also looked them over. The second guard, who must have been in charge, approached, ordering them to: "Pull over there!" He pointed. The driver glanced at Avraham and Laila, questioning the command. They both shook their heads.

The driver did as told, and they waited. Avraham had been right to question their luck.

"What is your destination in Jerusalem?" His narrow face and close-set eyes reminded Avraham of a rodent. The officer pursed his lips as he spoke, adding to the caricature Avraham had imagined.

"The home of Eliyahu Golomb," said Avraham.

"What is your business there?"

Avraham leaned over the driver. "We are hoping to negotiate property for a new kibbutz."

"And that is all?"

"Yes." After all, Avraham was telling the truth. They had no other possible reason that he could think of for being called to Jerusalem. He hoped his answer would be enough to let them go.

"Please wait." The officer walked away.

"Quick thinking," said the driver.

"It's the truth, and best I could do under the circumstance."

Laila sat still. Avraham could tell she was nervous.

"You handled yourself well," she said, resting her hand on his sleeve. It burned through to his skin. That was the first time she had touched him in a long time, and it was almost too much.

The officer returned. He, Laila, and the driver sat expectantly. "Your papers seem to be in order. You are free to go."

The driver pulled out of the parking space and headed for the point at which they would be allowed to pass. The road block was the only thing keeping them from their destination. Idling, they held their breaths, waiting for someone to think of another reason to detain them. The arm began to rise, and they drove under, never so glad to be on their way. Laila's touch faded quickly as they picked up speed and entered Jerusalem.

"Actually, we're not going to Mr. Golomb's home," said the driver. "We're going to the headquarters of the *Jewish Agency*. You were given Eliyahu Golomb's name for that very reason. You even had me convinced."

"Then who is Eliyahu Golomb?" asked Laila.

"He was instrumental in starting the *Haganah* and a respected man in Jerusalem. You will probably meet him today."

Interesting, thought Avraham.

Arriving in the Rehavia neighborhood of Jerusalem, an area modeled after European garden cities and the headquarters of the *Jewish Agency*, anticipation was high. Avraham helped Laila down from the running-board; his hands shook as his fingers wrapped around her waist, as small as it was. She barely weighed a pound, he thought. He watched as she retrieved her purse and overnight satchel they had been advised to bring.

Avraham turned to the driver. "Thank you for the ride. Hopefully you'll be available when we are ready to return."

"That will be up to my commander," said the driver. "It was my pleasure. I wish you well."

Avraham and Laila followed the drive's directions toward a limestone building divided into three wings, a stark edifice resembling a fortress more than an office building.

It was a well-known fact that limestone was exclusively used in Jerusalem for buildings. It was, in fact, *meleke* limestone that ancient Jews took from the quarries to fashion their city, and what the *Kotel* or the Western Wall was made of. Avraham had heard that in the beginning of the British Mandate, a law had been passed by the municipality making it mandatory to use only that limestone, even if it were just to face a building. Avraham had been intrigued by this decision, but he had not discovered the reason for the law.

Two armed guards with machine guns flanked the entry

way, making Avraham and Laila uneasy. The door opened and an official dressed in a freshly-starched uniform stepped out of the building, closing the door behind him. "May I see your identification?"

Avraham fumbled inside his jacket pocket and handed his papers to the officer who perused his identification carefully and handed them back.

"Yours seems to be in order. Now the lady's." The officer held out his hand.

Laila had her papers ready and passed them to the officer. He spent only a moment on hers.

"Please follow me," he said as he opened the door and ushered them in.

Avraham thought it odd, the officer hadn't identified himself. Perhaps it wasn't important, and Avraham and Laila would probably never see him again.

Avraham found the inside of the building to be stark and uninteresting. The stone walls were bare and menacing. There were no adornments, as if the building was only temporary.

"Please show your identification papers to the secretary when you arrive at General Avidar's office," said the officer; his voice was as starched as his uniform.

After boarding an elevator, they travelled to the third floor, where their escort pushed a series of buttons before the doors opened onto a very busy floor. Cubicles were set up in the center of the room, with small offices around the perimeter. A low hum indicated transactions were taking place, but not for anyone else's ear. Avraham hadn't realized the *Haganah* was this organized. He had always thought of it as just an army of fighting men. Laila and Avraham followed their escort to the back of the room where a secretary sat at a small desk, busily talking on the phone. She raised a finger,

The Laundry Room

signaling she would be right with them. Several minutes passed before she hung up. The officer had left them to their own devices.

"Laila Schwartzman and Avraham Lemberg ... to see the general. He's expecting us." Avraham's voice took on an authoritative tone. It was difficult not to be serious with this atmosphere. He was glad Laila was keeping her thoughts to herself.

"I'll see if he's available." She picked up the phone, pushed a button, and spoke briefly into the receiver. She nodded her head and placed the phone in its cradle. "He'll see you now."

The secretary rose, walked to a metal door nearby, and opened it. The door itself was plain; the room behind it was plain as well. There was nothing fancy about the office or the building. Efficiency, Avraham thought, must be the key word.

A man wearing a light khaki, short-sleeve shirt and darker khaki pants stood and walked from behind his desk to shake hands with Laila and Avraham. "My name is Yosef Avidar. Please, sit." He motioned to a small, wooden, table in the corner of the room, devoid of anything other than pads of paper and plenty of pens. "We are meeting here instead of *Haganah* headquarters because it is more prudent. It will appear we are discussing the establishment of a new kibbutz, instead of the real reason for the meeting."

Laila grabbed Avraham's arm, almost cutting off the circulation, and he saw that the blood was draining from her face. "I know that man," she whispered, her eyes flashing back and forth between him and Avidar. Her expression was unmistakably frightened. Avraham helped her to a seat.

"What's the matter? Are you unwell?" General Avidar directed his comment to Laila.

Avraham took note. "I would like to clarify something before we start," he said. "Laila says she knows you. Is that true?"

Laila had both men's attention. It took her a moment to respond; she must have had many conflicting thoughts running through her head. "Did you stop at my falafel stand, the day the King David Hotel was bombed?"

Avidar said nothing, and Avraham thought he must have been deliberating on how to answer.

"Yes, and I told you they were the best."

"Did you have anything to do with the bombing?" Laila was now sitting on the edge of her seat leaning forward, apparently ready to attack.

Again the general paused before speaking. "I would like to tell you why you are here before I answer your question." He didn't wait for them to respond. "Because of your ability, as a group, to work together and prosper under difficult circumstances, the *Haganah* has chosen your kibbutz to participate in an operation essential to the forming of the Jewish state."

Avraham and Laila exchanged glances. For Avraham this was a revelation; they hadn't been called in for a rebuke, and they weren't possibly losing the right to purchase Ma'agan Michael. He felt relieved for the first time in days; however, he wanted to know the answer to Laila's question. He had lost his unborn child due to that bombing, and he came oh so close to losing his wife. If this man had anything to do with it, he didn't care what he was offering, Avraham would have none of it.

"What we are asking is dangerous, time consuming, and hopefully no one will ever know you participated." His eyes came to rest on Laila. "I suppose if I want you on board, I will have to explain what happened that day."

The Laundry Room

Avidar took a sip of his coffee and began. "Secret papers had been confiscated from our bureau that contained information crucial to the welfare of hundreds of thousands of people—people helping other Jews escape to Palestine and more. It was imperative that the information be retrieved, and/or destroyed, before the wrong people began using the information against us. The operation to do that was planned for the evening of that day, when all workers and visitors in the area would be gone. It was to be confined to the basement and floors housing British personnel only. The British had taken over most of the hotel and few visitors remained. Most of Jerusalem did not know this. Too many branches of the *Haganah* were involved and communication broke down, thus the change in timing. We did make three phone calls to strategic centers of communication, but no one took us seriously, hence the causalities."

His eyes narrowed as he continued. "With the British pulling out in three years, conflicts between us and the Arabs have escalated one hundred percent, as we both jockey for position. There will be a full-scale war soon, and if we wait for the different Arab nations to unite, we will all be decimated. We must strike first."

Laila spoke, her face a road map of anguish. "I was there, as you know. I could have been killed. Avraham's wife lost her baby. You are talking to two of the most difficult people to convince. Avraham's wife will never be the same. I will never be the same either. How could you expect us to help you in any way?" At this point, Laila was shaking. Avraham covered her hand with his for support.

"I am humbly sorry for what happened to both of you. You are what we call *unfortunate victims*."

"There were ninety-one deaths and countless injuries. I would say that is a little more than *unfortunate victims*. It changed both of our lives," said Avraham.

"Are you living?" He turned to Avraham. "Have you had another child?"

"Yes, but that does not alter what happened. My wife was physically and mentally changed. We understand war is not pretty," said Avraham, holding back his true feelings, "but your planning tactics leave a lot to be desired." He couldn't believe this man was asking them to trust him. Did he take them for fools?

Avidar rose and began pacing the room. "Operations have changed drastically since then. The splinter group responsible for overreacting is no longer a part of our organization. We have clear thinkers, straightforward planners, and one goal only—to free our people from tyranny. If this is something you think your group might be interested in, and you can put your distrust aside, it could change the outcome of a bad situation. We would be working together. You would have a say in all operations." He stopped and looked them over carefully. "Am I making any headway?"

"Laila and I need to talk this over. You haven't told us what we would be doing."

"I have to know your feelings first before I can reveal the operation. After I tell you, I have to trust it will go no further because, again, it could jeopardize many lives."

"Can you give us a moment?" asked Avraham, looking at Laila for agreement.

"I'll be down the hall. Take your time. Come get me when you are ready to talk." Avidar rose and left the room.

"I don't feel good about this," said Laila. "Can he be trusted? I'm concerned that the *Haganah's* mantra is 'the end justifies the means'. He's asking us to make a decision for forty-three other people. They chose us to represent them, but they could not have known the magnitude of this conference." Laila shook her head and took a deep breath. "If it hadn't been for the bombing, I would have been more inclined to take this next step, whatever it might be. What do you think?"

Avraham rubbed his brow. Yes, he had been skeptical throughout the general's proposal, not knowing exactly what they would be asked to do; and yes, it was an honor to be singled out and appreciated for their hard work, but how on earth did Avidar expect them to make a commitment like this on behalf of the others?

"As you, I have a million questions and no answers. I never thought of myself as a hero, just an ordinary man doing ordinary things. I've shied away from the military, preferring to use my head for what I thought was a higher calling. But, if we want to survive in this land, we will all be called upon to make sacrifices. I could go on forever holding the *Haganah* responsible for our loss, but that would be nonproductive. They are basically all we have for protection. Someone is knocking on our door asking for help. Do we turn our backs on them?"

"When you put it that way, we don't have much choice. I say we hear him out and then make our decision."

"Are you sure?"

"Yes."

Avraham rose apprehensively, but at the same time, fired up with anticipation. He strode to the door and opened it, walked down the hall to where Avidar was waiting, stuck his head in, and nodded. The two men returned—Avraham, with trepidations—the general, with a mask of concern on his militant face. *His must be a difficult job*, thought Avraham— *David, fighting Goliath*.

The general took his seat across from the two. "And your

decision?"

"We are willing to hear you out," said Avraham, "but that is all. You are asking us to make a monumental decision without the benefit of knowledge, and for forty-three others."

"I realize this is not an easy task, and you are all so young. It's your youth and accomplishments that have driven our decision to recruit your kibbutz for this top secret mission. We are asking your group to help build and man an underground ammunitions factory near the city of Rehovot.

Avraham's jaw dropped to the ground. What did his kibbutz know of building ammunition plants, and what did he mean by "man?" This was the craziest thing he had ever heard. By the look on Laila's face, he figured she thought the same thing.

Despite Avraham's and Laila's obvious reaction, General Avidar went on. "Officially, the facility would be considered a training kibbutz for others interested in forming their own kibbutz. The idea for this operation has been a long time in the making, and I would be happy to tell you the whole story some other time, but I don't think it really matters. Given the time constraint imposed by the end of the British mandate, we have had to move up execution so that we can be ready in time. I can go into that later, also, but I think it wouldn't change your mind one way or another. Suffice it to say that only the top officials of the *Haganah* are aware of this plan. A caveat to this operation—you would not be able to tell anyone, including your families or best friends, what you were really doing. We are building a cover story that you would be expected to use."

Avraham and Laila stared dumbfounded at one another.

The general stood. "I have a few phone calls to make. I took the liberty of asking some of the members of the *Haganah* to join us for lunch if you agreed. I think you might feel more secure after meeting them. Please remain here, and I will return for you. I won't be long."

The general walked out without another word; when he was gone, Laila turned to Avraham. "He didn't even wait to hear if it was convenient or not for us to stay. If the meeting lasts too long, we'll have to remain overnight. I'll have to get word back to Itzhak. You will too."

"Zahar already knew we might be gone for more than one day, so she was prepared. I'll have Avidar make the call."

"Well, what do you think?" asked Laila, concern written in the folds of her brow.

"I'm not sure what we've gotten ourselves into. I feel honored on the one hand, and petrified on the other. I think this will be the kind of thing the men have been waiting for. I've seen signs of boredom around the kibbutz. The initial enthusiasm has worn off, and I believe the men will jump at the chance to serve their country, not to mention the excitement of working in secret. This is an once-in-a-lifetime opportunity."

Laila rubbed her temples. "I'm not so sure the women will be as enthusiastic. Agreeing to the general's proposal means bringing children into the equation."

"The children won't be near the factory. We'll see to that."

"Yes, I know, but if anything goes wrong, they could easily lose their parents."

Avraham had to admit he hadn't thought about that. Laila was so practical. Avraham would make sure he had all the answers before the general met with the kibbutz. Suddenly, it appeared to Avraham that what Laila was feeling was a lack of enthusiasm, and he wasn't going to let her ruin their chance of playing a role in the establishment of their own country. Before General Avidar had offered this opportunity, Avraham's single, most important goal had been to own a kibbutz; now there was a far greater challenge at stake, and he was fully committed. What had happened to Zahar could not be changed.

After about twenty minutes, Avidar returned again and asked them to follow him. They would be meeting with top officials in the *Haganah*. Avraham felt his pulse rise. Perspiration dotted his upper lip, and he could feel the excitement of meeting such important people take over his body. Avraham had no idea what the committee might add to what General Avidar had told them; but it might change Laila's mind, and it certainly wouldn't hurt when he had to try and convince the rest of the kibbutzniks to change their direction and at the same time, put them in harm's way.

The three took the elevator back to the first floor. Avraham could feel Laila's uneasiness all the way down. She was wound as tight as a violin string.

"Some of our guests were already here at a meeting," said Avidar as the elevator door opened. "The rest should be coming along in dribs and drabs."

Avidar ushered them into a long banquet hall, much more splendid than the rest of the building. The table was set with real china and goblets ringed in gold. Heavy mahogany serving tables lined the walls, covered in cut velvet wallpaper. Waiters in stark white uniforms stood around holding trays of wine and hors d'oeuvres. What a contrast to the rest of the building. Avraham was thinking a lot of important decisions had probably been made here. He pulled out Laila's chair and then seated himself. A distinguished looking gentleman walked in and took the vacant seat next to Laila. Avraham heard the man introduce himself.

Laila turned to Avraham and then back to the man. "Mr. Sharrett, I would like to introduce Avraham Lemberg. We are anxious to hear what you have to say about this venture."

The Laundry Room

"A pleasure to meet you." They shook hands across Laila.

The room began to buzz as the table gradually filled to capacity. In front of them sat a salad consisting of chunks of tomatoes and cucumbers bathed in a light dressing. Avraham couldn't imagine men being interested in such a salad. He thought it was more for ladies. But then, Laila knew more about food preparation than he did. The salad sort of reminded Avraham of the interior of the building ... bland. He was hungry and hoped for something more substantial for the rest of their meal.

"Excuse me," said General Avidar, clearing his throat. "We are all very busy people, and I know you have a million other places to be. I appreciate your fitting us into your schedule. Before we begin, I would ask the wait staff to return to the kitchen until we summon you back. Thank you for your service." Applause could be heard around the table.

Chatter filled the room as the waiters filed through a heavy wooden door, one that was locked behind them.

"Now then, I would like to introduce Laila Schwartzman and Avraham Lemberg, members of the newest kibbutz and one of the most responsible groups of young people I have met in a long time. You all know why we chose that kibbutz, now I need you to help me convince these two young people to risk their lives for their country."

Avidar went around the room introducing the esteemed members of the elite group. There was Zvi Berenson: with strong features, receding hairline, and cleft chin, he was the legal advisor to *Histadrut,* the leading trade union, whose job it was to organize economic activities among Jewish workers and instrumental in maintaining good relations between their fledging country and the rest of the world. Moshe Sharrett, who sat next to Laila, had squinty eyes, a bushy mustache, and bulbous nose. Apparently his family was among those who had founded Tel Aviv. He was the Secretary of the *Jewish Agency* and in charge of the political department. The man whose name had been used at the blockade, Eliyahu Golomb, was quite elderly, with strong features and a deep groove in the left side of his face. The only other woman in the room was Golda Meir, who resembled Avraham's grandmother. Her hair was pulled back in a tight bun, and her steel eyes reminded him of an eagle's. Avraham was interested to know why she had been invited.

"Now, down to business. I'd like to give you the opportunity to ask the members of the *Haganah* any question that will help alleviate your concerns," said General Avidar, directing his comment to Avraham and Laila. "You may direct your questions to someone in particular or open it to the group."

"Exactly what type of ammunition are we talking about?" asked Avraham.

Zvi Berenson answered, "You would be manufacturing nine-millimeter bullets. That is all. We have an overabundance of Sten machine guns, but not enough bullets."

"Aren't they highly combustible?" asked Laila.

"They are, but not as much as some others," replied Berenson.

"And you think a bunch of teenagers and young people can handle this?" Avraham was incensed. "This is crazy."

Golda Meir answered, "What do you think soldiers do every day that they are out there protecting your lives? They know the possible consequences, but in this case, the end justifies the means."

Avraham turned to Laila. That phrase had become Itzhak's favorite mantra. She must have known what he was thinking. She smiled for the first time that day.

The Laundry Room

"The difference is they are trained," interjected Avraham, trying to contain his anger.

This time Avidar jumped in. "You will receive the best training in the world. We would not leave you until we were certain you could handle the operation."

"Isn't it going to take a lot of machinery? If this is such a big secret, how will we do this without the British breathing down our throats every minute of the day?" asked Avraham, more intent on seeing how Avidar would answer than the question itself.

"All good questions. I see a future for you in the secret police." Avidar turned to Laila. "You've become quiet, all of a sudden. What are your thoughts?"

"You are asking us to make a decision that means life or death for our kibbutz. Neither Avraham nor I, and I think I speak for him, is in a position to do that. You are going to have to address the entire group yourself. They did not give us that kind of authority. That is why we have a general assembly, our secretariat, and committees. We are a democracy, not a dictatorship."

"Well said," Moshe Sharrett replied. "I respect your answer. That is exactly why we chose your kibbutz. We didn't point a dart at a board. Much research went into each of your backgrounds. A very impressive group of young people."

"So, do I take it you're ready for me to face the members of your kibbutz?" asked Avidar.

Again Avraham and Laila exchanged glances. "Yes," said Avraham, "but I cannot guarantee the result. You are going to have to make a good case for proceeding."

"And your thoughts, Mrs. Schwartzman?" Avidar said, eyes focused upon Laila.

"As I told Avraham, my feelings are mixed. I almost lost

214

my life that day at the King David Hotel, and it wasn't directly because of our enemies. I'm going to have to see some strong dedication to our group, not just someone giving us an assignment and leaving us to figure it out for ourselves. I'm sure we could, but it could be very dangerous."

Comments flew around the table. Apparently some didn't know Laila's or Avraham's story.

Golda Meir spoke up, "I can assure you, we have chosen only the best minds to see this operation through, and again, will not leave you on your own until we are positive you are ready."

"We'll see," said Laila.

"Very well." Avidar opened a leather-bound notebook and flipped through the pages. "How is two days from now?"

"That will be this Wednesday? Yes, that will work out fine. In the meantime, the kibbutzniks are going to be down our throat with questions. What are we to tell them?" asked Avraham.

Just then the door opened, and in walked an elderly gentleman with a full head of bushy white hair and stooped shoulders. He looked like he was carrying the world around on those shoulders. Avraham recognized him immediately. He could tell Laila hadn't.

"Excuse me, but I hear there was a meeting and I wasn't invited."

The room laughed.

David ben Gurion approached Avraham and held out his hand. "I understand you youngsters are going to save our country."

Avraham pushed back his chair and stood. "Well, sir, I'm not sure about that, but we intend to do the best job we can."

"And you, young lady. Are you of the same mind?"

The Laundry Room

Although only a little over five feet tall, ben Gurion's presence towered over Laila.

"You're asking a great deal of us without much detail. I would like to hear more." Laila said, remaining seated.

Suddenly, ben Gurion turned to the rest of the group. "Then, what are you waiting for? Fill them in. They can't very well convince others to do what they themselves are unsure of." He continued around the room shaking hands until he found an empty seat next to Golda.

"Fire away," he said as he sat down.

The next hour found General Avidar supplying more information than he looked comfortable giving. He left Avraham and Laila with: "Tell the rest of your kibbutz that I have a proposition for them, and no more. That includes your spouses. Let's see how good you are at keeping a secret. But now—what arrangements have you made for your return? We would like to have you stay for dinner. There are a few more people we would like you to meet."

Avraham checked his watch. It was past three o'clock. "We were hoping to go back today, but if you think it is necessary to stay ..." He ventured a look at Laila to see how she felt about the situation. She didn't look pleased.

"We have accommodations for special guests. We'll need two rooms. I'll take care of it," said Avidar as he left the room.

Laila and Zvi Berenzon must have picked up where they left off. Avraham found himself speaking to Yigael Sukenik, another important member of the group. Avraham forgot his position—there were so many names and professions floating around the room.

At that point, the door was unlocked and the waiters returned with a hearty meal of leg of lamb over couscous and roasted vegetables. Avraham dove into his meal while continuing his conversation.

"It's all arranged," said Avidar as he returned to the room twenty minutes later. "I've sent word to your kibbutz. Why don't you follow me if you're finished? I'm sure you could use some quiet time before dinner."

Avraham and Laila said their goodbyes and walked across the hallway to one of the wings, where the designated guestrooms were pointed out. Avidar explained what would happen at dinner, and then he left Avraham and Laila to themselves.

"My head is spinning," said Laila, standing outside her room. "How can I relax? I don't know what to do with spare time. I'm always busy."

"Why don't you just take a nap? That's what I plan on doing."

"I hope there is something to read in the room. I'll never close my eyes." She turned and walked into her room.

Avraham opened his door and entered a comfortable looking room—a suite, with a separate bedroom. As he looked at the bed he began to imagine Laila walking around her room, examining pictures on the walls, seeing what view there might be from her window; and then his other mind began to picture her falling back on the bed with him on top of her, kissing madly. The phone rang, hurtling him back to his senses. He walked quickly to the phone and picked it up.

A voice asked if he would like some water.

"Yes, water would be fine, thank you." Avraham lay down on the bed and drifted off. He wasn't sure how long he had been asleep when he heard a knock at the door. He got up to answer, and Laila was standing there, wrapped in a towel, her hair dripping with water. He grabbed her arm and pulled her into the room, closing the door a little too enthusiastically. She fell into his arms; Avraham held her as

The Laundry Room

she began kissing his neck, his chest. He pulled her onto the bed and began ravaging the towel off of her. He was excited and couldn't control himself.

A knock at the door woke him from his disturbing dream. Avraham sat up, alone in his room—sweating. He ran to the door and threw it open. A soldier was standing there holding a tray with ice and a bottle of water.

"Did I disturb you?" he asked.

Embarrassed by his disheveled appearance, Avraham said, "No, not at all. Thank you." Avraham took the tray and shut the door, depositing the tray on the side table next to his bed. He collapsed onto the bed and bent over, his head in his hands. *This can't be* he told himself. *I am a married man and she is a married woman; and besides, she hasn't shown any interested in me.*

All Avraham wanted was to return to the kibbutz. Why had they agreed to stay on? He knew why, and he was disgusted with himself. How was he going to make it through dinner?

###

"Your transportation is waiting," said Avidar. "I hope yesterday quelled some of your worries. You are returning armed with information. It should make my job that much easier. Now, I'm counting on you two for support when I lay out the plan. If you hesitate, that will be it. If they see you are not harboring any grudges, they will be more amenable to our plan. We must make this work."

"We will do what we can, but we don't promise anything. Each member of the kibbutz must decide for himself. There will be no pressure."

"You realize how important this is to the safeguarding of our country."

"We do, but we are only two people. You'll have to do a better job with them."

Avidar looked Avraham straight in the eye. "I can only do my best. I have convinced you to keep an open mind, have I not? I did not realize your involvement in the bombing before now. If so, I might have changed my tactics. I will be fully prepared come Wednesday."

"I have a question," said Laila. "Were you a general at the time of the bombing?"

"No. I was in a much lower position. I have been lucky."

Laila nodded.

Avraham left the premises with major concerns. How would he explain this to Zahar—working for the people who had stolen their first child and who were responsible for maiming her for life—his once-beautiful wife, who now sometimes repulsed him. He knew how that would sound to the casual observer, but he couldn't help it. It was her heart that kept them together. Yes, he might be shallow, he admitted it; but he would never let her know how he really felt. He owed her that much.

Avraham stole a glance at Laila, knowing that many of the kibbutzniks had not been in favor of her going, including him; but she had proved herself quite competent. He harbored a new resolve: stay away from her, and devote himself to his wife. That untimely dream had made its point.

Chapter 25

Laila

Pardess Hanna, 1945

Wednesday couldn't have come soon enough. Avraham and Laila had been grilled by everyone in the kibbutz at least once. She was worn to a nub from fielding questions and speculations. Laila and Avraham had decided to tell everyone that the kibbutz had been chosen, as an honor, to embark upon a venture that carried a number of risks. She and Avraham had felt it was better to introduce the idea as positively as possible. It was up to Yosef Avidar to do the rest.

Laila had mixed feelings about Avidar since she remembered seeing him at the King David Hotel the morning of the bombing. He had more or less admitted his participation during their interview. Her option, she decided, was that if she saw things going in the wrong direction during the briefing with the kibbutz, she could turn him in— but to whom? Who would even believe her?

Laila hadn't felt particularly well when she arose that morning, so she feigned sleep when Itzhak left. Marriage had something she had watched as a child, but never fully comprehended. Marriage was like the steps to a dance. One was always moving backward when their partner was moving forward, and vice versa. Each day brought with it a combination of highs and lows, but mostly highs. Their biggest problem so far had been the scene at the wedding and the fact that she had never mentioned the British soldier. She and Itzhak had spent their wedding night back-to-back. It was hard to put it out of her mind.

"How could you not have told me there was someone else?" he had demanded, as soon as they had entered their sleeping quarters.

"That's because there *was* no one else. I cannot help what was in his mind. We spoke maybe three times. That is it. I never encouraged him. He appointed himself guardian of Abba and me, and might have saved both our lives over the last few years, but I owe him nothing more than a thank-you. I never asked him to take on that role, and I had made it perfectly clear to him that there was no future for us early on. He never gave up. I might have admired that about him, but nothing else. Under other circumstances ..."

"A man does not go to the trouble he went to, to watch over you and your father and show up on your wedding day, hell-bent on destroying what he could not have, unless he had been given some encouragement." At that point, Itzhak was stomping around the tent.

"Ask Abba," Laila said, eyes pleading for Itzhak's mistrust to go away. "Abba even told him to leave me alone. I did not encourage him—not for a second. I took his kindness as a desire to show me that not all British were animals. That is it. If you insist on continuing these unfounded accusations, we'll be doomed from the start. I would ask for forgiveness, but I've done nothing wrong. Talk about forgiveness, what do you call Livia? Her tongue was still hanging out at our wedding, even though she feigned friendship."

Laila remembered Itzhak plopping down on the bed, glancing at her briefly with a look of disdain, and turned his back to her as he feigned sleep. It had taken a long, miserable week for them to right a terrible wrong. Things had simmered down, but there was still edginess to their relationship. Itzhak had ended up apologizing, but Laila wasn't sure he was convinced.

For what seemed like hours, she lay worrying whether things would work out. What disturbed her most was wondering how Itzhak would take Avidar's plan. What if he accused her of withholding that, too? If that turned out to be the case, she might have made a big mistake marrying him. She sighed. What was she doing projecting into the future? She was married, and it was forever. Laila rolled out of bed, slipped into wooden clogs—the rains had left the earth soggy —and clomped to the bathroom, feeling a bit woozy. What had she eaten that could have made her feel so awful? As she made her way into the bathroom, she wondered if the kibbutzniks would have to share bathrooms where they were going. There she went again, projecting into the future.

The dining room was a beehive of activity. Since equality was their watchword on the kibbutz, they did not have a queen bee, although there were some more equal than others. Chayim Sandler, whom they hadn't seen in some time, stood at the front of the room, shaking hands and schmoozing. He had been at a number of the kibbutz's early meetings, before they moved to Pardess Hanna. She wondered if he had been a plant.

The tension in the room was fraught with high anxiety.

The high pitch had gone from polite conversation to a low roar. Of course, only a few members of the secretariat had been sanctioned to be taken into Avraham and Laila's confidence so that it wouldn't just fall upon the two of them. Laila, along with Avraham and the other members of the secretariat soon joined Chayim along with Tal Rabin. Laila remained seated, hoping to play a very small role in the decision-making process.

When the door opened, Yosef Avidar entered in full uniform, showing off his intelligent eyes and square jowl; it was clear from his manner that he meant business. Laila grabbed Itzhak's overworked hand and gave it a squeeze. His nerves were on edge; she knew it by the set of his shoulders. He was anxious to move on. The kibbutzniks had worked for the government long enough and most of them felt it was time to take charge of their futures. It would be difficult asking the kibbutz to put off its dream, for who knew how much longer, with the new property within reach.

"Please pull your chairs forward so that I can speak to everyone without shouting." The chairs moved quickly as the general waited. "What I have to say is of utmost importance, and I don't want to have to repeat myself. Do I have everyone's attention?" Again, Avidar waited for everyone to settle down.

"It is partially because of Laila and Avraham that I am here today, but mostly because of you." His arms spread to take in everyone. "Avraham and Laila made me understand it was up to every member of your kibbutz to make major decisions. I respect that, so here I am, and want you to know they were sworn to secrecy when they left our meeting."

A second shuffle of chairs moved swiftly and then the room quieted to absolute silence. Ari sat to Laila's left. She could feel his body stiffen as the general continued his speech. What had once been a delicate arm was now as muscular as the rest of the men. Laila's stomach began to grumble, and Itzhak gave her one of those embarrassed looks, like everyone could hear. Laila had suffered bouts of nausea over the last few days, but she was hoping it would pass. A number of kibbutzniks had caught one thing or another, working so closely together, but none of their illnesses had ever gone on this long. It had been rough. Laila put one hand over her belly, trying to muffle the noise.

"My name is General Yosef Avidar. I am presently head of the *Haganah*, and I've come to offer you a chance to serve your country. I am asking that you postpone your plans to settle your own kibbutz, in exchange for taking on a clandestine operation that might contain an element of danger. It requires all of you to participate. As I said before, I have come to you because your kibbutz has made a name for itself, and because your leaders respect your desire to make decisions as a united group. We of the *Haganah* have studied your kibbutz extensively, and have found you to possess the right combination of skills: engineers, politicians, writers, scientists, business people, and hard workers. In addition to your skills, you have proven your loyalty to each other, and I believe you can be trusted to do what is best for yourselves and your country.

"If you have any qualms at this point, I ask you to leave the room and not come back. No one will think the less of you. If you choose to stay, you must understand that there is no backing out. You will know too much about the operation after that point.

"What I can tell you is that you will be leaving here and going to another location. Beyond that, I cannot say more until I have your word. I will leave the room and give you a half-hour to discuss this amongst yourselves. When I return, those in the room—those of you who have decided to participate—cannot look back."

A hand went up across the room.

"Yes."

"Can you tell us the time frame?"

"No."

Another wave of chatter rippled through the room until General Avidar raised his arm. "This is an open-ended task, so the time frame is unknown. Again, I remind you that what we are asking you to do is for your country. We are entering a difficult period with the British Mandate coming to an end. We haven't exactly been happy with their governing, but at least they have kept our neighbors somewhat at bay. That won't continue. There have been a number of skirmishes with too many deaths lately that indicate what lies ahead. If we do not get the upper hand now, we Jews can kiss our independence goodbye and maybe even our lives."

"We can't tell anyone?" asked Mazel, from her seat next to Itzhak.

"No. If you are seeing someone outside the kibbutz, that person cannot know," said Avidar.

"What do we say to our family when we leave?" asked Shaina.

"You tell them you will be training future kibbutzniks in a better place," he said, his voice curt and his brow heavily creased. It was obvious Avidar was tired of fielding answers. He held up his hands, indicating discussion was over. The murmur in the room grew louder as the general turned and strode out of the room.

As head of the kibbutz's general assembly, Avraham stood and motioned Laila forward. She had no alternative but to go.

The Laundry Room

"We have a lot to discuss; who would like to go first?" Avraham pulled a chair out for Laila, and then sat down. He shuffled some papers and handed her a pad of paper to take notes. Ordinarily she would have been insulted, but she had seen Avraham's chicken-scratch and understood his reluctance. She had, however, noticed a change in their relationship on the way back from the meeting. He had become standoffish around her. She hoped Zahar hadn't picked up on it. Laila would never want Zahar to think something had happened during their absence.

Their resident farmer, Zalman, stood up and waved his hand. With all the exercise he had been getting, he had slimmed down and wasn't as sloppy as when the kibbutzniks had first arrived. A few of the girls actually looked his way, nowadays. He did have big, brown doe eyes and rather thick lips, and Laila supposed there were those who might find that attractive. "I don't know. He hasn't given us much to go on. Do you know what he's asking of us? How do you feel about it?"

Avraham took a deep breath. "For my part ... and I don't want you to hold this against me if you decide to take part and things don't go well ... I'm in. So is Laila," he looked her way as to make sure she was still in agreement.

He should never have spoken for me Laila thought as she glared back at him and then, remembering what Avidar had said about being united, she nodded.

He then silently assessed the rest of their secretariat for their support. They nodded. "More than that, I cannot tell you."

Itzhak stood before Zalman got his answer. "I have heard talk of restlessness among you men. This is an opportunity to make our lives count for something more than catching fish. I'm not saying I don't want to do that, but I'm in, too." He looked at Laila with unabashed pride.

The excitement in Itzhak's eyes delighted Laila. She hadn't seen him this enthusiastic since they had finally consummated their marriage. She had begun to think the passion in his soul had been snuffed out like a candle. It thrilled her to see it rekindled and him so ardent. Apparently he had forgotten his earlier anger. Whether he had supported her or Avraham, it didn't matter. All she cared about was that he was supporting them.

Laila had a feeling Avraham would wait to tell Zahar who Avidar was, and what part he played in their personal tragedy. It might be impossible for her to forgive someone who had been involved in the death of her unborn child. For her part, Laila had no way of knowing how Itzhak would take the news. The bombing hadn't directly affected him, and might have been what brought them closer together.

To say sparks flew—tension grew—while the issue was debated would be an understatement, but when it was over, and the jury reconvened, the vote had been unanimous. Members of the kibbutz who had not interacted since they had first arrived were talking to each other now, asking how they felt about the pending decision. A show of unanimity, a bond of brotherhood, prevailed. Everyone was excited. Avraham strode across the room, opened the door, and motioned for the general to return. He stood firmly at the head of the table as if he would depart immediately if the vote were nay.

Avraham spoke with conviction. "We've polled our people, and we stand united. We are of one mind, and when the majority votes to proceed in one direction, the others follow. We are in. Are you at liberty to unveil our mission?"

The muscles in Avidar's face seemed to relax. Laila was thinking this was, indeed, a victory for him.

The Laundry Room

"Yes," he said clearing his voice. He took the seat to Laila's left. "Now that you have agreed, we will be moving quickly, because there is not much time to spare. Not far from the city of Rehovot is an old training camp. Our plans are to form a group of your most able-bodied men, with the help of our *Ta'as* engineers, and begin work on what will become an underground ammunition factory. You will be making bullets for the military."

Again, the room buzzed briefly, as people shared their initial shock with their neighbors and then quieted down with no guidance from Avidar. Laila could see their faces; all the members of the kibbutz were spellbound with a mixture of fear and excitement.

"Some background: in 1938 a group of concerned Jews began stockpiling old, castoff bullet-making machines from Poland because we had managed to confiscate hundreds of castoff Sten submachine guns left behind by the British, but we lacked the bullets to supply them. When the machines arrived in Beirut, they were stored until it became safe for us to move them. That was only just recently. Over time, gradually, we have smuggled them into our territory. This has not been without a measure of danger, as you can imagine. Jewish members of the British military found a way to carry them across the border, and anticipating a need to set up such a factory, we began the groundwork for a place the British were told would be a facility for training future kibbutzniks. The site, a fifteen-minute walk from the Rehovot train station, was, as I said before, once an agricultural training camp called Kibbutz Hill and not far from one of the British army bases. We figure they would never suspect us of doing anything out of the ordinary under their noses."

Ari stood. "How is it possible to build something so close

and the British not know?"

"We will be adding to a preexisting building, but underground. They will never know the difference, and the work will be done at night."

Ari shook his head but sat back down. Leora patted him on the shoulder.

Avidar continued despite the undercurrent in the room. "The upper building will become a laundry room. We have purchased a very large, fifteen ton, washing machine to muffle the noise that will be going on downstairs and have special ductwork that will conceal the polluted air rising from below. We have decided that you will offer the British the opportunity to clean their uniforms for a nominal fee. There will also be a bakery next door to afford access to machines, both coming and going."

"That means there will be a lot of foot traffic," Yussel Epstein blurted out.

"We've thought of that, too. You will offer a pickup and delivery service off the compound. That will cut down on traffic. Our plan is to conceal the underground entrance by means of the washing machine, which will swivel across the opening in the floor. A simple button will operate the mechanism. The other exit will be under a ten-ton baking oven, situated on runners."

The general hesitated a moment as the chatter elevated to a low roar. Avraham stood to quiet the group. "Let him finish. He must return to Jerusalem tonight."

While Avidar continued, Laila couldn't help but notice the excitement continue to build in her husband's eyes. It was as if he had come alive after a long sleep. She felt it too.

"The whole operation has been well planned. We expect things to go wrong from time to time, but we are confident you will be able to right those wrongs and come up with the

The Laundry Room

best possible solutions. Also, you won't be alone. We plan on leaving a few men with you, who have a vast amount of experience, to help you get started."

"How will we get the bullets to the soldiers?" Zalman asked.

"That will all be taken care of once we reach that stage. We will look to you, on occasion, for some of the answers to such questions. We feel that there is enough talent amongst you to make this work."

The general continued for the next hour, answering questions, sometimes having to consult a blue file folder for answers. It became obvious that much thought had already gone into this proposal.

As the discussion went on around her, Laila suddenly had a sobering thought. What if she were to become pregnant? What then? Would she want to put Itzhak and herself into such a position, where they might perhaps blow themselves and their baby to pieces? She put her hand to her belly, anxious to know Itzhak's thoughts.

Chapter 26

Avraham

Ayalon Institute, 1945

Work had begun on the munitions factory soon after the meeting with Yosef Avidar. Time was of the essence. Avraham threw himself into the work with abandon. He hadn't felt this exhilarated in years; it might have been the element of danger associated with the challenge and the possibility of getting caught. After that disturbing dream about Laila, Avraham had discovered a dark side to himself he was learning to deal with.

Avidar had kept his promise. A crew of *Ta'as* men, all experts in their respective fields, had descended upon the site of the *Ayalon Institute*, the code name for the project.

Eager workers quickly found their niches over the first few days. Avraham and Ari became the foremen, opting to work with the blueprints, lay out the foundation, and keep watch over the building's progress. They would be next in command to Moshe Wind, an expert builder from Jerusalem. Yosef Idelman, an engineer from Yagur, reconfigured the

The Laundry Room

original plans, which had been drawn up for the *Haganah* in 1938 by Professor Max Korein and Yehezkel Baram. It was Professor Korein who had decided which and how many of the machines the kibbutzniks would need in order to manufacture fifteen thousand bullets a day, and where to place those machines for maximum efficiency. Professor Korein also had prepared a catalogue which listed the machines and showed pictures of each, its size, and what it did.

The crew began work on two housing units, added a dining hall, toilets (the women had insisted), a barn, and large chicken coops. The most difficult part of the operation was constructing the factory. The building was to be cast in concrete, a faster way to construct, with dimensions of thirty-three meters long, eight meters wide and three meters high. The walls, once poured, would be fifty centimeters thick. In order to camouflage the two entrances to the factory, tin shacks were erected, allowing work underground. After the walls and ceiling were in place, a coating of asphalt sealed the building, followed by four meters of dirt.

At the end of each day, as the workers ascended from the factory, their clothing would be soaked from humidity trapped inside the underground chamber. Avraham was the first to address the issue. "What are we going to do about this? We can't work under these conditions. Someone will surely notice, and it can't be healthy, either."

Pesach Abramovitz, the plant manager, was perplexed. "Let me think. There has to be a way to dry out the walls." He went off muttering under his breath. They had discovered Pesach was a deep thinker, who often disappeared for hours at a time to work through a problem. He almost always came up with an answer.

Ari eagerly stepped forward. "I have some ideas." He ran

his dirt-stained fingers across his damp shirt. Ari's ideas had become valuable assets to speeding up the work on the factory. Between Pesach and Ari, problems were being ironed out so quickly that the entire construction was already ahead of schedule.

It had been several days from the time the work crew arrived before they had enough of the site built to even be able to bathe, and the water supply was still limited. Those not directly working on the factory itself were in charge of improving conditions for the forty-five young people who would be running the new kibbutz.

Ari broached the subject of his plan with Avraham. Avraham was a bit doubtful. "Let us see what Pesach comes up with," said Avraham.

"You are right," said Ari, "we cannot work in an environment that is as humid as the Sea of Galilee. We'll all get sick." Avraham and Ari walked to the dining hall, where several of the men had been assigned to cook for the rest. A lot of grumbling went on, because the meals were barely edible. Avraham wondered how someone could take perfectly good vegetables and turn them into slop.

"How are you sleeping?" asked Avraham, rubbing his eyes.

"Not well. The floor is hard, and the straw in the ticking sticks me through the night." Dark, swollen bags had formed under Ari's eyes. Already gaunt, Avraham thought he now looked like a stick figure in a comic.

"I think it's their way of making us work faster. I have never seen a building completed so quickly." Avraham sat on a stump, left over from a felled tree; Ari sat next to him. The two had become even closer over the past year. They respected each other and worked well together. When they had first met in college, Avraham had thought Ari might be

The Laundry Room

difficult to get to know; but to the contrary, he had opened up about his past and was forthcoming about his present. That was good, Avraham thought. They were going to need each other's strength to get through this ordeal.

The closer to the time they would begin this clandestine operation, the more concerned Avraham became. If he were single and had no one else to worry about, the danger they had placed themselves into would be a different story; but now that he had a family, he had certain responsibilities. He tried not to think about the consequences. They were doing this for their country, and wasn't that what he believed in?

He could see the changes in Zahar now that she was a mother. He was grateful for Laila, Leora, and the other women, who all supported each other. Theirs was a cohesive group, all working to the same end. Now that Laila was pregnant, Avraham thought she would need the women's support as well. When he looked at her, he saw what he suspected to be a slight change in enthusiasm for the project. Still, he was not her husband. It was up to Itzhak to rekindle that enthusiasm, not Avraham. As for him, he practiced restraint where Laila was concerned. Unfortunately, he couldn't control his dreams.

At dinner that evening, "What do you hear from Pardess Hanna?" Avraham asked Ari, pulling his thoughts away from Laila. Avraham was so hungry that, despite the caliber of food that was placed before him, he still devoured it. They had skipped lunch today in order to finish the factory. Tomorrow would be dedicated to working on a plan to dry out the basement.

"Leora writes mostly about the baby. They are preparing to leave Pardess Hannah as soon as we are finished with the factory." Ari emptied his second glass of water and reached for the metal pitcher. He refilled his and Avraham's glasses.

234

"They seem to be getting along well. She writes about the latest hostile raids on other kibbutzim, but assured me none of them were close by."

"Did Tal train any of the men left behind to continue the scouting missions?" asked Avraham, now picking at his food.

"No. I guess he decided it was best not to waste time training others, since we would be leaving soon."

"Probably a wise decision." Avraham finished eating and pushed his plate aside.

"We had more close calls during those expeditions, closer than I care to think about, especially when that imbecile decided to spray the woods with bullets. It's a good thing he didn't aim at the ground, because that would have been the end of it for all of us." Ari's body visibly shuddered.

"I don't even want to think about the possible consequences." Avraham stood—empty plate in hand. "I'd like to be settled, already. I'm excited about what we will be doing, but it still isn't permanent. I want to lay down some roots—be able to enjoy my family. I hear the same from Zahar. Tal has stopped by several times to check on them. That makes me feel better." He walked toward the kitchen; Ari followed. "I have to admit, I don't like being separated this long from Zahar and the baby."

"Neither do I," said Ari, his face revealed his concern. "Are we doing the right thing?"

###

The next morning, Pesach Abramovitz gathered the men to share Ari's suggestion which had been combined with his own in order to come up with the best plan of action to get rid of the high humidity in the factory. He went over the plans briefly as they would go into greater depth once Ari

The Laundry Room

shared his blueprints. "I have contacted *Ta'as,* and they are sending stoves to dry out the walls. They should be arriving within the next few minutes. I also sent for the bakery oven and the washing machine, so we can put them in place and camouflage the factory entrances. Yossi Nevo has designed the platforms upon which the machines will function. The oven will sit on a concrete base that will rise and glide on rails. We have calculated that we will need an opening there of 56x65 centimeters, by which to lower machinery. The washing machine will also sit on a concrete base, but swivel to the side for access. The opening there doesn't have to be large, just wide enough to let your people pass through. The washing machine will continue to work even when moved." Abramovitz wiped his brow. "Until the machines arrive, we will concentrate on dividing the area below and preparing the bases for the oven and washing machine. Ari, are your plans ready?"

"Yes, they are."

"Avraham, you and Ari go over the plans with the men. I will be with you in a moment." Abramovitz took one of his men aside and walked away.

As Ari looked for a place to lay down the plans, he shuffled through the many sets of blueprints until he found what he was looking for: the layout of the factory itself. As he pulled that particular plan from the pile, he cocked his head at the soulful sound of a train passing in the distance. "The Hill," the nickname the men had given their kibbutz, was only a few miles from the train station, and only a small knoll separated them from onlookers. Everyone stopped what they were doing and looked to Abramovitz for direction, since trains had passed so infrequently since they had arrived. Ari quickly folded up the plans, deciding not to share them until the men were underground.

Lynda Lippman-Lockhart

Abramovitz laughed. "You have nothing to fear from a bunch of animals headed for the Tel Aviv Zoo. The news reported the zoo had acquired its first giraffes." Moments later, spotted heads passed just above the knoll. The men couldn't help but laugh at the sight of long necks and small heads parading by. The levity of the situation brought with it a renewed vigor as the men went back to their jobs. It was just what they had needed.

Mounting the base for the brick oven ended up being a daunting task. The engineers had decided to incorporate its chimney into the air vent for circulation. That task would take some time to accomplish. One group of men went to work on it immediately. That was basically how they worked: someone would broach a problem, and someone else would come up with a solution. Many of their challenges could not have been foreseen; fortunately for them, Avraham thought, they had the brainpower to tackle just about anything.

While one group of men worked on preparing the oven, another group followed Avraham and Ari down the stairs that would be hidden under the washing machine directly above. Ari unfolded his blueprints and laid them on the floor. His eyes scanned the room and then his attention returned to the workers. "We have decided on eight rooms: the main hall for the stretching and cutting machines; a room for ovens, tubs, and chemical mixtures; the manager's office; metal works; a room for filling bullet cartridges—the assembly room; a shooting gallery for testing the bullets; a packaging room; and someplace to eat and to store gunpowder. Let's get started marking off the space."

The next few hours flew by as the crew worked on installing the washing machine and oven, until someone hollered down to Avraham that the dehumidifying heaters had arrived. The men climbed up the stairs, once again soaking wet from the humidity, and began unloading the heaters and lowering them below by using ropes as pulleys. It was a tedious task, taking most of the afternoon.

As the last piece of equipment was about to be unloaded, a vehicle careened down the road toward the kibbutz. The men stopped what they were doing and covered up the remaining machine, and nonchalantly stood in front of it and around the drive.

A British officer stepped out of his Jeep and looked around. He grabbed a crop from the side door and ran it across his palm, making sure everyone saw. He cut a dashing figure, with his mustache that curled around his nose and his single monocle.

The officer stepped forward, eyes locked on Pesach Abramovitz, who showed no sign of concern, and announced, "I'm here to inspect the kibbutz. I see you have made some progress how about showing me around?" Avraham blinked. The man really had spoken as if there was no punctuation to his sentences.

The men stood motionless. How much information had he garnered on the approach? This could be the end of their work and possibly the end of their lives, caught red-handed smuggling in machinery to make bullets.

Itzhak stepped forward. "Good afternoon. You must have ridden a long way. How about a beer? It's English."

The officer's brow furled, as if deciding whether it was wise to drink while on duty. He stood long enough for the men to break out into a sweat, but it appeared his thirst won out. He and his aide, a smaller version of his boss, followed Itzhak and Avraham into the dining room, chatting casually along the way. The men hurriedly unloaded the last piece of equipment while others kept watch.

When the officer reappeared, he was berating Itzhak. "I

had heard rumors of something brewing. It doesn't look like you've accomplished much."

Itzhak, who was quick thinking, had offered the two officers a warm beer. The commander took a sip and spit it out in site of those standing around.

"What's this? A hot beer? This is no way to treat your superiors."

Avraham could see his friend's mind working. Itzhak stepped closer to the officer. "Perhaps the next time, if you call ahead, we can send someone to Rehovot the day before your visit to get ice, and then the beer will be cooled to your taste when you arrive."

The officer slapped the crop against his thigh. "By George, what a splendid idea. Done." The second-in-command nodded, and with great fanfare, the two were off in a cloud of dust.

The men let go a collective sigh of relief. Avraham cuffed Itzhak on the back. "That was using your head. We now know who the diplomat is around here. From now on, you are in charge of handling the British!" They all laughed, patted Itzhak on the back, and returned to work. That story would be retold many times in the future when they needed a good laugh.

Chapter 27

Itzhak

Ayalon Institute, 1945

In the days that followed, the men encountered a number of problematic situations that had to be ironed out at the new kibbutz site before they could move in permanently and the women and children could join them. It was difficult enough to build an underground factory from scratch, but it was also necessary to find ways to conceal every aspect of the factory's operation as well. Yoel Ya'ari, a member of *Ta'as* and their electrician, had to devise a plan to counteract the overload of electricity to operate all the machinery. He was afraid the Anglo-Palestinian Electric Company would become suspicious of the power demand coming from their little kibbutz, so they told the electric company that they were also going to run a noodle factory, which needed more power than they thought. Itzhak helped construct a high-voltage pylon between the kibbutz and the orchard, with an underground cable that connected the kibbutz to the power source. A small room behind the bakery held the electrical panel to operate the current; and in order to move the giant washing machine aside to reveal the factory entrance, they added a hidden switch, which could be activated by inserting a stick into the outlet.

Many more innovative ideas were implemented to make the system work. The men had to be creative in their thinking, so that they could anticipate any unforeseen event that might crop up before it occurred. Fortunately, having some of the best minds in the country, and perhaps the world, at their service, the kibbutz was still ahead of the schedule imposed by the *Haganah*. Each time a problem arose, someone came up with an answer. Perhaps all their experience from poring over the *Torah*, questioning their interpretations, and discussing the possibilities had finally paid off.

After the first few days of actually living in their new quarters, Itzhak posed a question about sewage from the factory. "How will we dispose of our waste?" he asked at breakfast. "There may be times where we cannot leave the factory. Men and women will be working together."

"True," said Avraham. "We have to come up with a plan." A discussion ensued until it was time to go to work. Periodically during the day, one man or another would offer a suggestion, some of which were quite bizarre. Itzhak felt out of his element when it came to architecture and plumbing, but he still fielded suggestions. One of the men who had plumbing experience came up with the best plan, which he shared at lunch. "I say we install a pipe that hooks up with the existing plumbing, and have it empty somewhere deep in the orchard. That way it will be fertilizing the trees at the same time."

"Good idea," said Itzhak, finishing his meal, which he had devoured in minutes. There was little time to savor food, and

The Laundry Room

besides, it was not worth savoring in the first place. They should have made arrangements to bring an actual cook along, instead of having the men take turns. He couldn't wait to return home to enjoy Laila's cooking.

Itzhak had decided he was a very lucky man. His initial distrust had faded into the background. She had turned out to be a very loving person, and their time in bed was his favorite part of the marriage. She never ceased to amaze him with her little surprises ...

Itzhak suddenly realized he might be blushing, so he pushed those private thoughts to the back of his mind and focused on the present. "Let's get to work on the drawings." He called Ari over to the table. "What do you think of this?" The plumber went over his plans, and the small cadre of men decided it would work. The men then pored over the construction of such a system until they had to return to their tasks.

The group was now in its fifteenth day of construction and still ahead of schedule. The team worked like a well-oiled machine, and camaraderie was at an all-time high. Itzhak's initial misgivings were beginning to fade.

Days later, Yosef Avidar stopped by to monitor the progress of the factory's construction and catch the workers up on world events. He gathered them together in the shade of a eucalyptus tree, and held them in rapt attention throughout his report.

"We are making progress in our war for independence, but we can't let up our efforts to protect what appears to be the establishment of a Jewish state. We are so close, it is almost frightening; we have been working so long and so hard to accomplish our mission. It is more important than ever to finish the factory and get to work on supplying our military with its bullets. I commend you for your innovative ideas and the fact that you are days from completion. We, the *Haganah,* couldn't be more pleased with your progress. Any questions?"

Upon hearing the direction of Avidar's report, Itzhak knew what they were doing was more important than ever. The handwriting was on the wall; it was going to be up to them to see their dream of a Jewish state come into being.

"What about the British?" he asked.

"We see a relaxing of rules and regulations where the British are concerned. They have been turning a blind eye to many of our operations. They appear to have come to the opinion that we are not their enemies. It is true the British have proven to be an obstacle to Arab attempt to annihilate us, but more than once the British have seen the Arabs show their true colors: they cannot be trusted."

"Then why does what we are doing have to remain a secret?" asked Zalman.

"Because we cannot trust anyone, not even our own people. Strong drink loosens tongues, torture can bring forth information, and holding a man's children hostage will make him purge his very soul. What we are doing is to remain top secret. Do you understand?"

They nodded. Avidar had made his point.

"There is something else ... I hesitate to mention, but it will cement your resolve to keep this quiet. In January of 1942, the high command of the Reich met in Wanness, a suburb of Berlin, to discuss the 'Jewish issue' and what the Germans termed the 'Final Solution of the Jewish Question.' It turned out to be the calculated extermination of all European Jews, so that no one would be left to blame the Germans for what had happened. We heard rumors of such a meeting but never had proof until recently—never saw the decree in writing. So you see how important it is to make

The Laundry Room

sure we have a homeland where something like that can never happen again. No Jew should ever face a situation where he has nowhere to go."

Conversation picked up as Avidar strode back and forth before the group. Itzhak was disheartened but encouraged at the same time. He never could quite understand how human beings condoned the annihilation of a race or religion, even though he had studied war long and hard. He noted the sudden change in the men's voices as the reality of what they had just heard set in. So many of them had suffered at the hands of the Germans, and had prayed for America to get involved. But then, when America did get pulled into the war by the bombing of Pearl Harbor, it didn't seem like the conflict would ever end.

"*World War II* has come to an end, but our war is just beginning. Now it is up to us to make sure the land we have settledremains in our hands. That is why your job is so important. We are basically on our own. Oh sure, there are Americans and English who are supporting us monetarily, but they have no intention of coming over here to help us fight our war with the Arabs."

Itzhak stepped forward. "What I think I'm hearing you say is that *our* war will never end. We go from the Germans wanting us dead to the Arabs. I'm not sure which is worse."

"What is encouraging is that it seems the British and Americans are now on our side despite their own losses. However, to give you an example of what we can expect from the British, the *Struma,* a ship that should only have carried one hundred passengers, left the Black Sea on December 12,1941, with seven hundred sixty-nine Jewish, Romanian refugees, bound for Palestine—many of them children. As you well know, immigration had been closed to all Jews, so this was a dangerous plan, taken up by desperate people.

Before they left the port, the refugees were relieved of all their valuable possessions. The boat broke down several times before it had to be towed to the port of Istanbul, where it remained for two months. None of the passengers were allowed to disembark. Negotiations went back and forth between the Jewish Agency, the Foreign Office, the High Commissioner in Palestine, and the Turks. The *Jewish Agency's* plea to let the passengers continue on to Palestine was met with resistance from the High Commissioner in Palestine, as well as the Turks. When attempts to remove the children to Palestine failed, you can imagine the frustration and fright of the passengers. They were pawns in an unfortunate and inhumane war. Under pressure from the British, the Turkish government had the ship towed back out to the Black Sea, and the next day it was torpedoed by a Soviet sub and sank. We still do not know all of the ramifications of that massacre even after all this time."

Again voices were raised in anguish, hands wrung, eyes shut tight, and heads dropped to their chests. Itzhak was sick at heart. He couldn't believe what he was hearing. He wondered how many of the kibbutznik actually knew about this disaster. If Avidar was trying to spur them on, Itzhak thought, he had brought the right fuel. Most of the men had straightened up with new resolve.

"We are more determined than ever to get this project done as soon as possible, so we can begin our participation in this fight," said Avraham to the general. "If that is all you have to say, I suggest we get back to work."

Avidar nodded. "I could go on, but yes, by all means, return to your labor here. We are counting on you young people to help smash the resistance and establish our freedom. What has happened in Europe will never happen again, at least not in Palestine, if we have anything to say about it."

The men hurried back to their jobs, each with renewed enthusiasm fired by anger. If there had been any doubt in their minds about their mission, it had been erased forever.

In their discussions that night, they agreed not to mention the *Struma* debacle to their women. What purpose would it have served other than upsetting them?

The factory was completed in twenty-two days.

Chapter 28

Laila

The Alayon Institute, 1945

On February 12th, 1945, the first of the Pardess Hanna kibbutzniks arrived at what was to become their home for an undisclosed amount of time. Laila felt pangs of disappointment. Yes, their new home was somewhat better than the place they had left, but not by enough to outweigh the jeopardy they were putting themselves into. Laila kept reminding herself, while holding their son Dovele close to her breast, that they were doing this for their country. The sacrifice they were making was now as much for his freedom, as theirs; and Laila was sure those with new babies would agree.

Dovele, now three months old, had been a difficult birth. Laila had thought she would die before seeing her child, just like her mother had. After the ordeal was over, she was sure she would never give birth again. If it hadn't been for a nurse in Pardess Hanna, neither Dovele nor she would be making this trip. Watching Itzhak's strained face through the worst

The Laundry Room

of the delivery made her know she had to survive—if not for herself, then for him. She had seen life bleed out of his eyes. Afterward, Itzhak kept saying it was his fault. When it was made clear to him that she and the baby would live, he became more adamant about not continuing with their plans to establish the new kibbutz. He was ready to pull out and return to Jerusalem. Only by grueling persuasion, sometimes into the night, that Laila swayed him back to their original plan. She would not walk away from a commitment.

Several members of *Ta'as* met the new arrivals as they exited the bus and helped them get settled. Itzhak warmly greeted the men he recognized from working together on the factory.

One of the men picked up a valise Itzhak had carried off the bus and began walking toward the sleeping quarters. Itzhak, grabbed the man by the arm to stop him. "Laila, I'd like you to meet Pesach Abramovitz, who was instrumental in making this place livable. He was a big help from start to finish."

"So nice to meet you," said Laila, somewhat distracted by all that she saw. "I would like to see the children's quarters first, if you don't mind." Laila supposed she must have made an unfavorable impression from the start but she was more interested in where Dovele would be staying than where she and Itzhak would sleep. She could always find a way to make their quarters more habitable.

Pesach Abramovitz motioned Laila on. She and a few of the other mothers followed, while the rest of the weary travelers went in the opposite direction. Laila was pleasantly surprised. "How nice, a fresh coat of white paint; and I love the pink, blue, green, and yellow striped curtains." *At least they have two windows at either end of the building to let in the morning light,* thought Laila. It was difficult to make a solid stone building look happy; but the nurses, who had arrived earlier, had done their best. Two of Dovele's favorite nurses had come with them, so Laila felt better about the situation. Daphne took Dovele from Laila and lifted him into the air; he giggled.

"*Shana boychich*," she said, kissing him on the forehead. "Run along and get yourselves settled," Daphne said to the distraught women. "We can, at least, take the worry of the children off your hands."

Daphne was right; they did have things to do, and Laila no longer fretted about her son. He was in good hands. The other women deposited their children, and ventured out to find their husbands, who had been negotiating over who would get the best rooms.

Of course, Avraham would have first pick. As Laila was second-in-command, by virtue of title, Itzhak chose for them. She really didn't care. One was as good as another. Some of the other men would live in tents until additional buildings could be erected. Laila was curious to see where they would be working, and it wasn't long before she would find out.

After unpacking their Spartan belongings—they had disposed of anything that wasn't considered a necessity before leaving Pardess Hanna—Laila enveloped her husband in a tight squeeze. They kissed—savoring the little time they had to themselves—only to break apart when they remembered why they were there. Looking around, Laila accepted that they were down to the bare essentials. What did she need with heels, stockings, or dresses where they would be working? She had kept her wedding dress in a cloth cover and one or two other favorite outfits? She couldn't see much entertaining going on beyond simple gatherings. The kibbutzniks would probably be too tired anyway.

"This will work ... won't it?" Itzhak had asked, sulky

The Laundry Room

during the trip. He had held the baby most of the time, so Laila could get her rest. Even though youth had its advantages, she had not bounced back as hoped from the delivery, but she was sure she would before long. She was determined to do her part.

"I find myself second-guessing this decision," said Itzhak, about to leave the room.

"We will make it work," Laila reassured him, patting Itzhak's pale, gaunt face. They could be happy anywhere as long as they were together. "I know you would like to spend more time with the baby, but he is thriving and happy. We'll make the time we have together even more special."

"I know I always say this, but you're such an optimist." Itzhak hugged Laila back, and planted a sweet kiss on her forehead. His brow wrinkled as it often did when in a quandary; he kissed her again, but this time more deeply and with more passion. They remained locked in each other's arms until they heard conversation outside their room.

A knock interrupted the embrace. Ari and Leora entered and looked around. "Not any better than ours. We'll be meeting in front of the laundry room in ten minutes. Are you ready?"

"This can wait," said Itzhak, dropping something that Laila hadn't noticed he had in his hand. "Are you coming?"

"I'll be a minute. You go along." Laila stood in the middle of the room, gazing at what would become a constant challenge.

Leora hesitated, as if thinking she should stay, but must have understood that Laila wanted some time to herself. Sisters knew those kinds of things about each other, and they had become as sisters over time. Leora had come a long way, Laila thought. She had seen a new confidence in her after Leora gave birth. She was made to be a mother.

Left with her thoughts, Laila decided there was plenty of time to make changes. She had become a compulsive cleaner, something her mother—may she rest in peace—would not have believed. To make their room homier, she pushed the twin beds together as she had done in Pardess Hanna, folded hospital corners with the muslin sheets as she had been taught in the Scouts, threw a pale blue woolen blanket over the sheets, and arranged the yellow, pink and purple pillows she had found at the flea market in Rehovot for almost nothing—her only embellishment. Laila was happy they had stopped for a short tour of their closest city before coming here; several of the women, anticipating what they would find when they arrived, had purchased bright accents to add color to their drab surroundings.

Retracing her steps, Laila found Leora waiting for her on the patio. It was obvious Leora was as anxious as Laila about the next phase of their journey. For the moment, Laila realized Leora had become her lifeline to the outer world. Leora had been with Laila throughout her confinement and had brought her through the worst part of her labor. It had cemented their relationship. Leora took Laila's hand like schoolgirls: together, they entered the laundry room and faced their combined fate.

Itzhak made his way through the small, overcrowded room; Ari just behind. "A man called Lazar Yerman will be directing the tour," Itzhak whispered to Laila.

The laundry room was as austere as the rest of Kibbutz Hill. The floor and walls were cold, grey concrete and unembellished. Two rows of long, narrow, wooden benches, scuffed by time and abuse, lined the right wall of the rectangular room, almost making it look like a small meeting room. Two vintage sewing machines—complete with treadles —sat across from the benches, waiting for someone to crank

The Laundry Room

them back into action. Beyond them, a monstrous tub of a washing machine reminded them why it was called the "laundry room." Behind the fifteen-ton washer, in the corner, stood a copper water heater with pipes leading in every direction—an octopus came to mind, although Laila had never seen one in person—and to its right sat two huge vats to boil clothes. Overall, the room was depressing. Again, Leora squeezed Laila's hand.

Lazar went on and on, trying to impart information that Laila found tedious and disinteresting. The kibbutzniks were all anxious to see why they were there, not have to listen to a never-ending lecture.

Finally, Lazar opened a cabinet door and pushed something. Even though some of the group knew about the secret compartment, the other anxious onlookers watched in shock as the grey, hulking washing machine actually began to swivel to the right, rotating away from what Laila expected to be its permanent position. Instead, a gaping hole appeared in the floor, revealing a staircase leading down to the floor below. Laila felt faint. The reality of their mission finally sank in. She was happy to work for her country, but down there?

"It's important we practice descending quickly to the floor below," Lazar admonished. "Watch your footing, but do not hesitate. The quicker, the better. Your lives could depend upon it."

Hearing those words only added to Laila's apprehension. Again, she consciously asked herself if they had made the right decision, to join this project. It seemed she was doing that more these days, and she was supposed to be one of the leaders. But now, all Laila could think was that she had jumped in without taking a child into consideration. With youth came idealism and passion; now, however, she had been given a great deal of responsibility. Laila stood watching her comrades' expressions as they realized that what Lazar had said was the absolute truth. From here onward, every decision the kibbutzniks made meant life or death.

In record time, the men disappeared down the hole, while the women examined the mechanism that swiveled the machine on its track. Leora was first to take the plunge. Her marriage and subsequent motherhood had changed her from a frightened mouse to an assertive tiger. Laila thought that the change in her confidence would help her cope with what lay ahead.

Sophie was next, followed by Yehudith, and then Laila, who was watching every step. Carmel was right behind. Laila was impressed by the men's ability to manage the twenty-five foot spiral ladder without a mishap; she wasn't sure she would be able to manage. Half of the way down, her thoughts came to a standstill as Carmel's foot slipped, landing on Laila's shoulder. Laila clenched the ladder with one hand, and with the other, tried to reposition Carmel's foot onto the rung. The thought of both of them tumbling to the hard floor below spurred Laila to use every ounce of strength she had left. It didn't help that she was claustrophobic and afraid of heights, and most importantly, still recovering from a difficult birth.

Feeling her hand lose its grasp as Laila's own foot slipped onto Yehudith's shoulder instead of the rung, Laila flailed about trying desperately to readjust her position. When she thought she could not hold on another second, she felt Carmel's weight lift; but it was too late as Laila's hands, feeling like they were on fire, let go and she fell the rest of the way, landing on Sophie and Yehudith. Itzhak was there in a flash and tried to catch her, but failed. He managed to lift her off the two women sprawled on the floor, and carried her away from what could have been a disaster.

"Are you all right? What happened?" Itzhak asked, holding her tight, as if he was afraid she might break into a thousand pieces.

Laila fought back tears. She couldn't let the others see her like this, as she was one of the leaders—one of the ones they looked to for strength. "Carmel lost her balance. Her foot was pushing down on my shoulder, and I lost my grip. Are Yehudith and Sophie all right?" Laila stared at her raw, red hands, and blew on them to ease the pain.

Hearing her question, Yehudith answered for both of them. "We're fine; just a little shaken up. What a beginning!" The group laughed, lifting the embarrassment off the women.

Rivka, a size larger than Carmel waited till last. Now more reluctant than ever, she had to be cajoled into going down the steps.

"Come on, Rivka; you can do it," they all chanted.

"I don't know. What if I get stuck?"

"You'll be fine. There's plenty of room," said Itzhak in his most encouraging voice.

Laila was a bit leery about Rivka's descent because of her weight, but with many loving hands, the other woman made it. It occurred to Laila, though, that Rivka's talents might be used elsewhere.

With little space to stand, the expectant workers crowded in next to each other like a pack of camels at a watering hole. Menacing machines lined the walls of the long, narrow room. Everything seemed to be long and narrow. She didn't know what she had expected, but the place was clean and so was the air. For some reason, Laila had pictured it as dank and dark. Instead, there was plenty of lighting from florescent bulbs overhead.

For all that it was clean and well-lit; the factory was still essentially a tomb. This was going to be their workspace, but for how long? It had never occurred to her in her childhood, that someday she would be operating a machine that made bullets. She cringed.

As Laila reached for Itzhak's hand, she asked herself if she would be able to spend eight hours a day down there, devoid of sunlight and her son. Reassuringly, Itzhak squeezed back and kissed the nape of her neck, his favorite spot. No one noticed as all eyes were on the room.

Tal Rabin had been waiting for them below. He must have been there for moral support. Laila noticed that his hair had begun turning grey at the temples, and age lines had formed at the outer edges of his eyes. This project had aged him considerably, she thought worriedly. What would it do to them?

"*Shalom,*" Tal said with the utmost enthusiasm. "You have a lot to learn in a short period of time, so let's get started. You've met Lazar. He will be first in command, until you feel secure enough to handle the factory yourselves. From what I've seen, that won't take long."

Laila wondered if he was trying to win them over with flattery. She took a deep breath. It wasn't what she had expected. It was clean and not musty. Apparently Lazar read her mind.

"I see some of you already sniffing the air. Not bad, is it? We can thank Yossi Nevo, who physically carried out Engineer Olshinsky's original plans for the aeration of the building. Olshinsky managed to work out the air exchange with the two chimneys on either end of the building." He pointed to one of them. "One takes in air, while the other expels it. For those of you needing a technical explanation, see me later." Some caught on and laughed.

Clever, thought Laila. Once again, brilliant minds at work. Itzhak had recounted the details of the building of the factory when he returned to Pardess Hanna, but with no experience in architecture, Laila had found it difficult to appreciate what she was now seeing for herself. Suddenly she felt a whole lot better. Glancing around the room, she noted a change in posture of those who hadn't been a part of the building of the factory. No more stiff shoulders. People were now leaning forward, enthusiastically listening to what Lazar had to say. Where there had been resistance, she saw what she believed to be honest enthusiasm.

"I know you are probably thinking the air smells good right now, but what about while you're working? Nothing to worry about. It will be cleansed eight times an hour. If it turns out that that isn't good enough, we'll increase it." Lazar walked to the left side of the building. "We'll take a look at the bakery and the moveable ten-ton brick oven later. That was the entry port for the large machines, as most of you already know, and exit for repair and replacements."

"I noticed some of you examining the floor," Lazar said as he raised a foot to stomp on it. "We spared no expense. You will be using elevated shoes to protect you from the metal shavings and dust. We realize you will be on your feet for long periods of time, so we had a special floor designed to add cushion and eliminate some of the strain." Lazar stopped for a moment as if to let them take in what he had just said. Then he continued. "An old Yemenite from Petah Tikva kissed the ground when he was brought down here and told what would be going on. He promised to keep our secret, and to make a floor you could live with. I believe he did it. Tomorrow we will begin training. You are all to be here ready to go at seven. You each will learn to work all of the machines —just in case, even though some of you might never come down here again. We need workers above, too. It doesn't matter. You will decide who does what. I understand that you have a pretty good system in place already. That will help."

"What is the square footage of the room?" asked Schmuel, one of the men who had stayed behind in Pardess Hanna to help the women.

Lazar cleared his throat. "It measures ... thirty-three meters, or one hundred eight feet long, and five meters, or sixteen feet, wide. That is three hundred square yards, not feet," said Lazar, checking his facts on the clipboard. "The walls are two feet thick all around, and we are thirteen feet below the ground. Of course those working on the factory probably could have told you that."

Laila's mind began to wander. Instead of listening to what Lazar had to say, she took another look at the layout. She could not believe it took so many machines to make a single bullet. How was she ever going to learn how to operate them all?

"On the right are the machines, tubs, and vats for mixing chemicals." Then he pointed to a small office. "All business will take place in that room away from the filings and debris." He walked on. They followed. "That is the metal-works room, a room for filling bullet cartridges—assembly style; the shooting gallery for testing the bullets; a packaging room; and a dining area and storeroom for the gunpowder we will be using to make the bullets. We even stocked a library for breaks." A buzz of conversation followed.

Laila had never worked in a factory, but she had spent time at Abba's warehouse where they stocked and cleaned the carts.

The Laundry Room

"What about these machines?" asked Zalman. "They look pretty old."

"There is a story associated with those machines. Would you like to hear?"

Lazar did not need much prompting. "Around 1938, a very astute acquisitions director of the *Haganah*, Yehuda Arazi, went to Europe in search of weapons and ammunition. In Warsaw, he came upon a warehouse that contained old ammunition-making machines, not being used. He made a deal with the owner of the warehouse, who practically gave them away, selling them for the price of scrap iron. The machines were secretly moved to an abandoned factory in the city for repairs. Polish workers were hired, secretly, to work on the machines. One night while Arazi and his aide Katriel Katz were at the factory, the Polish police showed up, demanding a search of the premises. Arazi asked for a search warrant, which the officer did not have and asked to speak to his commander. The officer, fearing he had stepped into a hornet's nest, contacted his superior, who was at a party. Arazi, using his most official voice, berated the Polish commander for disturbing him at his 'home' and said 'this might create undesirable complications.' The commander asked what those complications were and Arazi said, 'I am not permitted to tell you anything more.' Knowing the factory belonged to a secret department of the army, the commander backed off. Arazi asked for several days to notify his superiors. The time was granted, and Arazi removed all papers, and the machines were shipped elsewhere. When the commander returned, there was nothing left to question. After that the machines traveled from Danzig to Antwerp on their way to the *Haganah,* but someone got wind of the transmission and reported it to the authorities."

"Did they ever find out who gave them away?" asked

Zalman.

"Not exactly, but Arazi's group managed to divert the ship and its cargo to Beirut."

"How did they do that," asked Leora, seemingly interested in the story.

"A young Jewish woman, named Shoshana, worked in the British Intelligence Center in Jerusalem. She managed to retrieve a copy of a secret telegram, whose message seemed questionable. It said something about a factory in Poland assembling thirty-four bullet making machines being packed and sent with an engineer named Walter to the *Haganah*. The British were asked to nab Walter and hold him for questioning. It seems 'Walter' was the code name for Yehezkel Baram who traveled with the machines. Shoshana contacted *Shai, the Haganah Intelligence Service*, with the information. It was Yosef Avidar and Aharon Ironi who received the message, sending it on to Yisrael Galili. He was a friend of Colonel Weiss of the Polish Headquarters. So Galili contacted Weiss, stating they had, in fact, shipped machinery capable of making bullets and it would not sit well with the British if they found out this machinery came from Poland. Colonel Weiss contacted the British, who immediately ordered the *Levant* to be boarded at port. Colonel Weiss also contacted *Shai* to tell them what he had done, giving them the head start on making other plans. Colonel Weiss determined where the machines might be diverted and arranged contact with the ship's captain, who then altered the course, landing in Beirut."

"What a story," Laila said, feeling more confident by the minute they were in good hands.

"That is not even the end of the story; however. I'll tell you the rest some other time."

Lazar's eyes rolled upward and to the left, as if going back to the actual building of the factory. "Now, as you well know, we had a number of challenges along the way that we've since worked out; one of which was the excessive use of electricity." He gazed around the room, eyes contacting with the men who had been involved with the building of the factory. "One of our brilliant minds came up with the idea of tapping into a transformer located in the orange groves and stealing power from our British friends." Laila knew that brilliant mind to be Itzhak's.

Lazar pointed out specifics as they continued their tour. His stories, for the most part, took the edge off their nervousness over what they would be doing and made the job seem more interesting than it might have been. Laila could feel her own muscles relaxing. Even Leora's shoulders had gone slack.

No, Laila had never pictured herself making bullets; or at least, not standing next to her husband in an underground cavern. At first, she had let Dovele be her excuse for feeling ambivalent, but the wave of enthusiasm from the rest of the kibbutzniks and the reminder of how important their job was to the security of their country, the more she had been swept up by the cause. It was obvious to her that Itzhak was enthusiastic and ready to begin.

Chapter 29

Ari

Ayalon Institute, 1945

Mixed emotions loomed over the forty-five in the morning; few had slept well. The heightened excitement from the previous day had driven most of their apprehension away, but what was left was enough to make them cautious. Silence was served with breakfast instead of the usual morning buzz. Couples, normally chatty, ate quietly, eyes focused on their food instead of searching out their best friends. Ari nudged Leora to finish her eggs and the banana bread she had made before they left. She had dawdled throughout the meal, moving the food in circles around on her plate.

"Sweetheart," said Ari, "what is the matter? Are you having second thoughts?" He hugged her. "If you get down there and decide it is not for you, you can do something aboveground. Everyone's job is important here, whether you are working below or somewhere else. You know that." He gave her an extra squeeze. "We all have to take some part in

The Laundry Room

is an important task." He pushed his glasses, which always managed to end up at the tip of his nose, back in place.

"I don't know." Leora tucked a few stray hairs under her kerchief and finished the last bite.

Ari hated that she had cut her beautiful tresses so they would not get in the way. She had the most beautiful hair of any girl he had ever known—like the sands of the Mediterranean and lush. Sometimes it looked like a ball of twine gone wild. He often lost himself in it, not wanting to find his way out. Laila's hair was blond like straw, Zahra's was as black as night, but Leora's hair was like no one's he'd ever seen before. "Try not to upset yourself. It will all work out." He patted her hand.

Leora lovingly ran the palm of her hand across Ari's face. "You always say the right thing." She smiled. "I'm fine. It's being away from Muttel so much that bothers me."

"When he is a grown man, he will be proud that you served your country." Ari stood, picked up Leora's and his trays and headed for the kitchen. Leora followed.

Outside, the others congregated in front of the laundry room, waiting for Lazar Yerman to show up. The days were getting hotter, earlier. Lazar and the other volunteers from *Ta'as* had taken up residence in Rehovot, until such time as they felt comfortable enough to turn the factory over to their students. Ari and the other men had stayed in Rehovot as well, during the time the factory was being built and the kibbutz added to. There was a small installation of British soldiers living and working there, too. Ari remembered how difficult it had been to explain their activities during that time. What he noticed was that the soldiers often politely pretended not to notice what they were actually doing. He had heard of the difficulties the British were having with the Arabs.

"Good morning," said Lazar, as he stepped out of his Jeep. "Everyone ready to do some laundry?" He winked. Some eyebrows rose.

Several of the men had volunteered to act as guards when they were not working below. They posted themselves at the entrance of the kibbutz so that they could warn the others of intruders. The group had practiced drills the night before, in case the British showed up. The kibbutz would operate as any other self-sustaining business, choosing one specialty while growing their own crops and providing sustenance for their members. Ari was impressed by the planning that had gone into the preparations for making this a viable kibbutz. So far, they had thought of everything. It was the everyday living that brought with it potential problems.

"Gather 'round," said Lazar. "We will descend as we did yesterday—men first. I would like to see the women beat yesterday's time. Timing is most important."

Someone pushed a button and the fifteen-ton washing machine began to swivel on its axis. Ari still found the concept a marvel. Who would think? The men disappeared quickly as before. When it was the women's turn, this time Rivka, who was working on losing weight, went first, followed by Leora and Laila. They were down in no time, patting themselves on the back while receiving praise from Lazar.

"You will notice some new faces this morning. These men are trained in the use of the machines. One will be posted at each. The instructors will work with a small group until at least one member of the group feels confident. I will give you fifteen minutes at each post. When we finish for the day, please decide which machine you prefer. There will be days when someone is sick and needs a replacement; that is why all of you must know how to operate every machine.

The Laundry Room

Remember, this is the only munitions factory producing bullets for the Sten gun across our territory."

Ari thought about what Lazar had just said. The pressure was on them to produce. He now understood how important it was that they do their job and do it well. He watched as small groups formed around different machines, and noticed the intensity of each individual as they watched the demonstration. Ari, Leora, Avraham, Zahar, Itzhak, and Laila stood at the shooting gallery, the last stage in the assembly of the bullet. It was here the bullets would be discharged. The room was made soundproof so as not to disturb the others inside the factory, nor to be heard above. It was also one of the most volatile rooms in the factory. If a person was at all claustrophobic, this would not be their first choice.

A short, wiry man of about forty, waited for them to get settled. "Hello. My name is Irwin Eisenberg. As you can imagine, this is a very important part of the bullet-making process. If the bullet fails here, the whole process must be redone. The test-firing area also holds the biggest risk. You will need someone with a steady hand and strong constitution. If you are the least bit squeamish, I suggest you try your hand elsewhere.

"Please note the red light above the counter on the left. If someone outside the kibbutz pays a visit, this light will go on and all work will cease. In order to drown out the noise from below, the washer and drier will be in use all day and possibly all night."

The six leaned in to hear what Irwin had to say. "What are we using for gunpowder?" asked Itzhak.

"Cordite. It was developed by the British some time before the nineteenth century, to take the place of gunpowder. They were looking for a smokeless propellant

264

and a low explosive. It works best for our situation."

Questioning glances passed between the women. Ari knew Leora would not be a good candidate for any of this. He could see it in her frightened eyes and stiff body. Although she had made great strides in conquering her fears over the past year, he knew this particular part of the process would be a test for her; and if she couldn't do it, he would make sure she would find another area to be of help. He didn't think firing a bullet was for him either, but he was determined not to show his own fear. He was sure he would find his station by the end of the day.

"Please watch carefully as I load the bullets, aim, and pull the trigger," said Irwin going through the motions, and causing the women's bodies to jerk several times, like an electric shock had shot through their bodies, each time a bullet was discharged.

One by one, the six were handed a primitive-looking Sten submachine gun and asked to shoot. Before aiming, Ari had to adjust his glasses again. *I need to have the frames fixed,* he muttered to himself, so they wouldn't keep creeping down his nose. He had tried his hand at fixing them and had almost broken them.

Ari took aim and squeezed the trigger. To his embarrassment, the gun bounced around in his hands, splaying bullets in all directions. Laila was next. Surprisingly, she handled the weapon like she'd been born to it. After the first few shots, she did not flinch at all. Ari saw pride in Itzhak's eyes. She was tough, for someone so young. Leora went next. Her hands shook as she attempted to take aim. Her relief was obvious when she finished. Ari patted her shoulder in sympathy.

"Why the Sten gun?" asked Laila.

"Ah, a thinking woman," said Irwin, directing his

The Laundry Room

explanation toward her. "We were able to confiscate hundreds of those guns, left behind by the British after skirmishes with the Germans or the Arabs. The ammunition was not as easy to come by, though, because it usually accompanied the person who dropped his gun and took flight. The gun is lightweight and easy to use, and readily available. We have thousands of them."

Their time was up and they moved to the first step of the process: the copper sheeting. Here, a short, ruddy older man waited for them to assemble around him. "My name is Saul Fromkin, and I will be showing you how to form the shells." He began by separating the copper sheets and laying one on the makeshift table, demonstrating how to cut it into strips to form the casings.

Ari was fascinated by Saul's expertise. His hands worked like a surgeon's, manipulating the sheet as if it were a layer of skin instead of a heavy, unbending piece of copper. Before long, the sheet had been dissected down to bullet sized wrappers.

Saul put each of his students through the wringer until they showed the ability to proceed to the next machine. He reminded them that the machines were antiques, abandoned by the Germans and purchased from Poland. Saul said the people who sold them must have thought they were going into a museum for display.

Ari came to understand that each process had its own machines and its own expertise. It would take time to become familiar enough to feel competent with what they were doing. It also never left his mind that one mistake anywhere in the process would mean disaster. It became clear being "the chosen" kibbutz for this operation definitely had its drawbacks.

The morning progressed until they were called to lunch.

Ari could not believe how quickly the time had passed. He was beginning to believe he wouldn't mind working down there, given the intensity of their job. He followed Leora up the stairs and to the nursery to play with Muttel. They would eat lunch together.

The child giggled when he saw Ari and Leora enter the room. It was Ari who received the heartiest greeting. Ari knew Leora did not mind because when Muttel did not feel well, he was all hers. Ari scooped the boy up and swung him above his head. Muttel giggled again. Ari brought him down to the floor and tickled him in his stomach, and the child giggled even louder.

Muttel was growing daily and would be tall and lanky like Ari. He was smart too, already ahead of the other children his age. Of course, Ari wasn't partial; he smiled to himself at the thought.

The nursery was the cleanest room in the kibbutz. The nurses were adamant that the children would be free from germs. Schedules were posted at the start of each day, so parents could visit without interrupting the children's routine. At first Ari had balked at not having his child with him at night, but seeing how well the children got along and behaved, he was inclined to go along with the setup. He knew, however, that Leora missed Muttel miserably.

This afternoon, he would suggest she not go below, but help in the nursery instead. He would miss having her by his side, but it was far safer above ground. If something should happen to him, at least Leora would be there for the child. He now realized how important his parents had been. Like most children, he had taken them for granted. He hoped Muttel wouldn't.

While they were in the nursery, Laila and Itzhak came for Dovele. "Why don't you bring Muttel and join us for lunch under the eucalyptus trees?" said Laila, cradling her son. "The children can play after we eat."

"What a wonderful idea," said Leora. "My head is spinning from all the instructions. Will we ever be able to run the factory by ourselves?"

Itzhak took Dovele from Laila, buried his nose in the child's sweet neck, and then reached for Laila's hand. "They are counting on us. The more we do, the better we'll be at it. Remember, if you want to fry an egg—you have to break the shell first."

The other three looked at Itzhak like they couldn't believe what he had just said.

Leora shook her head. "I don't know about that ... the part about getting better at doing something with practice, not the breaking egg thing."

Laila hugged Leora. "Say, why don't you consider working in the bakery or nursery, if you don't feel comfortable down there? It would be just as important. We have to project an image of normalcy, and you are such a wonderful mother. I would feel better knowing you were with Dovele."

Ari had a feeling he knew what Laila hadn't said. There was such a strong possibility they could blow themselves up, and then where would the children be?

"I've thought long and hard about it, believe me," said Leora, "but I did not want anyone to think I was a coward."

Laila leaned over and kissed Leora's cheek. "Nonsense, you will be doing the most important job of all, and I know the other women will be thrilled."

Ari watched the stress lines fade from his wife's face. This had been such a strain on her, especially with her aunt's failing health. Leaving Leora's aunt, Mrs. Malkin, had been difficult, knowing they would not see each other for perhaps years. Ari and Leora had talked into the night about the separation; and often, Ari questioned their decision.

Without warning, a blast of Yiddish music blew out of the loud speakers, alerting the kibbutzniks that someone was approaching. Ari heard the crunch of tires before he saw the vehicle. That had been another innovative measure: covering the road with gravel to alert the kibbutz of unwanted visitors. This was a truck—a British army truck. Those who had just exited the factory picked up rakes, hoes, and pitchforks, or took down a set of the dry, camouflage sheets from the clotheslines in front of the laundry room. Thank God they were above ground.

Two men climbed down from the truck, rifles drawn. They walked with authority toward the laundry room; the group gasped. Had they been discovered? What then? Leora started to say something; Ari grabbed her arm and shook his head.

The men approached Lazar, and time stood still. What were probably only seconds seemed like hours. Ari couldn't hear what was said, but a verbal exchange proceeded between the officers and Lazar. Lazar moved forward in an aggressive manner. Irwin joined him. More exchange. Lazar shook his head; Irwin raised his palms and shrugged. Lazar and Irwin took a step backward. The officers spoke heatedly and with conviction. Lazar and Irwin seemed to be answering their questions until the British officers laughed, shook their heads, and left.

When the truck was out of sight, the kibbutzniks converged upon Lazar and Irwin.

"What was that all about?" asked Ari, clutching Leora's hand.

"They were sent to find out why we had ordered so much copper," said Irwin, a big grin spread across his face.

The Laundry Room

"And what did you tell them?" asked Laila.

"That we made lipstick cases for kosher women, and that we needed a lot because that was part of our religion. I told them we would be happy to give samples when we were up and running. I hope God will forgive me about the 'religious' part."

Laughter broke out amongst the group. The men slapped Irwin on the back. His chest pumped out like an excited baboon.

Ari hoped the officers had not looked too closely at the women standing around ... none of them were wearing lipstick.

Chapter 30

Laila

Ayalon Institute, after lunch

All afternoon, the kibbutzniks worked with their mentors, establishing a routine until they became proficient at their stations. Laila was growing weary of the monotony of her tasks and allowed her mind to wonder over the past few years and how she had wound up a married woman. After all, she was barely twenty-two. Laila thought about the other women and how quickly they had all grown up, leaving vestiges of their childhood behind. Someone, not realizing Laila was miles away, gave her a nudge; and as she attempted to load the cordite into its chamber, a small bit of powder trickled down the side of the shell and onto her fingers. She froze. "Itzhak?" she cried.

Itzhak's eyes were as big as saucers, yet it seemed he was unable to move; while Laila's body shook uncontrollably, her eyes imploring Itzhak to help her. She was frightened the powder would burn her fingers. Would perspiration ignite the powder and blow them up? Laila was petrified. She was

271

The Laundry Room

Irwin, the firing room instructor, simply grabbed a rag and wiped the debris away. Laila looked up at him, grateful for handling the problem so easily. She was amazed at how something that looked so harmless could put the fear of God in all of them.

"You're okay. No harm done," Irwin said, patting her shoulder. "Let's get back to work."

Now that a "worst" had happened, would it be possible to relax enough to continue? Would she be more mindful of what she was doing in the future? Whatever the case, Laila decided not to dwell on the accident and get on with her job. She was, however, disturbed by Itzhak's inability to act. He had been transformed into a pillar of salt. Would he handle all crises like this?

As the panic died down, everyone went back to practicing their tasks, until their fingers ached and their backs screamed. Discussion flowed steadily, even when they couldn't hear what the others were saying. Between the hammering, the pounding, and the muffled rat-tat-tat of the machine gun, those silent moments that managed to creep into their midst were looked upon as a blessing.

At some point in the day, Zahar broke out in song—an old Russian folk tune reminiscent of days gone by. After the first chorus, the rest of the workers joined in, as the kibbutzniks needed something to take their minds off the consequences of their actions. Zahar's soprano voice soared above them all. It turned out they were a family of frustrated opera singers.

Oy, a nakht a sheyn
Di nakht iz geven azoy sheyn.
Oyf a benkele zaynen mir gezesn.
Di levone hot genumen avekgeyn.

272

Lynda Lippman-Lockhart

Oh, what a beautiful night!
That night was so beautiful.
We sat on a bench.
The moon began to fade away ...

During a break, Carmel, who had been Laila's roommate and who had revealed her harrowing story of escape during one of their bonfires, followed Laila into the empty office and unburdened her heart to Laila. "I'm really lonely," she said, her eyes pools of sorrow. "I'm not sure I can do this every day without someone to come home to, like you and Itzhak. I'm thinking of leaving." She sighed, her face awash with despair.

"I'm so sorry. I didn't realize." Laila motioned for the two of them to sit in the empty chairs on either side of a small table piled with papers. "We've all been so preoccupied with learning our tasks," said Laila, taking Carmel's hand in hers, "it didn't occur to me there was time enough to be lonely. What about Schlomo? He's a nice man ... never married ... very competent. Do you have an interest in him or anyone else in particular?"

"I like Schlomo well enough, but he doesn't know I'm alive. It's Yosef Avidar I'm interested in."

To say the name caught Laila off guard was an understatement. She was shocked. Carmel must be a fool to think Yosef Avidar would be interested in her. He had never stayed at the kibbutz long enough to form any attachments, which told Laila that, unless he was married to the military, he was already committed.

"I believe he has a family," Laila said cautiously. She didn't know that for a fact, but she couldn't imagine such a man remaining single. "Has he given you any reason to believe he was interested?"

"Not exactly."

"What do you mean *not exactly*?"

Carmel began twisting her handkerchief into a knot. Her eyes were directed at the floor. "He personally spoke to me at the last meeting."

Oh, my, thought Laila. She was reaching. "I think you might want to consider someone more your age ... someone you could have children with ... share your interests."

Carmel's eyes focused back on Laila. "But we share this place in common."

"How many times have you seen him since we left Pardess Hanna or arrived here? This mission of ours is just a side track for him. Please reconsider. What about Yussel Epstein, or ... ? I can tell you from experience, Schlomo's a good man and he's a big help in the kitchen."

Laila thought she might have come up with a good substitute.

"He's so shy. He never talks to me. They are all nice men, but I want Yosef."

"Let me see what I can do. I am not promising anything, mind you. What we are doing is very important, and I know you will be sorry later if you leave. What will you go back to?"

"Nothing. We'll see." Carmel's head dropped back to her chest as she rose and scurried out of the room.

Itzhak entered. "What was that all about?"

"Woman talk," said Laila, hunching her shoulders. She thought Carmel would be embarrassed if Itzhak knew what the two of them had been discussing. Being deceitful was not in Laila's nature, but hadn't it been "women talk" after all?

"I know you well enough not to push. If and when you want to tell me, you will." He kissed her on the neck, massaged her shoulders, and went back to his machine.

Laila sat pondering what she would be doing if Itzhak were not in her life. She would be lonely—probably miserable. Okay, so he wasn't perfect. Well, neither was she. She guessed marriage was a series of compromises until both people were content to move on to the next challenge. Alright, so sometimes Itzhak could be vague, like a wire sent over an angry sea, a garbled message; weak, unintelligible. Other times, however, he was clear as a bell, making his feelings resonate. Laila's girlfriends were her sanity, but Itzhak ... well, he was something else ... her love and happiness. And so with that warm feeling in mind, Laila was determined to find someone for Carmel.

At the end of the day, the workers stopped; someone pushed the button to open the door, and they all lined up to check their clothes and shoes for telltale signs that might reveal what they had been doing. Luckily all of the original forty-five members from Pardess Hanna were still there, along with the *Ta'as* volunteers. Although it was just them right now, there would come a time when there would be others living with them who were not privy to their activities. The tired kibbutzniks climbed the stairs for dinner and some fresh air. For now it was okay to be a little slack, but that time was coming to an end.

###

At dinner, one night shortly after they had begun their real work, Rivka stopped by Laila and Itzhak's table. "I'm worried about the noise coming from below. Is there anything you can do to muffle it?"

If Rivka was hearing the noise, Itzhak and Laila agreed, something had to be done and quickly.

"What about using mattresses to pad the area under the

washing machine?" Laila said, thinking out loud. She was embarrassed to say Itzhak and she had used the spare mattress in their room to block out the sounds of their lovemaking. Itzhak must have known what she was referring to and blushed—something he rarely did.

Covering his embarrassment, Laila continued before Rivka caught on. "I'll find out from Irwin if there is a mattress-maker nearby—perhaps in Rehovot; if so, we can have him make the mattresses to our specifications."

"Won't that draw suspicion?" Rivka asked. She was always worried they would be discovered. Actually they all were, but none so much so as Rivka.

Two days later, Ezra drove Laila in a horse-drawn cart to Rehovot. Itzhak was needed in the factory. Irwin had located a mattress-maker in the less fashionable section of town—a man who could keep his mouth shut. Laila was hoping he might be hungry enough not to ask questions.

On the ride to Rehovot, Ezra seemed pensive. "How do you manage spending all those hours underground, and being a mother?"

Laila was surprised at Ezra's question. Had he heard something? They had been working so hard since their arrival that she didn't think anyone had time to think. How was she managing? Well enough, Laila thought. Itzhak and she felt they had a purpose, working toward the establishment of their country: a country where others could live free to practice their religion the way they saw fit; a place where they would not fear being rounded up and shot. Laila supposed she was a bit idealistic, but she also knew it took idealism to make change.

"I am managing well. To be honest, I don't think about it

much. I'm happy with my life. I have everything I ever wanted—" She stopped abruptly. Hadn't she wanted to go to college and become something? On the other hand, she was young; she could still pursue a career after this mission was fulfilled—well, if she didn't get blown to pieces first. She had a beautiful son and a wonderful husband. Yes ... she was doing well. "And what about you?"

"I suppose I am fine. I would be better if Anna would agree to marry me. I don't know why she hesitates. We are getting along so well and working together each day without arguing. I love her with all my heart, but I sometimes doubt her devotion."

"Some women need more time. Don't push. If you do, you will surely lose her. Isn't it enough that you are together?"

"Would that be enough for you?"

Laila thought about Ezra's question. "No, I guess it wouldn't. I wish things were different for you. She'll come around, I just know it."

Ezra enveloped Laila in a brotherly hug. "Just being able to talk about it helps."

Laila patted his shoulder. "Anytime." They rode the rest of the way in silence. With nothing but time on her hands, Laila took the opportunity to examine the landscape, which was dry and barren. Why was it so difficult to make this area green? She realized the rain had a lot to do with it, and they had no real irrigation system in place, but the plots of land they had cultivated were doing fine. Their kibbutz worked hard each day, making a little headway in creating their own bit of Eden, knowing someday they would leave it behind for someone else. So that no one bore the brunt of the responsibilities, the kibbutzniks had instituted a system whereby the duties would be rotated weekly. That way, everyone could split their time between working above and

The Laundry Room

below ground. It would be interesting to see how long that lasted, with the escalation of efforts to gain their independence.

Following Irwin's direction, Laila and Ezra arrived at the shop, which resembled "The Hill": old, and in poor shape. Rain hadn't graced this part of the world in months, and the soil cracked and flaked wherever they stepped. Today Laila wore a sleeveless blouse, long skirt, and sandals because of the intense heat. She could almost picture the exodus of their ancestors, crossing the Sinai on their way to the *Promised Land*, hoping to find an oasis along the way. Despite the heat, she was happy for a break in her routine.

The limestone building, damaged in parts from being bombed repeatedly or stained by desert sands, was worse for wear. A mongrel rested alongside the open door: one eye open and one ear erect. He wasn't exactly a watchdog, because he wasn't barking, more a silent warning to those who might bring harm to his master. Ezra and Laila kept their distance as they entered the building. Laila had learned early not to be fooled by an unresponsive dog. One had surprised her when she was five, and she still carried the scars. She had also learned that if you don't appear scared, most dogs will leave you alone.

"Hell-oo-oo," she called assertively. Most men found it difficult to take her five foot-two inches seriously. Let the owner think he had someone to contend with before he actually saw her.

Laila heard a noise in the distance, but no one responded. Ezra and she passed glances between them.

A little louder. "Hell-o-o-o-o." Ezra hovered behind her, like her own personal watchdog.

From within, they heard a chair scrape the concrete floor, and then a loud thud followed by an unfamiliar curse. A door slammed in the background and an ox of a man, short and compact, resembling his cur, headed their way. He stopped in the door frame momentarily and growled, "What do you want?"

Laila stepped back, bumping into Ezra, who had not retreated fast enough. Laila found her authoritarian voice. "We're here to place an order."

With the mention of *an order* his demeanor changed dramatically. The taut muscles on his face relaxed to a pleasant smile. "An order, you say? Where are you from? I don't recognize you."

"Up on Kibbutz Hill."

"What size?" *Parv*, kosher butter, would have melted on his tongue.

Laila hadn't understood what he meant by *what size* at first, and then she blinked as it hit her. Of course he was talking business. She gave him the dimensions, and his hairy eyebrows peaked.

"Those are strange dimensions. What is their use?"

Laila panicked, looked to Ezra for help, and seeing she wasn't going to get any, blurted out, "Exercising."

"Ah. By the looks of your people on the Hill, I wouldn't think you'd need to exercise."

What exactly did he mean by that? How did he know what they looked like or anything else about them? Had the kibbutz become the latest topic of conversation?

"You can never get enough," interjected Ezra, stealing a glance at Laila to make sure he had said the right thing.

Laila returned a grateful wink, although she was afraid she might have chosen the wrong man to help her fight her battle. Ezra would rather write than fight. She had found it impossible to believe he had gone out on night raids: Itzhak had let slip what they had been doing, a few days after they arrived at the new kibbutz. Laila had made him tell her everything.

The three of them discussed sizes and cost, and Laila and Ezra were assured the mattresses would be ready in a week. On the way home, she and Ezra decided they were grateful they had gotten away with their lives.

A week later, Itzhak and Laila drove the horse drawn wagon back to Rehovot to pick up the mattresses. Ezra was busily working on organizing the underground reading room, for the times the workers might be trapped inside the factory and unable to come out of hiding. A plump woman in her sixties graciously helped them load the mattresses onto the wagon, and yakked nonstop through the entire transaction. Laila was disappointed because she had told Itzhak about the two bulldogs—one human and the other a bruiser of a dog. They saw neither.

On the way home, Itzhak was chatty. "I am pleased to see how well you have adapted to our new life. You're one surprise after another, and all pleasant. I have married a *Queen Esther*."

"Wow, what a compliment, but I don't know that I would place myself in the same category as a queen. She was a bold woman who thought nothing of herself, only her people." For some reason, Laila asked herself if she would be able to return such a compliment, considering Itzhak's reaction to the cordite spill. She knew she was being overly hard on him, but he kept disappointing her. Who was she comparing him to? Her father ... the green-eyed soldier? Itzhak had many positive attributes, Laila scolded herself, and she was going to have to stop finding fault.

Lynda Lippman-Lockhart

Laila was sure her reaction to Itzhak's complement brought questions with it.

"I can't help it if that's how I see you: wise beyond your years and timeless. Sometimes I wonder if I deserve you." Itzhak's face suddenly become an abstract painting—all lines and planes.

"Well, if you are fishing for a compliment, you are going to get one. It is I who feel blessed." Was she being totally honest? She supposed one imperfection does not define a person. She silently forgave him. "You are far more polished than I. You are smarter and better-looking." They laughed. Itzhak kissed her cheek, making the wagon teeter to the right and just miss a pot hole. The cordite incident was forgotten.

They had ridden for a while, the clip-clopping of the horses' hooves, the only sound, when Itzhak blurted out, "Something we have not discussed but should ... if something should happen to us and Dovele survives ... what then? My parents are out of the picture. Would your brother Judah take Dovele in and raise him as his own?" Itzhak's strained face revealed his concern.

"I've thought about that myself, but was afraid to mention it. You know how superstitious I am. I think, if Avraham and Zahar were to survive, or Ari and Leora, I would prefer either of them to be his guardians. He knows them, especially Leora. After that, I would think Judah would be fine. Should we ask Leora and Ari and then make it official by writing it down and giving it to someone outside the kibbutz to hold on to?" Laila gazed lovingly at her husband and decided this had been a good idea—spending the day together away from everyone and being able to have a real-life discussion.

"I think either Lazar or General Avidar would be happy to honor our request. You know, I'm glad we had this chat. It's been weighing heavily on my mind." Itzhak draped his arm around Laila's shoulder, pulling her close for another kiss.

"That's why I love you so much," said Laila, squeezing his hand as he held the reins. "You are so dependable."

"That's it? Not handsome or desirable?"

"You're all that and more." Laila nuzzled closer for another kiss. She and Itzhak ceased to be bothered by the mattresses flopping about in the back of the wagon, although it crossed Laila's mind that they might stop and try one out; but the thought soon faded with the sight of gathering clouds.

Chapter 31

Zahar

Ayalon Institute, September, 1946

The new factory had been running for several months now and one of the women who had put in her time below, asked to take Zahar's place in the nursery; and so, today Zahar was enjoying her day off playing with her children and mending worn clothing. Nothing was ever thrown away at their kibbutz, because someone could always find a new use for the item: an old skirt became curtains, while torn clothing became scraps for a quilt. It was an easy thing to do while also spending quality time with her children. Since Zahar had decided that work in the factory was not for her after spending a month below, she and Leora had been taking turns in the nursery. Zahar had no idea why Laila was so drawn to making bullets; it wasn't very ladylike. Of course, they were making a monumental contribution to the war effort, but Laila did have a child and that child had become whiny and difficult, and raising Dovele *had* become Zahar's business.

The Laundry Room

her room until it became so loud she couldn't miss it. She didn't recognize the voices, but that was nothing new. Young people frequently came and lived with them for a time, learning the skills needed to run a kibbutz on their own before moving on. With so many new people coming and going within the kibbutz, it had become more difficult to know who was in the know and who was not. For this reason the kibbutz had drawn on a prior experience the men had had while building the factory. Avraham had shared that experience with Zahar when he returned from building the factory. It seemed a train, carrying animals acquired by the Tel Aviv Zoo, passed close to the kibbutz one day. Only the heads of giraffes were visible from the kibbutz; and only the giraffes could see what the workers were doing; so in a moment of humor, the men had reversed the order of events so that now, those kibbutzniks who were out of the loop became "giraffes." Stories like that and more kept the kibbutzniks going. The young people needed a laugh now and then.

The conversation outside her room became even louder, and wondering what was going on, Zahar rose, placed the baby on her hip, and headed for the door. Ben followed behind, holding onto Zahar's skirt. She opened the door a crack and peered outside, and nearly fainted. British soldiers! Startled by the sight of the uniforms standing at her door, panic set in. What was she to do? Why were they there? What if they had heard the pounding below?

"Can I help you?" she asked, taking a step outside her room and readjusting the baby to her other hip—keeping her as far away from the soldiers as possible. What little exchange she'd had with the British since arriving at "The Hill" did nothing to help her forget the bombing, or the terrifying interruption at Laila's wedding.

"We were told we could find a place to shower here," said one soldier.

Zahar's face must have revealed her confusion. True, Zahar and Avraham were one of the few couples who had a crude shower attached to their room, but how did these men know?

"Is that true or is it not?" The soldiers had taken a step closer, and Zahar had taken a step backward into the room, her entire face now visibly apparent, scars and all.

The soldiers exchanged a moment of shock, but seemed to take Zahar's disfigurement in stride. She suddenly became self-conscious, turning her face away from the men. Not having dealt with strangers in some time, Zahar nonetheless recognized the pained expression on their faces. Hadn't they seen enough mutilated bodies in their travels? So be it, she decided. *If I'm such a horrible freak, they can just take their showers somewhere else.*

"Well, is it true or not?" asked the soldier, showing no signs of disgust.

"Of course it is true, but it will have to be one at a time. You see, we rotate our shower days because there is so little water," she explained, hoping they would understand not to waste what water they used. "You happen to be in luck; today is our day. Please make yourselves comfortable. The shower is all yours. I will fetch you some towels."

Zahar motioned for the men to follow her as she showed them the way to the bathroom—not that anyone could miss it. "I will be outside with the towels. You are welcome to stay in our room, out of the heat, while you wait."

The soldiers must have gotten over their initial shock of Zahar's appearance because they nodded and thanked her, taking a seat on her worn couch. She hurried out of the room, breathing heavily, about to faint, as she headed for the

The Laundry Room

nursery, pulling Ben behind her, the baby bouncing on her hip.

Once inside, she fell upon Leora. "A group of soldiers are in my room taking showers! I need towels. Do we have any extras?"

"Soldiers? British? What are they doing in your place—did you say 'taking showers'?" Leora's face reflected the panic Zahar was feeling. Naomi, Zahar's baby, reached her chubby arms out toward Leora, who took her willingly. Sometimes, Zahar thought, her children spent more time with Leora than their own mother.

"I have no idea, but they said someone had directed them here, and I did not know what else to do." By now Zahar's breathing had gotten under control. "Can you imagine how I felt when I answered the door?"

"You did the right thing. Leave Ben and the baby with me." Leora took Ben's hand and carried Naomi over to the cupboard where the linens were kept. She pointed to the shelf where the towels sat folded neatly, stacked and ready to go. "They were washed yesterday. Go, before they become suspicious. Don't tell anyone else, though. Somebody might panic and cause an alarm." Leora shooed Zahar off.

"Oh, and come back as soon as they are gone, so I know you are alright."

Trying to maintain her poise, Zahar walked back to her room like nothing was amiss. She nodded as she passed several of the "giraffes" and a few of her comrades, smiling when necessary, but her heart beat uncontrollably.

Then she heard her name. "Zahar, do you have a minute?" ventured Rivka, who was now working at the bakery and had flour on her cheek. Surprisingly enough, she had lost a great deal of weight in the past year and was looking good and healthy.

Lynda Lippman-Lockhart

Although the bakery had been part of the original design, it had become an unexpected gem, run by a young man who had never baked a thing in his life, but now managed to put out a fine loaf of bread. He was joined by another youth, Yosef, the son of a baker; he had been anxious to be a part of the factory but, because of his skills, was put to work in the bakery instead.

Yosef's father came to visit once and took note of the oven and how it was constructed. Zahar remembered hearing him say, "You will never put out a real loaf of bread with an oven like that." The two young men had been kneading the bread by hand all that time. Not too long after Yosef's father left, a package arrived for the bakery. His father had sent them a mechanical dough kneader which sped up the process and made even better bread. The aroma of yeast, cumin, caraway, and rye, or cinnamon, honey, and walnuts drew a crowd to the bakery every morning. The kibbutz had to be careful, though, that the word didn't get out and too many visitors would come, wanting to buy their breads and cakes.

Rivka cleared her throat. "Are you in Jerusalem?" Zahar didn't react. "That was supposed to be a joke. I asked if you had a minute."

"Sorry, I always have a minute for you." Zahar held onto the towels like they were her children.

Rivka's forehead wrinkled. "What are you doing with all those towels?"

Zahar panicked again. What was she doing with all these towels? "Okay, I have something to tell you, but I don't want you to go into a tailspin, scream, or faint. There are three British soldiers taking a shower in my bathroom. Someone told them we offer showers to the soldiers. Can you imagine? I didn't want to cause an alarm nor have the soldiers be suspicious of anything; so I let them come in, and I'm now bringing them back more towels."

Rivka's hands flew to either side of her face. "*Oy vez mear*. Oh woe is me. You must get them out of here and soon. If they see our people coming out of the laundry room ..."

"I'm doing my best," said Zahar, backing away from Rivka, afraid to waste any more time kibitzing.

"Do you need some help?" Rivka asked, catching up to Zahar.

"No, please. The less people know about this the better. Just go back to what you were doing. Oh, but what was it you wanted?" It was impossible to remain calm, but calm she must be. All she needed was for Rivka to go blabbing her mouth off and getting everyone riled up, and the whole kibbutz would be at Zahar's door.

"A recipe. I remembered you saying your mother made a wonderful Russian *babka*. Do you remember how she made it?"

"I'll have to think about it and let you know later." Perspiration was beginning to form between her breasts and spread to her armpits. She had to get back before the soldiers started looking for her. "I'll be right over with the recipe, after the soldiers leave. Is that all right?"

"That will be fine, and thank you." Rivka began to turn away. "Are you sure you're all right?"

"I'm fine, and thanks for asking." *What is the matter with that woman? Can't she see I'm a wreck, and all she can think about was a recipe for some cake?*

"If you're sure?" Rivka placed an index finger before her lips, as to show she could keep a secret.

"I'm sure."

"Okay," Rivka said and continued on her way.

Feeling even more stressed, Zahar jogged the rest of the way, continuing to nod and wave as she normally would when passing others. Those she passed must have thought she was *meshuge,* running to her room. When she reached her door, Zahar stopped, took a deep breath, and knocked. She did not want to enter if one of the men was not fully dressed. She hoped they were not going through her things. There weren't many, but what she had she prized.

The door opened a crack and a hand reached out to grasp the towels. Zahar gladly let them go. She backed away from the door, hoping Rivka kept her promise. Perhaps she should just go to the bakery; no, she needed to warn someone at the laundry room. Why had the alarm system not worked? Maybe the soldiers had come from the train station and through the back of the kibbutz, which was not guarded and should be.

Zahar hurried along, as if to an important meeting, and burst through the door to the laundry room. "You must warn them below to stop making noise." Out of breath and shaky, she dropped to the bench and breathed deeply.

Carmel immediately hit a button to stop work. She turned back to Zahar. "What is going on?"

"Three soldiers came to my door saying that someone told them *showers* were available at our kibbutz. I suppose they came the back way from the train station, hoping to clean up before reporting to their commander. I don't recognize any of them, but I let them in anyway. I didn't want to raise suspicion. They are taking turns showering right now. I didn't know what else to do."

"Good thinking. I wonder who told them our kibbutz was a place to clean up?" said Carmel. "I hope this doesn't become a habit."

"Maybe they thought since we did laundry, we had extra

water to waste on them." Zahar's nerves were frayed; how many times would she have to tell this story? At least her nerves had calmed down enough for her to be able to joke about soldiers using her bathroom. "Please don't tell anyone until I return. It could cause a panic. If anyone asks why you set off the alarm, tell them you'll explain later."

"I would have fainted dead away if they had come to my door—and the worst of the noise right under your room!" said Carmel, looking from side to side in case anyone might be listening. "I'll keep this quiet until you return. Don't forget to come back when the coast is clear."

Zahar took a deep breath, hugged Carmel, and left the laundry room. On her way back to her room, she decided a meeting was needed to address surveillance. People should not be able to drop in unannounced from any location around the kibbutz.

The fact that the soldiers had been able to enter the kibbutz undetected put a new fear in her heart. What about the children? Zahar glanced at the nursery as she passed, but it was quiet. With a relieved sigh, she continued on her way.

It had been hard on everyone, getting adjusted to a routine that seemed so foreign, but the kibbutzniks had learned to work together so well in the past that they had gently eased into their new task there. Someday, Zahar hoped to be able to look back on her participation at the Ayalon Institute and say she was glad that she had done something noble.

Wait until Avraham heard about her day. With the thought of Avraham, though, came a needling suspicion she had been feeling for a while now, that something was amiss between them. She felt something had changed after his trip to Jerusalem. Perhaps that happened with couples after a while, she mused. It was probably nothing.

Lynda Lippman-Lockhart

When Zahar returned to her room, she knocked. The door opened wide, and three very clean and happy men exited. "Thank you for your hospitality. We will be sure to tell others how cooperative you were to strangers. Point us, if you will, in the general direction of British headquarters."

Zahar was happy to do so and see the back of their heads. *Please don't do us any favors* she said under her breath. As they left the kibbutz, several pairs of eyes followed the soldiers down the road and past the guards. Those same eyes returned to Zahar as she entered her room to see if all was well. To her dismay, she found a lapis brooch of her mother's gone. She wept silently. Something else had been taken away from her by the British.

As she left to give Carmel the all-clear sign, Zahar was engulfed by her comrades, besieging her with questions. She raised her hand and motioned toward the dining room. Once inside, the questions, like bullets, came at her from all directions.

"Just a minute," she said. "I'll tell you what happened all at one time. I'm a wreck, so let me catch my breath. Oh, someone must alert Carmel it is okay to get back to work."

Zalman ran to relay the message, and when he returned, Zahar told her harrowing story. She knew she would tell it many times before the day was through.

When she finished, she took a closer look at her friends. She saw something that hadn't been apparent before: they were pale and drawn, not like the robust, tanned young people who had moved in months ago. Zahar had been aboveground enough to enjoy the sunshine and retained a healthy tan, but those below, like Avraham, Laila, and the rest, were not as lucky. Avraham had complained of headaches and his eyes often ached. Laila was often fatigued, her limbs weak most of the time. It looked like that was another question for Zahar to pose that night, although she would ask Avraham first. Surely, there must be something they could do to remedy the situation.

Avraham trudged into the room that evening, hot, sweaty, and tired. He fell onto their bed and placed his muscular arm over his eyes. Zahar dropped to the bed and felt his forehead. It was cool.

"What is the matter, dear?" she asked him. "I'm worried about you and the rest of the factory workers. Something is wrong; I can see it better than you who work together down there. Can we ask Yosef or Lazar for help?" She applied a damp cloth to his forehead. "You're not getting enough rest and spending too much time below. Please, for my sake and that of the children's, ask someone for help."

"I'll be all right after I take a shower. Speaking of which, I heard what happened today. I was so proud of you for staying calm and handling the situation so well. Of course, I would expect nothing less of my girl." He grabbed Zahar's arm, pulling her down on the bed to lie next to him. "I never dreamed this would be so demanding. I'm sure most of it is emotional stress, never knowing when something will go wrong, and lately we have had a couple of close calls. I don't know if I mentioned, Zalman sliced his hand the other day and had to be taken to the hospital in Rehovot for stitches. The doctor asked how it happened, and he said he had done it on a metal bedframe. It's getting harder and harder to keep this place a secret, but you know, I'm finding the most difficult is keeping the factory a secret from the "giraffes.""

It was one thing after another: a problem—a solution. Could they always come up with the right answer? When it had become necessary to explain the heaps of oil soaked clothing associated with the factory, the men came up with a metal-works division that manufactured springless metal bedframes. The metal workers' division had become so popular, dozens of young men vied for a position in the new factory. It was another buffer to the noise from below, and a good place to put the "giraffes."

"We're forced to live a life of lies," finished Avraham," and it's taking its toll on all of us."

Zahar knew what the stress was doing; she felt it in her own marriage. Something had to be done to help those working below. It was becoming more obvious every day that the majority of the kibbutzniks were not, in fact, working out in the fields or in the citrus groves, where they ought to be if this were a normal kibbutz.

When Zahar didn't reply, Avraham tousled her hair as he left the bed for a shower. "Don't worry your sweet self about it. I will be fine. Did the Brits leave me any water?"

"You're very funny. You have no idea how frightened I was." Zahar heard something as Avraham left the room, but she wasn't sure what he had said. She wasn't so sure how *fine* he would be, either.

The following week Dr. Kott, the *Haganah's* chief physician, arrived at the Ayalon Institute. After deliberating over the ailments, he asked to see their working conditions for himself. He had been given clearance by *Shai*, the intelligence service, and when shown the munitions factory was amazed by what he saw.

"How many hours do you spend down here a day?" he asked, eyeing the workers with concern.

"At least eight ... sometimes more," offered Laila.

The Laundry Room

"Aha." Dr. Kott strode the length of the factory, scanning the walls and ceiling. "I believe you are plagued by 'miners' disease,' or the lack of vitamin D. You need exposure to quartz—blue light—several times a day. He scribbled some notes. "I will send an infrared lamp that will add color to your skin and reduce the symptoms. If the British happen to see it before it is installed, they will probably think it is a lady's hair drier. It has a large hood and tall stand. You men will get a taste of what it's like to be in a beauty parlor for a few moments every day."

The women laughed. The men scowled.

"A diet of milk, vitamins A and D, and as much meat as possible should be added to the menu."

From that time on, a storehouse of food was kept below, but that became expensive because the food spoiled quickly without refrigeration. The men suggested that once a week, those below would polish off the food before it went bad; and so, at the end of every week, they made a banquet of the rations, and Zahar took care that a fresh supply of food was always replenished.

Zahar was amazed at the difference in the workers' skin tone within the next few weeks. She also noted how much better she was feeling, having spent more time down below over the past two months supervising the food situation. She even found she had more energy with those few visits a week under the sun lamp.

Avraham was almost back to his old self, too, and their sex life picked up somewhat, but Zahar wasn't sure she was ready to become pregnant just yet. Her miscarriages had caused her so much pain. At least she had her husband back. What next?

Lynda Lippman-Lockhart

Museum Workshop

The Laundry Room

Underground workshop Entrance

Chapter 32

Laila

Ayalon Institute, 1947

Laila woke before dawn, rested after several nights of sleeplessness in a row. So as not to disturb Itzhak, she rolled out of bed to land on her feet. The first sign of a new day crept through the burlap curtain she had made out of potato sacks—ones that hadn't smelled too bad, and were made of material slightly less rough than usual. Her feet found their worn slippers, and she padded out the front door, to enjoy the sunrise.

The sky held the promise of a beautiful day, with a backdrop of navy blue blended with splashes of pink and purple. The clouds resembled wisps of angel hair loosed from its restraints. Laila's only regret: she would be underground while the rest of the world enjoyed the sunshine, the camaraderie of good friends, and their children; but that was second to what she must do. They took pride in their work—their efforts in the fight for freedom. It was essential to Laila that she reminded herself daily.

The Laundry Room

Dovele was growing as fast as the newly-planted legumes, and it tore her to pieces not to be able to spend more than her allotted time with him. Parents had between four o'clock and bedtime most days. Like a puppy, her son would bounce from one wall to another when she entered the nursery, and mope when she left.

Laila had had her doubts about raising children by *Beit Yeladim* standards, actually letting others raise your children, although statistics showed the "children's house" accomplished most of what it set out to do: create happy, self-sustaining children, whose parents were less stressed, and make sure that time spent together was maximized into quality time. From what Laila was told, the concept came about as the result of having minimal space allotted to each couple in the first kibbutzim to be created. Regardless, after her four hours with Dovele each day, she would have to return him to his *metapelet*—caregiver.

Even after all this time, Laila was still working her way through the concept. Itzhak and she had taken care of their other responsibility, should something happen to both of them. Making a will had brought a bit of relief, yet Laila could not fathom ever leaving her child.

The door creaked as it always did when opened, and Itzhak stepped outside, drawing Laila to him. She breathed in his musky morning scent as they stood locked in each other's arms, drinking in what promised to be a balmy day. It occurred to Laila that she might have taken for granted this time of day and not having a child to worry about, and decided perhaps those who had developed the childrearing concept might have stumbled upon something more than worth considering.

"I hate to break the spell, but we have work to do." Itzhak spun Laila around and kissed her soundly on the lips. He had been more amorous lately, and Laila suspected she might be pregnant again. When Zahar had lost another child, it had broken all their hearts. Leora, Anna, and Laila shared each other's joys and sorrows. Zahar had taken to spending more time in the children's quarters, and was now raising Laila's son along with her own.

"You're right, as always, but it's too beautiful to leave just yet, with the sun rising over the orange grove, and sunbeams filtering through the trees." She drew in a deep breath filled with the scent of orange blossoms, savoring it as she let it swirl around like a good wine.

"Ezra better watch his step. You may surpass him as poet laureate of the kibbutz."

"Now you're teasing me." Laila pinched his side. He giggled like a small boy.

"Yes, I am, but good-naturedly. Do we have time for a little...?"

"...but not time to worship the sun?"

He said nothing, just smiled and pulled her lovingly back into their cave.

After breakfast, Laila and Itzhak made their way to the laundry room. Several clotheslines had been strung up in front of the building, and each day a new set of sheets would be set out to dry, blocking the entrance to the building. That simple act had made it much easier for the workers to appear and disappear without question. Once the factory was established, a number of new recruits looking to learn skills necessary to begin their own kibbutz had been added to the Ayalon Institute. Like the rest, the new kibbutzniks had no idea what the original forty-five were doing, nor where they went each day, and it was becoming increasingly difficult to prevent them from finding out.

The Laundry Room

Itzhak and Laila deposited their shoes in cubbyholes at the bottom of the stairs and donned their elevated ones for work. Laila took her place at her station, to begin the day's work at a task she could now do blindfolded. She wondered if someday she would dream of this time and the impression it had made upon her life. She had become an expert in copper, experimenting with its thickness, length, size, durability, and weight. But, with the buildup in fighting, it had become increasingly difficult procuring the copper sheets. The cordite was something else. Most of their base products were acquired by sabotaging British freight trains, transferring ammunition to strategic British camps across Palestine. Laila had not been content to just fill bullets; she wanted to know how cordite was made, and so she asked Irwin, who happened to be there that afternoon.

"It is a compound developed by Sir Alfred Able and Sir James Dewar," he explained, "with properties of nitroglycerine, nitrocellulose, and Vaseline—highly flammable. The compound is carefully mixed with acetone, which emerges as spaghetti-like rods called cord powder or what they called *cordite*. Instead of exploding, it burns. Is there anything else you would like to know?"

"Thank you. Not now, but I appreciate your taking the time to explain cordite to me." Laila and Vida went back to work. Laila was teaching Vida, who had been working above in the laundry room but wanted a little more excitement, how to fill the casings.

Zalman was in charge of the furnace for pressure casting the copper, while Ezra managed the press that cut and formed the bullet casings. He passed his completed strips to Ari and Leora, who had taken the day off from the nursery today. Leora was carefully stretching the strips into cylinders, the one job she had told Laila she didn't mind.

Lynda Lippman-Lockhart

Laila was happy that Leora was able to devote two days a week to the factory. They hadn't seen much of each other, and Leora had said she was concerned she wasn't doing enough. Leora's aunt, Mrs. Malkin, had passed away a few months ago, and Leora had taken it badly. Her aunt had been the last of her family and her identity. She had clung to Laila and Zahar for comfort. Laila thought Ari might have been hurt by her choice of helpmates; hopefully the two of them would work it out.

Laila felt a tap to her shoulder. "What do you think of engraving a symbol of our work on the bullets? It would be nice to know we had left our mark on the enemy."

"Brilliant," hollered Ezra above the din. "Do you have something in mind?" Zalman passed his question onto Avraham, who paused in his routine, but only for a moment.

"I like that idea, but what would we engrave?" asked Avraham, eyes returning to his. Laila had decided Avraham was the hardest worker of all. It was almost as if the devil were after him.

A discussion ensued, as always. Everyone had an opinion.

"How about 'AE' and the date? An 'A' for *Ayalon*, and 'E' for *Eretz Israel*, in hopes that the bullets will help establish our own country," offered Ari.

"We should bring this up before the general assembly, but I'm sure everyone would agree," said Laila. After their break, Anna joined Laila and Vida moved on to help Schmuel close the bullets with brass strips.

Vida began singing a much loved Yiddish tune—one of their favorites. Leora and Laila picked up the harmony. The noise in the factory made normal talk nonexistent over the hammering, chiseling, and firing, but they didn't care. They had an assembly line par excellence—lacking in everyday conversation but high in enthusiasm.

The Laundry Room

Laila still remembered her grandmother singing the song Vida had begun, and she and her grandmother crying through the song:

On a wagon bound and helpless
Lies a calf, who is doomed to die.
High above him flies a swallow
Soaring gaily through the sky.

The wind laughs in the cornfield
Laughs with all his might
Laughs and laughs the whole day through
And halfway through the night

Dona, dona,
Dona ... dona ... do... na ...

Now the calf is softly crying
"Tell me wind, why do you laugh?"
Why can't I fly like the swallow?
Why did I have to be a calf?

The wind laughs in the cornfield
Laughs with all his might
Laughs and laughs the whole day through
And halfway through the night

Dona, dona, dona ...

Calves are born and soon are slaughtered
With no hope of being saved.
Only those with wings like the swallow

Lynda Lippman-Lockhart

Will not ever be enslaved.

The wind laughs in the cornfield
Laughs with all his might
Laughs and laughs the whole day through
And halfway through the night

Dona, dona, dona ...

Now the calf is softly crying
"Tell me, wind, why do you laugh?"
Why can't I fly like the swallow?
Why did I have to be a calf?

The wind laughs in the cornfield
Laughs with all his might
Laughs and laughs the whole day through
And halfway through the night

Dona, dona, dona ...

For the first time, the significance of the words made sense to Laila. Her parent's generation was the calves and hers was the swallow.

It was hard to return to work, but return they did. The singing continued for the next hour or so, helping to quell the monotony of their tasks.

Laila changed places with Vida and handed Schlomo a small, round disk, which he stretched into a cylinder, soon to become a cartridge. He chiseled a furrow for the cap and a hole for ignition. Carmel was right by his side; she had given up on Yosef Avidar and latched onto Schlomo, who was a

303

nice man, but certainly not quite as commanding.

In the small office across the way, Avraham and Zdich, who had held out until the last minute to join the group going to the Ayalon Institute, pored over the inventory while the rest pounded out one bullet after another.

Laila never stopped worrying about Itzhak and Lazar as they took turns firing off rounds of bullets, making sure each batch of their handiwork held up to their scrutiny. The workers lived with the knowledge that each step of the process could lead to cataclysmic results. For that reason, Laila believed, the kibbutzniks didn't have time for petty problems within the kibbutz. There were almost no quarrels between members in their day-to-day lives. They all depended upon each other for their lives, and no one was willing to upset the applecart. Even she and Livia were civil.

By the end of the day, Laila could tell that something was brewing. She felt a charged energy that was lacking on most days ... almost celebratory, but no one ventured to ask. At lunch, instead of ascending the stairs, they were surprised with a small banquet, catered by the group in the filling and packing department, who must have anticipated the first production of a series of 100,000 bullets. This banquet was unlike the end-of-the-week buffet in that the food had been brought in from Rehovot—compliments of Tal, especially for the day. The excited workers fell upon the food like vultures on a roadside carcass and for their other reward, they each received a gift of a small bullet to commemorate the milestone—one with *"AE47"* engraved on it.

A sense of pride welled up in Laila's heart. She and her friends were doing something very important, and although the gift was well-meaning, Laila thought it almost silly to think they needed something as mundane as a replica of a bullet to remind them that their labor here was worthwhile.

Lynda Lippman-Lockhart

"And what do you think of that?" Itzhak said, hugging Laila to him. "We did it. Who would have thought a bunch of kids could accomplish something like this?"

Laila knew he was referring to his father.

Some of the women, as custom dictated, spat through their fingers to scare the evil spirits away in case they happened to be listening. It was an ancient, superstitious antidote for bragging. Emma had often done it, and Laila had always thought it foolish and "Old-Worldly". She thought about the first time that she saw Emma make the sign; Emma had always taught Laila not to spit in public, and here she was doing just that.

There are customs that go back so far no one knows when or why they began—we just carry them on. My Emma did it and her Emma before her. Ours is not to question. And so Laila never questioned, but never found it necessary to keep an old custom going that she didn't believe in.

The workers hugged and kissed and sang their hearts out. Today they chose *Hatikvah,* "The Hope," their national anthem. Laila knew it had been written by Naftali Herz Imber in the 1880's to describe the hope that the Jews would return to the Holy Land someday. Feeling patriotic, the workers formed a circle—arms locked in solidarity:

In the Jewish heart
A Jewish spirit still sings
And the eyes look east
Toward Zion,
Our hope is not lost,
Our hope of two thousand years,
To be a free nation in our land,
In the land of Zion and Jerusalem.

The Laundry Room

The rest of the day flew by, with the kibbutzniks in a cheerful mood.

"I am so glad I was here today," said Leora, a proud smile appearing on her face. "It made me feel more like I was a real member of the Resistance. I wish Zahar could have joined us. I think she is getting homesick, although for what home that might be I have no idea. Her parents are both dead, like mine."

"I think she sees no future here. "The Hill" is just an interval in all our lives, but it is a necessary one. I understand that now far better than I did in the beginning, and I am glad I'm here. But for Zahar ..." Leora's face lit up. "Let us find some time to take her into Rehovot for a day of fun." Laila did understand and shared Zahar's feelings. She wanted nothing more than to finally be settled in a kibbutz of their own, one where they could see the fruits of their labor.

Laila was thinking perhaps Zahar's sentiments were Leora's too. "I'd like that. Let's plan a day." Laila watched Leora walk away a little lighter and happier. After all, that's what friends were for. Itzhak and she had taken a day off here and there to pretend they were a normal couple; and although Rehovot was close by, it still made them feel far from the restrictions placed upon them at "The Hill."

At the end of the day, cardboard packages of fifty bullets each were loaded into cartons, containing one thousand bullets each. It was Laila's turn tonight to make sure the packages were picked up by their transport system. Zalman, Itzhak, and she placed the packages near the window, where the driver would find them. The pickup trucks had been purchased from British surplus and reconfigured for their purpose—to hide contraband. *Sliks,* or caches, had been built into the front, under the seat, and in the rear of the trucks.

Lynda Lippman-Lockhart

The caches were nicknamed "rabbits" because they hid below the surface. A rakish man named Michael Shor, whom Laila thought must have nerves of steel, usually drove the "tender". His trips were spent dodging both the British and the Arabs, but he was always there to do his duty.

Not long after the evening excursions began, the kibbutz had found itself having to improvise; the British had become wise to them, so they'd added a large spray tank and additional storage space under the truck. Since the truck appeared only at night, it was then named the "dwarf", referring to something unseen.

The next morning after a pickup, there would be new copper strips waiting to be made into bullets. The kibbutz asked no questions. They felt it better to remain in the dark, although Laila couldn't help but worry about the trucks being blown up along the way, or possibly leading the enemy to them.

The boxes stacked as specified, Zalman, Itzhak, and Laila were about to leave when the red light blinked: on, off, on, alerting them to stop what they were doing and be silent. This had only happened a few times before, and usually in the middle of the day, when the workers were fully engaged. Itzhak turned to Laila, placing a finger to his lips. Zalman, a heavy man, moved on cat feet until they were in close enough proximity to whisper.

"What do you think?" asked Zalman.

"I don't know, but it shouldn't last long." Itzhak motioned for them to follow him to the firing range, where they wouldn't be heard; but not to take any chances they would still wait out the time in relative silence.

An hour passed. Itzhak crept out of the room to check the light; he returned shaking his head.

"Oh God. What about the children?" Laila cried out. Both

The Laundry Room

men shushed her with their index fingers.

"They will be fine," whispered Itzhak. "It might be one of the British surprise visits. I'm sure everything's just fine; and besides, I haven't heard of them indiscriminately killing innocent children—it was the Germans who did that."

Laila wasn't so sure. A million scenarios ran through her head, none optimistic. She thought it might be a Jewish trait to think the worst, but then, look at their history.

Laila kept a running commentary with herself until she couldn't stand it one more second. "We have to do something!"

"What do you suggest?" asked Zalman, face showing signs of intense irritation. "You see that light. Those are our instructions."

"But they many need help up there," she cried out hysterically.

"You're working yourself up into a state that won't help anyone," said Itzhak, pulling her close, rocking her like a baby. "You've always been the strong one in the family. I'm counting on you to help me get through this. There is nothing we can do but wait."

Laila knew Itzhak was using psychology on her, but it didn't work. She broke away from him and tiptoed to the far end of the firing room. He followed. He reached for her hand; she let him have it. Now was not the time to squabble. She knew he meant well.

Laila watched Zalman think—cogs grinding out answers. He had made himself a part of their family, mostly because of Dovele. Laila didn't understand the connection between him and her son, but it seemed to be healthy for both of them; however, she would never consider naming him as Dovele's caretaker. Zalman was too much a child himself; perhaps that was why he had not found a wife.

Whispering her thoughts, "All I can think about is that I'm glad we made arrangements for Dovele."

"What do you mean?"

"Just in case we don't make it out of here."

"Laila ... we will make it out of here. Everything will be fine. It's nothing." His eyes betrayed his words.

"And what if it isn't?"

"We'll do the best we can. I'm not going to let anyone destroy what we have. You can count on that." Itzhak kissed her long and hard, and she relaxed into his strong arms, wanting to believe that what he said would be true. He had become the husband she had hoped for, but it had taken time and patience. It wasn't easy turning Romeo into an Abba.

"You two lovebirds, cut it out; you're making me jealous," Zalman whispered loudly. "We need to make a plan, just in case."

Zalman joined them, upending a crate. "There's a whole host of scenarios of what could happen, and I think we need to be prepared for all of them."

"What's on your mind?" said Itzhak.

"I think we should gather all the guns we can find and load them to full capacity. Then I think we should prepare some bunkers to hide behind, instead of sitting here like a bunch of asses with our heads in the ground."

"I believe you mean an ostrich with its head in the sand," retorted Laila.

"However it goes. You know what I mean," said Zalman, already at work.

Itzhak took stock of the firing range, knowing where everything was, and nodded. "I agree. You two take the rest of the factory; I'll work on this room."

Laila was happy for something to do besides waiting to be

The Laundry Room

discovered. They worked like Trojans until they felt they were ready for whatever might come their way.

The hours ticked by until two in the morning, when Itzhak left the firing range again to check the light. He returned with the good news—it was off. They breathed a sigh of relief as they gathered their belongings. Laila had on her above-ground shoes when the light flashed again. Her body slumped. She cast a glance at Itzhak, who shook his head in dismay. They sat down on the crates that were to be picked up by the transporters, and contemplated what to do next. Something had gone wrong. She felt it in her gut.

Zalman motioned them back into the soundproof room. "Now what?" he mouthed.

"I don't know," whispered Itzhak. "Why would the light go off and then back on?"

"Could it be a short?" said Zalman. "But if it were, don't you suppose someone would have come looking for us by now?"

"I would think so. What about your roommates?" Laila asked.

"They wouldn't even notice I was missing. They don't particularly like me," said Zalman, eyes downcast.

"What do you mean?" said Itzhak. "Everyone respects you."

"Respect and liking are two different things." His head dropped.

Laila had had no idea. If they got out of there, she would have to do something about it—whatever that might be. Of course, she realized she couldn't always fix other people's lives; besides, it was up to them to find their own answers. On the other hand, when had that stopped her?

Laila watched as the two men went on like teenagers.

"Now is not the time to worry about being popular," she said. "We have to decide on a plan. I don't want to have to put words to what I'm thinking; but we have to get out of here."

"Laila is right." Itzhak was now pacing the room as he often did when in high gear.

Seeing neither had a plan, Laila said, "Since I'm the smallest, I should go up and look around. Maybe they won't notice me."

"Not on your life," said Itzhak. "I'll go; at least if I run into someone, I can shoot them ... if I have to."

Zalman shook his head. He hadn't offered, even though he had no wife or child to support. Laila was disappointed in him.

Itzhak grabbed a few Sten guns, handing Laila one and the other to Zalman, whose face had gone pasty. He stood stone-cold, studying both of them as if trying to read their minds. Then Zalman said: "Follow me." Itzhak and Laila shared a brief moment of wonder. The three crept toward the stairs, and Laila witnessed a complete metamorphosis of a human being. She was shocked. Zalman did have metal running through his veins. She had changed her opinion of him in a split second.

Near the top of the stairs, the three heard something. Itzhak held out his hand to stop and pointed toward the window. It rose slowly. Their guns rose to the ceiling, ready to fire. A pair of gloved hands appeared, reaching for the crates they had stacked earlier, only to disappear into the night. The window slid into place. Normally copper sheets would have been lowered on ropes. The stunned trio weren't sure whether to be relieved or worried. Had that been Michael Shor, or were the British on to them? Dizzy and nauseous, Laila prayed silently that everything was okay above—that the children were safe and her beloved friends alive.

The light flicked off. It was time to go. She followed her husband unquestioningly to their fate.

Chapter 33

Itzhak

Ayalon Institute, 1947

A return to normalcy took weeks after the British incident, and Laila, Itzhak, and Zalman's close call that night in the factory. Apparently someone had tipped the British off about kibbutz activities, and the Brits were determined to catch the kibbutzniks in the act. Fortunately for the kibbutz, Laila, Zalman, and Itzhak had waited to surface until the search of the area was over. It was agreed upon that a new system should be implemented that would keep those who remained below, after hours, better informed.

The constant strain of being on guard finally caught up with Laila. "Itzhak, sweetheart, I am going to take the day off and spend it with Dovele and Tova. I just don't have the strength or will to climb down those stairs today."

"That's a good idea. You deserve some time off. You've been pushing yourself unmercifully; and besides, the children will love it. I'll let them know you won't be reporting for work today. Just relax and enjoy yourself." Itzhak kissed

The Laundry Room

the top of Laila's unruly locks and headed out the door.

On his way to the factory, a number of new challenges came to mind that had cropped up with the passing of time, one of which was simply dealing with the residue from clothing and shoes. Itzhak found Laila constantly sweeping the fibers from the cordite out of their room and grumbling about the mess the fibers made. The other problem concerned how to handle the number of new recruits to the kibbutz. The kibbutz now numbered over one hundred members, and it was getting increasingly difficult for the factory workers to disappear and reappear each day without one of the "giraffes" noticing. If there were those who suspected something, they never said, but Itzhak wasn't sure if that was a relief or a cause for concern. It was certainly worth bringing up at the next meeting of the secretariat.

As Itzhak was about to enter the laundry room, on his way down to the factory, Ezra stopped him.

"Do you have a minute? I'd like to discuss something."

"Sure."

The two young men took a seat in the patio. Itzhak wondered what was on Ezra's mind. Even though Itzhak sometimes felt put upon by having to solve so many dilemmas, he still found the process of finding the puzzle pieces and assembling them in the right order, kept his mind active—ready for the next challenge.

Ezra leaned in to Itzhak and spoke in a whisper. "I'm worried about all the visitors we have been having. We must do something about it."

"I agree, but what?" The two friends hadn't seen much of each other lately, and Itzhak missed their discussions. One of them was often working underground while the other was out in the field. Itzhak's mind was already at work.

"We have to find a way to make it unpleasant to visit."

314

Lynda Lippman-Lockhart

Apparently Ezra had taken on the task of worrywart.

"What do you mean?" asked Itzhak. The idea had crossed Itzhak's mind, but he had not acted upon it. Apparently he wasn't the only one concerned about the unwanted visitors and the interruption they caused to those in the factory.

"Yesterday alone, we had ten intruders wanting one thing or another. The "giraffes" are encouraging people to visit, and we obviously can't tell them not to."

"So what do you suggest?" asked Itzhak, suddenly tired of having to come up with another answer. Why hadn't Ezra gone to Avraham? Then Itzhak realized he would have been miffed knowing Ezra hadn't come to him first. What was the matter with him? Maybe he needed a day off as well.

"We could post a sign stating there was an outbreak of 'hoof-and-mouth' disease, which would place us under quarantine; or, we could say that due to contagious children's diseases, all visitors must dip their shoes in disinfectants so as not to bring anything else inside." Itzhak was pleased with his proposal.

"We could use one of those excuses for a while, but we would have to come up with a host of others, depending upon how much longer we have to stay here. Also the 'giraffes' would wonder what was going on and why we were doing this." Ezra stroked his newly grown beard, his eyes hooded in thought. "I think we need to pose the question and air your suggestions at our next meeting. It is next week, isn't it?"

"Yes, as far as I know," said Itzhak. He didn't think putting up a few signs was something that had to be voted upon; however, it had been Ezra who had posed the question. Perhaps Ezra wasn't so keen on his ideas.

Ezra seemed to be especially uncomfortable today. Itzhak doubted that the visitors were his main concern. "What's

315

The Laundry Room

going on, Ezra?"

Ezra's head dropped to his chest and hung there for a moment. He lifted it slowly. "Anna has been so busy lately that we haven't talked much. She is giving me mixed messages; and I've seen her talking to Levi, that new recruit."

"I don't think you have anything to worry about. He talks to everyone. Laila says he often talks her ears off, but he is very interesting. He made a dangerous escape from Poland, and doesn't mind sharing it with anyone who will listen."

Seeming to want to change the subject, Ezra asked, "Any news from the home front? I missed the last meeting you know. I've been sick. That's why I haven't been below."

"I wondered about that, but I haven't had time to think, either. Oh, the army has stepped up the need for bullets, and the factory is now running nonstop. Laila and I have been taking opposite shifts, because we've been working around the clock, but she's off today because one of the kids is sick— another reason to quarantine the kibbutz. When will you be returning?"

"Tomorrow." Ezra did not look overly enthusiastic.

"Good ... we need you."

"I'll be there."

The general assembly met to discuss visitors. As Ezra had told him the week before, the kibbutz had had their share of them lately, which interrupted work and added to everyone's stress level.

"There must be a way to keep people from wanting to come here," demanded Zalman. Itzhak tried not to roll his eyes. Zalman always interjected himself into the discussion, but rarely had an answer.

"What keeps people away better than disease?" Itzhak

ventured. "We could post signs stating we were under quarantine. With so many children, it's possible to come down with some childhood disease or another. Besides, with a number of us working off the kibbutz, we could say that they were bringing disease back with them."

"Not a bad idea," said Avraham, who seemed to want to move on to something more pressing.

"I say we give Itzhak's idea a try." If it had been anyone other than Zalman who had seconded the motion, it would have passed; but no, Itzhak thought, they carried on like they were deliberating a passage from the Torah, interpreted differently by each.

Rivka, now a member of the secretariat, brought the idea to a vote and it passed. The next day signs were hammered to the entry fence: *Hoof-and-Mouth Disease, Poultry Plague, Infant Illness: QUARANTINE!*

After the meeting, Ruth, who was not on the secretariat and had been in Rehovot all day running errands, caught up with Itzhak. "You know, I have worn out another pair of shoes. We can't keep sending them back to the same shoemaker. He'll become suspicious."

He wished Ruth had brought up the issue before the meeting and not after it. "You're absolutely right. We need our own shoe repair shop. I'll see what I can do."

Itzhak hurried back to his room. Laila was sitting at the small wooden desk in the corner, hunched over paperwork. He walked over to her and placed his hands gently on her tight shoulders, massaging out the kinks. He knew the right spots from experience. Married life had become precious to Itzhak, who knew every day was a gift. He tried not to dwell on the possibilities, but it was hard to keep them away. In the past, when Laila had mentioned Carmel's plight of wanting someone in her life to come home to each night, Itzhak couldn't help but feel sorry for her; but now that she and Schlomo had recently married, Itzhak knew Laila had been right about having someone in your life. He knew he would be lost without Laila.

"Sweetheart, do you have a minute?" The dim light from the single bulb above cast shadows about the room. Itzhak was mindfully aware of Laila's attempt to make their place more comfortable. They had found the desk at a secondhand store in Rehovot on one of their rare days off. The small lamp upon the desk had come from a peddler who'd passed by the kibbutz a year ago, and several pieces of pottery were gifts from Ari, who had expanded his talents to include throwing pottery. Not that that was surprising.

Laila turned her chair around. "Anything for you, my love. What is it?"

"Ruth just posed a question I believe needs an answer." Itzhak pulled up an old wooden chair next to Laila.

"And that is?" Laila grabbed a handful of her thick, sandy blond hair and twisted it into a knot.

"She said she has worn out another pair of shoes and fears the shoe repairman in town will become suspicious if we keep coming to him over and over with the same problems." Itzhak valued Laila's ideas, and wanted to make sure she was informed about the meeting, which she had missed because the baby was ill.

"It's too bad she didn't bring up the shoe problem earlier; then you could have brought it before the secretariat."

"Since they just met, it will be another month before the issue can be addressed, and I don't think we can wait that long." Itzhak sat on the bed, across from Laila. "You know they all asked about you. I told them you were under the weather." Itzhak and Laila were not ready to disclose the good news just yet. It was difficult being around Zahar when

Laila was pregnant. Itzhak knew Laila felt too much like she was flaunting her good fortune in front of her dearest friend, when Zahar had such difficulty conceiving.

"Is there anyone amongst us who might have some training in repairing shoes?" Laila turned her chair around so that she faced Itzhak.

"You mean a shoemaker? I never thought of that. I can always count on you for a logical solution." He actually had thought of it, but was reluctant to say so. It was important to Laila to have a say in what happened within the kibbutz— more important to her than him.

"What about Mendel? He's pretty clever." Mendel had been injured during the building of the factory and couldn't navigate the stairs, so he'd gone to work in the bakery instead and had been there ever since.

"Mendel? Perfect. You know him better than I. Would you ask?" Itzhak reached over and took Laila's hands in his.

"I'd be happy to. Now, how did the meeting go?"

"You know, the usual—a lot of arguing and a lot of compromise."

They spent the next hour reviewing issues addressed in the meeting Laila had missed and chatting about what else had transpired that day; they hadn't had a moment to themselves since they'd gotten up that morning. Itzhak noticed signs of exhaustion in her face and was worried. It was important that Laila take care of herself, so she would have a successful delivery. She needed time away from the factory, but she hadn't taken it until he'd insisted. His wife had a stubborn streak he couldn't defuse.

At breakfast, Laila cornered Mendel Fischer, the most versatile of the group. Itzhak placed himself so he could

The Laundry Room

eavesdrop without interfering.

"What do you think about becoming a cobbler?" Laila asked, taking the direct approach midway into their conversation.

"I don't know the first thing about fixing shoes, but it couldn't be too hard. I didn't realize there was a need." Mendel sipped his coffee as he listened to what Laila had to say. He seemed to come alive with her suggestion.

Itzhak continued to watch Mendel's expressive face as Laila plied him with questions.

"That is because you work in the bakery, and you don't wear out your shoes as we do," Itzhak heard Laila say.

Itzhak couldn't stand it another moment, so he jumped into the conversation. "We can have someone from headquarters find a shoemaker to teach you the basics. I'm sure you could pick it up in no time." Laila flashed an irritated look at him, as if to say, *Hadn't you asked me to do your dirty work? And here you are jumping in as if I'm not capable!*

Itzhak raised his hands, palms out, and stepped back.

"I'm flattered you both have so much faith in me. As I said before, it never occurred to me that such a thing was a problem. Yes, I'll be happy to give it a try. Never let it be said I don't like a challenge. Who would have though I would be working in a bakery?"

"That's all we ask," said Laila reassuringly. Itzhak kept his mouth shut after that.

Days later, Tal brought someone to teach Mendel how to do the most essential repairs. As time passed, not only did Mendel become proficient in repairs, but he began creating his own sandals, strong enough to withstand the terrain yet comfortable enough to wear all day long. The kibbutzniks never went without shoes again. No matter what the challenge, the kibbutz had someone for every task, and both the kibbutz and the factory were operating at their most productive. Itzhak couldn't have been prouder.

###

A week later, as it happened, Rivka's sister, Evita, arrived for a visit—unannounced. She was the antithesis of her corpulent sister, an Auschwitz escapee with not a spare inch of fat on her bones. After a few days, she became very vocal. Itzhak, Laila, and Ari were finishing up breakfast when Evita confronted Laila.

"What is the meaning of only a few of you who come to breakfast at 8:30 being given eggs and milk? That isn't kibbutz equality," she demanded, hands on skinny hips.

Ari, who must have noted Laila's loss of words, jumped in to help her out. "Only those who work in sanitation get milk and eggs," he said, and then looked to the others for support.

Those seated close enough to hear the conversation nodded, having difficulty suppressing their laughter.

"Oh? So I'll volunteer to work in sanitation." Her face set in triumph, she marched out of the dining room.

"What are we going to do if she persists?" asked Laila.

"We'll have to tell her the truth," said Itzhak, finishing the last of his healthy breakfast of scrambled eggs with onions and peppers.

"What if she's not willing to keep our secret?" asked Laila.

"We'll have to kill her!" said Itzhak, face devoid of emotion.

Everyone else got the joke, but Ezra shook his head. "Somehow, right now, that isn't funny."

"Seriously, I don't think she will divulge our secret. I'm

sure Rivka will make her see the light." Itzhak picked up his tray and headed for the trash. As far as he was concerned, the matter of Evita was settled.

The following morning Evita came to breakfast, apparently expecting the promised eggs and milk. Itzhak and Laila approached her before she could begin a tirade. They escorted Evita outside and around the building to a secluded spot under a eucalyptus tree.

"Please sit down," said Laila.

Evita's eyes rolled. "What now?"

Itzhak glowered at her. "You are forcing us to tell you something that puts you and this entire kibbutz at great risk. We have tried to work with you, protecting you from the truth, but we no longer have a choice." Itzhak crossed his arms. "Before I go on, you must promise that what I tell you will die with you."

Evita looked stunned. Her eyes grew large. "My sister knows this secret of yours?"

"Yes."

"And she did not tell me?" she asked indignantly.

"She couldn't," Laila jumped in.

Laila and Itzhak sat for a moment while Evita worked through her dilemma. It did not take long.

"All right, you have my word." She sat, wringing her hands, perspiration forming on her upper lip.

"This kibbutz is the site of a clandestine ammunition factory. We make bullets for the *Haganah*."

Evita's face grew pale.

Itzhak leaned in close to her, his voice low. "If you breathe a word of this to anyone, you put your sister and the rest of us in jeopardy—not to mention the children. There are many who live and work here who do not know what we are doing. You may not speak of this to anyone but your sister from this point on, and only when you two are alone. Please do not put her on the spot by asking details. We realize this will be difficult, but there is no choice. You forced our hand. If you cannot keep this information to yourself, we will be forced to turn you over to the *Haganah*." Itzhak leaned back upright and waited for a reply.

Evita did not speak for a moment. Her eyes traveled back and forth between Laila and Itzhak. "You're serious, aren't you? Very well," she said. "I am no longer in sanitation. I prefer working in the orange groves anyway." Her mouth turned up into a half-smile. "I'm actually relieved. I was beginning to think everyone thought I had leprosy."

Itzhak was shocked by her reaction. Evita was obviously tougher than Laila and he had thought.

Laila hugged Evita, but the woman remained rigid. She was probably processing what she had just heard.

Itzhak still didn't have a good feeling about Evita, but only time would tell.

Chapter 34

Laila

Ayalon Institute, summer of 1947

Laila rarely took time to contemplate her situation, but for some reason, while dropping an orange into a burlap sack, her mind wandered. There were those who might think what they were doing was heroic, full of drama, but it had become as any other job, something a person just did. The kibbutzniks were young, impressionable, and fighting for their own cause. The fact that what they did could destroy all of them made the kibbutz that much stronger.

And then there were the British, who were adding pressure by initiating more frequent visits. Apparently the kibbutz hadn't made itself visible enough in the surrounding towns, so they got to work sending small groups out to mingle with neighbors. Funny, the green-eyed soldier had not surfaced in a year. Perhaps he had been sent to the front, or maybe killed. Laila shuddered at the thought and an orange slipped out of her hand, falling to the ground.

"What is going on up there?" yelled Leora.

"Sorry. My thoughts were elsewhere."

"Please take me with you the next time you wander off; you just missed my head." Leora chuckled as she bent down to pick up the orange.

"Sorry. It won't happen again."

"Just kidding."

"I know."

"Where were you?" Leora squeezed the liquid of the slightly wounded fruit down her throat.

"I let my thoughts go where they shouldn't—our present situation and the volatility of our job." Laila didn't mention the fact that she had also been thinking about the green-eyed soldier, who still found his way into her thoughts, but not as frequently anymore.

"You're right; better off not thinking about it. It doesn't accomplish anything. If you start questioning ... well, what are the chances that others won't? We are doing our job."

"Huh. You're way too pragmatic. I told you my thoughts were nonsense."

They went about their work without further discussion. At the end of the day, Leora and Laila arrived back at the kibbutz to find a group of *Palmach* trainees who looked like they had singlehandedly fought a war.

As they drew near, the women could hear the soldiers' story. The men had just arrived and looked tired, worn, and starving.

"Would you mind starting over?" asked Rivka. "Laila is a member of our secretariat and would be interested in what you have to say." She pulled Laila through the crowd, pushing her to the front.

Laila introduced herself and slithered away in embarrassment, headed for Itzhak, who stood next to Ezra

The Laundry Room

and Anna. Rivka never noticed her departure; she seemed enthralled by the handsome soldiers.

One of them eyed his companions. "We're thirsty. Could we have something to drink first?"

"Why don't we move to the dining room where it is cooler, and everyone can hear?" Rivka suggested.

Laila couldn't believe Rivka's *chutzpah*. Why, she had just jumped in and taken over. Was she campaigning to take over running the secretariat? And if she did—so what?

"This way," Rivka said. The rest followed, as confused as Laila at Rivka's sudden take-charge attitude. She had always been a follower, albeit with a big presence.

"Good idea," said Ari, who had just finished his shift and was on his way to lunch.

Once inside, the soldiers were given refreshments and quizzed mercilessly about current events.

"Let them tell their story so we can all hear," demanded Zalman.

One of the soldiers stood, holding onto a cool beer the kibbutz now kept for the British colonel, who visited monthly but always called ahead. "The British set up a dragnet, in search of anti-British activities and anything written they could put their hands on. This was in response to the most daring attack on bridges we have ever staged. The British caught a number of officers, but no top officials. We were taken captive to a detention camp and later released because the British couldn't prove anything. A few of us were sent to Kibbutz Hefziba, not far away. For some reason, Tal Rabin suggested we come here."

Avraham approached Itzhak and Laila, motioning them to follow. Out of earshot, he said soberly, "I think the reason Tal sent them here was to lend a hand. We need more men.

We are exhausted, and I, for one, am afraid someone will eventually make a mistake. We don't have time to contact Tal, so what do you think?"

Itzhak, now an influential member of the secretariat, turned to Laila. "I agree. I don't think we have anything to fear. They have already proven themselves. Avraham, will you speak to them?"

"Don't you think we should poll the rest of the secretariat?" Avraham asked.

Laila could see Itzhak's mind working. "We don't have that much time."

"Go ahead," she said. "I'll go below and poll Sol, Carmel, and Schlomo."

"Hurry. Most everyone else is in the dining room," said Avraham, already on his way.

The polling was unanimous. The three met back at the entrance to the dining room and discussed how they would broach the subject with the soldiers.

"I think it should come from you men," said Laila, stepping forward. "I'm not sure fighting men take kindly to a woman's counsel." Not everyone was as democratic as their kibbutz.

After dinner, Itzhak and Avraham asked the three soldiers to step outside. The men exchanged dubious looks and followed. Laila trailed behind, keeping her distance but close enough to hear.

Avraham appeared nervous. Every time members of the kibbutz shared their secret, they took a calculated risk. "We believe we know why Tal sent you," he said. "We have to ask that what we are about to say be kept in the strictest confidence and not repeated outside our immediate group. We are taking a big chance, but we believe, as soldiers, you

The Laundry Room

are trustworthy."

The soldiers shared another uncomfortable moment. One spoke up. "As long as you aren't going to shoot us, we are fine with whatever you have to say."

"You have nothing to worry about from us. Are you in agreement?"

Again the men exchanged glances and nodded.

"Very well, then," said Avraham. "We are running an underground munitions factory. We supply the majority of 9mm bullets for the Sten guns you are using."

Eyes widened.

"The factory is working around the clock and some of us have had little sleep. We think Tal sent you here to give us a hand. We could use even more help if you think there are others, back at the camp you came from, who might be trusted."

"First of all," one of the soldiers stepped forward with a new tone of respect, "and I speak for myself—I would be honored to work with your group. I have heard nothing but praise for this kibbutz. I had no idea ..."

"We're glad to hear you had no idea, or we would be in trouble," said Itzhak with a smile. "What do you think?" He turned to the other men.

One of the soldiers spoke up. "I too would be delighted to join the kibbutz and help take some of the stress off your hands. It will be a welcome change from being shot at."

Avraham and Itzhak nodded in agreement. Laila, on-the-other-hand, was amused that the soldiers obviously had no idea what they were getting themselves into.

After they showed the soldiers the factory, the most senior of the soldiers said, "We will stay as long as we are not needed elsewhere; but first, we must returned to Kibbutz

Hefziba to see how many others wish to join us."

Days later, the original group of soldiers returned with thirty other recruits, who were filled with a renewed enthusiasm and eagerness to help.

The kibbutz was grateful for that.

One morning, shortly after welcoming the new recruits to the kibbutz and while the dew was still on the ground; Laila stole a moment to herself. She stood in the doorframe of their room, mug in hand. Glancing over her shoulder, she took a moment to admire her latest handiwork. Although it had not increased in size, Laila had made her and Itzhak's space as comfortable as possible. The original burlap curtains had been replaced with a lapis-blue silky material, tied back with an accent in green and blue glass beads. Their bed was now covered with the same material as the drapes. Laila, had happily, replaced the old Oriental rug with a newer one, but with matching blue, green, black, and white motifs. While feeling deprived of nature's beauty most of the day, she tried to bring some of it into their room. Itzhak said he felt he was sleeping in a sheik's tent in the middle of an oasis, and expected to see harem girls dance their way through the door any moment.

Itzhak had risen early that morning and was already on his way to the fields. It was his day to work outside and hers to spend with her children. Tova, Laila's second child, had been an easy birth and had been worked into Laila's schedule like eating and drinking. No more panic over everything she did or ate, like Laila had done with Dovele. It seemed that Tova, whose name meant "good", had known from the beginning that her mother would have little time for her, so she did her best not to ask for much.

The Laundry Room

Laila finished her tea and dressed for the day. Since she would be with her children, she chose her only colorful skirt and peasant top, instead of her work "uniform" of sleeveless shirt and baggy shorts. Summers had been brutal down below, and the workers had needed to make adjustments to their clothing. Luckily, fashion was not a watchword for the kibbutz.

Laila anticipated her children's excitement upon arrival, and decided to set out earlier than expected. She could no longer see her feet, as another sister or brother was on its way. She finished tiding up the small room, changed the sheets, and gathered the towels. She would drop them by the laundry, where she would spend only a moment kibitzing with Leora.

Outside, Zalman and Ari were in the midst of a heated discussion. Rivka, with her sister's help, was hanging up the day's camouflage in front of the laundry room. Laila passed Sara, a "giraffe," who was carrying a sack of what looked like dirty clothes. Laila wondered if Sara knew she was headed in the wrong direction. Laila dropped off the laundry, hugged Leora and continued to the nursery, promptly forgetting about Sara. In the distance, she saw Dovele's thick black hair caught in a sudden gust of wind and his little hand waving frantically. Laila waddled to him and enveloped him in her arms. He kissed her cheeks and then her stomach, a new habit—from where, she had no idea. She guessed he was kissing the new baby.

Zahar appeared from behind the nursery door. She was wearing a bright green top and long skirt. She was also pregnant, and Laila prayed that Zahar would carry the baby full term. Laila looked beyond her for Leora, and then reminded herself it was Leora's day in the laundry room. While she was looking, Tova managed to wiggle her way out the door and threw herself at Laila's legs. Laila picked up her daughter and nuzzled her nose in the pink skin of her neck—the sweetest part of a baby, as far as Laila was concerned.

"Good morning sister," said Zahar.

Laila loved when Zahar called her that. Laila hadn't seen her real sisters in such a long time. "How much longer?" she asked.

"A month, I suppose. I feel like I'm carrying twins this time. How are you feeling?"

"Better than usual."

They laughed easily, chatted about nothing, and then Laila took Dovele in one hand and Tova in the other, and led them back to the room. Laila felt it her duty to teach the children life's lessons. They worked on letters and colors. Dovele was a quick learner; Tova, was not yet ready for any of this. Laila and Dovele practiced the alphabet, sang songs, and colored ... their favorite while Tova explored the floor and everything within hand's reach.

Dovele looked up at Laila with concern. "Where's Abba?"

Laila loved that he called Itzhak "Abba." Laila had noticed Dovele turning his attachment away from her and toward his father. At first she was jealous, but she realized it was normal for a boy; and besides, she still had Tova and would be busy with the new baby. Laila wouldn't have as much time for him as before. She also felt pressured to return to the factory.

"Abba's in the field and will be back early enough to give you a bear hug." Naturally, Dovele had no idea where they went each day or what they did.

Dovele giggled and they returned to their game. Tova and he got along so well. Dovele was a natural teacher. He had so much patience. He would grab her hands and move her in a circle, singing songs—her chubby legs keeping time to Laila's

The Laundry Room

voice. They would fall to the floor in spasms of joy.

About that time, Sara—the "giraffe"—passed the room, still clinging to that bundle of clothing, but this time headed in the right direction. Laila figured Sara must have stopped to chat along the way. Laila often worried about Sara and her inability to fit in. Rivka, Leora, and Laila had all tried to become her friend, but with no success. She was a loner.

It was then that Laila remembered she had a few more things of Itzhak's that needed cleaning—they had so few clothes. With Tova on her hip and Dovele hanging onto the basket, they headed for the laundry room. Laila spotted Zalman basking in the sunshine, kibitzing with a friend. Laila felt a strong tug on the basket.

"Emma ... Zalman."

"Go, child. Hug your friend Zalman."

The child ran, calling Zalman's name over and over until he was snuggled in the man's arms, Zalman kissing the boy's tousled locks. Zalman picked up the boy and swung him around. Laila and Avraham questioned the draw, but they never questioned it. She supposed it was good for both of them. Laila left Dovele outside to play with Zalman; Tova remained on her hip. Laila entered the building, noting Sara had already dropped her clothing into an oversized basin. Sara reached for the soap powder, turned on the faucet, and commenced scrubbing. Laila dropped her bundle on the floor, stopping to talk to Leora.

Without warning, the washing machine began to swivel on its hinges, leaving that gaping hole in the floor. One by one, like ants pouring out of their underground tunnel, the workers ascended, passing Sara, and continuing on their way, forgetting that she knew nothing about the factory.

Sara screamed, "People are coming out of the ground!" and careened out of the laundry room, collapsing to the hard concrete of the patio—gibberish spewing like lava from her mouth. Fast-thinking Leora grabbed a pot of soapy water and ran after her; Laila followed, Tova bouncing on her hip. Leora rushed past Laila, and in the middle of the patio, poured the pot of soapy water over Sara's head to stop the screaming. The women lifted the poor woman and carried her back to her room. Carmel, her roommate, would have the duty of calming her down that night.

The next day, Sara was taken out to the field where she was briefed. She and Laila sat talking for hours as Sara worked through what had taken place.

As they talked, one question kept going through Laila's mind: how would the kibbutz be able to make sure something like that never happened again?

Chapter 35

Avraham

Ayalon Institute, early into 1948

It was early Sunday morning, and Zahar and Avraham had given themselves permission to sleep in. They had worked hard the day before, and every muscle in their bodies screamed for rest. The Jews were in a full-scale war with the Arabs, and receiving little help from the British. The Jewish army was depending upon the kibbutz more than ever for those 9mm bullets.

Avraham lay quietly, staring at the unscarred side of his wife's face. He wasn't sure she had figured out why he preferred this side of the bed. At least, he hoped not. It was at moments like these that she seemed as before, his beautiful girl; but when she turned, he had the everyday reminder of what she had been through. Their second child had been stillborn, and it all but destroyed her, and so when Zahar carried Naomi full-term, the whole kibbutz celebrated. Even with the new baby and the joy she had brought, Zahar's depression had not completely gone away. So, lying there day. They would go to Rehovot, where he would buy her something special. His resolve: focus on family and not Laila. He needed to rid himself of those improper thoughts that would only destroy his marriage and continue to make him unhappy. His fantasies had gone on longer than they should have. He loved his wife—that was true. She deserved his full devotion.

It was at that precise moment that an explosion rocked the compound.

Avraham and Zahar grabbed sheets off the bed and wrapped them around their nakedness on the way to the door. Avraham shielded his wife with his body. She was shaking. Avraham understood her fear after experiencing that horrendous explosion at the hotel. Now, the two of them watched in horror as people ran from one building to the next, looking for the source of the explosion.

"Please stay inside," said Avraham as he maneuvered Zahar back into the room. "I'm going to find out what is going on." Avraham threw on some old clothes, and was about to run out of the room when Zahar grabbed his arm.

"Please be careful. I love you." Tears ran down her cheek, as she tried to wipe them away with the back of her hand.

"I will. I love you, too." Avraham joined the rest of the men as they scoured the kibbutz for any sign of destruction. But they found no evidence that the kibbutz had been compromised.

Itzhak ran up to Avraham, out of breath, eyes ablaze. "Do you think it might have been the train station?

Avraham returned to his room. "We're fine, nothing was destroyed. We're not under attack, but something happened close by. Are you okay?" he asked, holding her close.

"I'm okay. What happened?"

The Laundry Room

"I'm not sure, but we have not suffered any damage. I'm on my way to the guard's station. I'll be back as soon as I can. I'm sorry you had to be upset for nothing." He was truly sorry. It seemed life was an uphill battle, and the kibbutzniks were constantly being tested for strength and resilience.

"Go. I'm fine," said Zahar. "You would think I would have gotten used to unexpected adversities by now, but it's always a shock." She kissed his cheek.

Avraham ran to the main gate, thinking the watchmen might have a better vantage point. As he approached the towers, one of the guards jumped to the ground, opened a hidden cache in a brick wall next to the tower, and gave a hidden screw a half turn, setting off flashing red lights across "The Hill." The secretariat had determined the code: one flash meant to stop production because there was a stranger in the area; three flashes meant "stop work and be on the lookout"; and many flashes meant to evacuate the factory and scatter. The signal system was used only in extreme emergencies.

Today, the flashing lights began in earnest, warning the kibbutz something dire was afoot.

"What happened, Avraham?" Itzhak and Laila were close behind.

The sentry was busy closing the gates. He spoke over his shoulder. "At first I thought it was a train wreck, but now I think someone blew up a train. You'd better alert the others; we will probably be having visitors."

"What should we do to prevent them from coming?" asked Laila, scantily clad in her night clothing. She must have realized her condition and tightened the shawl around her.

"I suggest we send some of our nurses and a few able-bodied men down to the station to help, so that the soldiers don't come here looking for aid," said Avraham, noting Laila's discomfort and her attire. "I'll go with them," he said, having trouble taking his eyes off of Laila.

"Do you think that wise?" asked Itzhak. "We can't run the risk of something happening to you."

"I think it's the best plan," said Avraham, heading back to the kibbutz. "They have too much to worry about to be concerned with a few volunteers, and they will probably welcome some help. Laila, get the nurses organized."

"But I want to come," said Laila.

"I need you here to coordinate supplies and to watch in case any injured people wander this way."

Laila frowned. "I understand. I'm on my way." She hurried away toward the nurses' quarters, but Avraham was aware of her displeasure.

A few minutes later, two of the nurses, Avraham, and Lebel Frumkin, who had volunteered to come because he had medical experience, were seen carrying a white flag and medical provisions, headed toward the train station. When they arrived, it was to a horrible sight—bodies everywhere. The kibbutzniks could hear guns in the distance.

Noting more help was needed, Avraham sent Lebel back for more volunteers. The extras showed up with bandages and such, and met Avraham at the wreck. Only then did he see Laila busily taking over. He had told her to stay put, but she had disregarded his directive. That would not do. She continued to be a thorn in his side.

Avraham found a British soldier who must have been guarding the station. "How can we be of help?" he asked, gathering some of the volunteers around him.

"I don't know," said the soldier, scanning the area. "Help whoever you can. I have to report this to the proper authorities. Now if you will excuse me—" He was obviously distracted and half-panicked, wondering what to do first. He left Avraham and the volunteers to figure it out for themselves.

"Ezra, you and Anna take Lebel and one of the nurses and create groups depending upon need." Avraham stopped and ran his hand across his brow, as if visualizing the plan. "Zalman, you and another nurse set up an area for the supplies. The rest of you, do whatever you can to make sure no one goes back to 'The Hill'."

Avraham started analyzing the situation and what needed to be done next. The nurses worked feverishly, trying to keep the victims alive, using the triage system to help separate the badly wounded from those who could wait. Ambulances from Rehovot finally appeared, and the kibbutz volunteers helped carry the wounded to them, to be transported to the nearest hospital.

Avraham's biggest concern throughout the ordeal was that some of the less-wounded men might turn on them, thinking that the volunteers were the enemy; but when they saw that the volunteers meant them no harm, the injured seemed happy enough to have someone taking care of them and let them continue without incident.

As Avraham scanned the wreckage, he happened to spot Laila busily administering to a wounded soldier. He couldn't help but marvel at how diligently she went about her duties, unaware that her own life could be in great danger. Perhaps he had been a little too gruff, ordering her about like an underling, since she was one of his most valuable of the leading members. Avraham would take up the matter with her later, he decided. This was no time to pull rank.

When the worst was over, Avraham and Lebel approached one of the officers. Avraham took a deep breath before he spoke. There was no way to know how this very distraught man might take what he had to say. "I'm hoping you will remember our selfless assistance and leave "The Hill" alone. We are not harboring any criminals, nor are we looking for any trouble."

The officer said nothing, but apparently respected their wishes, for they were never bothered about the incident.

Days later, when Tal Rabin arrived, the kibbutz learned what had precipitated the attack. He called the kibbutz together to share his information.

"On February 22, a bunch of Arabs and British deserters drove British Army trucks containing explosives onto Ben Yehuda Street, one of the busiest areas for shopping in Jerusalem. Fifty-eight Jews were killed, and one hundred forty injured. The Arab high command took full responsibility for the incident, sending out an edict that if the Jews did not adhere to the rules of war, they, the Arabs, would continue to set off more explosives.

"So, *Lehi,* our underground rebels, took it upon themselves to punish the British for doing nothing about the earlier incident. They bombed a train going from Cairo-Haifa used by British officers, killing twenty-eight soldiers and wounding thirty. In retaliation, the British raided a nearby Jewish, alcohol factory and removed all rifles from the workers. After the British left, a group of Arabs came in behind them and massacred the defenseless men."

"I say we do something to better protect ourselves!" shouted Zalman.

"What do you suggest?" asked Avraham.

"I don't believe the British will continue to leave us alone," said Zalman in earnest. "They might be placed in a position to show the Arabs they aren't on our side. I say we build an underground arsenal. I'm sure Tal can confiscate a

The Laundry Room

few of those Sten guns for us. The army will never miss them. No one seems to care about our welfare, so it's up to us to act before we're all slaughtered."

"I'll see what I can do," promised Tal. He left shortly afterward.

The next day the men searched the kibbutz for a good place to put their arsenal. Avraham met some of the men outside the bed-framing building and declared he had found the right spot, so Ezra ran and got two shovels and they began digging under the workshop table in the framing building. They dropped a small wagon down the hole, throwing in a few rifles for good measure. The men decided they would add to the arsenal whenever they could.

If the British did raid "The Hill," that's all they would find. As it turned out, the arsenal was never used or discovered.

Chapter 36

Laila

Ayalon Institute, June 1948

By the morning of March 24th, 1948, the kibbutz had become more than an underground factory; the kibbutzniks had become a major part of the war effort to gain independence. Production had sped up to maximum capacity, the members working through the night with the knowledge that if they failed, so failed the Jewish army. Laila was seeing less and less of her children, and was just about ready to collapse. Itzhak and she had just come up for breakfast and were standing outside the dining hall when a bullet snapped by Laila's head.

Itzhak grabbed her, pushing her through the door and to the ground. Those who had been standing around or were already in the dining room dove under tables, some too late. Sophie Bresler, who had been standing next to Laila only minutes before sharing stories of her nieces' latest exploits; lay bleeding, clutching her midsection. The sight of that much blood once again propelled Laila back to that horrible

The Laundry Room

participants in a government subplot—the bombing of the King David Hotel.

Suddenly aware of her surroundings and under a table, Laila felt the room spin out of control. She gasped for air and clung to Itzhak, who must have realized the effect the attack was having on her. He positioned himself between Sophie and her, while he went about trying to stop the bleeding before Sophie bled to death.

"Sophie's been hit. I need for you to pull yourself together and help me," Itzhak's voice quivered. "You're going to have to let go of me so that I can reposition myself. It is going to take both of us to keep her alive. Can you do that?"

Laila nodded and gradually unclenched her fists, letting go of Itzhak's shirt. Realizing how badly Sophie was hurt, Laila forced herself out of her own panic and into a more useful mode. Laila locked eyes with Itzhak, took the encouragement she needed, and crawled around him until she was behind Sophie.

What Laila saw made her sick. She hadn't been able to really look at Sophie, and now the reality of her situation hit Laila in the gut. It was imperative that they get Sophie to a hospital.

Laila glanced about the room, seeking help. Most of the others seemed to be in shock, lying prone on the floor; so that left Laila and Itzhak to do what was necessary to keep Sophie alive. This incident was another reminder of why the kibbutzniks had to finish what they had started. There had been a number of minor attacks before now, but no one had ever been hurt. Not until today. This was serious.

"Help me, Itzhak. I don't want to die," Sophie moaned.

"We won't let you," he said, doing his best to stop the bleeding. "Please, hold on while we figure out what to do." This time his eyes seemed to be searching Laila's for help.

Just then, Laila felt a hand on her back and jumped. "I need to use the bathroom," whispered Rivka. "Would you come with me?" She had directed the question to Laila.

"No one is going anywhere," snapped Itzhak, eyes glaring.

Laila knew that when Itzhak's eyes stormed he was angry, and there was a tempest brewing. Her husband was usually well-balanced, but when the scales tilted, so to speak, watch out.

"It is too dangerous," he hissed, "and besides, it is in another building, which means you would have to go outside, and becoming a moving target. Find a bucket or something." He turned his attention back to Sophie, who had lost consciousness. Bullets popped like corn, ricocheting off the stone structure, piercing glass, splitting wood, and leaving the dining room in shambles. If those caught off-guard lived, it would be a miracle.

Laila continued to pray that someone in Rehovot would hear the commotion and come to their aid. They huddled together, hoping the snipers wouldn't come any closer. Even with Sophie bleeding in front of her, all Laila could think about were the children; they would be so scared. At least Leora and Zahar were with them today.

This wasn't supposed to be happening. The kibbutz was a front for peaceful assembly. They had caused no trouble, had been helpful, and had adhered to all the rules. The kibbutzniks couldn't fight back because they weren't supposed to have guns, and even if they could use them, they couldn't get to them.

The sniper fire continued for more than an hour, but it never got any closer. Laila began to believe most of it was for show. She continued to hold a pressure bandage on Sophie's wound as she watched Ari and Leora crawl toward them. "Were you able to see who was firing?" Ari asked.

The Laundry Room

"No," said Itzhak. "Help me move Sophie to the back of the room. We'll need something under her so we can slide her instead of lifting her."

"I thought you were with the children!" Laila attacked Leora.

"I was—I'd just left to see Ari when the bullets began," responded Leora, her eyes filled with worry.

"Does that mean Zahar is alone?" Laila countered.

"No, Yehudith is helping out today. She said she needed some time with her children."

"Oh, thank God. I would hate to have Zahar have to handle this alone." Laila thought she had heard a little sarcasm in Leora's words about needing "time with her children." Could it be the women resented all the time Laila was giving to the cause?

"Yehudith is a strong woman, probably a lot stronger than I. She'll keep order." Leora placed her hand on Laila's shoulder as if letting her know she had meant no harm.

The four scanned the room for something to slide under Sophie, not expecting what came next—a bullet sped past, shattering what was left of the window pane and spraying broken glass in their faces. A shard lodged in Laila's scalp. Again she flashed back, this time to the burning ember that had set her hair on fire that day when the hotel blew up. She slid her free hand through her hair, hoping to pull out the shard, not thinking of the consequences. Her hand came away full of blood from the wound. Her stomach churned.

Itzhak, intent on moving Sophie and unaware of Laila's injury, dashed to the side of the room where they kept fresh dishtowels and other linens, and found a tablecloth. He dove under a table as another barrage of bullets sprayed the back wall. Fortunately those under fire hadn't made it that far, or they would have all be dead.

Itzhak slid back under the table and must have seen the bloody side of Laila's head. "You're bleeding. Were you hit?" bellowed Itzhak. "Here, let me help you." Itzhak took one of the towels and wrapped it around Laila's head.

"I'm all right ... it's just glass. It's Sophie who needs our attention. Here, let me help you with the tablecloth."

Leora cried, "Let us help," and scooted close to her friend. It appeared all was forgiven.

Some of the men began turning tables on their sides, creating a barrier and staggering them for fortification. Laila didn't feel any less vulnerable. Her head throbbed and she was just barely keeping herself together. Where was the *Haganah?* They needed more protection.

The onslaught continued in intervals. Just when they thought it was over, another barrage of bullets would hit the building. The kibbutzniks in the dining hall were all praying the attack would end. Sophie was no longer responding to anything they were doing.

When Laila thought all was lost, someone answered their prayers, and the shooting gradually came to an end. The small group in the dining room stayed put, waiting to see what would happen next. It wasn't long before British uniforms became visible, and the kibbutzniks were rescued.

Laila had never been so happy to see those khaki greens. Now Sophie and anyone else who had been wounded would be transported to the hospital, but first Laila had to check on her children. The baby was only a few months old, and Laila was just beginning to feel like her old self. Turning to Itzhak, she said, "I have to make sure the children are all right first, and then I'll be with you. If I don't return, go without me." She kissed his forehead and grabbed Leora's hand. They ran like crazed animals to the nursery.

When Leora and Laila finally reached the nursery, the

The Laundry Room

door was locked. Laila pounded. "It's Laila and Leora; please let us in. It's over and we are all safe." She almost forgot the secret word which was necessary to enter. "Eucalyptus!" she screamed. Laila could hear the bolts slide back and the door open. They rushed in, almost stumbling over Yehudith. "Are ... they ... all right?" Laila asked. At this point, she could hardly speak.

"They are fine," said Zahar, holding one of the babies who continued to cry. "A little frightened, but fine." The rest of the children were wrapped around her and Yehudith's legs. "What happened? When we heard the first shot, we bolted and barricaded the doors."

Leora had scooped up her youngest, who was now clinging to his mother.

"We're not sure, but we think it was a group of local Arabs who were taking potshots at us. They hit several people, Sophie being one of them. We're taking her to the hospital right now. Would you mind watching the children until I return?" Laila glanced from Zahar to Yehudith.

"Of course ... go," said Zahar. Then her eyes widened. "You've been hit—you're bleeding! Here, let me get something to stop the bleeding." She ran to the closet and found a clean, white towel, removed the soiled one that had been temporarily wrapped around Laila's head, and applied the new one a little more securely.

"It was a shard of glass, not a bullet." Laila knew what she was thinking. She kissed Zahar on the cheek, ran to kiss her children, and hugged them tightly to her breast. "I love you. Be good for Zahar and Leora. I will be back soon." Her middle child had that unmistakable look of terror on her face, while Dovele tried to be stoic. She handed the baby over to Yehudith.

Cries of "Emma ... Emma ..." trailed behind Laila as

Dovele and Tova followed her to the door. It broke her heart to leave, but she felt she must. Her children, small though they were, were going to have to toughen up if they were to survive this land. Laila bent down again and hugged them one last time. "Behave, my children. Emma will be back—I promise." Laila turned to Zahar. "Sophie is in bad shape. She needs someone she knows with her, not some strange man."

"I understand. The children will be fine," she said picking up Tova and grabbing Dovele's hand.

Laila reached the ambulance just as it was about to leave. Itzhak pulled Laila in through the back door. "How are the children?" he asked, worry lines running across his face.

"They're fine. I'm afraid I made them unhappy bursting in like that and then leaving, but they will recover. How is she?"

Itzhak shook his head. He either did not want to say or couldn't.

Itzhak and Laila were determined to stay with Sophie until she was out of the woods; she needed someone to comfort her. Laila was afraid they might lose her; she had lost so much blood. Sophie mumbled, "Uri, Uri," over and over. Uri was a Jewish soldier who stopped by "The Hill" whenever he could. He and Sophie had planned to marry at the end of the year. Laila prayed that day would come.

Sophie's condition was touch and go all the way to the hospital. The debris-filled road was bumpy and difficult to navigate, not to mention dusty, making it almost impossible to keep Sophie from added infection. Laila and Itzhak sat on either side of her to absorb the shock. Laila held her hand while Itzhak reassured her she would be okay. They weren't even sure she heard them or knew they were with her.

The ambulance arrived to bedlam. The injured from other kibbutzim had already been unloaded and lined the corridors. Sophie was rushed into surgery. It appeared the hospital was not equipped to handle a catastrophe of such magnitude, so Itzhak and Laila pitched in where they could, even though their skills were limited. The train bombing and their attempt to help had begun their schooling in the art of triage. By late afternoon, they learned that Sophie had taken a further turn for the worse. Itzhak and Laila were losing hope.

In the middle of changing the bandage on Laila's head, she looked up to see Uri headed their way.

"What happened?" he said, rushing toward them, visibly distraught.

"We were attacked—snipers."

"I heard. That is why I am here, to help."

"Do you know about Sophie?" asked Itzhak.

Uri's face turned ashen as he teetered; Itzhak caught him. "What? Is she all right? Where is she?"

Laila spoke to him as she would a child. "She was injured during the attack, and is in the operating room right now. They are doing whatever they can for her." Laila felt like the messenger who brought bad news. "A miracle brought you here. She needs to know you're here. I'll take you there."

Laila and Uri hurried through the halls, which were filled with wounded people all vying for attention. Laila's heart went out to those who would not make it through the day. She barely knew where she was going—barreling down one hall and up the next until she saw a sign directing them to the operating room. Uri was on her heels, never more than a step behind. She tripped once; he caught her and pushed her forward. By the time they arrived at the operating room, they were both fighting back tears of frustration and worry; Laila knew the thought of losing Sophie must be tearing Uri apart.

A nurse approached. "Who are you looking for?"

"Sophie Bresler," Uri said, his voice shaking.

"What relation are you?" By the look of things, the nurse was exhausted and in need of a break.

"We're engaged." At this point, Uri was hanging onto Laila.

"Please stay here," said the nurse, looking down at a chart. "I'll see if one of the doctors can speak with you. She disappeared behind a double, swinging door.

"What if she dies?" Uri wailed. "What will I do? I have thought of nothing but our wedding and how beautiful she will be. Her parents are coming from Safed. What will I tell them?"

"You'll tell them she is going to be fine and the wedding will go as scheduled. You must think positive." Laila gently grasped Uri's arm. The words came, but Laila's heart was breaking for him. She had lived through so much in her short life, and wondered if she would ever find peace in any land.

The doors the nurse had disappeared behind suddenly flew open as a doctor exited, wiping his brow with his forearm and pulling away his mask to reveal a weary face. His furrowed brow led Uri and Laila to believe the worst. Laila felt Uri's body sag.

"We are doing all we can for Miss Bresler. She has lost a great deal of blood and may already have an infection. She has a rare blood type, and we have none of her type on hand for a transfusion."

Laila looked at the doctor and then at Uri. "What is it?"

"AB negative."

"I'm O Negative, a universal blood donor," Laila said, tightening her grip on Uri's arm. "Where do we go?"

"Just a minute; you've been wounded, and there's that

The Laundry Room

infection—"

Uri stepped forward. "I have some connections. What can I do? Sophie and I are engaged."

The doctor rubbed his eyes. It was obvious the ordeal was getting to him. "There is a miracle drug called 'penicillin,' which is widely used in other countries, but nearly impossible to acquire here in Palestine. If you could get your hands on it, we might have a fighting chance. But you should know that all communications have been severed, so we have no way of sending out word. We are on our own. I've got to go." The doctor started walking toward the door. "I'll alert one of the nurses to take you down to the blood draw area," the doctor said to Laila. He then turned back to Uri. "Whatever you can do ..." He disappeared behind the double doors.

Laila was thinking that Uri would have to find a way back to "The Hill" in order to use his connections, but the only vehicles available were the ambulances. "Go find Itzhak. He may have an idea. I have to stay—"

Uri was gone before she finished her sentence.

Hours or days later—she didn't know which—Laila heard her name as if through a tunnel. "Laila? Laila, how are you? How is Sophie?"

Laila looked up from the bed in the hallway to see Uri, Itzhak, and Leora headed her way. Laila tried to sit up, dizzy and more than a little foggy from the trauma of giving blood when she was already wounded. She grabbed Uri's shoulder. "She'll be better now that you're back. Were you able to get the miracle drug?" Laila prayed silently, knowing that without the medicine, Sophie would likely die.

Lynda Lippman-Lockhart

Itzhak held up a large package, which he handed off to the nurse. She took it and scurried off. Uri and Leora both dropped to the wooden bench next to Laila. Itzhak, disheveled and out of breath, sat on her bed and held her hand. "How are you? I haven't stopped worrying about you since I left. I'm not sure how much more our family can take. I worry about the children not being with us during times like this, and the emotional toll on you. This has been awfully hard on you. I want this all to end now."

"Me too, but I'll be fine; and as for the children ... well, they'll soon forget. Remember, being young has its benefits. Now, tell me what happened." Laila pulled Itzhak down for a kiss. She had never realized she could love someone as much as she did Itzhak. Yes, her parents and siblings had been her life, but this was different. And, as much as she loved her children, she knew they were only hers temporarily, on loan to her until they grew up.

"It is a long story; I'll tell you later. Right now, all I want is to hold you and catch my breath. I'm so proud of you, you can't imagine. You are the strongest, bravest woman I know. I love you very much."

"Thank you. The feeling is mutual."

Laila had been so absorbed in Itzhak's return that she hadn't noticed Uri trying to catch his breath. He looked like he was about to have a heart attack.

"Are you okay? Do you need a medic?"

"I'll be fine after I catch my breath. We haven't stopped moving since we left. When this is over, I'm going to sleep for a week." They all laughed for the first time since the nightmare had started.

The small group of anxious people waited for the next few hours, huddled together, sharing memories of Sophie and planning their future until an unfamiliar doctor appeared.

351

The Laundry Room

Uri stood, his body tense, his face a roadmap of worry.

The doctor removed his mask and head covering and smiled. "I think Miss Bresler is going to make it. Her fever has gone down, and she is responding well. Let us clean her up and put her in a room; then you can see her. That will make her happy. Are you Uri?"

Uri nodded.

"Your name is the only word she uttered throughout her suffering." He paused. "Could I have a word with you?" The doctor led Uri down the hall.

Itzhak, Leora and Laila looked on. Laila wondered what sort of news had to be given in private. When she saw Uri break down sobbing, she knew he had been told something awful. What could it be? The doctor patted him on the shoulder and walked away. Uri stood unmoving. When he returned, Laila and the others could see he had been ripped apart.

"The bullet ... Where she was injured ... We'll never have children."

Laila pulled him close as he dropped his head to her shoulder. Itzhak joined them. They cried for the young couple's loss. When a nurse appeared to take Uri to Sophie; Laila, Leora, and Itzhak said their goodbyes and left, relieved but brokenhearted.

Perhaps now the *Haganah* would find a way to protect them from their enemies while they did their part for the war effort. It had been three long years, and Laila was ready for the work to end. They were all anxious to get on with their lives.

When things finally died down, the kibbutz implored the British government to let them have weapons for defense;

352

they refused. This kibbutz was supposed to be a "safe" zone. Because of the denial of permission to bear arms, the kibbutzniks fortified their tall fences, fully enclosing the sentry towers. A number of the kibbutzniks wanted to avenge the raid, but the general assembly discouraged them from leaving. They were needed where they were, to fight the war in a different way. The kibbutz had reached a peak production of ten thousand to fourteen thousand bullets a day.

Together, this group of young people had proven themselves over and over again. Surely, they would be granted their own kibbutz once the war had ended. Forty-five young people had defied the odds, never losing even one member of their extended family. The *Haganah* had asked a lot of them, and they had answered the call. They had served their country bravely and without question.

Epilogue
Laila
Ma'agan Michael, 1974

The war ended in June of 1949, when a truce was finally declared. The underground factory was no longer needed, so the machines were moved to Tel Aviv until a new and improved factory could be built. Of the people who had worked together, day in and day out, most—that's one hundred fifty-four members and forty-four children—moved to Ma'agan Michael, where they live and work today. Attrition has played with those figures somewhat, losing members one day, gaining the next.

Ma'agan means "anchorage", and "Michael" was derived from Michael Pollack, a philanthropist who donated money to the Palestine Immigrant Colonization Association, an organization that helped place those who had lost their homes and often families to war. To the young people who had given so much, this new home was their anchor, giving them a sense of permanence. For Laila it was the "hope" she had once prayed for.

Lynda Lippman-Lockhart

Itzhak became a real fisherman, along with Ari, Ezra, Schmuel, and a dozen others. Their little coterie would leave early in the morning and return late afternoon, sometimes loaded with monkfish, albacore tuna, buri, lavrak, amnon, sea cod, striped mullet and denise. Sometimes they came back empty-handed, but that happened less and less often as they became proficient at their new trade.

Standing next to the Mediterranean Sea, looking out over the water and reminiscing, Laila couldn't help but think about their last days on "The Hill." The kibbutzniks had been through so much, for a bunch of young kids who knew nothing about the world except what they each had experienced separately; but together, they were mighty, invincible, and some were even called heroes. Laila never saw herself as a hero. She did what she was called upon to do. Idealistic though they might have been; that idealism had helped them all through the worst of times.

Laila mused over the first time Avraham had pulled the trigger on the *Sten* gun, and they all took a collective breath, worrying they would blow themselves up sooner or later. It was a miracle that it never happened. What did they know— nothing? They were wet behind the ears, her Abba would have said. He had died before Laila was able to tell him of her part in the war effort. She knew he would have been proud. Judah couldn't believe his little sister could keep a secret and for twenty years, but she had.

Laila's children opted to leave the kibbutz and live in Jerusalem and Haifa, respectively. They wanted to strike out on their own—experience life as their parents had. How could she argue with that? She would have been a hypocrite if she'd tried to stop them.

Laila glanced back over her shoulder at what was now theirs. The kibbutz owned seven hundred fifty acres for

The Laundry Room

farming cotton, fodder, bananas, avocados, and citrus fruit. Their barn held five hundred fifty cows that gave off 2.5 million liters of milk a year. They harvested fish from their four-hundred-twenty-five-acre pond, which yielded six hundred fifty tons of carp, St. Peter's fish, mullet, and silver carp. Further down the road was their plastics factory and "Suron", a factory that used chemicals to etch high-tech metal parts.

Laila was proud of all of their accomplishments, but it sometimes tired her to think about them. Oh sure, there were times when she almost regretted the loss of those precious years; but she knew, in her heart, they had been good ones, ones that had cemented her relationship with her husband and brought with them a contracted peace for all. Israel was a miracle, built upon bent shoulders and parentless kids. How could they help but be anything less than a fearless nation?

Laila received her degree in the sciences, but still worked in the Suron factory. Itzhak took over Avraham's position as titular head of the kibbutz, while Laila faded into the background. With the end of the war and a shift to new land, it was time for new blood and new ideas.

Today, standing by the sea, Laila had a vivid flash of the past and the day the war came to an end. She had just come up from the factory at the end of her shift, when she heard the commotion. From past experience, Laila naturally feared another attack, but instead she saw people dancing, slapping each other on the back, and singing songs of joy.

"Laila, the war is over," beamed Ezra, hugging her until she couldn't breathe. "We have won! *The Declaration of Independence* has been signed, and Israel is now our country. Would you please go below and tell everyone the news!"

Could it be true? Had they won? She was so elated until she turned to go back downstairs but saw, in the distance, a figure that looked vaguely familiar. He no longer wore a dress uniform, but Laila recognized him, just the same.

He walked toward her, his gait that of a man not so sure of himself anymore. Laila stood anchored in place. How could it be? She had not seen him since her wedding day. What could he possibly have to say to her all these years later, especially now that the war was over?

"Good day," he began, not quite as confident as before. "I am sure you have heard the news. It seems you have outsmarted us British and the Arabs, and established your own country with little help from anyone. I congratulate you."

"Yes, I just heard. What are you doing here?" Laila know she sounded rude, but she didn't know what else to say. The green-eyed soldier had caused friction between Itzhak and her from the start. If Itzhak saw him now, his presence would only flame the fire. He had to leave before Itzhak came to join in the celebration.

"I'm not here to cause trouble. I am leaving, going back to England in a few days, and I wanted to say goodbye. I also wanted to apologize for my behavior at your wedding. Can you ever forgive me?"

Laila cringed, thinking about that day; then she realized nothing was gained from holding old grudges. "Of course. That was years ago. We were children. We are both mature adults now, and I can only wish you the very best. I hope you find someone who will make you as happy as Itzhak has made me. We have three children. It is time you returned home to start your own family, but I must ask you to leave ... quickly. I don't want any trouble."

"I understand," he said, and a look furrowed his brows

that Laila thought must have been pain. "May I hug you?"

Hug me? Laila was afraid someone would see and tell Itzhak, but everyone else was hugging, all one hundred fifty-four adults and forty-four children.

Laila stepped forward; the soldier enfolded her, and she melted into his arms. They clung to each other. Laila could feel his heart pounding in his chest, his body trembling; his breath was warm on her face. He held her like he would never let go. He whispered. "You never complained through the whole ordeal. Your only concern was for the other woman. Your strength and determination is what kept me going. I admire your character and will never forget you."

It was then that a pin in his lapel pricked her, and she pulled away. "Please go," she said breathlessly. "I wish you well." Laila turned and ran toward the laundry room, temples pounding—never looking back.

"My name is Ethan," he called.

The End

Author's Notes

Writing a novel is much like being a horticulturist; in that an idea, like a seed, must germinate, be fed, nurtured, and cultivated before it brings forth the fruit of your labor. The idea of a trip to Israel had been that seed, planted in my subconscious for some time. It was Rabbi Daniel Treiser of Temple B'nai Israel in Clearwater, Florida, and a host of others on the trip, including our guide Jeremy, who supplied the much needed soil. The seed was then cultivated by that trip, planned by an Israeli travel company, Arza, and loyally tiled by my husband Robert W. Lockhart, who has been my support system since the day we met. The seed basked in the Israeli sun, germinating after visiting the Ayalon Institute, a munitions' factory—now a museum—outside of Rehovot, Israel, and took root six months later in the form of the first sprout or manuscript. The manuscript was then nurtured by my readers: my sister Elaine Stupp, loyal friends: Beverly Mitlin, Marsha Moran, and Carol Leaman, all of whom proffered helpful suggestions. The plant was then pruned by my editors: Professor Tom Bernardo, Eckerd College; Professor Dylan Phillips of Winthrop College; Heather Bungard-Janney; and most especially my sister Elaine, who tidied up the garden. The two harvesters responsible for making the end product possible are Yehudith Ayalon—without who there would be no story—and Michael James of Penmore Press, my publisher, for believing in me and giving me the opportunity to be published. Yehudith is the bouquet,

Michael the florist, and Midori Snyder my sounding board.

I credit my whole family for making me more insightful when delving into the human heart; and dear friends Elaine and Bob Felberg who have stood in the background cheering me on over the years. I would be remiss if I didn't mention Bogie, my loyal standard poodle, who has patiently sat by my side throughout the whole process and who was the inspiration for my children's book *Oodles of Poodles of Dark Corner*. Most importantly, I would like to thank the Ayalon Institute for bring this story to light and honoring forty-five unsung heroes.

I would like to give a nod to Office Depot for graciously running off a number of copies of my dry-runs, the United States Post Office for carrying my query letters and their subsequent rejection letters, and especially the Historical Fiction Conference held in St. Petersburg, FL, for helping me find my publisher. Never let it be said that it doesn't take a village to write a book or feed the world.

About the Author

Lynda Lippman-Lockhart

Lynda Lippman-Lockhart grew up in St. Petersburg, Florida, and graduated from the University of Florida with a Bachelor's Degree in Education. She then earned her English degree from the University of South Florida. She was director of a nursery school for four years, and taught high school English for twenty-six years. Upon retiring, she began her next profession, writing. Her literary skills were honed at workshops at the University of Iowa, Lesley University and Eckerd College. She won first place for her short story "The Pink Bathtub" at the Florida Writers Conference. Her first novel was *Oodles of Poodles of Dark Corner*, inspired by her standard poodle, Bogie. Lynda has two children and six grandchildren. She and her husband Robert live in Florida.

If You Enjoyed This Book
Please write a review.
This is important to the author and helps to get the
word out to others
Visit

PENMORE PRESS
www.penmorepress.com

All Penmore Press books are available directly through our website, amazon.com, Barnes and Noble and Nook, Sony Reader, Apple iTunes, Kobo books and via leading bookshops across the United States, Canada, the UK, Australia and Europe.

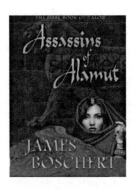

ASSASSINS OF ALAMUT
BY
JAMES BOSCHERT

An Epic Novel of Persia and Palestine in the Time of the Crusades

The Assassins of Alamut is a riveting tale, painted on the vast canvas of life in Palestine and Persia during the 12th century.

On one hand, it's a tale of the crusades—as told from the Islamic side—where Shi'a and Sunni are as intent on killing Ismaili Muslims as crusaders. In self-defense, the Ismailis develop an elite band of highly trained killers called Hashshashin whose missions are launched from their mountain fortress of Alamut.

But it's also the story of a French boy, Talon, captured and forced into the alien world of the assassins. Forbidden love for a princess is intertwined with sinister plots and self-sacrifice, as the hero and his two companions discover treachery and then attempt to evade the ruthless assassins of Alamut who are sent to hunt them down.

It's a sweeping saga that takes you over vast snow-covered mountains, through the frozen wastes of the winter plateau, and into the fabulous cites of Hamadan, Isfahan, and the Kingdom of Jerusalem.

"A brilliant first novel, worthy of Bernard Cornwell at his best."—Tom Grundner

PENMORE PRESS
www.penmorepress.com

Historical fiction and nonfiction
Paperback available for order on line
and as Ebook with all major distributers

Force 12 in German Bight
by
James Boschert

Considering that oil and gas have been flowing from under the North Sea for the best part of half a century, it is perhaps surprising that more writers have not taken the uncompromising conditions that are experienced in this area – which extends from the north of Scotland to the coasts of Norway and Germany – for the setting of a novel. James Boschert's latest redresses the balance.

The book takes its title from the name of an area regularly referred to in the legendary BBC Shipping Forecast and one which experiences some of the worst weather conditions around the British Isles. It is a fast-paced story which smacks of authenticity in every line. A world of hard men, hard liquor, hard drugs and cold-blooded murder. The reality of the setting and the characters, ex-military men from both sides of the Atlantic, crooked wheeler-dealers, and Danish detectives, male and female, are all in on the action.

This is not story telling akin to a latter day Bulldog Drummond, or even a James Bond, but simply a snortingly good yarn which will jangle the nerve ends, fill your nose with the smell of salt and diesel oil, your ears with the deafening sound of machinery aboard a monster pipe-dredging ship and, above all, make you remember never to underestimate the power of the sea.

'Roger Paine, former Commander, Royal Navy'.

PENMORE PRESS
www.penmorepress.com

Historical fiction and nonfiction
Paperback available for order on line
and as Ebook with all major distributers

BRUNO JAMBOR

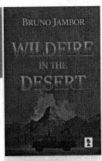

"The time for the wildfire has come. Flashing through the desert, it will consume cities, and nations, and continents."

WILDFIRE IN THE DESERT

by Bruno Jambor

Manuel's secluded life near Baboquivari Mountain shatters when he hides his nephew Rodrigo's truckload of drugs to save his life. Drug cartel members track them, and local police show keen interest in them. When they shelter a mysterious man they find near death, the situation becomes impossible.

The only one with a solution is a local citizen who lived several centuries before, who swore that when things deteriorate, depend on celestial favors. An astronomer and an engineer join Manuel's group to practice using those favors following the advice from the past.

The unusual circle of friends enters a bewildering world where allies are enemies and remedies for the present were laid out in past centuries. Will they be able to use the celestial favors to escape the deadly ambush of their hidden enemies?

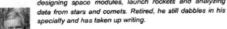

Order Now: www.PenmorePress.com

Bruno Jambor *has worked in the space industry for over thirty years, designing space modules, launch rockets and analyzing data from stars and comets. Retired, he still dabbles in his specialty and has taken up writing.*

This is his first novel. He lives with his wife at the foot of the Rockies, in Colorado, where the deer and the antelope play, but the skies are less clear all night due to city lights.

He cultivates what the deer let him grow, which is mostly pinion pine, penstemon, and sage.

NOW AVAILABLE at all Leading Booksellers & On-line e-Book Distributors.

TPB | $17.50 USD
978-1-942756-06-4
6"x9" | 03/15
228 PAGES
RIGHTS: WORLD

EPUB MOBI | $9.95 USD
978-1-942756-07-1
RIGHTS: WORLD

Penmore Press

Penmore Press

Challenging, Intriguing, Adventurous , Historical and Imaginative

www.penmorepress.com

CPSIA information can be obtained
at www.ICGtesting.com
Printed in the USA
FFOW01n1950050515
13065FF